fAMILY PORTRAIT

Graham Masterton was born in Edinburgh in 1946. After training as a newspaper reporter, Graham went on to edit the new British men's magazine *Mayfair*. At the age of 24, Graham was appointed executive editor of both *Penthouse* and *Penthouse Forum* magazines.

Graham Masterton's debut as a horror author began with the wildly popular *The Manitou* in 1976. Altogether Graham has written over a hundred novels ranging from thrillers and horror, to disaster novels and historical sagas, as well as four short story collections.

fAMILY PORTRAIT

GRAHAM MASTERTON

Published in Great Britain in 2011 by
Arrow Books in association with Hammer

1 3 5 7 9 10 8 6 4 2

First published in Great Britain by Arrow Books in 1985

Arrow Books in association with Hammer
The Random House Group Limited
20 Vauxhall Bridge Road, London, SW1V 2SA

www.randomhouse.co.uk

Addresses for companies within The Random House Group Limited can be
found at: www.randomhouse.co.uk/offices.htm

The Random House Group Limited Reg. No. 954009

A CIP catalogue record for this book
is available from the British Library

ISBN 9780099561842

The Random House Group Limited supports The Forest Stewardship
Council® (FSC®), the leading international forest certification organisation.
All our titles that are printed on Greenpeace approved FSC® certified paper
carry the FSC® logo. Our paper procurement policy can be found at:
www.randomhouse.co.uk/environment

Typeset by SX Composing DTP, Rayleigh, Essex
Printed and bound in Great Britain by
CPI Cox & Wyman, Reading, RG1 8EX

One

As soon as he saw her standing under the lime trees, her thumb lifted, her red nylon rucksack propped up against the railings beside her, he knew that she was a suitable victim. He drove thirty or forty yards further on, and then drew the huge black Vanden Plas limousine in to the kerb.

He sat there, without moving, the engine still warbling, watching her fixedly in the rear-view mirror. He saw her pick up her rucksack, take two or three steps towards him, then hesitate, obviously uncertain if he had stopped for her or not. She's pretty, he thought. She's perfect. His fingers, resting lightly on the steering-wheel, had immaculately buffed nails.

It was a foggy, spectral morning. Beyond the railings, silent and steamy, slid the River Semois. On both banks of the river, the crumbling old buildings of Bouillon crowded the hillsides like the abandoned nests of house-martins and winter wrens. It was November in the Ardennes, close to the French border. A time of wet leaves and dripping trees and penetrating silences. A time when the clouds were so low that you could easily begin to believe that the rest of the world had disappeared altogether.

Now the girl was jogging up to him, her rucksack

1

slung over one shoulder. He took a cigarette out of a gold cigarette-case, but didn't light it. As the girl came up to the car, he wound down the window, and waited for her. There was a sharp smell in the morning air of smoked meats and tobacco and river-water.

'*Merci, monsieur,*' the girl panted. '*Je suis en voyage à Liège.*'

'*A Liège?*' he smiled. Even while he was sitting in the car, the girl could tell that he was very tall, almost six foot three. He had a bony, aristocratic-looking face. Grey, brushed-back hair, hollow cheeks, lidded eyes. A thin, refined mouth. He wore one of those grey hand-tailored suits that seem to be designed exclusively for the owners of lavish Italian hotels. His pale cream shirt was of a quality that would categorize it as 'gentlemen's linen'. On his knobbly left wrist he wore a Piaget wrist-watch that was so thin and so understated that it must have been impossibly expensive.

'*Allez-vous vers Liège?*' the girl asked him. Her accent was strongly American, and now that she was close up to him, he could see how American she looked. Dark-blonde hair, plaited into long pigtails; wide china-blue eyes; and a full-lipped innocent-provocative mouth that was simply crammed with healthy white teeth. She was younger and smaller than he had first thought, although under her yellow quilted anorak she appeared to have the kind of rounded figure he always preferred.

'You're American?' he asked her.

'Yes,' she said, and then frowned at him curiously because his own accent was American, too. The clipped, careful consonants of the better parts of New England. Cape Cod, perhaps, or rural Connecticut. 'And you? You're an American? If you don't mind me asking you.'

2

'Please,' he said. 'Get in. I can't take you all the way to Liège, but I can certainly get you to Rochefort, and you should easily be able to hitch another ride from there.'

'I think you saved my life,' the girl told him. 'I thought I was going to be standing there for ever.'

He leaned across and opened the passenger door for her. She tossed her rucksack into the back seat, and climbed in. 'At least I managed to have a bath and wash my hair this morning,' she said.

'Ah,' he replied. He was fragrant himself with Christian Dior cologne.

'This is a beautiful old car,' she remarked, as she closed her door. 'Look at that panelling. Real wood.'

'It's a Vanden Plas Princess limousine, four-litre,' he told her. 'It was built in England in the 1960s for Count Louis de Rochelle. He lets me use it from time to time, when I feel the need to get out and about.'

'You're friends with a count?'

He smiled again, rather vaguely this time. 'My family and I have been living in part of his château for the best part of the post-war years. He spends most of his time in the South of France, so we don't see very much of him. He gambles, you know. He inherited more money than was good for him, and he feels the need to throw it away.'

He pulled away from the kerb without making a signal. The car's transmission whined noisily as he drove up to the road junction on the west side of the Bouillon bridge. 'I ought to introduce myself,' he said, holding out his hand. 'I am Maurice Gray.'

'Should I know you?' the girl asked him. He had announced his name as if she ought to.

'No, of course not,' he said. 'I may be a native son, but I have been living on foreign soil for too long now for anybody to remember me. I read only last week in *Time*

3

magazine that my very last acquaintance from the old days had passed away.'

The girl was about to remark that Maurice Gray didn't *look* so very old. Fifty-five, maybe? Sixty at the very most. But then she decided that it was probably politer not to, and so she simply smiled and nodded, and said, 'Well, *tempus fugit*,' which was a terrible college cliché, but better than saying anything embarrassing. Her mother always said embarrassing things, like asking doctors of philosophy to look at her bunions, and she had always promised herself that she would never be the same.

She said, 'I'm Alison Shrader. Ball State University, Muncie, Indiana.'

'Well, well,' said Maurice Gray. 'Muncie. I once knew an optician from Muncie. He committed suicide shortly after the war.'

Alison didn't know what to say to that. They drove over the old stone bridge, while beneath them the river mist swirled like the most regretful of memories.

'You've eaten?' asked Maurice Gray.

Alison pointed back towards the far bank of the river, where there were two or three seedy-looking cafés. 'I had breakfast in the Café de la Citadelle,' she said, pronouncing the name as if it were the grandest restaurant in Belgium. 'Black pudding, and a glass of Stella. It was great. Well, not bad. Edible.'

Maurice Gray smiled. 'I hope you know what black pudding is made of,' he remarked.

'You don't have to remind me. But it's nutritious, isn't it, and I couldn't afford anything else. I'm trying to keep my budget down to a hundred and fifty francs a day.'

'Very commendable,' said Maurice Gray. 'You can live like royalty on a hundred and fifty francs a day, if you know where to eat, and your friends are rich.' He

4

steered one-handed through the back-streets of the town, reaching inside his jacket for his cigarette-case. 'Would you care for a cigarette?'

'I don't use them, I'm afraid,' said Alison. 'But please don't let me stop you.'

'No, no,' said Maurice Gray. He opened the case and tucked his own unlit cigarette back into it. 'I respect the rights of those who don't smoke.'

Alison said, 'That's a beautiful case.'

'Yes,' he replied. 'It was given to me by my father, to take to the Sudan with me. One side is very highly polished, you see, so that it could be used as a heliograph.'

He tilted the case from side to side, pretending to send morse messages across the desert. 'Camels . . . dying . . . send . . . champagne . . .'

They slowed down while a noisy moped, carrying an old man in a beret and his heavy-legged wife, wavered around in front of them. The wife was perched on the luggage-rack, her arms filled with loaves of French bread and celery and sausage.

'You really live in a château?' asked Alison.

'Not a very elegant one, I'm sorry to say. Well, not many of them are. They have all been pillaged over the years by successive armies, and most of them have been knocked about a bit. Ours is no exception.'

They drove out of Bouillon and up the winding hill towards the main highway to Liège. On either side of them, the fields were pale with fog, and the white Friesian cattle lay in the silvery grass like a landscape painting by Bruegel. At the top of the hill, there was a huge sculptured memorial to the casualties of World War Two, a rusting, welded collection of abstract swords and ploughshares. It looked jagged and primitive in the fog, the symbol of a pagan battle.

Alison said, 'I guess I'm on a pilgrimage, sort of.'

'A pilgrimage?' asked Maurice Gray. He glanced down at her faded jeans, at her mud-stained trainers. She had a perky, classically American profile. Marilyn Monroe and Candice Bergen and Bo Derek all shaken up together into a cocktail of freckles and freshness. 'What sort of a pilgrimage?' he wanted to know. 'Spiritual, or temporal?'

'My father fought here, during the war,' said Alison. 'He was in the Battle of the Bulge.'

'Ah,' said Maurice Gray. His eyes were curiously dead.

'He was wounded at Liège,' Alison went on. 'A German mortar-bomb, that's what he said. The fragments went into his head.' She touched her left temple with her fingertips as if she could feel the shrapnel herself.

'I never knew what he was like when my mother first met him, of course, but she always said that he was lively, and funny. I can only remember that he was very distant, very remote. You could look at him, and talk to him, and you could tell that he was thinking about something else. He never said what. Mom used to say that when he came back from the war, she felt that she had lost him, just as much as if he had been killed. She had lost the man she married. Instead she had a person who *looked* like her husband and *talked* like her husband but just wasn't anybody at all. I think she got herself pregnant with me just to see if she could bring him back; you know, mentally bring him back, from whatever kind of psychological plane he was living on.'

Maurice Gray was silent for a while. Then he said, lifting his hand in a slight gesture of regret, 'There were very many tragedies during the war. It is quite right that you should come here to remember them.'

Alison wiped her breath away from the car window

with the end of her red knitted scarf. 'My father's dead now. He died last year. I felt I had to go see the place where he was wounded; the last place where he was actually *himself*. I thought maybe the surroundings would help me to understand him. I don't know. I thought in a peculiar way that maybe he would still be here. Does that sound stupid?'

Maurice Gray shook his head. 'Who are we to question what parts of the human presence might survive, long after they are traditionally supposed to have expired?'

Alison said, 'My friend was going to come with me. Then she changed her mind. Well, her parents made her change her mind. They said they didn't approve of ghost-hunting.'

'Well,' smiled Maurice Gray, 'they are not exactly the height of sophistication, are they, the people of Muncie, Indiana?'

'*I'm* from Muncie – thanks very much.'

'Of course. But there are always shining exceptions to every prejudice, of which you are a very fine example.'

They had turned off the main highway now and were driving along the straight, narrow road which led to Rochefort. Away from the river, the fog had begun to clear; and a liquid sunshine illuminated the fields and the grey-painted barns and the yellow-and-amber trees.

'Is your château far from here?' asked Alison.

'Not far,' said Maurice Gray. 'It is just outside a small village called Vêves. I don't suppose you will have heard of it.'

Alison shook her head. The sunlight suddenly filled the interior of the car and sparkled on the highly polished walnut dashboard.

Maurice Gray said, 'You are in a hurry, I suppose, to get to Liège?'

'Not especially. I have another week here in Europe.'

'Well, it was just a thought,' said Maurice Gray.

'What was?'

He smiled at her ruefully. 'I was wondering perhaps if you would care to visit my château and have lunch with me. I very much dislike being on my own; that is why I stopped and asked you if you wanted a ride. I love company, and bright conversation. But, you mustn't feel obligated. If you prefer, I will drive you straight to Rochefort, without feeling at all upset.'

Alison couldn't help smiling back at him. 'You're so old-fashioned. I mean, I'm not saying that rudely. I love it. But your manners are so – I don't know – they're just like a movie. *Gone With The Wind*. Something like that.'

'Well, I have been living here in Europe for quite a long time,' Maurice Gray explained. 'I suppose the charm of their manners does rub off on one. They are all very charming people.'

Alison unzippered her anorak. With one surreptitious look sideways, Maurice Gray caught the swell of a breast beneath a soft white sweater, the sharp glint of a silver crucifix.

'It's real warm in this car, if you don't mind my saying so.'

'The heater has only two settings: Antarctica and Hades.'

Alison laughed. 'Do you really want me to come to lunch? I won't be upsetting anybody?'

'Whom could you possibly upset?'

'I don't know. Don't you have servants, or something?'

Maurice Gray inclined his head. 'Yes,' he said, 'we have servants. But our servants are there to *serve* us. We don't have quite the same domestic problem as people do in the United States. Our domestics are

8

helpful and obedient, just as they used to be, back in the old days; the days of grace.'

'Well, as long as it's okay.'

Maurice Gray raised a hand as if he were about to lay it on Alison's thigh; but then he refrained, and returned it to the steering-wheel. 'I promise you,' he said, in the quietest of voices, 'it's very much okay.'

It took them an hour to reach the high massif overlooking the valley of the River Meuse. The clouds had gathered again, and the sky was steely-dark. All the same, they could see for miles and miles all around them, as if they were on the roof of the world. Forests and fields and distant mountains, and the wind whipping chaff across the road.

Maurice Gray turned right, down a narrow side-turning signposted Vêves. He could sense that, for the first time, Alison was beginning to feel uncertain about having accepted his invitation for a ride; and so he smiled reassuringly, and hummed a few bars of a silly French song called 'Le Pingre de Paris'.

The road wound downwards between the sloping fields. The sky grew so threatening that Maurice Gray had to switch on his headlights. It began to rain, transparent droplets that quivered on the windscreen.

'My father always said that he wanted to come back here,' said Alison. 'It's really wild, isn't it? I feel like I'm right inside some kind of fairy-tale. You know, Sleeping Beauty, with the thorns growing up around the castle.'

'You shouldn't read too much,' Maurice Gray remarked. 'Reading is bad for the spirit. You remember what somebody once said – "Those who read the symbol do so at their peril."'

'I'm not sure what that means,' said Alison.

9

'It means that there is always a risk in exploring beneath the surface,' Maurice Gray replied.

They passed the Château de Vêves, a high round-turreted castle which was supposed to have been Walt Disney's inspiration for the fairy castle in *Snow White*. Maurice Gray remarked that he couldn't imagine Walt Disney in his shiny wide-trousered suit standing here in the depths of the Ardennes, admiring the Château de Vêves. 'Those who live in Hollywood never admire anything; especially anything that promises to be immortal. When they capture a beautiful place on their accursed film, a castle, or a palace, they destroy it, as surely as if they had arrived with a wrecking-crew. It is the same with people. Whomsoever they film, they kill—just as effectively as if they had pointed a loaded gun at their heads, instead of a camera.'

'I'm really not at all sure what you're trying to say,' said Alison.

Maurice Gray lifted a finger. 'It's very simple. Your image is what you are. Can you understand that? The image that you present to the world is what you actually are. Why do you think that African tribesmen used to be so frightened of being photographed? They knew what our vanity has allowed us to hide from ourselves. They knew that every time somebody paints your portrait or takes your picture, they do just that. They literally *take* something from you: something of your image, something of yourself. Your face grows old, not from within, not from age, but from without, from use and abuse by other people. Your face grows old from being looked at, from being photographed. You still don't understand me? Well, you will. Your face is the same as a car tyre, if you will forgive me for making such an uncomplimentary metaphor. It is scuffed and worn by everything with which it comes into contact. Not from inside, but from external friction. Why do you think that Arabian women wear the yashmak? It is not from modesty. It is to protect them from the gaze of others, to keep them young.'

Alison said, 'I really don't know. I mean, I really don't. You're trying to say that people's faces grow old just because other people look at them, and take their photograph and stuff?'

Maurice Gray slowed down, and then turned right, through a shower of loose grit, up a steep and overshadowed lane. Beneath the low-hanging trees on her left, Alison could see an unnaturally green field, in which sheep were grazing. Ahead, there was darkness – a tunnel of trees. Maurice drove into the darkness with a lack of concern born of long experience. For a moment, they could see nothing at all. But then they emerged on to a wide white gravel forecourt, and right in front of them stood a huge Gothic château, with a tall central tower. Amongst the spires and the turrets and the blue-slated attics, there must have been at least a hundred windows; and on the lower floors there were tall French doors, rows and rows of them, shining like quicksilver in the dark of the morning, leading to ballrooms and reception rooms and hallways.

It looked as if a massive London railway station had been magically and thunderously transported to the forests of Belgium and set down here on the crest of a high natural hill, overlooking a romantic garden, with a circular pool, and a gushing fountain, and groves of ash trees. The effect was both dramatic and overbearing: man attempting with wealth and arrogance to impose his will on nature, and for some reason she couldn't really work out, Alison began to feel isolated and depressed. Maurice Gray stopped the car in front of the grey stone steps, and she wished very much that she had the nerve to ask him to take her back to the highway, so that she could continue on her way to Liège.

'This is incredible,' she said, looking around.

Maurice Gray stood a little way off with his hands tucked neatly into the pockets of his jacket, like pink letters waiting to be posted. He smiled, and said, 'You like it? It's pretty vulgar, really. But come and have some lunch. I can show you around afterwards. Do you like hare? The game here is quite tremendous.'

They mounted the steps and walked into a huge echoing lobby lined with white streaky marble. There were palms in pots, and a dusty red Chesterfield, but the whole place had the strange feeling of being abandoned.

Alison's sneakers squeaked on the marble. Then stopped squeaking. 'Maybe we'd better forget lunch. Why don't you just drive me back to the highway? I'm sure I can easily hitch a ride to Liège. I mean, you don't have to bother any more.'

'It's no bother at all,' said Maurice Gray. 'Please don't be put off because it's all so overpowering. Come upstairs – let me show you the tower. It's really very unusual.'

'Listen, I'm embarrassed,' said Alison.

Maurice Gray's voice echoed. 'You don't have anything to be embarrassed about. Why should you be embarrassed? Please.' He spread his hands wide and smiled at her encouragingly. 'I'm only asking you for lunch.'

Alison nervously rubbed the back of her thumbnail against her teeth, and said nothing.

'Please,' said Maurice Gray. 'The servants will be here in a while.'

Alison looked around the hallway. Dust silently fell in the premature twilight; dust that must have been falling for scores of years.

She said, 'I'm sorry, this is all wrong. I feel like I'm intruding.'

'Of course you're not,' Maurice Gray reassured her. He held out his beautifully manicured hand. 'It was I, remember, who invited you. That can hardly be called an intrusion.' He smiled, but his smile was as chilly as white wine. 'Come on. While we're waiting, I can show you the tower.'

'I don't think I want to,' said Alison. 'I mean, I know it sounds stupid, but something about this place has got me really spooked. I guess I never knew anybody who lived in a house quite so *old* before . . .'

'Old?' asked Maurice Gray. 'This place isn't old. It was only completed in 1911. Now, you could hardly call that *old*. But don't be put off. I know that it's rather cavernous. None of my family like it either, except for my sister, and she's always had delusions of grandeur. But it's home, you know; and in the summer it can be quite charming.'

'I think I made a mistake,' said Alison, a little panicky now. 'I really think that I'd better leave. Please. It's just me being hysterical. But the whole thing has kind of overwhelmed me, do you know what I mean, and I really would prefer it if you could take me back to the highway.'

'Without lunch?' asked Maurice Gray, in surprise. Smooth-haired, grey and tall.

'Please. I'm not very hungry.'

Maurice Gray smiled. 'Well, for goodness' sake, the last thing that I want to do is to hold you here against your will. If you don't want lunch, all right, I under-stand. I realize that I have been rather too forceful.

Please forgive me. I've taken advantage of you. I was lonely and bored, and I didn't stop to think what effect I might be having on you; talking strange talk and bringing you all the way out here to such a grim-visaged château. I'm sorry. Please forgive me. Say that you do.'

'Well, I forgive you,' said Alison, uncertainly.

'That's marvellous. You mustn't be afraid of this place. Let me show you the tower; it's really quite splendid.'

'Well, okay,' said Alison. 'But aren't your servants around?'

'In the kitchen, I expect,' Maurice Gray explained off-handedly. He led the way through two enormous oak doors into a long, high, marble-floored hallway. To their right, a grand staircase descended from the upper floors. On every wall, there were oil portraits of displeased-looking men in period costumes.

'The family de Rochelle,' Maurice Gray remarked. 'Nothing to do with *our* family, I hasten to tell you! Look at their piggy little eyes! It takes centuries of avarice to produce eyes like that. The greediest dynasty in Europe, I would say.'

He mounted the echoing staircase, and Alison had no choice but to follow him. The backs of his black Italian shoes were perfectly polished. He stopped on the first landing and showed her a cabinet of Sèvres porcelain. 'You see this dinner service? It was originally made for Louis XVI. It has four hundred and eighty-five pieces, and every single one of them was painted by hand.'

They had reached the second landing when a side door opened and a young Belgian appeared. He was thin and slight, with hair that stuck up on the crown of his head like a cockatoo, and a pointed nose.

'Ah, Paul,' said Maurice Gray. 'I was wondering where you were. I have brought this young lady back for lunch, if you could arrange it.'

The young man stared at Alison with watery grey eyes. Then he nodded, and said, in a strong Flemish accent, 'Of course, Mr Gray. I shall call you when we are ready.'

Alison felt more at ease now that she knew she was not alone with Maurice Gray. Being brought out to a strange Gothic château in the middle of the Belgian forests was a little too much like the prelude to a horror movie; and even though she kept trying to persuade herself that Maurice Cray was a perfectly respectable man, and that it was daytime, and that there were plenty of other people around, she still felt oddly unreal as she climbed up yet another flight of stairs. Looking out of the windows of the tower, she could see the gravel court-yard outside, and the bright green gardens, and the inky-coloured sky. Maurice Gray's car, parked by the steps, looked as tiny as a toy.

'I have a room of my own up here,' Maurice Gray told her. 'It is the only place where I can find any solitude. I can look out over the forests and imagine that I am the emperor of all that I survey.'

'You sure have a fantastic view,' said Alison.

They reached Maurice Gray's room. It was compara-tively small, no longer than 20 feet, and no wider than 15 feet. It had a leaded Gothic window facing west-wards, towards the hills bordering the Meuse. There were waxed oak boards on the floor, covered with a blue-and-grey Persian rug. There were no pictures on the walls, and it was only sparsely furnished: an oak bed, covered with a white bedspread of Brussels lace, and a desk, with a chair.

'Kind of monastic, if you don't mind my saying so,' Alison remarked.

Maurice Gray nodded in amused agreement. 'I suppose you're right. But after one has tasted absolutely every kind of food, and drunk absolutely every kind of wine, and experienced absolutely every kind of romantic experience – well, what can be left but monasticism?'

'Can we go down now?' Alison asked.

'Of course. But first let me show you the view from the clock room.'

They climbed the last flight of stairs – a tightly winding spiral of decorative iron treads. The clanging of their feet echoed all the way down to the hallway at the foot of the tower. At the top, there was a small dark room in which the mechanism of the tower's four clock-faces slowly ticked – cogs and springs and spindles, all of them softly gleaming with oil. Only one shaft of light penetrated the room, from a tiny observation hole beside the east clock-face.

'Have a look out of there,' Maurice Gray suggested. 'You'll be quite amazed at what you can see.'

Alison bent forward and peered through the hole. A sudden ray of sunlight illuminated her right eye, as if she were being examined by an optometrist. An eye as blue as cornflower. Maurice Gray stood behind her, his hands by his sides, his head slightly lifted, a man practising his haughtiness in the privacy of his own clock room.

'I can see the fountain,' said Alison.

'And what else?' asked Maurice Gray.

'The stables. Well, they *look* like stables.'

Maurice Gray drew out of his inside pocket, where it had been sheathed, a short broad-bladed knife. He held it up and it shone brightly in the gloom of the clock room.

'What do you see just beyond the stables?' he asked her.

'An orchard, I guess. A pear orchard.'

'Yes,' said Maurice Gray. 'The finest Williams.'

The clock mechanism ticked and whirred. Maurice Gray stepped forward, his knife held lightly in the open palm of his hand.

He said, 'It's almost noon. We ought to go down now, before the clock starts chiming. We don't want to have ringing ears for the rest of the afternoon.'

Alison asked, 'Is that an herb garden, there, past the wall?'

Maurice Gray leaned forward, as if he were going to peep through the hole. Instead, he pushed his knife straight into Alison's back, with an audible crunch. The knife cut between her fourth and fifth lumbar vertebrae, severing the posterior columns of the spinal cord, which control direct touch and conscious muscle sensations. Alison said, '*Ah,*' in a choking voice, and collapsed to the dusty wooden floor.

Maurice Gray stood over her for a moment. He left the knife where it was, embedded in her back. He had stabbed her with the intention of paralysing her, not of killing her. To withdraw the knife now would start her bleeding. He fastidiously wiped his fingers, and then he bent over so that he could see her face.

She was white. Worse than white, almost blue. Her gasps for breath came quick and short and uneven, like the breaths of someone having a nightmare. Her eyes were still wide open, but she was unable to move.

'Well, now,' said Maurice Gray. 'The perfect stroke.'

The door of the clock room opened behind him. It was Paul, his Belgian servant. Paul had taken off his jacket now, and rolled up his sleeves. He was smoking an American cigarette. He didn't even bother to look down at Alison. Instead, he took the cigarette out of his mouth and flicked the ash on to the floor.

'You are back very soon, *monsieur*,' he remarked to Maurice Gray. 'As you can see, I had some luck.'

There were no words wasted between them. Together, they picked Alison up, Maurice Gray taking her feet and Paul holding her under her arms, and carried her carefully down the spiral staircase. Alison whimpered, just once, but neither of them took any notice. Outside, it began to rain again, and drops pattered noisily against the windows, as if they were clamouring for sudden attention.

'I found her in Bouillon,' said Maurice Gray. 'She has been hitch-hiking in Europe alone. Nobody will miss her for months and months; and, by then, anybody who might have seen her will have forgotten.'

'*Mademoiselle* will be pleased,' said Paul, not altogether respectfully.

They carried Alison into Maurice Gray's room and laid her on the floor, on the Persian rug. Paul stripped off the white lace bedspread, revealing a white starched surgical sheet. Then the two of them lifted her on to the bed, face down, the handle of the knife still sticking up from the back of her yellow anorak.

'Did Mr Forbes call?' Maurice Gray asked, taking off his jacket and hanging it over the back of his chair.

'Not yet, *monsieur*.'

Maurice Gray looked closely into Alison's face. Her eyes stared back at him in helpless terror. *What have you done to me? What's happened? Please – I can't move. Please – I can't feel.* Maurice Gray smiled, and said, 'Can you imagine how frightening it must be, to be totally helpless? But don't worry, my dear, this will soon be over. Soon, you will be at peace.'

Paul unlaced Alison's shoes and set them neatly

down on the floor, at the foot of the bed. Then he reached around her, unbuckled her belt, tugged down her zipper and wrestled off her jeans. They were dark-stained and damp: when Maurice Gray stabbed her, she had lost control of her nerves. Paul stood silently by while Maurice Gray himself drew down Alison's small pink cotton panties, and held them for a moment against his face, breathing in the aroma of young girl, and helplessness, and fear.

They cut up the back of her anorak and her sweater with scissors, as far as the handle of the knife, so that they could take them off without having to extricate the blade. Alison wore no bra, so now she was naked, except for her silver crucifix. There was a pattern of five moles on her back, just above the broad flare of her hips. The handle of the knife stuck out of her with shocking incongruity.

'The dressing,' said Maurice Gray.

Paul opened the top drawer of the desk and took out a sterile-dressing pack. Maurice Gray snipped it open, and laid it on the bed. Then he grasped the handle of the knife and slowly drew it out. Dark crimson blood welled up instantly out of the cut and poured down on either side of Alison's waist, but Maurice Gray quickly pressed the dressing against the wound and taped it.

'Good,' he said, more to himself than to Paul. 'Now, may I have the instruments, please?'

Paul had already taken out of the second drawer a small mahogany instrument-case, lined with dark blue velvet. He laid it down beside the blood-streaked knife, and Maurice Gray opened it up. There were rows of surgical scalpels, as well as clamps and suture needles. Without hesitation, he picked out one of the scalpels, and held it up between finger and thumb.

'They were all sharpened this morning,' said Paul, as if he were afraid of being criticized. Maurice Gray gave him a testy, equivocal smile, and then bent over Alison's bare back.

'You could bring me a brandy,' he suggested. 'This is going to take an hour or two, at the very least.'

'Do you want anything to eat?' Paul asked him.

Maurice Gray glanced at him. 'I don't think they're hungry at the moment. I would rather anaesthetize them than excite them.'

Paul nodded to show that he had understood. It was obvious that at times like these, he felt that he could show his contempt for Maurice Gray. At times like these, Maurice Gray was at his weakest. Every man is, who is indulging his most compulsive desires.

Maurice Gray worked with the flowing capability of long experience. He cut a line from the back of Alison's neck, all the way down her spine, until he reached the wound where the knife had penetrated. He cut through nothing but the scarf-skin, the epidermis, which is only a tenth of a millimetre thick. He drew no blood, because he never once penetrated the lower layer of skin in which the blood vessels are carried, the corium. He hummed again two or three bars from 'Le Pingre de Paris'.

Out of his instrument case, Maurice Gray took a flat triangular blade rather like a surgical pie-slicer. He inserted it sideways into the incision he had made in Alison's back, and gradually began to lift her outer skin away from her body. The skin made a soft tearing noise as the lowest layer of the epidermis, the Malphigian layer, was torn away from the corium.

Alison was unable to move, unable to speak, but she was quite capable of feeling pain. Although there are no major nerve-endings in the outer skin layer, thousands of fine sensory nerves terminate in the Malphigian layer, and the agony of having these quickly torn away was stunning. Her eyes bulged in sheer cringing horror at what Maurice Gray was doing to her, and her breathing became as harsh as a carpenter's saw.

Maurice Gray carried on cutting systematically and with some elegance. He removed all of the skin from Alison's back without tearing it, holding his own hand underneath it so that he could see how fine and soft it was. Beneath the lifted skin, Alison's back was as scarlet and raw as chopped steak.

Paul switched on the bedside lights as Maurice Gray peeled the skin away from Alison's shoulders, and around her neck. Then, between them, they turned her over, so that she was lying on her back, staring helplessly and desperately up at the ceiling.

'Quite beautiful, don't you think?' asked Maurice Gray, standing back for a moment. Alison was full-breasted, narrow-waisted, her stomach still flat with youthfulness. Maurice Gray rubbed a few of her fine blonde pubic hairs between his fingers as if he were rubbing tobacco leaves. 'Quite beautiful. And scarcely a blemish.'

He cut a circle around her throat so that the skin of her face and her scalp was separated from the rest of her body. Then, with his triangular blade, he raised the skin from her collar bone and her upper chest, and then at last tore it intact from her breasts. Alison closed her eyes. The pain was intolerable now. Her lips opened and closed slightly, and from experience Maurice Gray knew that she was probably saying a prayer.

O God, let me please be dead.

He carried on cutting and tugging, gradually drawing away from her gruesomely reddened body a ghost of skin that had once been Alison, an extraordinary translucent cloak. It always reminded him of Peter Pan's shadow, in J. M. Barrie's play, a shadow that was gradually unstitched from its owner, until it took on a life of its own.

His scalpel worked deftly around Alison's navel, releasing the convolutions of skin. He cut around her fingernails, and pulled the skin off her hands like thin, wax-coloured gloves. He parted her vulva with his thumb, and cut into the inner lips, so that he could lift the skin away from her mound of Venus. Then he was slicing and lifting the epidermis away from her thighs and her knees. He finished with the soles of her feet, where the skin was much thicker, almost a millimetre. The sound of the skin tearing away from her feet was like sticky-tape being lifted off the back of someone's hand.

Outside, it was growing very dark now. The rain was pattering harder against the window. Alison lay on the bed, her whole body peeled of skin, and already anointed with yellowish glistening lymph. Only her face remained to be skinned; and this would take far more time and concentration. Maurice Gray carefully lifted the intact body-skin and handed it to Paul, who laid it out on a clean sheet on the floor. Maurice Gray was sweating, and had to take out his handkerchief and dab at his face.

'The best you've ever done, *monsieur*,' Paul remarked, with mock obsequity. He always said that, even when Maurice Gray had accidentally torn the skin or made an inaccurate incision.

'Just take it to *mademoiselle*,' he instructed sharply. 'Tell her that the face will not be long.'

'*Monsieur*,' Paul nodded. 'Whatever you say, *monsieur*.'

When Paul had left, Maurice Gray leaned over Alison and looked down into her face. She stared back at him blindly, and he knew that she was suffering beyond any kind of human understanding. If only he could tell her just how much *he* had suffered; he and every other member of his family. It was a life for a life, a skin for a skin. He felt genuinely sorry for her. Genuine remorse. But if she had ever known how agonizing *his* life had been, how fearful, how threatened, how damned, she would at least have had some comprehension why she had to die so painfully; even if she could not have found it anywhere in her heart and soul to forgive him.

He probed the tip of his scalpel into the side of her eye, coaxing the skin away from her upper cheek. All the time, her eye watched him, knowing what he was doing, unable to resist. He made the usual neat incisions under the nostrils and around the mouth. The skin of the lips came away like the discarded chrysalises of exotic moths.

At last, the mask of skin which had covered her face was removed, and she lay on the bed completely flayed. Her body was bright scarlet now, and slimy with weeping fluid. Beautiful and tortured, he thought. A naked sacrifice to the future.

She opened her eyes only once more. He understood the message that was there. He nodded, and smiled. He took the scalpel in one hand, blew her a kiss with the other, and then drew the scalpel quickly and deeply across her throat.

He stood back, his right hand covered in blood. A good way for anybody to die, he thought. A short hour of terrible suffering, followed by a quick release. The suffering that she had endured would ensure her access to heaven, so that she could sit beside Catherine and Joan of Arc. The quick release would make sure that she didn't have to linger unnecessarily in Purgatory.

Paul came back carrying a white napkin in which to

enfold the facial skin, then disappeared again. Maurice Gray went downstairs to the second landing, along the noisily boarded corridor and into the bathroom to wash his hands. The blood streaked the white ceramic of the basin. In the mirror, Maurice Gray thought that he looked rather tired. It would not be very long before somebody else would have to be found. He and Cordelia always needed to look for new people at almost the same time. She, late in the fall; he, in the depths of winter. It wearied him. It hurt him, too. But what else could they possibly do?

He clasped his hands over his face, as if in meditation. The years weighed on him so heavily now.

He walked along the landing until he reached the library. It was a small library, considering the size of the château, densely packed with books, a few of them old and cracked and leather-bound, but most of them modern. Almost all of them were concerned with beauty and cosmetics and surgery. Linus Pauling and Michael De Bakey. But Maurice Gray looked at none of the books. Instead he went straight across to the carved oak cabinet in the corner, unlocked it and took out a decanter of brandy. He filled a glass with shaking hands.

' "Those who go beneath the surface do so at their peril," ' he quoted to himself. ' "Those who read the symbol do so at their peril." '

He went to the window and looked out over the grounds of the château. He had told Alison lies, of course. The château had once belonged to the Count de Rochelle, certainly, but the Gray family had bought it from him years ago, when it was decrepit and deserted and half of the roof had collapsed. Who knew what the Count de Rochelle was doing now? He was probably dead, or drunk, or half dead, or half drunk. Maurice

Gray crossed himself, and prayed without any hope that the Lord would forgive him for what he had been forced to do.

He sat in the library for nearly two hours, while Alison Shrader lay dead upstairs, and the sacrifice that she had made was carried through the house. Maurice Gray had been quite right: Alison had become a saint in her hours of suffering. Unrecognized, unknown, uncanonized, but a saint all the same. Maurice Gray drank three large glasses of brandy until his ears began to buzz and he was no longer sure that he could keep himself steady.

At last, when it was dark outside and the window-panes were poured full of ink, he heard gramophone music echoing along the corridors. *L'Arlesienne*, by Bizet, one of Cordelia's favourites. He heaved himself out of his chair, but even as he did so, Paul arrived at the library door, with a tinkling glass of Perrier water and a supercilious smile.

'Miss Gray is ready to see you now, *monsieur*,' said Paul.

'You'll, er . . . ?' asked Maurice Gray, nodding upwards towards the room where Alison Shrader now lay dead.

'Of course, *monsieur*. What do they say in *Snow White*? The deepest and darkest part of the forest. Game for the game.'

Maurice Gray took the Perrier off the tray and thirstily drank three-quarters of it. Then he gently but firmly pushed Paul aside, and walked along the corridor to Cordelia's room. He knocked at the double oak doors.

'*Entrez!*' Cordelia called.

Maurice Gray opened the door and stepped inside. The room was large, three times the size of the library, but the curtains were tightly drawn, so that it was impenetrably dark.

'Can't we have a light?' asked Maurice Gray, patiently. He kept his hand on the door-knob.

'Tomorrow you can see me, when everything's settled,' said Cordelia.

'You're – all right, then?'

There was a long silence. Maurice Gray knew that he had said the wrong thing. Cordelia was upset.

'It was beautiful skin,' said Maurice Gray.

'It was adequate,' retorted Cordelia.

'You're not unhappy, though? You're pleased with it?'

'It was adequate.'

Maurice Gray knew that there was little point in arguing with Cordelia when she was in one of these moods. He opened the door wider and said, 'I shall see you at breakfast?'

Cordelia was silent for a very long time. Then she said, 'Maurice, I can't stand very much more of this.'

'Very much more of what?'

'You know what I mean. This exile. This isolation. This way of life.'

Maurice said nothing. He had heard this complaint from Cordelia so many times before. And so many times before he had argued that the risks of going home were far too great; that in Belgium, at least, they could continue to survive without being discovered; that their victims could be dragged into the forests, to be buried in shallow graves, and eventually devoured by the wild pigs. Unknown, undetected, forgotten – as they were themselves.

Cordelia said, 'Tomorrow I shall talk to Father again.'

'That's your privilege, of course.'

'For God's sake, Maurice. Don't be so unctuous. You're my brother, not my priest.'

'I'm trying to be your protector.'

Another silence. Then, 'I know,' she said. 'I'm sorry. But I really do want to go home.'

'It would take only one person to recognize us, and the same thing would happen again.'

'Not if we have the portrait.'

Maurice Gray lowered his head and said, with all the quietness of monumental impatience, 'You know as well as I do that there is no chance whatsoever that we shall ever find it. We were routed, Cordelia; that is the only word for it. Routed, and exiled.'

'I shall go to Luxembourg again. I shall talk to Eustachio Rossi.'

'I cannot prevent you.'

'No, you can't,' replied Cordelia. 'And, yes, I shall.'

Two

He told Edward that he would probably be back by five, or six at the very latest.

'But supposing somebody wants to buy something?' asked Edward.

'If somebody wants to buy something, then sell it to them,' said Vincent, shrugging on his dark blue Bijan overcoat. 'This is a business, you know. Not a museum.'

Edward looked around the gallery with distinct unhappiness. 'Perhaps I should wait until you get back. Pre-Raphaelites aren't exactly my strong suit.'

Vincent tugged on his black leather gloves. 'They're only pictures, for Christ's sake.'

'Well, I guess,' Edward agreed. It was typically irreverent of Vincent to refer to seventeen million dollars' worth of mid-Victorian masterpieces as 'only pictures'. There were three Rossettis, two Holman Hunts, and a previously undiscovered portrait by Millais. But then Vincent came from a family which had been buying and selling works of art long before Rossetti, Millais or Holman Hunt had ever picked up a paintbrush. Vincent's grandfather used to get drunk with Monet; and his great-grandfather had been a friend of Sisley. Vincent himself had been one of Mark

Rothko's closest supporters, and he regularly had lunch with Richard Anuskiewicz.

Edward opened the door for him, and a sharp blast of December cold penetrated the warmth of the gallery. The door was electronically locked: anybody who wanted to come inside and look at the pictures had to press the doorbell first, and hopefully peer through the toughened security glass. A siren whooped; a tractor-trailer blared its horn. There was a smell of winter and traffic and burning bagels. Vincent said, 'Just one thing: don't let anybody take the Millais yet. Dick hasn't had the chance to photograph it. Oh – and if Aaron Halperin calls, tell him I shall be coming up to the country this weekend. I've got two Johnsons I want him to clean.'

'Okay, commander,' said Edward, lifting a hand in salute, and then closed the door. He stood there for a moment, watching Vincent walking away, and then he turned and propped his hands on his hips and looked around at all the paintings on the gallery walls as if they were disobedient children who had been left in his care.

'God damn it,' he said. He very much disliked being left in charge of the gallery on his own; somebody difficult always came in. Like the last time, when an elderly Iranian exile had wanted to buy four John Kanes, all at once, in cash, and have them delivered to the Pierre Hotel by taxi. By *taxi*, for God's sake. And then there had been the time before that, when a well-dressed silver-haired man, apparently wealthy and apparently sane, had suddenly and furiously struck out with his umbrella at an original Paul Fairley bronze. Art, for some reason, always seemed to prove an irresistible magnet to eccentrics; and Edward always seemed to be there alone when those eccentrics made their entrances.

For the first half-hour, Edward prowled the gallery's

mushroom-coloured carpets, inspecting the paintings as if he were challenging them to misbehave themselves. Nobody rang the doorbell: it was mid-morning and freezing, three below zero and threatening to sleet, a slack time for the selling of great art. After lunch was always far more profitable, when wealthy men were returning to their hotels from the Four Seasons or the 21, full of rich food and richer wine, and anxious to impress those pretty young ladies with whom they shouldn't really have been having lunch at all.

Edward walked around the gallery's second-floor landing. He drummed his fingers on the balcony railings. A slight, athletic, curly-headed young man of twenty-five, in a charcoal-grey suit with a contrasting waistcoat, and the sort of Ivy League necktie of which *Playboy*'s fashion adviser would have approved. He was stylish, and reasonably smart, but somehow he always managed to look as if he would have been much more comfortable in a jogging suit.

Edward was the middle son of three. His older brother had gone straight into the family brokerage business. His younger brother had dropped out altogether and gone to sell catamarans in San Diego. But Edward – mainly because he hadn't been able to think what else to do, and also because he had wanted to impress his father that he was independent – had somehow found himself here, at the Pearson Fine Art Gallery on East 61st Street, with the questionable title of 'executive curator'. The truth was that he was Vincent Pearson's telephone-answerer, letter-typer, excuse-maker, diary-keeper and general gofer.

Edward liked art, especially Impressionists, but had no artistic talent of his own. If he could have portrayed this winter on canvas, however, he would have rendered it lamp-black all over. In October, he had crashed his beloved Dodge Charger on the New Jersey Turnpike, wrecking it beyond repair. In November, he had lost his fiancée Laura to a broad-shouldered tight-suited hotshot lawyer, who had looked to Edward more like an Armenian meat-packer than an attorney; and two days after that he had been mugged outside his apartment and robbed of all his credit cards.

It was hardly surprising that as he paced around the gallery this morning, he felt more than a little ill-starred.

It was while he was looking down from the second-floor balcony, however, that he first caught sight of the woman. She was looking in through the gallery's left-hand window, where a small Holman Hunt entitled *Amos and the Basket of Summer Fruit* was displayed, on an artistically arranged rumple of emerald green silk.

She was pale-faced, but even from this distance – even through the reflections of the toughened-glass window – she was obviously beautiful. She wore a dark fur hat and a dark fur coat. One hand was clasped at her collar, as white and perfect as a sketch by Leonardo.

Edward watched her for a while. She seemed strangely agitated, because she kept turning away from the window and then turning back again. Every now and then she would raise her hand as if she were trying to shield her eyes from the glare of the gallery's spotlights.

Not another brick-thrower, Edward prayed. Even if she didn't manage to crack the window, he would have to call the police, and then there would be crowds, and questions, and all the usual wrangling. One woman had smeared a pecan pie all over the window, simply because she objected to the 'indecency' of two pink-painted metal cubes entitled *Uncertain Nudes*.

But this woman kept her distance from the window and didn't produce any bricks from her handbag. She didn't go away, though, in spite of the cold and in spite of the jostling lunchtime crowds; and it was quite clear that it was the gallery window to which she was drawn.

After five minutes or so, Edward came down the stairs into the main body of the gallery and approached the window so that he could get a better look at the woman. She was tall – much taller than he had first imagined – and very striking. She had the lean, well-bred face of an upper-class European woman, possibly English, more likely French. Her eyes were large and feline and heavy-lidded; her mouth was slightly parted, and Edward could detect the glint of slightly overbiting teeth. For some reason, teeth like that had always appealed to him. A woman with a slight overbite always looked to him as if she was on the verge of experiencing some faintly erotic pleasure.

He continued to watch her, and every so often she would turn and stare directly back at him, but there was no indication in her expression that she had seen him, or that she was at all concerned that he was observing her so intently.

At length, however, just when he began to think that she was going to leave, she quickly approached the gallery door and pressed the bell with the flat of her hand.

Oh, well, thought Edward. Here we go. Eccentric of the month. He came forward with his warm, executive-curator's smile and unlocked the door. Cold mink brushed against his hand as the woman stepped inside. Edward conscientiously locked the door behind her, and then turned. The woman was white-faced, her head tossing in agitation, like a thoroughbred mare that can smell smoke.

'Are you the owner?' she demanded. Clear, cut-crystal English.

'I'm the executive curator. The owner's out right now.'

'Will he be long?'

'Well, I guess. He told me not to expect him before five; and, with him, that usually means six.'

'So,' said the woman. Then, more quietly, 'So.' She stalked slowly towards the nearest painting, *The Wedding Feast*, immaculately painted, immaculately varnished, sheen upon sheen, until it was almost impossible for the eye to penetrate it.

'Rossetti,' she said.

Edward nodded. 'I can tell you the price if you want.'

The woman raised her head and looked around at some of the other paintings. 'Excellent. An excellent collection.'

'Thank you,' said Edward.

The woman frowned at him as if she couldn't understand him. 'I wasn't complimenting you. I was complimenting the artists. It is artists who create. Collectors only collect. And galleries – galleries are the money-changers in the temple.'

Edward tried to look unperturbed. 'I'm afraid that Pre-Raphaelites aren't exactly my forte,' he said. The woman, as he spoke, turned her back on him. He added, 'I'm more of an Impressionist man, myself.'

The woman said, with her face hidden, 'I have always associated the Impressionists with weakness. They seek to interpret light, rather than form. Light is nothing; light has no substance. Only skin and bone have any true meaning. Flesh, and muscle.'

'That's one point of view,' Edward replied, trying to be polite. After all, the woman was obviously wealthy, and obviously highly eccentric. Who knows? She might make an offer for one of the Holman Hunts, and then he would genuinely have earned his title of 'executive

33

curator'. He followed her with his hands clasped tightly behind his back as she walked around the gallery's semicircular floor, glancing at each of the paintings in turn.

'Upstairs,' he said helpfully, 'we have a previously unattributed Millais. A portrait of Wilkie Collins, painted just before he married Effie Ruskin.'

'Yes,' said the woman; and Edward had the peculiar feeling that she was talking about the painting as if she knew it.

'It's, ah –' said Edward, raising his hand towards the balcony. 'Would you care to take a look at it?'

The woman said, 'No.'

'Oh,' said Edward. There was an uneasy pause. Then Edward said, 'Is there anything else you're interested in?'

'Yes,' said the woman. She inspected the paintings one more time, then turned back and stared at Edward. 'Waldegrave. Do you have any paintings by Walter Waldegrave?'

Edward leaned forward, as if he hadn't quite heard her. 'Waldegrave? I'm sorry.'

'He was English, born in London. He painted landscapes, mostly. Very few portraits. But there is one portrait in particular which I am very keen to acquire.'

'Can you . . . describe it?' asked Edward.

'It measures five feet wide by three feet deep. It is a very *dark* portrait; and it shows a family of twelve, in a red-lined drawing room.'

Edward flushed for a moment, and then very slowly shook his head. 'I'm sorry. You'll have to talk to the owner.' He felt embarrassed, and for some reason peculiarly fearful. On his second day at the Pearson gallery, Vincent had taken him back to the stockroom, where there were two or three hundred mid-Victorian paintings stored in slide-out racks, all kept at a constant temperature and humidity. Vincent had shown him some of the finest, some that were merely entertaining daubs, some that he was anxious to sell to anybody at almost any price, some that he could hardly bear to part with.

When Edward rolled out one large canvas, however, Vincent had stepped straight across the aisle and rolled it back out of sight again. 'Not to be sold, that one,' he had said briskly. 'That belongs to the Pearsons' private collection.'

Edward had rolled it a few inches back out again. 'I can see why,' he had said. 'It's a marvellous piece of work. But aren't they all hideous? I wouldn't like to meet *them* on a dark night; especially not *en masse*.'

'It was my grandfather's,' Vincent had explained, insistently pushing it back out of sight. 'For some reason he was very superstitious about it. He used to say that it was like a family charm – that as long as we kept it, it would keep us safe.'

'In that case, I can see why you do,' Edward had remarked. 'But why do you keep it here? It would look absolutely terrific in your apartment.'

'It always used to hang over the living-room fireplace when I was a boy,' Vincent had told him. 'But lately, it's begun to deteriorate. I'm sending it up to Aaron Halperin next week to have it restored.'

'It's kind of spooky, isn't it?' Edward had replied. 'I mean, all these ugly old people. Do you think Waldegrave painted them from life?'

Vincent had shrugged. 'They were probably nothing more than a fantasy. A figment of the artist's nasty imagination. Waldegrave was pretty odd towards the latter part of his life; mixed up in witchcraft and demonology and all that kind of hocus-pocus. Mind you, Stuart Heathcliff thinks that this painting was nothing more than a satire on Waldegrave's critics. Every art-commentator who had ever given him a bad notice, collected together and made to look as ugly as their reviews.'

'Must be worth something, just as a piece of history,' Edward had commented.

'Yes; but it's not for sale,' Vincent had replied, with an emphasis in his voice that made it clear that he was not inclined to discuss the painting any further. Edward had hesitated for a moment, then made a face, and followed Vincent out of the stockroom.

But here, only two months later, was this white-faced woman in furs asking him about the very same painting. Twelve people, in a red-lined room; although according to what *she* had said, the twelve people were not critics, not art-commentators, but a family. Perhaps Waldegrave hadn't liked them, either. Perhaps they were his in-laws.

The woman said, 'I was given to understand on good authority that Mr Pearson is the present keeper of the Waldegrave portrait. I have in fact been trying to locate it for a very long time.'

Edward found himself smiling rather inanely, although he didn't really mean to. It just seemed to be the only response that his face was able to come up with. 'The name Waldegrave does ring a bell,' he remarked.

'Walter Waldegrave,' the woman enunciated clearly, without taking her eyes away from Edward's face. Such extraordinary eyes, that looked at him, and yet didn't seem to be looking at him at all. They were more like mirrors than eyes. 'Born seventh March 1843. Died, thirteenth April 1886. That was a Tuesday, you know, and in Connecticut it was raining.'

Edward thought: here we go. The first cracks in the

apparently sane exterior. The next thing, she's going to be stripping her clothes off, or attacking the paintings with a bottle of Indian ink.

He said, 'I really don't know anything about such a picture. I've seen all of Mr Pearson's collection, even his watercolour portfolios, and I'm afraid that . . .' He lifted his hands to show that he was no longer able to help.

'You've seen it, haven't you?' the woman asked him. 'I can tell, by the look on your face. You've seen it. What kind of a condition is it in? Is it undamaged? Is it still unmarked?'

'I'm sorry,' said Edward, 'we're really talking at cross-purposes here. It would be much better if you came back later and talked to Mr Pearson.'

The woman paused, and then she said, 'I am prepared to pay you a very great deal of money for it, if necessary.'

'Well, I'll tell Mr Pearson that. I'm sure that he'll give you the promptest possible attention.'

'You're very loyal, aren't you?' the woman asked him. 'A very loyal executive curator. Well, I suppose I can't blame you. There was a time when men were dashing. These days, they're too concerned about losing their jobs.'

Edward said, 'Shall I tell Mr Pearson that you'll be calling around again?'

'If you wish.'

'Shall I tell him your name?'

'You may, if you want to.'

Edward went across to the little desk where they kept their cards and their pens, and where customers perched on a rococo chair to write out their cheques. He picked out a pen from the ivory holder, and said, 'Yes?'

'Tell him that Ms Vane called. Ms Sybil Vane. I won't leave my number. I'm staying with friends at the moment, and I don't think they'll much appreciate being disturbed by calls from trade.'

'And when do you expect to be able to come back?'

'Tomorrow,' the woman told him. 'I'm not sure whether it will be morning or afternoon. But certainly tomorrow.'

'Thank you,' said Edward, and led the woman to the door.

'You're very security-conscious,' she remarked, as he made a point of glancing into the street before he unlocked the door.

'Well, we have to be. This isn't exactly Woolworth's.'

The woman smiled at him. 'You've been charming,' she said. 'I shall look forward to seeing you again tomorrow.'

'Goodbye, madam,' said Edward dutifully.

He locked the door after she had left, and watched her cross 61st Street against the traffic. In a moment, she had disappeared. He turned back into the gallery and walked over to the desk, where the card lay with the name *Ms Sybil Vane* scrawled across it. He picked it up, fanning it between finger and thumb.

There had been something remarkable about that woman. Something not quite real. She had been cold, and testy, and not particularly polite, and yet there had been a quality about her, a chilly charisma, which had left Edward feeling that he would like to see her again, if only to look at her. She had left a strange perfume in the air, too. It was like nothing he had ever smelled before. It smelled like closed rooms, crowded with flowers. It smelled like spices kept in sealed ceramic jars. It smelled like the love-juice of a woman, inhaled long after she has left, from a small embroidered handkerchief.

He could almost fantasize that under her long black

mink coat, she had been naked. Pale shining thighs, black silky stockings.

He suddenly felt very young and immature, the same way he had felt at high school when he had tried to ask Sally Vanderhogh for a date; yet elated, too, and slightly frightened.

He turned around and there was a man outside in the street watching him through the glass door. Their eyes met for a moment; then the man had gone. He thought of the woman saying, *'That was a Tuesday, you know, and in Connecticut it was raining.'* And it was his memory of that remark, the strangely matter-of-fact way in which she had said it, that disturbed him more than anything else.

'In Connecticut it was raining.' Perhaps she wasn't an eccentric, after all.

Three

The sleet was falling so furiously now across the reservoir that they could scarcely see the shore. Gordon had retreated under his Army-surplus rain-cape, so that all Wesley could see of him was the glowing butt of his cigarette, and the twin reflections that it sparked off in the lenses of his circular spectacles. Wesley remained where he was, well forward, in the prow of the boat, casting and reeling in and recasting in spite of the slanting sleet, his waterproof hat hanging down over his ears like a sodden cabbage, determined that he wouldn't row back to shore until he had caught himself at least one more perch. The fish had been laughing at him today, and Wesley wasn't the kind of man who cared to be laughed at, either by fish or by women. Gordon couldn't have cared less who laughed at him, but then Gordon hadn't been through two divorces, and Gordon hadn't lost his ten-year-old son in a boating accident, either, as Wesley had.

The police had dragged Candlewood Lake three times, but they had never found the body of Wesley's son. That had been six long years ago now. But Wesley still took his anger out on the fish. Nobody ever mentioned it, not out loud, but the terrible implication of Wesley's anger was that the fish had actually eaten his son.

He had to blame the fish, of course. He couldn't blame himself.

Gordon lit a fresh cigarette from the butt of the last, and noisily cleared his throat. 'Weather forecast didn't say nothing about no sleet,' he remarked, as if that would cheer Wesley up.

'Weather forecasters don't know shit,' said Wesley, as he tugged at the line. 'Anybody with half an eye could have seen there was sleet coming. You can tell it by the clouds.'

Gordon said, 'You want a sandwich? Marjorie packed me some pepperoni.'

'I'll have a beer, if there's any left.'

'Sure.'

Gordon shuffled around inside the makeshift tent of his khaki rain-cape, and at last produced a can of Miller. He was wet and bone-cold and uncomfortable, but he knew better than to suggest to Wesley that they row back to the shore yet. When you went fishing with Wesley, you stayed out on the reservoir until Wesley was satisfied that he had massacred enough fish. Only then did you head for home. The compensation was that when you went fishing with Wesley, you always caught yourself three times as many as when you went fishing with anybody else; and Wesley would give you the whole of his catch, too. Wesley never ate fish. Nobody ever asked him why.

The sleet rattled across the surface of the lake in grey, chilly salvos. It was almost impossible to make out the shoreline now, except for a dark serrated line of pine trees. Wesley sniffed, and wiped his dripping ginger moustache with the back of his hand. Then he tugged open the ring-pull on his can of beer, and drank. 'Crazy, isn't it?' he said. 'I'm sitting out here on three hundred million gallons of water, having another half-million gallons dumped on me from Heaven Above, and I'm thirsty.'

Gordon blew smoke, and said nothing.

For a long time, there was no sound but the sleet, and the persistent slapping of wavelets against the side of the boat, and the sharp whirring of Wesley's reel. 'Fucking fish,' said Wesley, after a while.

Gordon tossed his cigarette butt into the reservoir. 'You still seeing Marlene Adams?' he enquired. He never got into discussions about fish.

'Sure I am. I took her down to Bridgeport last week, to see the Johnny Cash concert.'

'She like Johnny Cash?'

'All country music. Dolly Parton, Waylon Jennings, Smokey Valley Boys, you name it.'

'Never would have thought it, not to look at her.'

Wesley finished his beer, and crumpled the can in his left fist. 'All women like country music. It's sentimental, that's why. Give them something sentimental, and that's all they need. Something with tears in. You know what her favourite is? That one about the little girl who turns up on the doorstep with her little puppy and then dies in the night.'

Gordon sniffed philosophically. 'Well, never would have thought it. Not to look at her.' He paused for a long time, and then he said, 'The little girl, you mean?'

'What?'

'The little girl dies in the night?'

'And the puppy, both.'

Gordon nodded, and checked his watch. It would be growing really dark soon. He wondered if he ought to eat his last pepperoni sandwich, or leave it until later. From inside Gordon's dark, dripping cape, Wesley looked in the sleety twilight like Captain Ahab searching for his nemesis. Hunched and determined and unforgiving. *Moby-Dick* was the only classic book that Gordon had ever read, apart from *No Orchids for Miss Blandish*, and he had scarcely understood a word of it. He liked to tell people that he had read it, though, and quote from it from time to time.

'Better to sleep with a sober cannibal than a drunken Christian.' That was his favourite line.

He was still debating with himself about the sandwich when Wesley suddenly jerked his line. 'Shit!' Wesley shouted. 'I've got something. Something real big!'

Gordon tried to tug his raincoat off, and scramble forward; but Wesley shouted at him, 'Stay where you are! Don't rock the fucking boat so much!'

There was a short *zizz* of line going out; then Wesley began to reel in. 'It's big,' he said excitedly. 'Biggest one today, easy.'

Gordon crouched in the middle of the boat, straining his eyes against the icy rain and the darkness. 'Can't see nothing,' he said.

'There! Look, there! You can just see the splash!'

'Still can't see nothing.'

'Well, come here and give me a hand, pinhead. This thing weighs a fucking ton.'

Clumsily, Gordon made his way forward and helped Wesley to grasp the handle of the fishing-pole. Whatever Wesley was reeling in, it was tugging against them with enormous, sluggish resistance; but to Gordon it felt more like a dead weight. It wasn't struggling, it wasn't fighting against them, it was just dragging in the water like a half-submerged log. If it was alive, anything that size would have whipped both of them straight out of the boat. Gordon had gone out blue-marlin fishing off the Florida Keys once, and he knew just how powerful and just how lively those suckers could be.

'It's a log,' he told Wesley. Wesley's ear was dripping and pink, like a freshly opened clam.

'Don't talk crap, this ain't no log. This is the big one. This is the fucking big one.'

Nepaug, like all lakes and reservoirs, had a legendary monster-sized fish. The local fishing enthusiasts called it Old Whiskers, but Wesley never referred to it as anything else but 'the big one'. Half the fishermen in Litchfield claimed to have hooked Old Whiskers on their lines, at one time or another. All of them, of course, had been forced to cut him free.

Gordon said, 'Still can't see nothing. If this was a fish, this would be struggling. This ain't struggling none. This is a log.'

Wesley turned and stared at him, white-faced. 'You're trying to tell me I don't know no fucking log when I catch one? This ain't no fucking log! This is it! This is the big one!'

Almost hysterically, Wesley wound and wound and wound at his reel. Gordon tried to help him, but Wesley angrily pushed him aside. Now, through the sleet, Gordon could make out herring-bone ripples in the water, where Wesley was reeling his catch towards them. It was dark, and it was big, and it sure looked like a log. Gordon took off his glasses and wiped them on his damp, crumpled handkerchief.

The dark shape in the water now floated towards them under its own momentum. Wesley must have known by now that it wasn't a fish, that it was only a lump of wood or a tangle of weeds and trash, but he kept on winding until the line was taut and the object bumped against the hull of their boat.

'Now, you bastard!' he cried, almost sobbing, and whipped back his fishing-pole so that the thing reared out of the water.

44

Gordon screamed like a woman. The object, as it jumped up, almost as if it were alive, was a human body. The horrifying thing about it was that it was hairless, and raw-red all over, the grisly scarlet of fish-bait. Its eyes were lidless and its teeth were bare and it stared at them in expressionless agony before it splashed and wallowed back into the water again.

'*Jesus Christ!*' shrieked Wesley. '*Jesus Christ!*' He scrabbled for his knife to cut the body loose from his line, but at first he couldn't manage to sever it, and he was shaking and whining and cursing all at once. The body spun around and knocked against the boat again, and Wesley yelled out, '*Get away! Get away! For Christ's sake, get away!*'

In the end, unable to cut his line, he tossed his entire fishing-pole overboard and sat, rigid with horror, watching the body gradually float round and round and away from them.

Gordon stumbled to the stern of the boat and yanked at the starter of the old Evinrude motor. Unusually, with a deafening burp, it burst into life first time. Without a word, Gordon turned the boat around and steered it through the curtains of sleet back towards the shore-line. Wesley didn't say anything either. Wesley didn't even look at Gordon, but knelt in the waist of the boat, his hands clutching the gunwales until his knuckles were white, his head bowed, only his shoulders betraying the spasms of fear and disgust that were rippling through him with every breath.

And worst of all, the unspoken words: My son must have looked like that after the fish had been at him. O God above, my son must have looked like that.

They reached the wooden jetty on the north-west bank of the reservoir. Gordon tied the boat up with freezing banana-fingered hands, his face contorted against the sleet. Wesley remained kneeling, staring at Gordon's lunchbox as if it somehow contained the terrible secret to everything that had happened.

Gordon took his arm. 'Wes, Wesley. Come on now.'

Wesley looked up. His face looked as if it had been disassembled and then put back together again.

'Come on, Wesley, we've got to call the police. That was a body out there.'

Wesley said, 'It wasn't . . . ?'

'No,' Gordon reassured him. 'It wasn't Donnie. Donnie's long gone, remember. And Donnie was a boy. That was a man, or maybe a woman. Somebody full-grown.'

Wesley stood up unsteadily, and allowed Gordon to half lift him up on to the jetty. Gordon's Chevrolet was parked a little way off, its windscreen heaped with frozen slush. Gordon helped Wesley to cross the sloping bank of the reservoir, and into the passenger seat.

'The way that thing came jumping out of the water,' said Wesley. 'By God, Gordon, that scared the living shit right out of me, I promise you.'

'Well, me too,' said Gordon. 'But let's go call the police.'

There was a garage at Warren. It took them over half an hour to reach it across the rough wooded tracks, but during all that time they hardly spoke. The windscreen wipers squeaked monotonously from side to side, clearing triangles through the sleet. Gordon smoked as he drove, his eyes squinched up against the gathering darkness. Wesley sat sideways in his seat as if he were an invalid, as if every nerve in his body had been rubbed raw.

Wesley stayed crouched in the car while Gordon called Sheriff Jack Smith, at Torrington. He watched

Gordon with glazed eyes as Gordon stood in the sleet-swept telephone booth, gesticulating with his cigarette. When Gordon came hurrying back to the wagon and opened the door, he said, 'Well?'

'They're coming. We have to get back to the reservoir.'

Wesley shook his head. 'I don't want to go, Gordon.'

'You have to. You can stay in the wagon if you want to. You don't have to – you know, look at it or anything. They won't make you do that.'

Slowly, pathetically, Wesley began to sob. He clamped his hands over his face but the tears ran down his wrists. Gordon watched him for a while, biting his lip, feeling helpless; but then he tugged the gear-lever into drive, turned it round on the forecourt and headed back towards the Nepaug Reservoir.

The sheriff's car arrived within an hour, its blue lights flashing in the darkness. The sleet had eased off now, replaced by a thin, wet, penetrating drizzle. Both Gordon and Wesley stayed in their seats as the sheriff walked across towards them, his flashlight bobbing and ducking with every step. He opened Gordon's door, and said, 'How are you doing, gents? This isn't the day for it.'

Gordon climbed down and nodded back towards Wesley. 'Wesley's taken it kind of hard, Sheriff. It's shook him up. I guess, you know, it kind of reminds him of what happened before. He didn't take that easy, either.'

Sheriff Jack Smith was stocky and short, with a big good-looking head that had always reminded his wife Nancy of Richard Burton. He wore a dark blue water-proof hunting cap with furry ear-flaps, and a dark blue raincoat. He was thirty-eight; the most outspoken and pragmatic sheriff that Litchfield County had elected for years. He believed in drug programmes and constructive welfare work and community service for young offenders, and he had never shot anybody in his life. He knew that he was the legal custodian of a countryside in which the native farming population was falling fast, in which the old values and the old customs were disappearing. After all, this part of Connecticut, in the 1980s, had a lower population than it had been able to boast in the 1780s.

Jack Smith also knew that his liabilities included looking after the mainly empty properties of wealthy New Yorkers who came up to Connecticut only at weekends; as well as keeping an eye when they *did* come up on their big-city tastes for cocaine, and for women who weren't their wives, and for domestic disturbances.

Ten to one, he thought, as he stood in the sifting rain by the shores of Nepaug Reservoir, ten to one this floater doesn't come from Litchfield; nor died here, neither.

'Dan Maskell's coming over,' Jack told Gordon. 'He's bringing the inflatable boat, and a searchlight. He should be here in just a while.'

'Wesley thought that he'd hooked a fish,' said Gordon.

'Whereabouts was it?' asked Jack, flicking the beam of his torch out into the darkness.

'Just floating around in the middle there someplace. But you should have seen it. It was kind of red all over, like it was painted or something, or burned. Did you ever see anybody burned?'

'Frequently,' Jack told him. His brown eyes gave nothing away.

'Well, I don't never want to see nothing like that, not again,' said Gordon, shaking his head. 'That damned thing's going to give me nightmares for the rest of my life.'

After about twenty minutes, Dan Maskell arrived in a police pick-up with an inflatable dinghy on the back, and a collection of generators and searchlights and nets and boat-hooks. While the dinghy was being blown up, a four-wheel-drive Datsun arrived from the medical referee's office, and Wallace Greenstreet stepped out, haughty and tall as a stork, in a London Fog raincoat that looked as if it had been used by a team of small boys as a little-league football.

'Sorry to drag you out, Wallace,' said Jack, taking out a stick of Wrigley's Spearmint and folding it into his mouth.

Wallace briskly rubbed his hands together. 'This time, I have to admit that it was quite a relief,' he told Jack affably. 'My sister had just arrived, with that half-witted husband of hers. When you called, he was just about to strike up a conversation on the relative merits of rented rug-cleaners.'

'Gum?' asked Jack.

Wallace fastidiously shook his head. 'What do we have here? Have you located it yet?'

'Give us an hour or so. It shouldn't be hard to find.'

For the next twenty minutes, Jack and Dan puttered around the reservoir in circles, systematically searching the surface for Wesley's unexpected catch. Their flash-lights criss-crossed through the rain; their voices echoed. Jack felt as if he were searching a flooded cellar.

They came across the body quite suddenly. They bumped into something. Jack shone his flashlight at it, and there it was. Scarlet, as Gordon had told him, and tangled up in fishing-line. On first sight, it reminded Jack of a dead seal he had once seen on a beach in Newfoundland, skinned for its pelt. It was lying face-down, and that usually indicated a male. The smell of decomposing flesh was very strong, in spite of the cold and in spite of the rain.

'Let's just take it in tow,' Jack told Dan. 'Get a hook around that fishing-line, then we can bring it in behind us.'

Dan Maskell's face hung in the torchlight like a wrinkled Hallowe'en pumpkin. He was fifty-three years old, a professional policeman with thirty-two years of service. He had dragged so many dead bodies out of cars, out of lakes, out of garages, out of bedrooms, out of rivers, out of woods, that one more dead body just didn't make any difference, as far as he was concerned. He caught hold of Wesley's floating fishing-pole and made it fast, and then turned the inflatable dinghy back to shore.

'We're not looking for anybody special, are we?' Dan asked. Usually, when a gang personality disappeared in New York, Jack's office would be sent a message to look out for his corpse. They had once found Vittorio Seccone, in a burnt-out car, deep in the woods around the foothills of Ivy Mountain.

Jack glanced back at the red body they were towing. 'Nobody that I know of. Besides, this doesn't look like the Cosa Nostra had anything to do with it. Too grisly. Only amateurs ever get this grisly.'

They brought the body into shore, and carefully carried it along to the end of the jetty. Jack and Dan both wore gloves; but even so Jack could feel how slippery the flesh was. They laid the body on to Wallace Greenstreet's stretcher, and inspected it by the light of their torches.

'Is this the body you saw?' Jack asked Gordon.

Gordon could scarcely look at it: the mask-like face, without eyelids or lips; the red slimy chest; the genitals like a handful of pig's-liver. He nodded, and said,

'Unless there's another one floating around out there, exactly the same.'

'Don't bet that there isn't,' put in Dan Maskell, lighting up a wine-flavoured cheroot, and then obviously wishing that he had taken his gloves off first.

'Will Wesley make an identification?' asked Jack.

Gordon shook his head. 'Wesley's got this idea . . . well, you know. It's all to do with Donnie. He saw this thing come rearing up, and all he could think about was Donnie.'

Jack steadily chewed gum. 'All right, then,' he said. 'I'll talk to Wesley later. Why don't you take him home, give him a couple of drinks? I'll call by later and see how he's shaping up.'

'Okay,' said Gordon, clasping Jack's shoulder. 'Thanks for everything.'

As Gordon drove away, Jack and Wallace and Dan gathered around the stretcher. Dan had manhandled the floodlight out of the dinghy, and set it up on its tripod a few feet away so that they could examine the corpse more closely.

'Well, a male, all right,' said Wallace, lifting the slippery mass of the genitals with his index-finger. 'Caucasian, judging by his blue eyes, although you can't tell by the skin. The entire epidermis has gone, including the melanocytic cells that would have shown us whether he was black or white.'

Jack said, 'The fish haven't gotten to his eyes yet.'

'Indeed,' said Wallace, 'and that would indicate to me, as it obviously has to you, that this body hasn't been floating around in the water for very long. Possibly, only a few hours.'

'Then how the hell did his skin get like this?' asked Dan. 'He isn't burned, is he? And he hasn't been nibbled by fish.'

51

Wallace looked at the body more closely. 'What you see here is the corium, or true skin. The outer skin, the epidermis, has completely gone. Not just in patches, as you might expect from a burn or an accident, but completely and perfectly. Look here, and here. Those are marks from a knife. A surgical scalpel, probably, or something similar.'

'I still don't follow this,' said Jack. 'What are you trying to say to me?'

'I can't be conclusive, of course,' said Wallace. 'Not by the side of a lake in the middle of a downpour. But I'd say that this poor fellow was almost certainly skinned.'

Jack's chewing slowed down. He looked at Wallace acutely. '*Skinned*? You mean deliberately?'

Wallace nodded.

Jack stuck his hands on his hips and looked the body up and down. '*Skinned?*' he said. 'Holy Moses.'

'Do you think he was still alive when they did it?' asked Dan. 'Is there any way of telling?'

'Well, none, not really,' said Wallace. 'But I would certainly guess that he was still alive; and probably conscious, too. Otherwise, what on earth would have been the point of doing it? This is torture, in my view. Deliberate, calculating torture; and carried out most expertly, too. Whoever took this man's skin off was a real expert.'

Jack looked down at the ghastly, glaring-red face. 'What the hell would anybody want to do something like this for? I mean – you can hurt somebody just as much without peeling them apart like an apple.'

'Well, you're the one who has to look for the motives,' said Wallace. He unfolded a black plastic sheet and laid it over the corpse with the nonchalance of a housewife making a bed. 'Maybe it was part of some Mafia ritual. Maybe they wanted to make an example of him.'

'But if they wanted to do that, why did they throw him in the reservoir? *We* only found him by accident; and it was highly likely that he would never have been found at all. What's the point of going to such lengths to make an example out of someone, and then dumping their body where the chances are that nobody's going to see what you've done?'

Wallace buckled up the straps around the corpse, and then looked at Jack with one of his bland, don't-ask-me expressions. 'I'm only the medical examiner, remember? All I can give you is fact, not conjecture. The fact is this man was flayed, probably while he was still alive, and probably by somebody whose skills were as good as a top-flight plastic surgeon. Anyway, they might have disposed of the body, but you remember that old Jewish joke, about "when they circumcised you, my friend, they threw away the wrong bit"?'

'What the hell are you talking about?' Jack demanded.

Wallace raised a hand to calm him. 'I'm simply saying that they might have disposed of the body, but they still have the skin.'

Jack stared at him. He stopped chewing. 'And you think they might have used his skin . . . as an example? Kind of exhibited it? Here's the skin of Don Whatever-His-Name-Was; if you don't watch out, the same thing could happen to you?'

Wallace shrugged. 'As I say, Jack, the motivational conjecture is up to you.'

As they talked, another car drew up, an elderly Volkswagen, and a young man in a duffel coat climbed out and hurried towards them, swinging a camera.

'Hi, Dennis,' Jack greeted him. Dennis worked for the *Litchfield Sentinel*.

Dennis was lanky and tall, with an incipient black

moustache, and a crowd of angry pimples on his chin. 'Somebody dead?' he wanted to know.

'No, no, that's Deputy Cohen under there, rehearsing his part in *Frankenstein*.'

'A floater?' asked Dennis, unabashed.

'Found floating,' Jack corrected him.

'Not drowned, then?'

Jack shook his head. 'Killed first, floated later. So far, I'm treating it as homicide.'

'Can I take a picture?'

'Not this time.'

'Aw, come on, Sheriff. The public's right to know.'

Jack said, 'Knowing doesn't necessarily include prying. Nor does it necessarily include the taking of obscene pictures.'

'What's obscene? That's a body, not the gatefold of *Hustler*.'

Jack said, 'Give me your camera.'

'What?' asked Dennis.

'Give me your camera,' Jack repeated, and held out his hand. Reluctantly, uncertainly, Dennis passed it over. Jack said, 'Now you can look. Go on. Make up your own mind whether it's obscene or not.'

Wallace, with thinly concealed amusement, noisily folded back the plastic sheet to expose the corpse's head. Dennis stood staring at it for almost half a minute. Then he looked away and nodded, and came back to Jack to retrieve his camera.

'What did they do to him?' he asked, in a sporadic voice. 'What the hell did they *do* to him to make him look like that?'

'The way it appears to us, now, they hurt him a very great deal,' said Jack. 'If you want more details, come to my office tomorrow morning.'

'You've got it,' said Dennis, and left. They watched

his tail-lights jiggle away across the fields and into the woods.

'Poor kid,' Dan remarked. He scratched his stomach, as if he had just taken his girdle off. But Jack said, 'All right. That's it. We've got work to do. Wallace – get that body to the morgue. Dan, you can start taping off this whole area, all around the landing-stage. I'll call up the forensic guys and get them out here straight away. We need to look for footprints, clothing, splashes of blood, anything.'

'Supposing we find his skin?' asked Dan.

Jack looked at him, his face baleful in the floodlight, the crags of his cheeks overemphasized by intense light and intense shadow.

'Don't ask questions you don't want to hear the answer to,' he replied. 'Now, come on, let's get going.'

He went back to his car, a three-year-old Cherokee with a dent in the door. He called Torrington, and asked for the forensic department. Then he had himself transferred to his home telephone number. Nancy answered almost straight away.

'Nancy? It's Jack.'

'Oh, darling. Are you going to be late?'

'Very, by the look of it. We just brought in a body from the Nepaug Reservoir.'

'Oh, no. Was it a drowning?'

Jack said, 'I can't talk about it now. I'll see you later. But give my love to Benny, won't you? And lots of love to you, too.'

Dan came up, holding Wesley's fishing-pole.

'Do you want me to stash this stuff in your car?' he asked. 'You can take it round later.'

Jack hung up his intercom. He unwrapped another stick of chewing-gum. 'I'm not sure that poor old

Wesley is going to want to see any of that fishing-tackle ever again.'

Dan stood and waited, with the cold rain falling all around him; and really neither of them knew what the hell they were going to do.

Four

By three o'clock that afternoon, there was still no sign of the woman who had called herself Sybil Vane. Vincent came out of the stockroom where he had been wrapping up the two Johnsons that he wanted restored, and said, 'It looks like your lady is a no-show.'

Edward had been sitting with one buttock perched on the edge of the desk, watching the doorway almost all afternoon. It was impossible for him to explain to Vincent how disappointed he felt by Sybil Vane's failure to appear. He felt almost as if he might have invented her; the frustrated fantasy of a young man who had just lost his fiancée to an Armenian meat-packer. Correction, attorney.

'She was quite clear that it was a Waldegrave she was after?' asked Vincent. He had taken off his coat, and in his seven-button waistcoat and his starchy white shirt, he looked as relaxed as Edward had ever seen him. He was handsome, in a rather too clear-cut way, with curly grey hair, a squarish, Italianate face and a very short straight nose. He could have posed for Michelangelo's *David*, except that he didn't look as effete as that. His girlfriend from the Metropolitan Museum of Modern Art, Charlotte Greene, called him 'god in a three-piece suit'. They didn't sleep together. She might have called him something else if they had.

Edward said, 'She described it exactly. Twelve people, in a red-lined room. She knew Waldegrave's dates, the date of his birth, the date of his death. She said that she'd been looking for the portrait for a very long time.'

Vincent checked his watch. 'Well, I can't stay very much longer.'

'I could always tell her to come back next week,' Edward suggested.

Vincent fastened his cuff-links. 'I don't think there's very much point. I'm not going to sell her the painting, whatever she offers.'

'She said that she'd pay you really well for it.'

Vincent straightened his necktie, lifted his coat off the back of the rococo chair, and shrugged it on. 'I'm sorry,' he said. 'It's simply not for sale, and that's all. Apart from which, it's beginning to fall to pieces. You know what those mid-Victorian amateurs were like. They never mixed their paints properly. Too much turpentine, too little pigment. And Waldegrave was one of the worst.'

'What shall I tell her, then, if she comes?' asked Edward.

'Tell her precisely that. Tell her the picture is not for sale. Tell her that it's in terrible condition, in any case; and that even if she *were* to buy it, she'd most certainly be wasting her money. Quite seriously, I give that picture two years, if that. It's always happening, even to the best paintings. Just before you came, I had to take a John Frederick Lewis off display. A beautiful picture, *Saturday Morning in the Hareem*, one of those Oriental studies. But the paint was falling off it like dandruff.'

Edward challenged him, a little impertinently, 'You're not going to tell me that you're superstitious about it? The Waldegrave, I mean?'

Vincent smiled benignly, and picked up the two Johnsons, one under each arm. 'Of course I'm superstitious about it. Why shouldn't I be? My grandfather said that if we held on to it, it would keep the family safe. And if that's what my grandfather thought about it, then that's good enough for me.'

'But you don't *really* believe it?'

'Stop psychoanalysing your employer. Do you want a Christmas bonus, or not? And make sure that you set the alarm properly before you leave. I shall be back in the city very early Monday morning and I shall probably call around at your apartment to collect the keys.'

'All right,' said Edward. Neither of them commented on the fact that this was the first time that Vincent had trusted Edward to lock up the gallery himself. Edward began to feel the beginnings of a pleasant familiarity between them, the budding of an amicable working relationship which might well develop into a close friendship. Vincent was formal in his manners, traditional in the way that he dressed; but Edward sensed his genuine appreciation of the people who worked for him and the people he loved.

Vincent left the gallery to walk down to the car park on 61st and Third, where he collected his dark green Bentley Eight. He drove back to the gallery and parked it outside, so that Edward could carry out the two Johnsons for him.

'If Milo Kasabian calls, tell him he can reach me in the country,' said Vincent. 'And if Charlotte calls, tell her I'll be with her in five minutes flat, traffic permitting.'

He looked up and down the street. 'Still no sign of your mysterious Ms Vane?' he asked.

Edward shook his head.

'Think it'll snow?' Vincent asked him.

'It's my birthday next week,' said Edward. 'It never snows before my birthday.'

Vincent drove off, and Edward returned to the gallery, unlocking the door with his special security keys. He checked his watch. Only another hour, and he could go home. But Vincent made a point of keeping the gallery open at all advertised hours, citing the family story of the evening that Nubar Gulbenkian had walked into the gallery at one minute to five and asked if it was too late for him to purchase a Thomas Hart Benton painting of *Susanna and the Elders.*

Edward went through to the office and plugged in the electric kettle, so that he could make himself a cup of coffee. Vincent didn't approve of percolators: on a tray on top of the filing-cabinet there was a copper Belgian coffee pot, and a copper container of coffee.

Edward was sitting at his desk in the front of the gallery reading Charles Holmes' biography of James Thurber when the doorbell rang. The ringing startled him; so much so that it left a salty taste in his mouth. He put down his book and walked over to the door, already taking his keys out of his pocket. It was Sybil Vane; white-faced as before, and wrapped in her furs.

He unlocked the door. She came into the gallery as fluidly as an animal. She looked around, and asked, 'He's here?'

'Mr Pearson? I'm afraid you've just missed him. He had to go up to the country for the weekend. I thought you might have been able to call by a little earlier. He left, what, only ten minutes ago.'

'Well, what a pity,' the woman said, although she sounded distinctly unconcerned. 'I was looking forward to meeting him.'

'I'm sorry,' said Edward. 'Can you call back Monday? He'll be here Monday.'

'Did you talk to him about the Waldegrave?'

'Yes, I did.'

The woman came up close to him. She inspected his face as intently as if she were reading the open pages of a book. Again, Edward could smell that extraordinary perfume, pot-pourri and closed rooms and oil of musk and sex. Her even breathing ruffled the fur on her wide collar.

'Did he admit that he *does* have it? The Waldegrave?'

'Well, yes, he does have it. It's been in his family for seventy years.'

'Seventy years, yes,' nodded the woman. 'Seventy-three, to be exact.'

'But . . . I'm afraid, well, he won't sell it.'

The woman pressed her fingertips against her lips, as if she were afraid of what she might say. Then she turned away.

'I did ask him,' Edward told her.

'And?' the woman queried, without turning back.

'He said it was something of a family heirloom, not for sale. Apart from which, it's not wearing too well. Mr Waldegrave wasn't too handy at mixing his paints, apparently. They're all flaking off. Mr Pearson said he wouldn't give the painting longer than two years, even with restoration. He said you'd be wasting your money, if you want the honest truth.'

The woman stared at him and her eyes were like mirrors seen at night. 'Two years? Is that what he said?'

Edward made an apologetic face. 'I'm sorry. But he was quite adamant. It's not for sale.'

'You told him I would pay whatever he asked? You told him how important it was?'

'I'm sorry,' Edward repeated.

The woman tapped her fingertips together worriedly. Then she became conscious that Edward was watching her, and she smiled, a little crookedly, and said, 'Ah, well. If Mr Pearson cannot be persuaded to sell, then Mr Pearson cannot be persuaded to sell.'

'If there's anything else I can interest you in,' Edward suggested, to be encouraging. He felt strangely upset that he could not oblige her; he felt almost as if he needed her approval. Now she would have to leave the gallery disappointed, and above all, disappointed in *him*. He couldn't understand the feeling at all, but he was feeling it, and it was strong enough to make him unusually anxious.

'I have been searching for this particular portrait for so long,' the woman explained, more to herself than to Edward. 'I have been trying to restore an old collection, you see, that used to belong to my family. Only a few paintings remain to be located, no more than eleven or twelve. The Waldegrave, however, is by far the most important. I must tell you, Mr –?' she paused and raised a questioning eyebrow.

'Merriam,' Edward told her. 'Edward Merriam.'

'Not the *Norfolk* Merriams?'

'No, I'm afraid not. The Rochester Merriams.'

'I'm sorry?'

'You wouldn't have heard of them,' Edward smiled. 'They weren't in society.'

'Ah,' said the woman. Then she lifted her hand towards him. He took it and wondered if he were supposed to kiss it. Her fingers were very cold, and there were enough diamond rings on them to have lacerated any man's face to ribbons, like a marmoset's claws. He looked at her and she was waiting for him; and so he pressed his lips lightly against the smooth skin. The hand of a very young woman:

no wrinkles, no liver-spots, no protuberant veins.

'My name, of course, is not really "Sybil Vane",' she said. 'That was just my little joke.'

Edward said nothing, but watched her and waited for her to explain. Perhaps it was a joke against herself, he thought, a gibe against her own vanity.

'My name is Cordelia Gray. If you were thirty years older, you would have heard of the Grays. In those days, everybody had. But we have all been in Europe for a while. Well, for some years, to be exact. It is quite remarkable how quickly one is forgotten. You have no need to be ashamed that your family were not in society. Society is nothing but a basket of snakes, with memories that are no longer than their own tails, and as little heart.'

Edward said, cautiously, 'I'm pleased to know you.'

'Well, Edward,' said Cordelia, 'the pleasure is quite mutual.'

'How long have you been back from Europe?' Edward asked her.

'Less than a month. We have been staying in Newport, for a while. Newport, Rhode Island. But we hope to be moving back into the family home in Connecticut before long. That is why I have been trying to track down all of our old paintings, and all of our old furniture. So much of it was dispersed when we had to go away.'

'That's quite a project, putting an art collection back together again,' said Edward.

'Yes,' said Cordelia. 'So far, however, it has been very successful.'

'Until now, with the Waldegrave,' Edward put in.

Cordelia nodded, brushed fur away from her face. 'Until now, with the Waldegrave,' she agreed.

There was a short silence between them, but it was crowded with unspoken approaches. When they spoke again, they both spoke together, and laughed. Edward said, 'Please, after you.'

'I suppose it sounds very forward of me,' said Cordelia. 'But I was wondering if you yourself might be interested in helping me.'

'You mean, to put your collection back together again?'

Cordelia nodded. 'It wouldn't take up very much of your time. It certainly wouldn't affect your work here. But I would pay you very well for it; and perhaps you would like to come up to Connecticut and help me to hang it, and to catalogue it.'

Edward said, 'It's a very tempting offer. I mean, it sounds like fun. But I'd have to say that I couldn't necessarily get hold of the Waldegrave for you. I mean, that couldn't be part of our arrangement.'

'Of course not,' said Cordelia. 'I understand what Mr Pearson has said to you; and if the painting is not in a fit condition in any case . . . well, perhaps we had better forget about it. But I would certainly appreciate your assistance. Do you think you could be interested in doing that for me?'

Edward hesitated for a moment, then gave her a cheerful, assertive nod. 'Okay. I think I'd like that. If you can get hold of a list of your collection for me, then we can talk it over.'

Cordelia lifted her wrist and looked at her watch. 'I have to go now; I have an appointment. But are you staying in the city this weekend?'

'I usually do.'

'Are you free for lunch on Sunday? At twelve, perhaps? There is a small restaurant on East 60th Street called Les Images. I will meet you there.'

'All right, then,' said Edward. 'As long as you let me pay.'

Cordelia came close to him and touched the lapel of his suit as if she could convey extra meaning to him through her fingertips. 'I wouldn't dream of it. The invitation is mine.'

Edward stood staring at the door for a long time after she had gone. He felt as if he had drunk too much dry white wine. There was a sourish taste in his mouth, and a tight sensation around his scalp. He took a sip of his coffee, but it was cold now, and he grimaced with disgust.

There was no doubt that the presence of Cordelia Gray had an unusual effect on him. It was almost like free-basing, although Edward admittedly had only done that twice. He could imagine it was what miners sometimes felt, when they were being gradually overcome by firedamp, then breathed fresh air again and realized how close they had been to asphyxiation.

He set the alarm and locked up the gallery. He stood for a while in the doorway. The night was cold and noisy, the streets were crowded, and the red tail-lights of passing cars were drowned in a wet black asphalt lake. He walked to the corner of Fifth Avenue with his coat-collar turned up, his hands in his pockets. For a moment, across the street, he thought he saw the face of the man who had peered in through the gallery door yesterday afternoon, after Cordelia Gray had left. A truck passed in between them, and the face was gone.

Edward whistled for a taxi. Three splashed right past his toes, ignoring him, until a third pulled up, driven by a saintly-looking Puerto Rican who appeared to be three parts high. Santana vibrated on his stereo, 'Samba Pa Ti'.

'Wentworth Apartments,' said Edward. 'West 63rd and Eighth.'

'Faster than a speedin' bullet,' the taxi-driver told him.

Edward sat jostled in the back of the taxi as it headed west across Central Park South, and tried not to think about lunch on Sunday. She was only a middle-aged woman, after all. A middle-aged woman from a cobwebby Connecticut family; and all she was interested in was her art collection. So why get so provoked? Why think about her eyes, and her soft-smooth hands, and that faint *zizz* of one silk-stockinged thigh rubbing against the other?

'West 63rd and what was it?' the taxi-driver yelled back.

Five

They drove north-eastwards out of New York into an evening of overwhelming darkness. Vincent had to use his headlights on the Major Deegan Expressway, and they illuminated a cold and hostile future-world of concrete underpasses, distant apartment blocks, scrubby trees and abandoned Thunderbirds robbed of their wheels.

Charlotte Greene sat beside him, the hem of her Oleg Cassini skirt drawn up higher than it ought to have been, revealing very slim legs in very shiny dove-grey tights. She hummed along with the Vivaldi. Vincent always played *The Four Seasons* when he drove back to Connecticut from New York. He said it prepared his mind for the country; for real trees; for people who didn't snarl at you; for fairgrounds and quiet roadside restaurants and red-and-yellow corn fields; and for logs which you had to knock the bugs off before you stacked them on to the fire.

Charlotte said he was being pretentious, but Vincent didn't particularly mind about that.

She was the youngest woman member on the Metropolitan Museum of Modern Art board. Also, by far the most beautiful. Vincent would have taken almost anything from a woman with her qualifications. He

67

liked his women companions to be intelligent, rather than beautiful. When they were both, like Charlotte, it was what he described as a 'heavenly bonus'.

Charlotte said he was arrogant and stuffy. But Charlotte also knew that he was unusually kind, and that no matter how assertive he was, he would never hurt her.

Her taste in art was too advanced, as far as he was concerned. She liked splodges of colour on huge canvases, and stacks of bricks, and old bathtubs with inexplicable messes of enamel down one side. But, physically, she was just his type. She was tall, with a figure like one of Karl Lagerfeld's fashion models, with a shaggy mane of straw-blonde hair. Her eyes were a startling violet colour; her face was a perfect heart-shape, with the slightly weak chin and the full pale mouth of a true High Renaissance virgin. Vincent had called her 'Venus' the very first time that he met her, which had annoyed her but also flattered her. Yet they had been friends from the moment that they had first clasped hands, and they frequently lunched together and went for weekends together up to Vincent's country house in New Milford, Connecticut.

They had never become lovers, though. Somehow their close and intimate friendship had never crystallized into an affair.

This was probably because they were too much alike. They had both sensed that if their relationship became physically entangled, it would never survive. They valued each other's continuing company more than they valued the prospect of a short and incandescent moment of sex. They kissed often. At New Milford, they shared the sauna and the jacuzzi together. But there were always separate beds. Charlotte was between lovers, in what she described as 'a breathing space', and

68

at the moment she was far more interested in her work for MOMA than she was in men.

Vincent was occasionally dating a twenty-one-year-old girl called Meggsy, an editorial assistant at a small midtown publishing house which specialized in art books. Meggsy liked Meat Loaf, and wore tinted designer spectacles and DD-cup bras, and was far too young for him. She had been brought up in Akron, Ohio. Vincent took her along to prestigious dinners and openings just to tantalize the older members of the New York art establishment, and to infuriate the gays.

Charlotte said, as they drove through the Lake Taconic valley, with the sky dark as a dragged-over blanket, 'Did that woman come to see you?'

'What woman?' asked Vincent.

'You know. The woman who wanted the Waldegrave.'

Vincent glanced at her, taking in her nylon-shiny knees, then said, 'No. It was one of those dead-end enquiries, that's all. Just like those out-of-towners who spend twenty minutes standing in front of a Monet, and ask you how much it is, and promise to call back the following morning with a certified cheque to pick it up.'

'Seems odd, though,' said Charlotte.

'What does?'

'Well, if you want to impress a gallery, you don't ask for a Waldegrave, do you? You might ask for a Marsden Hartley or a Man Ray. You might even ask for a Glackens. But you don't ask for a *Waldegrave*. That's like walking into Sardi's and asking for tuna on toast, and expecting them to be impressed.'

'Well, I don't know,' said Vincent. The lights on the instrument panel shone on his face with an unearthly tinge of green. 'Maybe it was a severe case of reverse snobbery.'

Charlotte smiled. 'It just strikes me as peculiar that she should want it so much.'

'There's a man in Houston who collects used tyres. Waldegrave did have his fans. Queen Victoria once asked him to paint the view from her library at Osborne.'

'And did he?'

Vincent shook his head. 'He died about three months later. He was drowned in the sea off the east coast of England.'

'Poor old Walter Waldegrave.'

'It was probably the Lord's punishment for painting so badly.'

Charlotte was silent for a while. They passed a yellow traffic-sign which read *Danbury, pop 54,900*. They passed the Danbury fairground on their right-hand side, followed by warehouses and suburban rooftops and rows of parked school buses. Charlotte said, 'Why won't you sell it?'

'The Waldegrave? I just don't want to.'

'You don't *really* believe that it keeps your family safe. How could it?'

Vincent made a face. 'I don't know. But if you had something from your grandmother – a ring, maybe, or a necklace – and your grandmother had always made you promise to keep it safe, because it would be bad luck to you and your children if you sold it – well, what would you do?'

Charlotte shrugged. 'I'd keep it, I guess. But not out of superstition. I'd keep it out of love, and respect, and in memory of my grandmother. Not that she *did* give me anything.'

'Well, that's what I'm doing,' Vincent told her. 'I'm keeping the Waldegrave out of love, and respect; and also because I don't like to sell anything bad. Which the

Waldegrave is. It's terrible. Badly composed, badly painted and falling to pieces in front of your very eyes. I wouldn't sell it to anyone, not for anything.'

Charlotte said, 'Why did your grandfather want to keep it, if it was so bad?'

'Search me.'

'But he was a very good art dealer, wasn't he, your grandfather? I mean, he was the one who really built up the family business?'

'That's right.'

'So why should he want to keep a painting as bad as the Waldegrave, unless he had a special reason for it?'

'Charlotte,' said Vincent, a little testily. 'I really don't know.'

'But didn't your *father* ever tell you? He must have known.'

'My father was too busy travelling to Europe and walking out with well-known and occasionally notorious actresses.'

'Is that what Thomas is going to say about you?'

'Of course not.' Vincent rounded on her. 'You're not an actress, and you're not notorious. And you don't come from Europe.'

Charlotte said, 'I still think it's strange, this woman wanting the Waldegrave so badly. And I think it's strange that you didn't sell it to her.'

'I'm a man of integrity,' said Vincent, half seriously.

Charlotte reached across and touched his cheek, then his lips. 'Is that why you never take me to bed?'

At Danbury, they turned north, through Brookfield, until they reached New Milford: a small, neat, colonial town built on the side of a low hill overlooking the northern end of Lake Lillinonah. There was a town green, a town tavern, a gingerbread-fronted newspaper office, the New Milford Savings Bank and a white-painted church with a weather-vane. In the middle of the green stood a cannon from 1775, and rows of benches where the older residents liked to sit on autumn days with the crimson leaves silting up around their feet.

Charlotte called it 'Stepford Wife Country', and swore that every man who lived here was either a geriatric or a chauvinist pig, and that every woman was a domesticated robot.

Vincent, whatever he thought about it, had to call it home. Because five miles further on, up a winding turning, sprawling and turreted and shaggy with ivy, stood the huge country house called Candlemas, the Pearsons' rural seat; and however much time he spent in New York, and London, and Los Angeles, Vincent always had to come back here, if not to rest and refresh himself, at least to pay homage to his roots. His great-grandfather had lived and died here; his grandfather had lived and died here; his father had lived here and died on Omaha Beach. He himself had been born here, on the day that Britain had declared war against Germany.

They drove between the tall wrought-iron gates, which this evening had been chained back in preparation for Vincent's arrival. The house stood at the end of a long brick pathway, lit by glass-globed carriage lamps. There were lights shining at the downstairs windows, and fragrant woodsmoke was blowing from the chimney-stacks. Vincent had called Mrs Miller two hours before he left New York, and asked her to open up the house and light the fires. Mrs Miller lived about a half-mile back towards New Milford, in what had once been an old 1920s roadside restaurant, with her crippled son, Ben. Ben always grumbled that Mrs Miller had enough work to do, cleaning up at the New Milford supermarket, without drudging for the Pearsons. But Mrs Miller had been 'doing' for the Pearsons for nearly thirty-five years, and she felt that Candlemas and the Pearson family belonged to her by right and by duty. She couldn't have countenanced the thought of Harriet Whitney cleaning up for Mr Pearson; or Betty Elsmore poking around in 'her' linen cupboard.

Mrs Miller appeared at the front door as soon as Vincent drew the Bentley to a crunching halt on the gravel driveway. She was a small woman – serious, bespectacled, martyred – with fraying white hair and a mannerism of patting at her left shoulder whenever she spoke, as if to reassure herself that she was still there.

'Well, well now, spot on time,' she said, as Vincent carried their suitcases into the hallway. 'But it's a dreary day, isn't it? I've made a pot-roast for you. It should be ready in a half-hour.'

'Mrs Miller, you will get your reward in Heaven,' said Vincent, setting down the cases in the hallway, next to the huge colonial side-table. 'I shall have a word with the Archangel Gabriel, in person.'

Mrs Miller gave Vincent a flattered but flustered smile. She didn't approve of blasphemy. Hadn't she prayed enough that Ben would find the strength to walk; hadn't she sprinkled his wasted knees with water from Lourdes; hadn't she suffered enough of his anger and frustration? And now to be told as a joke that she would find her place in Heaven. Well, young Mr Pearson wasn't half of what his father had been.

Charlotte said, 'The house looks lovely,' and Mrs Miller patted herself and sniffed and tried to pretend that she wasn't pleased. 'There's steak in the pot-roast, sirloin steak, and champignons de bois,' she said. There wasn't even the slightest hint of a French accent in the way she said *Cham Pig Nons De Boys*. That was the way it was written on the card in the supermarket, and that was the way she was going to say it.

Mrs Miller always preferred Charlotte to any of Vincent's other 'lady visitors', as she referred to them. Charlotte was the only one who actually used the guest bedroom that was prepared for her, soap and towels and everything. The others only pretended, when Mrs Miller knew perfectly well that they were sharing Vincent's four-poster colonial bed in the big master bedroom overlooking the garden. As far as Mrs Miller was concerned, the master bedroom was the 'marriage bedroom', and always had been. Mrs Pearson had slept there for twenty years, alone, after her husband's death. Mrs Pearson had died there. It seemed like sacrilege to fornicate there, on the bed which had known such gladness, and such sorrow.

'How's Ben?' Vincent asked Mrs Miller, walking through to the long, low-ceilinged living room. A log fire was crackling in the cast-iron grate, and all the green velvet curtains had been drawn tight. 'Charlotte – would you like a drink?'

'Ben's not a happy boy,' said Mrs Miller. She untied her apron. 'He says the space shuttles are affecting his legs; not to mention his alfalfa rhythms.'

'Alpha rhythms,' said Charlotte, carefully.

'That's just what I said,' Mrs Miller agreed. 'He says everybody in the world has different alfalfa rhythms; some get disturbed and some don't.'

Vincent laid his hand on Mrs Miller's shoulder. 'Just tell him that if there's anything I can do . . .'

'The doctor gave him pills for it,' said Mrs Miller, although Vincent knew that she disapproved of medication, and especially of placebos. If the doctor was giving Ben placebos, that meant that he was deranged; and Mrs Miller absolutely refused to accept that her son was deranged. He was injured; he was suffering from stress. But he certainly wasn't deranged. Those times that he swore; those times that he sat in his wheelchair screaming at his fate; Mrs Miller could accept all of those, just so long as he wasn't deranged.

'It's the space shuttles,' she insisted. 'The way they affect the atmosphere . . . it gets him down.'

'Can you come up here and clean on Monday?' Vincent asked her, moving his hand away gently.

'Well, surely,' said Mrs Miller. 'I can fix you breakfast, too, if you want.'

Vincent shook his head. 'We have to get back to New York real early. You know what it is. Another day, another ten thousand dollars.'

'I remember your father,' Mrs Miller told him. She didn't have to say anything else. Vincent could remember him too; although mostly through photographs and black-and-white home-movies, and stories that his mother had told him. Six years ago, Vincent had gone to Omaha Beach, and stood knee-deep in the water, and known for sure that his father had gone.

He would go through the whole of his life missing his father. So would Mrs Miller, who had somehow expected the world to be different, after World War Two. More like *When a Girl Marries* than *Peyton Place*.

After Mrs Miller had driven off in her old beige-painted Rambler, Vincent went back into the living room and poured himself and Charlotte a large glass of Jameson's whiskey each. He sat down by the fire and raised his glass in a toast. 'Here's to us. And may the space shuttles leave poor Ben Miller well alone. Especially his alfalfa rhythms.'

'Poor woman,' Charlotte remarked.

Vincent said, 'She's not as much of a poor woman as

she likes you to think. She just enjoys the sympathy, that's all.'

'It was good of her to make us a meal,' said Charlotte, curling up her legs on the tapestry-covered sofa.

Vincent swallowed whiskey, and shrugged. 'She only does it because she wants to feel that she's in charge. I don't think she ever forgave my mother for dying and allowing me to inherit the house.'

'Oh, don't be so hard on her,' said Charlotte. 'How can you say that?'

'I can say it because it's true. But she's an excellent housekeeper, so who's complaining?'

They went upstairs to shower and change. They shared the same bathroom without embarrassment, although when they were naked they were both more conscious of the understanding at which they had silently arrived: that they would not be lovers. Vincent stood in front of the mirror, wrapped in nothing but a large blue Turkish bath-towel, shaving. Charlotte undressed, folding her clothes on the black papier-mâché chair. She was small-breasted, 'thin as a wire', as Vincent put it; but very elegant in her leanness. Her nipples were as darkly red as damsons; her skin was still lightly tanned from her September holiday in Colorado; her pubic hair rose up like a blonde cockerel's crest.

Vincent changed into a cream silk Pierre Cardin shirt and a pair of grey Italian trousers. That was his idea of dressing casually. Charlotte wore a long loose paisley dress by Geoffrey Beene, tied with a thin leather belt. Vincent kissed her on the cheek, and said, 'Well, the picture of chic.'

Charlotte kissed him back. 'I couldn't possibly disgrace your sacred ancestral home in my green jeans and T-shirt.'

They went downstairs again to play some music and finish their drinks.

They were just about to go through to the kitchen to see about supper when the telephone rang. Charlotte picked it up, and then handed it to Vincent. 'It's for you. It's Mrs Miller. She sounds upset, for some reason.'

'Mrs Miller?' asked Vincent, standing up so that he could disentangle the telephone cord.

'Oh, Mr Pearson. I didn't mean to trouble you, but it's Ben.'

'What's the matter, Mrs Miller?'

'He was all right when I first got home. He was real quiet. He was having his TV dinner and he was watching the *Dean Martin Comedy Hour* and he was fine. But then he dropped his dinner all over himself and all over the floor and he's acting so *strange*, Mr Pearson, he's acting so *strange*. I don't know what to do.'

'Did you call the doctor?'

'I left a message on his recording machine. I told him it was urgent.'

'Well, listen, Mrs Miller,' said Vincent, reassuringly, 'I'll come right over. He's not having any difficulty breathing, is he? He doesn't look like he's choking, or anything like that?'

'He's acting strange, that's all. I can't even begin to tell you.'

'You hold on, Mrs Miller. I'll be right there.'

Vincent put down the phone. Charlotte said, 'What's wrong? She sounded really distraught.'

'She said that Ben was acting strange. I'd better get over there and see what's wrong.'

'Do you want me to come with you?'

Vincent went to the hall table, opened the deep middle drawer and took out one of the thick Arran sweaters that were always kept in there in case one of Vincent's weekend guests felt like a walk. He tugged it over his head, and said, 'I won't be long. Why don't you get supper ready? There's a case of Beaune in the cupboard next to the larder; open a bottle up and help yourself.'

'The Stepford wives strike again,' Charlotte complained. 'What is it about Connecticut that turns perfectly sane and sensitive men into boorish dominators of women?'

Vincent kissed Charlotte at the doorway, then walked across the driveway and climbed into his Bentley. His hair was still slightly wet from the shower, and his scalp tingled in the cold. He started the engine up, and drove back through the gates and down the sloping track that led to the main road.

He switched on the car radio as he drove back towards New Milford, catching the end of the eight o'clock news. '. . . *said that a second body discovered late this afternoon in a storm drain at Oyster River Point had been mutilated in exactly the same way, and that there was every reason to believe that the perpetrator in both cases was one and the same . . .*'

He switched the radio off again. On his left, next to a small run-down trailer park and a Getty garage, fenced off from the road with low, peeling pickets, was the one-time restaurant which Mrs Miller had lived in for the past eleven years, ever since Ben's accident. Vincent's headlights swung across the shabby, boarded front, the overgrown yard, the rusting tables and chairs that had been sitting at the side of the restaurant ever since it closed. There was still a faded sign on the door, which said *The Copper Kettle* in fancy Gothic lettering.

Vincent parked the car and climbed out. A dog was barking over by the trailer park. In the nearest trailer, somebody was watching television with the volume turned up to cataclysmic. Mr Dunfey, probably; Vincent had met him before. Deaf as a wall, but wouldn't admit it.

He went up the uneven wooden steps and knocked at Mrs Miller's door. Mrs Miller answered it almost immediately. She was wearing a long flowery apron, and she looked white and worried.

'I'm so thankful you came,' she told him. 'I had a call from the doctor not more than a minute ago. He was over at Washington, but he's going to get here just as soon as he can.'

Vincent stepped into the house. It was crowded with cheap furniture and wallpapered everywhere with red and white Regency stripes. There was a musty brown smell common to all really old houses, mingled with the sourer undertones of food and cigarette smoke and bedsore liniment. There were wheelchair ramps built over the steps which led down to the kitchen and up to the parlour. The downstairs toilet door was half ajar, and Vincent could see the chromium handrails which Ben Miller needed whenever he used it.

'He's in here,' said Mrs Miller. 'He's no better. He was sick, a minute ago. I'm worried he's going to choke himself.'

Ben Miller was sitting in his wheelchair in the middle of the parlour, his head arched back, his neck swollen. The room was suffocating with the smell of vomit, and there was a plastic washbasin on the floor, full of bleachy water.

Ben was nearly twenty-seven, but eleven years in a wheelchair had given him the appearance of a large, distorted child. His hair was spiky and scruffy, he was badly shaved, and most of his front teeth were missing, from eating endless candy bars. His eyes were closed and he was gargling in the back of his throat.

'Has he been like this all the time?' Vincent asked Mrs Miller.

Mrs Miller twisted her apron with worried hands. 'He doesn't open his eyes, but he keeps talking, saying things. I don't know what they mean. Every now and then he hits out. Mr Pearson, I don't know what to do for him. I don't know what's wrong. I was so frightened that he was going to have some kind of a seizure and I wouldn't be able to help him.'

Vincent stepped cautiously forward and looked at Ben more closely. Ben was muttering to himself, occasionally twitching his head. His eyes were fluttering under his eyelids as if he was having a nightmare.

'Ben?' said Vincent. He touched Ben's shoulder; but all Ben did was shudder. 'Ben? Can you hear me? This is Vincent Pearson.'

Ben suddenly thrashed wildly at the air with both arms, lurching forward so violently that he almost toppled out of his wheelchair. Vincent caught his shoulders, but Ben twisted away from him, and then hunched himself forward, his head buried desperately under his hands.

'They gah!' he babbled. 'They gah! They gah!'

'Ben! Please! It's Momma!' begged Mrs Miller, and knelt down beside him, trying to prise his intertwined fingers apart. 'Ben, listen to me. Nothing's going to hurt you. Nothing's going to get you.'

'They gah! They gah-gah!' Ben repeated, his voice muffled.

'Help me get his head up,' said Vincent. He took hold of Ben's wrists, and gradually, using almost all of his strength, he managed to tug Ben's hands apart. Then he braced his thigh against the back of Ben's wheelchair, and levered Ben up into a sitting position.

Ben's face was purple and contorted, like an orangutan.

His tongue was hanging out. His eyes rolled around madly.

'Ben,' wept his mother. 'Ben.'

'*They gah, they gah,*' he spluttered, twisting around in his chair and clutching at his mother's dress. '*They guh – they guh – they gah –*'

'Ben, Ben, Ben,' crooned Mrs Miller, and the tears were running freely down her cheeks. She looked up at Vincent and her distress was so intense that she couldn't even speak; she could only shake her head. Vincent held on to Ben's contorted torso as firmly as he could, although Ben was shuddering and writhing so much now that it was almost impossible to prevent him from sliding progressively downwards in his chair. His thin helpless legs were folded up under his bulky body like broken coat-hangers.

For nearly five minutes Vincent and Mrs Miller hung on to him, wordlessly, while he battled against demons that none of them could see.

'*They're guh – they're bah; they're bah!*'

'Ben,' wept his mother.

He twisted his neck around and stared at her in catatonic fury. 'They're back!' he foamed. 'They're back! They're *baaaaack*!' He sounded as if he were tearing shreds of flesh off the back of his throat.

'They're back, they're back, they're back!' Ben garbled. His hands beat a furious tattoo on the arms of his wheelchair. 'Oh, God, save me, they're back! Don't let them get me! Please, Momma, don't let them get me! Please, Momma, please, Momma. Oh, Momma, I've seen them! Oh, Momma, I've seen them!'

Ben suddenly flung his head back, and his spine became locked in a rigid curve so strongly that Vincent was unable to straighten him. Ben clenched his teeth until blood began to run down on either side of his mouth, and his whole body began to shudder as if he were right on the point of spontaneous explosion. There was a moment of utter convulsion, then he began to shake his head frantically from side to side, faster and faster, flinging blood and sputum all around him, like a mad dog.

'Oh, Momma, I'm so frightened! Oh, Momma, oh, God, *I'm so frightened!*'

Then, wretchedly, he wet himself, in a subdued fountain that poured through his grey tracksuit trousers and down his thighs.

Vincent and Mrs Miller held on to him until at last his tremors began to subside. After a while, he dropped into a shallow, restless coma, his eyelids twitching, his nerves jerking, his breathing rough and laboured and intermittent.

Cautiously, Vincent released him and stood back. Mrs Miller got up on to her feet too, and stepped back, watching her son in perplexity and anguish. Every now and then, Ben flailed one of his arms and growled something unintelligible. Whatever he was dreaming about, whatever phantoms were pursuing him through the dark and serpentine corridors of his unconscious mind, they were terrifying and relentless, and they wouldn't let him escape.

'*They bah . . .*' he muttered.

Vincent helped Mrs Miller to carry Ben through to his bedroom on the opposite side of the hallway. There was a narrow bed with a yellow candlewick bedspread, a varnished bureau and a bedside locker with a fringed lamp on it. Beside the bed there was a neat stack of recent *Playboy* magazines. Mrs Miller may have been modest and religious, but she could hardly deny her paralysed son a look, at least, at what his accident had taken away from him.

He had been up on the roof of the Parker house, nailing shingles. The ladder had slipped, and he had fallen like a swimmer, head first, arms gracefully out-stretched, straight into the concrete path. The surgeons had been sure that he was going to die. He had told his mother often enough that he should have died. He had also told her that he would have preferred to have been more seriously brain-damaged, so that he could have spent the rest of his life contentedly smiling at the ceiling, and not understood how much he was missing.

They laid him on the bed. Mrs Miller was shaking; but she unbuttoned the cuffs of her blouse, and rolled up her sleeves, and set about tugging off Ben's tracksuit trousers, so that she could clean him up. Vincent helped her. He knew that she needed to do something practical and matter-of-fact, just to help her calm down. She brought a bowl of soapy water and a face-cloth, and wiped Ben's bony, wasted legs with the deftness of someone who has had to do it many times before.

'He's had a lot of bad turns, since the accident,' she said. 'He never used to have them before; only childish ones, like the bogeyman, and wolves in the cupboard. But, since the accident, he's always having them.'

'Not as bad as this, though?' asked Vincent.

'Never as bad as this.'

Vincent helped her to push Ben's legs into a fresh pair of pyjama trousers. Mrs Miller drew the blanket over him, and laid her trembling hand on his forehead to see if he was running a fever.

'He don't seem too bad now. He seems to have settled.'

Vincent watched Ben dozing. 'What kind of bad turns?' he asked.

'Like nightmares, almost; except that he's awake. Some to do with trying to walk, of course. But others too. Real strange things that he can't explain. So scary, some of them, that he has to sit up in his wheelchair all night, because he's afraid to go to sleep, just in case the nightmare gets him when he can't protect himself.'

'What did the doctor say about them?'

Mrs Miller picked up the bowl of water, with the face-cloth floating in it. 'I guess we could leave him now,' she said. 'He must be exhausted, with all that shouting and twisting about.'

Vincent followed her through to the kitchen. She emptied the bowl into the sink, and then rinsed the sink out with scalding water.

She said, as she turned off the tap, 'The doctor told me that people who nearly die, the way that Ben did – well, sometimes they get this kind of second sight. Do you know what I mean? Because they've actually died, because they've actually gone beyond the end of their own life, they've seen what it's really like when you pass away.'

Vincent looked at her for a moment. 'And that's what gives them these waking nightmares?' he asked her.

'Seems like. They can't tell for sure. You have to die yourself to tell for sure.'

'Well,' said Vincent, 'that doesn't sound like a very encouraging commercial for the afterlife, does it?'

'No, no,' said Mrs Miller. 'It's not the afterlife itself that gives them the turns. Dr Serling said that almost every patient who comes out of a coma starts weeping because they didn't make it to the other side; and that they spend the rest of their lives yearning for death, because they've seen it for themselves, and they know how beautiful it is.'

'What does give them turns, then?'

Mrs Miller busily wiped the pine-topped kitchen table. 'What gives them turns is what they've learned about the world, and what's in it. That's what gives them turns.'

'I don't understand.'

'Well, I don't suppose anyone does,' said Mrs Miller. 'Has Ben ever described them to you, these turns?'

She shook her head. 'He says he can't. He says he doesn't want to. But I remember one night about two years ago when things were really bad and he couldn't sleep, *wouldn't* sleep, rather, and he begged the doctor for Benzedrine to keep him awake. I asked him then what was wrong and he said that it was nightmares and daydreams, both; except that they never seemed like dreams at all – they seemed like they was real. Only somehow they wasn't real, either.'

She paused, slowly wiping her hands on her apron, and then she said, 'It was like seeing the world for the first time, he told me. He said, "Momma, there's so much evil in the world, and everybody walks past it, just like it was invisible or something." He said that his accident had given him special spectacles, if you know what I'm trying to say. Before the accident, he could sit in a room and it seemed like it was full of his friends. But afterwards, it was just like wearing special spectacles. Suddenly, he could see that there were devils in the room, too, and evil people, and spirits so lewd he wouldn't describe them, not to anybody. And yet all his friends were still sitting there, unconcerned, like they couldn't see nothing.'

They heard a car outside, then a door slamming.

'That should be Dr Serling now,' said Vincent.

Mrs Miller held his arm. 'You know that sometimes I can be sharp, Mr Pearson. Sharper than I mean to.'

Vincent patted her hand. 'You don't have to worry about that, Mrs Miller. You're the best housekeeper in Litchfield County. Probably the whole state.'

'Thank you anyway for coming down to help me so prompt,' she told him. 'And, listen, all that stuff about the special spectacles and the devils and such – please don't repeat it. Ben finds it difficult enough as it is to make any friends around here. If they thought he was deranged as well as crippled . . . well, he'd no doubt lose the two or three friends that he does have.'

There was a brisk knock at the front door.

'I won't repeat it,' Vincent promised her. He kissed her cheek. 'Now, listen, I'd better get out of Dr Serling's way, and yours, too. And there's a pot-roast waiting for me, back at the house. If there's anything you need during the night, though, don't you be worried about calling.'

Mrs Miller said, 'God bless you.'

They were simple enough words of thanks, and yet there was an unusual inflection in Mrs Miller's voice, which, as he drove home afterwards, made him frown at himself in the rear-view mirror.

'*God* bless you,' she had said. As if she was trying to make quite sure that he wasn't blessed by anyone or by anything else.

Six

Captain Hoskins led the way to the morgue, his large bottom moving busily, one side of his crumpled shirt-tail hanging out. 'My first thought was a surgeon,' he said. 'One of your high-class tit-reshapers, gone crazy. That does happen, you know. They work under a lot of strain, these people, and they get to think of the human body with contempt; do you know what I mean? Like when you and me look at a car, we see the shiny outside of it, but what does an auto mechanic see? He sees rust and dirt and wires and junk, and that's the way these surgeons look at the human body.'

Jack Smith said nothing, but obediently followed Captain Hoskins along the long, waxy-floored corridor, his head slightly bowed because he was thinking, and because he was upset. One skinned corpse per week was quite sufficient, so far as he was concerned. Now the West Haven police had found another, on the beach, and from Captain Hoskins' preliminary descriptions, it sounded even worse than the body they had fished out of the Nepaug Reservoir. And he couldn't even offer Captain Hoskins any educated guesses as to who might have killed and skinned these people. He had been able to find no clues at all to the Nepaug Reservoir murder: no footprints, no tyre tracks, no clothing-fibres, no drops of blood. Nobody had come forward to say that they had witnessed anything suspicious: no hunchbacks dragging sacks through the night; no screams; no dark mysterious limousines.

But somebody had picked up a twenty-three-year-old student from the University of Connecticut at Storr, an economics graduate called Karl Madsen, while he was hitch-hiking from Canaan (where his parents lived) to Storr. And that somebody, or somebodies, had taken Karl Madsen to some place unknown, and stripped him completely of his outer skin, and then left him floating in the Nepaug Reservoir. The medical examiner said that he had never seen anything like it, ever. Only the epidermis had been removed, with consummate skill, and if you wanted a comparison, that was like peeling the rice-paper off the back of an almond cookie without tearing the rice-paper and without disturbing a single crumb of the almond cookie; only ten times more difficult.

Captain Hoskins said, 'The seagulls were at him, when he was found, so it's kind of hard to tell what he was like when he was originally dumped. But there isn't any question, somebody skinned him, and the opinion seems to be that they skinned him alive.'

'What makes you think that?'

Captain Hoskins pushed open a plastic swing-door marked POLICE MORTUARY. 'I don't know. It was something to do with the way the blood was clotted. Like, wherever the seagulls hadn't been able to get at him, he was one huge scab. I don't know. You'll have to ask the doctor.'

They entered the wide, tiled, echoing mortuary. There was a strong smell of industrial disinfectant, and another smell, sweetish and sickly, which no amount of scrubbing and disinfecting could ever completely conceal. It was instantly recognizable to anyone who had ever fought in a war, or worked in a hospital, or opened up the trunk of an abandoned car and found a week-old body lying in it.

A young morgue assistant with spiky hair and out-size rubber shoes came out of the office to meet them. He wore spectacles taped with bandage, and there was a red spot on the end of his nose.

'You want to see the guy with no skin on?' he asked, helpfully.

'If you'd be so kind,' Captain Hoskins replied, with exaggerated Oliver Hardy courtesy.

The assistant walked across to the end wall, where the remains of all those who had recently died in West Haven in violent or suspicious circumstances were evenly chilled at 2 degrees C, just above freezing point, the same temperature as Safeway chickens. The assistant rolled out one of the middle drawers, and said, 'Help yourself. Hope you didn't eat breakfast.'

Jack only needed one look. The body was a raw, garish scarlet, just like the corpse of young Karl Madsen.

There were no eyes; the gulls had taken those. The mouth was stretched back in a hideous toothy smile.

'Okay, roll him away,' said Captain Hoskins.

They left the mortuary and walked out across the car park towards Captain Hoskins' car. It was a windy, damp morning, with the leaves clinging in the puddles, and the clouds moving past them as quickly and silently as if they had been back-projected. Captain Hoskins buttoned up his sheepskin jacket and said to Jack, 'This is going to be a weird one; and if you and me can't come up with something, then the shit's going to fly, believe me. If there's one thing Commissioner Neuman doesn't want, it's "The Connecticut Cutter".'

'You didn't pick up any clues at all?' asked Jack. He put a Barclay between his lips, and sniffed.

Captain Hoskins said, 'They found him lying on his back, on the beach. There was no blood, no footprints, no fingerprints, no hair-samples, no fabric-fibres, no nothing. Just the same as yours.'

Jack lit his cigarette, and tersely blew smoke into the wind. 'The question I keep asking myself is, *why now?*'

'What do you mean?'

'Well, suddenly this guy starts abducting young men, and peeling their skin off. I mean, *why now?*'

'Search me,' said Captain Hoskins. 'Everybody has to start sometime. You could ask that selfsame question about anything you like. Why did you join the police department on the day you did? Why did everybody suddenly decide to vote for Ronald Reagan last year? Why did Columbus decide to sail to America in 1492?'

'But that's exactly the point I'm making,' said Jack. 'I joined the police department on the day I did because of specific reasons: because of my age; because of the length of the course at the police academy; because I wanted to take Nancy on vacation to Key West before I actually started duty. The same goes for the people who voted for Ronald Reagan, and for Christopher Columbus. There were reasons why these things happened when they did, and there's a reason why these young men were murdered when they were.'

Captain Hoskins thrust his hands into his jacket pockets and looked away. Jack knew him from way back. He didn't put any faith in theorizing, or lateral analysis. He preferred clues that could be seen, and touched, and held up in a court of law, with a label dangling from them, *Exhibit A.*

'If we can answer *why now*, we should be able to answer *why*,' Jack went on. 'And if we can answer *why*, we should be able to answer *who.*'

' *"Who"* is a total fruitcake, that's who,' said Captain

Hoskins. 'A genuine, certified product of the Allen Street Bakery.'

'Well, you're probably right,' said Jack. 'But he has incredible skill, no matter how crazy he is. Do you know what the medical referee at Hartford told me? He even took the skin of Madsen's balls, like tomatoes. Can you imagine that?'

Captain Hoskins said, 'I wish to hell that I couldn't.'

They agreed to keep in regular touch with each other, in case one or other of them came up with an eye-witness, or a viable clue. Then Captain Hoskins drove off to his headquarters, and Jack climbed back into his Cherokee, and drove back towards Litchfield County, and the small town of Harwinton, which was home. The sight of the body in the West Haven morgue had depressed and unsettled him; but it also gave him a lot more to think about. The homicide at Nepaug Reservoir hadn't just been a single isolated killing. It hadn't just been a one-off example of gruesome curiosity, a sadistic experiment to see what a human body looked like, stripped of its skin, or how much a man would scream if he were flayed alive. It had been done for a purpose; and the purpose had a pattern, even though so far the murderer had only struck twice. Once meant random; twice meant a reason. And no matter how much he prayed that it wouldn't, Jack had a feeling of dull professional certainty that it would happen again, and even again, before they would begin to understand who might have done it, and why. And *why now?*

Something must have changed in the murderer's life to trigger him off. It wasn't just a change in locality; Jack had checked with the FBI computers in Washington, and not one person in the entire United States had been found dead of injuries caused by expert skinning-alive, right back to the year when FBI records had started, back in 1908. The murderer must have been triggered by a change in circumstances, a change in basic psychology, a change in *needs*. If only Jack could think what these changes were related to; why it was suddenly necessary for the murderer to pare off people's skin. The only historical parallels he had been able to discover had been the use of human skin for the binding of books on necromancy, in the Middle Ages, and the flaying of Jewish prisoners in concentration camps so that their skin could be used for lampshades and cigarette-cases and other ornaments.

Perhaps the only pertinent clue to be found in the history books was that those who had skinned other people in the past always seemed to have done so not just for the cruelty of it, but because they actually *wanted the skin*. They displayed another characteristic, too – and that was an attitude of complete superiority over their fellow human beings. They had taken the skins because they regarded their victims as nothing higher than animals whose hides are generally considered to be fair game. After all, nobody with any compassion for his fellow men could have used a book or a cigarette-case covered with human skin; or sat reading by a lampshade that had been bought at the cost of a human life.

Jack reached home shortly before lunch. The wind was drier now, the puddles were nothing more than dark stains on the pavement. He turned down Torrington Park, which was a small development of six new houses in a landscaped dead-end, a kind of unglamorous Knot's Landing, with kids' tricycles left in the roadway, and washing flapping in the back yards, and the next-door kids slowly and greasily dismantling a jacked-up Imperial Le Baron in the front driveway. Jack parked in front of his house, the second from the end, and stiffly climbed out. He could see Nancy in the living room, talking to her friend Pat Lerner. He hadn't seen Pat for a while, and he thought it darkly appropriate that she should have turned up in a week so crowded with malignant happenings. Apart from being a grade-school teacher, and an obsessive macramé-maker, Pat was a 'sensitive'. She could read fortunes (tea-leaves or Tarot); she could contact dead relatives (although they rarely seemed to say anything sensible); and she could predict the weather by listening to the chirruping of crickets. Jack and Nancy had known her for so long, however, that it never occurred to them that Pat's spiritual sensitivity was anything else but a rather clever knack, like being able to play the accordion, or juggle with oranges.

Jack smiled and waved, and Nancy came to open the door for him. She was small and pretty and brightly blonde, and Jack absolutely adored her voice because she always sounded as if she were about to burst into tears, even though she wasn't. She worked mornings at the Harwinton grade school, teaching the under-fives. He loved her very straightforwardly: he had never had to lie to her about anything, except once, three years ago, when he had disarmed a man in Washington Depot who was threatening his wife and children with a shotgun. If Nancy had ever found out what he had done that day, she would never have let him go back to work again.

'You're *early*,' she said, kissing him. She was wearing jeans and a blue-checked shirt – what he called her hayseed look. 'Pat came over to read me my fortune.'

Jack hung up his coat in the hall. The house wasn't large, but Nancy always kept it neat. There was a natural-stone fireplace, with glass ornaments on it, and a reproduction of William Ranney's *Pioneers* hanging on the chimney-breast. There were horse-brasses and an aquarium, and a brown antique-style dining-suite.

'Foretelling the future again, hey?' Jack asked Pat, rubbing his hands together to warm them up. 'Do I get new cars this fiscal year?'

Pat shook her head. 'So far, all I've turned up for Nancy is a long sea voyage, an unexpected letter, and a new husband.'

'Well, that's an encouraging start,' smiled Jack, sitting down in his favourite colonial-style armchair. 'When do I leave?'

Pat was kneeling in front of the beechwood coffee-table, dealing out cards. She was a thin woman, with long dark braided hair and a sharp, almost Red Indian profile, although she was Jewish. Pat's husband sold Pontiacs. Pat busied herself with every neighbourhood charity that she could lay her hands on, as well as the business of everybody in Harwinton who was under seventy and still capable of adultery, or at least of being suspected of adultery.

'I'm using different cards today,' said Pat. 'Usually, I read Nancy's fortune with the Tarot, but today I decided to see what Mademoiselle Lenormand's pack has to say about her.'

Jack leaned over. 'Could I see those?' He picked up two or three cards and examined them. One had a painting of stars on it, shining in the night sky, and a rhyme which promised that *a chance of luck befalls tonight*. Another showed a golden crucifix, with a warning that *a cross weaves pain, historically sad*.

'I've never seen these before,' said Jack.

'Do you want me to tell your fortune?' asked Pat.

Nancy came back into the living room and said, 'Would you like some coffee? Pat and I were just about to have some.'

Jack said, 'Sure. I might as well have a last cup before your new husband moves in.'

'The cards didn't really say that,' Nancy told him, sitting on the arm of the chair next to him and putting her arm around his shoulders. 'She's only trying to stir up marital discord. It's her favourite hobby. That, and the Heart Foundation, of course.'

Quickly, Pat laid the thirty-six cards out on the coffee-table, four rows of eight, and one row of four. 'This is you, the Cavalier, card number twenty-eight,' said Pat. 'Your immediate fortune is represented by the cards' that are closest to you; the other cards have a lesser influence on you, the farther away they are.'

Jack inspected his cards carefully. 'What's this? A wheatfield? I'm going to give up being a cop, and take up farming?'

'Well, that doesn't mean anything much,' said Pat. She looked the cards over and frowned, and then suddenly she gathered them all up again.

'What's wrong?' Jack asked her. 'That means I don't have any fortune?'

'I set it out wrong, that's all.'

'Well, come on, try it again. I want to see whether I get those cars or not.'

Nancy said, 'Sounds like the coffee's ready,' and went off into the kitchen. After a moment, she called, 'Would you like some cookies? We have pecan chip, or chocolate chip, or coconut.'

'I'm watching my figure,' Pat called back, as she shuffled the cards, and then dealt them out again. 'It's not getting any thinner, but I'm watching it.'

Jack shifted forward in his chair. 'Well now, what do the mystic cards have to say this time? Hey look, I'm going to be a farmer again. You didn't shuffle them well enough.'

'I shuffled them,' Pat protested. 'Jack, I swear I shuffled them.'

'They're all the same. They're all exactly the same.'

Nancy came in with a tray. 'Maybe that's what your fortune is, no matter which way you shuffle them. "There are more things in heaven and earth, Horatio".'

'Horatio?' asked Pat, looking up in surprise. 'Is that what you call him?'

'It's a quotation,' Nancy told her.

'Well, lookit, I'm going to be a farmer, that's what the cards predict, and that's all there is to it,' said Jack. 'And I'd better hurry this cup of coffee, because they're going to want me back over at Bristol by two.'

Pat said, 'Jack, this card doesn't mean that you're going to be a farmer.'

Jack lowered his cup of coffee and looked at her. Her voice had been unexpectedly stark.

'It's not bad news, is it?' he asked her, with a smile.

'There's a scythe in this card. There, look, resting against the wheat. And the interpretation is, *The scythe looms bare, danger stalks too. Of strangers beware, they can harm you.*'

Jack set his cup of coffee down on the table. 'Pat,' he said, 'why do you think I'm a policeman, instead of a mail-carrier, or a bus-driver, or an insurance salesman? I spend fifteen hours of every day dealing with strangers who can hurt me. That's not news. That's not even a prediction.'

Pat was still relentlessly serious. 'You must be careful of knives and sharp objects. Unless you watch out, somebody is going to cut you, quite seriously.'

Jack said nothing for a long time, but picked up the card with the picture of wheat on it and examined it closely. Then he tapped it sharply with his fingernail and laid it back on the table. 'What do the rest of the cards say?' he asked Pat.

'They're not good cards,' Pat told him. 'Maybe the vibes are wrong. Maybe they're not *your* vibes at all. You haven't been close to any really bad criminals recently, have you?'

'Only my accountant.'

'Please, Jack, don't make a joke of it.'

Jack picked up his coffee again, and swallowed two hot mouthfuls. Nancy was always nagging him for gulping his coffee too quickly. 'I went to see a cadaver this morning,' he said.

'A cadaver?' asked Pat. 'You mean a murder victim?'

'That's right.'

'And did this . . . cadaver's death have anything to do with knives? Or something sharp?'

'I can't tell you that, not at the moment. It's still confidential. I haven't even talked to the commissioner yet, although I very soon shall.'

Pat let her finger wander to the next card, the card which was positioned directly above the Cavalier's head. Number seven, the serpent. A poisonous green snake, coiled on a rock. The card warned, *'Vile is the serpent who lulls with a bite . . . flee every moment she turns on the charm . . .'*

'What does that mean?' Jack asked.

'It means that you have to be wary of a very cunning and alluring woman,' said Pat. 'She will seem to be seductive, but in fact she will be out to do you very great harm, even kill you.'

Jack glanced at Nancy, and then said, 'Go on. What about this one, on my left? The owls, sitting in a tree?'

'Grief,' said Pat.

Nancy interrupted, 'I had that card, and you said it meant a long sea voyage.'

'From you, the card was far away. That means a voyage. But from Jack, look, it's very close. That means grief.'

'Anything else?' asked Jack. 'I mean, just in case I start to feel cheerful?'

'Below you, here, the mountain,' said Pat. 'That signifies that somebody is lying in wait for you; that you will have a very difficult time, in the next few weeks; and that just when you believe that you have achieved what you set out to achieve, just when you think that you have won, this "beast in his lair" will strike out at you.'

Jack finished his coffee, and rubbed his hands together again, although very much more slowly and thoughtfully this time.

'Did you ever know any of this stuff to come true?' he asked Pat.

'This is only the sixth or seventh time I've used this particular deck,' she said. 'But all I can say is, it's alarmingly strong. It gives off a truly remarkable power.'

'And you believe in it?'

'I don't see any reason not to. It's been used for well over a hundred years now, with a lot of success.'

'Tried, proven, empirically evaluated success?'

Pat gathered up the cards. 'There isn't any such thing, Jack. Not for the testing of cards, nor for the catching of criminals, nor even for baking of chocolate fudge cake.'

'Wash your mouth out with soap and water,' Jack teased her. 'You're supposed to be watching your figure.'

Pat was tucking the cards back into their box when one of them dropped to the floor. Jack reached down to pick it up, but when he handed it back to Pat, he suddenly noticed that his hand was full of blood. Blood was running freely down his sleeve and pumping out all over his suit and the lemon-yellow carpet and the coffee-table and everywhere, all in the space of a few silent, shocked, horrified seconds. It took Jack a moment or two to realize what had happened. The edge of the fortune-telling card had sliced painlessly into the palm of his hand, just where the radius and ulnar arteries joined, and his heart was busily squirting blood out of him at seventy squirts a minute.

Nancy stared at the blood splattering across the coffee-table, and couldn't understand at first where it was coming from. It seemed almost as if the ceiling had opened up and it was raining blood out of the sky. But then Jack tugged the tray-cloth from under the coffee-cups, tipping cups and spilling coffee amidst the blood, and pressed it firmly against the palm of his hand. Instantly, the tray-cloth was soaked dark red, but the pressure of Jack's thumb was enough to suppress the squirting.

'Jack!' Nancy cried out. Pat dropped her cards, and stared at him in horror.

'It's okay,' he reassured Nancy. 'The edge of the card cut my hand, right into an artery. It's deep, but it's not too long. All you have to do is fetch me a bandage from the first-aid kit, and a large handkerchief, and something like a pen or a pencil.'

Pat watched in silence as Nancy bound Jack's hand with a bandage, then knotted a handkerchief over the wound, and pushed a pencil through it so that she could turn it around and around, and tighten it up as a tourniquet.

'That should hold it,' said Jack. Although he was calm, he was beginning to feel faint now, and unsteady from shock. 'Now, if you could drive me down to the hospital, I'm sure that the emergency department can sort me out.'

Both Nancy and Pat helped him into the passenger seat of his Volkswagen. Nancy reached across to buckle him in, and he tried to smile bravely at her. 'You look like death,' she told him. She kissed his cheek.

'I just cannot *believe* that a playing-card did that,' said Pat, as they drove out of Torrington Park. 'It seems unreal.'

'It happens all the time,' said Jack. 'You know the Silver Lake paper mill? They called us up there about two years ago; one of the workers had lost half his arm, cut clean through by the edge of a large sheet of kraft paper. I mean, by comparison, this is nothing.'

'I'm so sorry,' said Pat, 'if I hadn't been doing those stupid cards. If I hadn't been so *clumsy* –'

'It's not your fault,' Jack told her. 'I should have watched what I was doing.'

His hand was stitched and bound up properly in the casualty department at Harwinton Clinic. A young nurse with a wide smile and huge breasts and freckles brought him a cup of coffee. The doctor gave him an anti-tetanus shot, sneezing uproariously as he did so, and then took out his handkerchief to worry at his nose. 'The things you can catch, Sheriff, when you work in a hospital. You wouldn't believe it. And the classier the hospital, the classier the disease.'

The doctor let him home after two hours. They dropped Pat off at her house in Wilson View, then they went back to Torrington Park. Nancy had already called Deputy Norman Goldberg at the Torrington police headquarters and told him that Jack would be late.

'I think I could use a drink,' said Jack, as they opened the front door and stepped into the hallway. The reproduction wall-clock was just chiming three.

'You know what the doctor said: no alcohol. It dilates the arteries and starts up the bleeding again. How about some coffee?'

'I'm awash with coffee.'

They went into the living room. It looked as if somebody had been murdered in there. Jack's blood was sprayed all over the carpet, all over the table, all over the chair. There were several bloody footprints, as well as squiggles of blood on the wall, and tear-shaped drops on the pale gold curtains.

'I don't know,' said Nancy. 'You've never been tidy, have you? You can't even *bleed* tidily.'

Jack put his arm around her, with stiffly bandaged fingers, and kissed her. 'I'll call the rug-cleaners right away. You know those people over at Bristol? They cleaned all the blood out of Norman's carpet.' Norman Wagner, who lived about a mile away, had accidentally taken off his left thumb with an electric knife while carving the Thanksgiving turkey last year.

Nancy picked up the bloody tray-cloth, and Pat's cards.

'Here's the card that cut you,' she said, and handed it across to him.

Jack took it, holding it carefully between finger and thumb. He didn't want a repeat performance with the other hand. On the back of the card there was a red pattern, with a drawing of a wide-eyed owl in the centre. He turned it over. On the front, there was a picture of wheat, and a scythe resting against it. The bottom third of the card, which included the blade of the scythe, was blotchy with Jack's blood.

'The scythe looms bare, danger stalks too. Of strangers beware, they can harm you.'

Jack turned the card around a couple of times, then shrugged and handed it back to Nancy.

Nancy said, 'You don't think – well –'

Jack shook his head. 'It was an accident, that's all.'

'Well, Pat's been right before.'

'Right about what? Mrs Piatkowski's dog, catching the distemper? A rainstorm, on the day of the PTA bring-and-buy?'

'Yes, I know they were small things, but –'

'But what?' Jack demanded, with a smile.

Nancy laid the card down on to the blood-sticky table. 'I don't know. But *something*. Something's going on. Something's going wrong. I can feel it. Can't you?'

Seven

Bantam, 14 December

It was late morning by the time Vincent reached Aaron Halperin's house, which was on a dark and tangly hill just outside Bantam, on the Litchfield road. Aaron lived in a rambling semi-collapsed building that had once been part of an eighteenth-century coaching inn. It was dominated by a huge bare oak; and as Vincent drove up to the house through the briars and the unkempt bushes, the oak stood high above the rooftops, raising its branches to the sky like a soundlessly shrieking giant.

Vincent parked outside Aaron's studio, which was a long low shed at the back of the house. He lifted the two Johnsons out of the boot, and walked across to the lighted porch. There was a blue pottery sign there which said *Halperin*, and a notice underneath which announced *Ars Longa, Vita Brevis.* Aaron always translated that as 'He who has protruding buttocks should avoid wearing small briefs.' Vincent rang the old-fashioned doorbell, and heard it jangle at the far end of the studio, where Aaron usually worked.

After a few moments, the door juddered open and Aaron appeared, his arms outstretched. 'My wandering boy!' he cried. He was big and ginger-bearded, with gold-rimmed glasses and a nose that looked as if it had been marinated in cherry brandy. He wore a white floor-length apron, which was streaked all over with scores of different colours: ultramarine and alizarin crimson, Naples yellow and brilliant green, Terra Verte and lemon chrome. Aaron used his aprons instead of a paint-rag; and Vincent always used to say that instead of washing them, he ought to sell them off as works of art.

'I was expecting you earlier,' said Aaron. 'But don't worry, I've got plenty of wine. Home-brewed. You can drink it or clean your paintbrushes in it; it's just as effective for either purpose.'

He brought over a magnum-sized bottle of dark red wine, labelled *Bantam Beaujolais*, and poured out a generous glassful for Vincent. Vincent sniffed it, and remarked, 'Well, an interesting bouquet.'

Aaron finished his own glass of wine, and splashed himself some more. 'We don't call it bouquet around here; we call it odour.'

Vincent set down his glass, reached into his coat pocket for his gold penknife and slit open the brown wrapping-paper around the Johnson paintings.

'These are really beautiful. You'll enjoy working on these. They need general cleaning, more than anything else; but I think the seascape could do with a little restoration around the top left here. You can see that the paint's beginning to flake quite badly.'

Aaron held them up, one after the other. 'They're good. Two of the best Johnsons I've seen.'

Vincent walked along the length of the studio while Aaron examined the paintings more closely. Aaron's work-table ran almost the whole length of the building, and was crowded with palettes, brushes, bottles of linseed oil and turpentine, gesso, rolled-up canvases, glue, fixative, and literally thousands of tubes of oil paint, in every colour imaginable, mostly French and

British, all crumpled and squeezed-up and heaped together.

Beside the end window, which faced north, there were fifteen or sixteen easels, all jostling together, and all bearing canvases which Aaron was in the process of restoring. Although he was recognized as one of the finest restorers of nineteenth-century oil-paintings in the country, Aaron found it impossible to work on any one picture for longer than seven or eight days at a stretch, and he always kept at least a dozen going at once, so that he could refresh himself by changing from a landscape to a nude, from a portrait to a still-life, whenever he began to feel jaded.

Vincent picked up a small landscape by John Frederick Kensett, and angled it so that he could see it better. 'Is this the one you're doing for Milòs?'

Aaron glanced up. 'That's right; it's almost finished. It's a beauty, isn't it?'

'You said you were having trouble with the Waldegrave,' said Vincent.

'Yes. You really should take a look at it. The dang-blang thing's driving me crazy. I'm beginning to wonder if it's worth restoring at all. You're going to spend five hundred dollars and wind up with a painting that's worth about five cents. Maximum.'

He put down the Johnsons, and walked around the end of his table, towards one of the larger easels which stood in the corner. The painting had been removed from its frame, but all the same it was enormous, nearly five feet wide and four feet deep. It was draped all over with an old green velour bedspread, with fringes.

'First of all,' said Aaron, beckoning Vincent over. '*Smell* it.'

Vincent stepped nearer, and cautiously sniffed. The air in the studio was so aromatic with paint and turpentine that he couldn't distinguish the smell at first; but eventually his nostrils sought it out. A thick, sweetish smell, like chicken-skin that has decayed and gone green, only somehow more pervasive, and more clinging.

'Jesus,' said Vincent. 'That's terrible.'

Aaron said, 'You ain't seen nothing yet,' and dragged the bedspread off the canvas. There it was, much as Vincent had remembered it when he was a young boy, twelve white-faced people posing stiff and straight-backed and formal in a crimson room; black-suited and black-dressed; the men clasping their lapels with all the severe dignity of morticians; the women with their hands tucked together in their laps; two of them holding black lace fans; the other caressing a small dark creature that could have been a cat. Vincent had never been able to make out exactly what the creature was, and his grandfather had consistently refused to tell him, although he had always asserted that *he* knew. It could have been a rat, Vincent supposed; but it could have been nothing much more than a black tangle of fur. A muff, maybe, or a fox wrap.

The pose was the same, the room was the same, but the faces had altered beyond recognition. All the white paint was crumbling off them, making them appear decayed and leprous. Some of them were so badly disfigured that it was impossible to make out any of their facial features at all; noses had flaked away, eyes had deteriorated into murky grey sockets. They had the appearance of a family who were fatally and irrevocably diseased, a twelve-strong company of death.

Vincent frowned, and stared at the painting closely.

'It really does smell bad, doesn't it?' he commented. He carefully picked at one of the faces with a surgical scalpel, and examined the paint under the light. 'What causes this? Do you have any ideas at all?'

'I've never seen anything like it before in my whole career,' said Aaron. 'Usually, this kind of appearance is associated with disintegrating canvas at the back, which in turn destroys the paint film on the front. But in this case the canvas is totally one hundred per cent sound. I've examined the paint under the microscope, and I've taken about twenty ultraviolet pictures of each face. Sometimes you might get decomposition of the surface paint if someone has painted over the original picture at a later date. As you know, that happens pretty often with portraits. Someone puts a new face on an old body, or changes the clothes, or the background scenery. But all of this particular painting is completely original.'

'Did Waldegrave use some kind of unusual additive, maybe?' asked Vincent. 'Was there something he might have mixed into the paint which has started to go bad?'

Aaron swilled wine around his mouth, swallowed, and shrugged. 'Occasionally that happens. I've come across vegetable dyes, and ox-blood. Gauguin used to mix some of his yellows with turmeric. But this paint seems just like ordinary, well-mixed, turpentine-based oil-paint.'

Vincent stared at the Waldegrave for a very long time. There was something about its rotting facelessness that depressed him and made him feel uncomfortable. He lowered the bedspread back over it again, and turned round. 'Is there anything else you can try?' he asked Aaron.

'I've sent a small sample over to the laboratory at Hartford, so that they can give me a complete analysis. But I don't think they're going to come up with anything new. This painting of yours is falling to pieces and nothing that I can do or anyone else can do is going to be able to prevent it.'

'Well, wait until you get the results from the lab,' said Vincent.

'It's the goddamned *smell*,' Aaron complained. 'Van Gogh won't even come in here. He thinks it's a skunk. And if I've been working on it, he won't let me stroke him until I've washed my hands.' Van Gogh was Aaron's marmalade tom-cat.

'Can't say that I blame him,' Vincent remarked, sniffing at his own fingers.

'It's strange that it should have started to disintegrate so suddenly,' Aaron said. 'I mean, why *now*, all of a sudden? You've had that picture in the family for donkey's years, haven't you?'

'As far as I'm concerned, it's a relic,' said Vincent. 'But my grandfather always used to insist that we kept it, and kept it safe. He said it was like a talisman, it protected the family from evil.'

'That doesn't sound like your grandfather. He wasn't a superstitious man, was he?'

Vincent shook his head. 'I guess that everybody has their one good-luck charm, though. Their rabbit's foot, or their four-leaf clover.'

'Or their clove of garlic,' Aaron added.

'You're right,' said Vincent. 'That picture does look rather like the annual convention of vampires.'

Aaron poured Vincent some more wine, even though Vincent protested. 'Aaron – it's very good. Plenty of body. Plenty of fruit. But I'm driving.'

Aaron said, 'It's too late. You've already drunk one glass. That means you're irrevocably condemned to a crushing hangover, and probably a drink-driving charge thrown in.'

Vincent lifted both hands in resignation. 'In that case, Aaron, *prost*! And may your mother soon be happily married.'

Aaron took the wine-bottle by the neck, and led the way through to the house. It was untidy, the house, but warm, with crackling log fires everywhere, and scores of fascinating old pictures on the walls, most of them early American watercolours and framed Puritan samplers. Aaron's three daughters were playing chequers in the small side sitting room; Marcia his wife was baking biscuits in the low-ceilinged kitchen; and his only son Michael was playing Hunchback on his computer. Aaron adored chaos, and lots of people, and laughter.

'Come and sit by the fire,' he told Vincent. 'Marcia's going to be bringing in those biscuits pretty soon; and it seems like a shame to drive all the way up here, and miss them. Did you ever taste hot Kinkawoodles?'

'I never did,' Vincent smiled.

'Well, it's very interesting,' said Aaron. 'Back in the eighteenth century, all those fussy New England ladies used to make up silly names for their cookies, just for the fun of saying them. There's Kinkawoodles and Snickerdoodles and Jolly Boys and Rhyming Jacks.'

Vincent said, 'How did a nice Jewish boy from Newark, New Jersey, ever get so interested in the gastronomic history of the *goyim*?'

Aaron laughed. 'Maybe if I eat enough *goyish* cookies, I'll get to turn into one. You know? Dr Jekyllstein and Mr Hyde.'

Then, however, Aaron turned serious. 'That painting, you know; I looked it up in the records of the Royal Academy, in London; because that's where it was first put on public display.'

'That's right,' Vincent nodded. He had seen for himself the discoloured Royal Academy label that was still sticking to the back of the canvas. In brownish ink, it certified inclusion of Waldegrave's *Family Portrait* in the Summer Exhibition of 1883, fourteen years after the

Academy had moved from the National Gallery in Trafalgar Square to its present location at Burlington House.

Aaron crossed the room and brought over three old leather-bound volumes, which he spread out on the hearthrug around his feet. Vincent noticed that the toe-caps of Aaron's shoes were speckled with thousands and thousands of tiny droplets of multicoloured paints. 'Here it is,' said Aaron. '"*Family Portrait*, by Walter John Waldegrave. Dimensions, 62¼ inches by 47½ inches. Oil. Painted February, 1883, at Northwood House, near Harrow."'

'Anything else?' asked Vincent.

'Nothing very much,' Aaron replied. 'Waldegrave is listed in Duxford's *Biographies of the Notable Painters*, which was published in 1902, by Blackie. Here we are:

"Walter Waldegrave, born 7 March 1843, at Bourne, in Lincolnshire. First made his mark as a painter at the age of eighteen when he was employed by Peter Robert, Lord Willoughby de Fresby, to restore frescoes and ceiling-paintings at Grimsthorpe Castle, not far from Bourne. At this point in his life he became interested in occult and religious subjects, and painted a notable series of six allegorical pictures depicting the voyage of the spirit after death. These pictures were shown at the Underwood Gallery in London in 1865, but were taken down after only one week because of complaints about their pernicious and blasphemous content. They were returned to Grimsthorpe Castle to be sequestered in the vaults, where they remain today. Waldegrave returned to London in 1867 and made his living for several years as a minor portrait painter. Very few of his portraits from this period of his life survive, although his portrait of Mrs Adrian Hope is a notable exception. In early 1880, Waldegrave became familiar with Oscar Wilde and Frank Miles, who at that time were sharing apartments together in Salisbury Street, close to the Strand. Frank Miles introduced Waldegrave into Society, and in 1882, he travelled to America with Lily Langtry. In 1883, Waldegrave painted what were probably his best three works: *Family Portrait*, *Lady Archibald Campbell* and *Ellen Terry*. In 1885, at the age of forty-two, Walter Waldegrave inexplicably gave up painting and returned to Lincolnshire. His drowned body was found on the beach at Skegness in April, 1886."

'Is that all it says?' asked Vincent. 'It doesn't give any more details about the family portrait?'

'There's a footnote,' said Aaron:

"*Family Portrait* was exhibited at the Royal Academy of Arts Summer Exhibition of 1883, but it was removed from the exhibition at the painter's request only three days after the public opening, for no specified reason. There has been considerable conjecture over the years as to the identity of the family who are shown in the portrait, and to the location, since the room in the picture is *not* Northwood House, where it was painted. Waldegrave himself would only say that his subjects were a family of quality, and that the room was painted from reference. *Family Portrait* is now assumed to be in private ownership."

Vincent sipped his wine and then set the glass aside. Bantam Beaujolais was every bit as potent as Aaron had promised, and he couldn't drink any more. 'You know something,' he said, 'there's a story here. A real story. A young country painter gets his first experience restoring wall-paintings at somebody's private castle; then he gets interested in the occult; then he paints a series of pictures which scandalize everybody; then he makes friends with Oscar Wilde and Frank Miles; paints three well-known pictures; and winds up five years later, drowned.'

Aaron said, 'I was trying to find out if he used some special kind of paint. But all I could dig out about his technique was this: look here, a passing reference in Andrews and Milner's *Nineteenth Century Realism*:

"Some portrait painters were renowned for their photographic likenesses: and perhaps the most accomplished of these was Henry DeVere, whose portrait of Richard D'Oyley Carte was considered by some critics to be 'too realistic to be good'. Then there was Walter J. Waldegrave, whose most distinctive painting *Family Portrait* was considered by Whistler to be 'so animated, that it was almost frightening.'"

'Well, it's certainly taken on a life of its own,' Vincent agreed.

Aaron closed the books, one by one, and sat back. 'Every painting's different. Every painter has a different way of applying his paint. Sometimes, when I'm in-painting, I can feel the personality of the original painter flowing right through me. I know that he would approve of what I'm trying to do. I know that he would appreciate my care. But this painting, this Waldegrave, it's like a swamp. Do you understand what I mean? The more I work on it, the more it falls apart. I feel like a medical examiner, trying to dissect some decomposing body. The faces in that picture, they don't even feel like paint. They feel like rotting flesh.'

'If you feel that badly about it, don't work on it any more,' said Vincent. 'Throw it in the trunk, and I'll take it away.'

'No, no, it's a challenge. It's something new. Let me wait until I hear from Hartford.'

'If that's what you want.'

Marcia came in with the Kinkawoodles: hot, crumbly cookies tasting of almond. Marcia was slim and funny and very New York, although she always swore that she had renounced the city for ever. She sat cross-legged in front of the fire, and stroked Van Gogh, and wanted to know what was the latest from the city.

'It's Christmas,' Vincent told her.

'I know. Santa Clauses ringing bells and smelling of sherry. Bagels. Lights. Christmas trees. Skating at Rockefeller Center. Taking the kids to Macy's to be scared to death by Father Christmas.'

'Bantam, Connecticut's okay,' smiled Vincent.

'Sure,' said Marcia, resting against Aaron's paint-bespattered knee. 'The things you do for the man you love.'

Van Gogh struggled away from Marcia's lap, and padded off into the kitchen. Vincent and Aaron ate more Kinkawoodles, and Vincent managed to drink more wine. Marcia began to explain how she was going to redesign the upper floors of the house, which had fallen into disrepair, and how she was going to make the living room more flowery and comfortable, then Aaron suddenly lifted his head, and said, 'Was that a scream?'

'A scream?' asked Vincent.

'I don't know. I thought that I heard somebody calling out.'

Vincent put down his glass, and stopped crunching at his cookie. 'I don't hear anything.'

'I'm sure of it,' said Aaron.

He got out of his chair and walked through to the kitchen. 'Where's Van Gogh?' he asked Michael.

Michael was eating a peanut-butter sandwich, which he had made for himself. The peanut-butter jar was left open, the knife was left sticky on the worktop, crumbs were scattered everywhere.

'I don't know,' said Michael, with his mouth full.

Aaron walked quickly through to the studio. Unsure at first of what was going through Aaron's mind, Vincent followed him. The door of the studio was still open, as they had left it, and the lights were still shining. It was unnaturally bright in there, after the dim winter light of the sitting room; as if they were standing under one of the spaceships from *Close Encounters*.

'What's the matter?' asked Vincent. 'What's wrong?'

'I don't know,' said Aaron. 'I heard someone screaming, that's all.'

'Are you sure? It wasn't Michael's video game, was it, or one of the girls?'

'I heard someone screaming,' Aaron insisted.

They looked around; at the easels, at the crumpled tubes of paint, at the stacks of frames and canvases. They could see their reflections in the murky glass of the studio windows, pale and hesitant.

'There's nobody here,' said Vincent. 'You must have imagined it.'

Aaron stood still and silent for a long time. 'Well, maybe I did,' he said, softly.

Marcia came through, still munching a cookie.

'What's the matter, honey?' she asked Aaron, and linked her arm through his.

'Nothing. I thought I heard a scream, that's all. It was just my overworked imagination.'

'Aaron,' crooned Marcia, sharing her cookie with him. 'You don't need any imagination.' She smiled at Vincent. 'Believe me, Vincent, he doesn't need any imagination.'

'Sure, sure he doesn't,' said Vincent, with his hands in his pockets. He took a last look around the studio. He had a feeling that he ought to go over to the Waldegrave and take off the drapery, but he didn't particularly want to.

'Imagination is the thief of sanity,' he misquoted, and switched off the studio lights behind him.

Eight

New York, 15 December

Cordelia Gray was waiting for him at a small table at the very back of the restaurant. Her lipstick was assertively scarlet and she wore a striking grey hat with a grey ostrich plume in it. The restaurant was crowded, but pretty, with mirrored walls and pink tablecloths and glass vases full of freesias.

'I hope I'm not late,' said Edward. Cordelia offered him her hand and he was slightly surprised that she obviously expected him to kiss it. He kissed it, closing his eyes as he did so.

'I have asked for champagne; I hope that wasn't too forward of me,' Cordelia told him. Her perfume was slightly different today, but there was still something about it which made him feel heady and disturbed, as if he were sitting in a closed room while a snake slid sensually up his trouser-leg.

'Champagne's perfect,' he said.

Cordelia smiled, tight-lipped. 'Krug, 1973. For the price of one bottle, you could feed an entire Ethiopian family for a month.'

Edward ran his hand through his hair. It had been windy outside, on 60th Street. 'Is that supposed to make me feel guilty?' he asked her.

'Guilt is a complicated affair,' Cordelia replied. 'There

are those who ought to feel guilty, but don't; and there are those who feel guilty when they have no need to. Then, of course, there are those for whom the concept of guilt has no meaning whatsoever.'

They ordered *potage du Père Tranquille*, a creamy lettuce soup, on Cordelia's recommendation. 'It is named after a mysterious Capuchin monk,' she said. 'But it is also named for the drowsy effect which lettuce is supposed to have on those who eat it.'

They followed this with grilled sea-bass. 'Very plain, excellent for the strength, and perfect for the complexion.' Cordelia wanted no dessert, only cheese and fruit, but Edward asked for crystallized chestnuts.

At the next table, a party of executives from Cleveland were drinking too much and laughing too loudly. One of them was loudly extolling the virtues of his new Mercedes-Benz. 'So it's German. What's wrong with German? That doesn't mean they used your grandfather's hide to make the seat-covers.'

Cordelia smiled with secret self-satisfaction, and sipped her champagne. 'I am pleased that you came, Edward. If it hadn't have been for you, I would have had to eat alone today, and I cannot bear to eat alone. It is almost like a punishment, don't you think? Each mouthful is a reminder that you have nobody with whom to share your meal.'

'I'm growing used to it,' said Edward.

'You live alone?'

'My girlfriend used to live with me. Up until last month, that is. Then she upped and married someone else. Danny Monblat. Now she's Mrs Laura Monblat, if you can imagine that.'

'Laura Merriam would have sounded far more mellifluous.'

'Yes, well,' said Edward, with resignation. 'I think I've gotten over it now.'

'Did you really love her?' asked Cordelia.

Edward looked up from his dessert. 'Yes,' he nodded, 'I loved her.'

'But you don't love her any more?'

'I don't know. Even if I did, what difference would it make?'

'You think she's beautiful, though?'

'Yes, as a matter of fact, I do,' said Edward. He spooned up more chestnuts, and wondered where all these questions were leading to.

Cordelia ate her food in an extraordinary way. Edward had first noticed it when she had started to eat her sea-bass, but of course he had been too courteous to remark on it. First she picked out a piece; then, as she lifted it up to her mouth on the end of her fork, she cupped her other hand right over it, so that it disappeared like a conjuring trick. After glancing at her several times during the course of the meal, Edward began to realize that he never once saw her open her mouth and put a piece of food directly inside.

She chewed oddly, too. Somehow, even though she didn't appear to be moving her jaws, her cheeks rippled. That was the only way in which Edward could possibly describe it. He thought it would be rude of him to stare at her too closely, however. She probably had false teeth, for all her elegance and beauty, and found chewing difficult. After all, she must be at least – well, how old? Thirty-eight, thirty-nine? Or maybe older. It wasn't easy to tell. Her skin was still smooth, smooth as a young girl's; and there were no wrinkles around her eyes. And yet there was an air about her which made him think that he was sharing this table with a very much older woman. He looked at her again and realized with perplexity that he couldn't actually make up his mind what her age could be.

'So, Mrs Danny Monblat,' said Cordelia, fastidiously cutting herself a tiny slice of Brie.

'That's right,' said Edward. He didn't really want to discuss it. It still hurt.

'And now you live quite alone?'

'The hermit of Wentworth Apartments.'

Cordelia passed her hand over her mouth, swallowing the fragment of cheese which she had cut. As she did so, however, a small white morsel dropped from behind her hand on to her plate. Instantly, she pinched it up between finger and thumb, and conjured it back into her mouth.

She did it so quickly that Edward hadn't properly been able to distinguish what had happened. Yet he had been left with an uncomfortable feeling that he had seen the morsel *twitch*, as if it were alive. He stared at Cordelia in the hope of a gratuitous explanation; but Cordelia stared back at him as remotely and as blankly as ever, with those eyes that were simply mirrors.

He cleared his throat. 'Would it be impertinent of me to ask you the real reason why you invited me to lunch?' he asked her. 'I mean, I know you're interested in having me rebuild your family's art collection. But it isn't a little tiny bit to do with that Waldegrave picture, is it? A little bribery and corruption?'

'Corruption?' smiled Cordelia. She swallowed a piece of bread, and for one second Edward thought that he could see the same rippling that had made her cheeks move when she ate, only this time it was running in a silent torrent down her bare throat. 'What do you know about corruption? And I'm talking about *real* corruption.'

'Not much, I suppose. Just what I read in the papers.'

'You are beautifully ignorant,' said Cordelia. 'Tell me, shall we go for a walk in the park, and talk about the family collection there?'

Edward finished his glass of sambuca. 'Yes, I'd like that. As long as you don't mind the wind.'

'The wind?' laughed Cordelia. 'Why, I remember once I was out on a boat off Long Neck Point, and the wind –'

She stopped in mid-sentence. She stared at Edward with an expression that he couldn't understand at all. Caution? Fear? There was something curiously anxious about it. She lowered her eyes, and said, much more quietly, 'The wind was very strong, you know. Almost gale-force.'

She paid the bill (in cash, he noticed – freshly printed fifties); then they walked westwards to the park, against the wind, while grit and newspapers whirled all around them, and the smoke from hot-chestnut stands and bagel carts fled through the crosstown streets like cindery ghosts.

Cordelia held his hand as they walked through the park. Joggers passed them by with monotonous sneaker-slapping; children squealed and called for their parents to watch them in voices that sounded to Edward like distant sea-birds. Three blacks passed by with a ghetto-blaster thumpling out Chaka Khan.

Cordelia said, 'I hope you've decided to say yes.'

Edward smiled. 'I've thought about it very favourably. It sounds like an interesting job. I'm not sure that I can spare the time away from the gallery, that's all.'

'You could be seconded to me for a while. I'm sure Mr Pearson wouldn't object to that. I would pay him for the temporary loss of your services.'

'Well, as long as he doesn't mind . . . then yes, I'm interested.'

'And the Waldegrave?' she asked.

Edward squeezed her hand. He felt oddly light-headed, as if he had been breathing in laughing-gas. It was probably nothing more than the two bottles of Krug champagne they had managed to drink between them, followed by wind and cold and fresh air. 'I'm sure that I can persuade Vincent to sell you the Waldegrave. He's stuffy and traditional, that's all. He should have been alive in the 1880s, not the 1980s.'

'You don't live far from here, do you?' asked Cordelia. Her voice sounded as if it was reaching him from the other end of a tunnel. 'Wentworth Apartments, wasn't that it?'

'That's right. You know that block where they shot *Rosemary's Baby*? Well, it's right next door to that.'

'I would love a cup of hot tea,' Cordelia told him, pressing close to his arm. 'Do you have tea?'

'China, if you like China. Lapsang souchong.'

'That's my favourite.'

They left the park and caught a Checker cab right outside the Plaza. The taxi-driver thought he was Enrico Caruso, or at the very least Mario Lanza, and sang 'Vesti la giubba' in a wavering baritone, all the way to the Wentworth Apartments on West 63rd. Cordelia sat very near to Edward in the back of the cab, her black-gloved hand holding his left arm with possessive tightness. He smiled at her from time to time, but wondered why he felt so detached, and so woozy.

Edward paid the fare. The taxi-driver peered at the twenty-cent tip as if an overflying pigeon had dirtied the palm of his hand. 'Don't you like opera?' he demanded.

'I love it,' Edward told him. 'That's why you only get twenty cents.'

Cordelia, waiting on the pavement in her long black overcoat, her lapels lifted up to enclose her face like the petals of a black tulip, smiled at Edward; and reached out her hand. Edward thought that he had been rather witty. The taxi-driver grumbled, 'Asshole', and screeched away from the kerb in a temper.

They pushed their way together through the heavy glass-and-mahogany doors of the Wentworth Apartments into the hushed and dusty lobby. Above them, a huge glass chandelier hung like the transparent skeleton of a giant spider that had died in its own web. The thin winter-afternoon sunshine barely penetrated the windows, which were leaded to look like the windows of a Gothic castle. There were even shields on the wall, bearing coats-of-arms.

Edward said, 'It's incredibly pretentious, I'm afraid. But my grandfather bought an apartment here in the 1930s, and we kept it on.'

Cordelia stood still for a moment and looked around her, breathing in the musty air. 'I like it,' she said. 'It reminds me of . . . I don't know. I can't remember what it reminds me of. But I know that I have been somewhere like this before. Somewhere almost *exactly* like this.'

'Perhaps you've been *here* before,' Edward suggested, a little uncertainly. 'It's not the most memorable block of apartments ever constructed.'

'Perhaps,' agreed Cordelia.

They walked the length of the lobby to the lifts, which were embellished with bronze doors bearing ostentatious heraldic devices, lions rampant and crowned helms. Edward drew back the gate so that Cordelia could step inside.

Cordelia hesitated for a moment. 'I haven't been too pushy with you, have I?' she asked; although it was plain by the intonation in her voice that she didn't expect any other answer but 'no'.

'No,' said Edward.

She held his left wrist, encircling it with black-leather fingers. 'There are always times in your life when you must allow destiny to carry you forward, wherever it wants to take you; and not try to swim against the current.'

Edward closed the doors, and the lift rose upwards with a deep, subdued humming. Unlike most women, Cordelia didn't look once at the mirror in the back of the lift. She kept her eyes on Edward.

'Do you wonder what kind of a woman I am?' she asked him. 'A woman who insists on buying a young man lunch, and then asks to be taken back to his apartment for tea?'

'You want me to rebuild your art collection for you,' Edward reminded her.

Cordelia said nothing for a moment; then laughed, baring her teeth. Edward noticed that they were neither crooked nor false. In fact they were original and perfect.

The lift reached the seventh floor and quietly stopped. Edward opened the gates, and they stepped out into the corridor. Edward walked a little way ahead, turning his head back now and again to make sure that Cordelia was following him. Each time, she gave him that strange smile. She was quite right, of course: he was wondering what kind of a woman she was. But he was far too flattered by her offer to bring the Gray collection back together again, and far too intrigued by her extraordinary claustrophobic eroticism, not to allow this strange afternoon to go any further.

He reached his apartment, 797. He unlocked the door, and then courteously stood back, so that Cordelia could enter it first. Inside, it was warm and gloomy; so

Edward reached around the door and switched on the table-lamps. One of the radiators on the far side of the living room was knocking loudly; it always had done. Edward's grandfather had complained that it sounded as if the Count of Monte Cristo were imprisoned in the next apartment, and was tapping on the pipes. The living room was steeped in brown. There were dark brown velvet curtains; dark brown mock-Stuart chairs and tables with twisty legs; a rug the colour of dried tobacco-leaves. Up above the carved oak fireplace hung a portrait of a man in a brown coat, with a misshapen brown beret to match. The fireplace itself was home to a small collection of house-plants: two brown ferns, two knobby little cacti and a leprous yucca.

On the coffee-table, copies of art and design magazines were heaped in untidy stacks. A banjo was propped up against the arm of the old-fashioned tapestry sofa. There were no flowers, anywhere. Only ashtrays, and empty wineglasses.

'Well, this is rather fine, but I can tell that a man lives here on his own,' smiled Cordelia.

Edward looked around, his hands self-consciously propped on his hips. 'Yes, I suppose you're right. I rather miss having Laura around. All those little touches, like fresh-pressed tablecloths, and bowls of pot-pourri. The last party I had, one of my friends actually *smoked* all of my pot-pourri. He said it was better than Colombian gold.'

Edward walked through to the kitchen and noisily opened up the hatch which led through to the living room. He filled the kettle, and then he scrabbled through the cupboard to find his small tin of Lapsang souchong.

'If I were to rebuild your collection,' he said, 'when do you think you would want me to start?'

He looked through the hatch and saw Cordelia Gray. He slowly lowered his hands to his sides and stared at her.

She had taken off her long black overcoat. Now she had turned her back on him, and was slowly and deliberately unbuttoning her tailored grey dress. She kept her hat on, her grey plumed hat. Her dark hair was sharply and beautifully cut on the nape of her neck. With an easy movement, she let the dress slide from her hips, then gathered it up and folded it over the arm of the tapestry sofa.

No words were spoken. She stood in the centre of the living room, her skin as white as an unprinted page; and just as he had fantasized, she wore black underwear. A black lace bra, a black garter-belt, and sheer black stockings, with seams, sleekly encasing each long slim leg. A tiny black *cache-sex* barely covered her between her legs, and was drawn tight between the cheeks of her white bottom with black braided silk.

She turned now and faced him. He could see the dark red smudges of her nipples through the lace of her bra. The feathers of her hat nodded in the dimness of the afternoon, like funeral feathers.

'This is no time to talk about art,' she said in a whispery but distinctive voice.

Edward said nothing, but momentarily ducked his head aside, and let out a short 'Hah!' of surprise and pleasure. Then he smiled at her, bashful and gratified but still amazed at what was happening to him.

She reached behind her and unhooked her bra; it dropped from her shoulders, baring small rounded breasts. Then she unfastened her garter-belt and peeled off her stockings. She was naked now, except for the small black triangle which concealed her sex.

'Bring me a knife,' she said.

125

'A knife?' Edward queried.

'Just bring me a knife. The longest and sharpest knife that you have.'

Edward frowned. Then he obediently opened the cutlery-drawer, and took out his Sabatier carving-knife, ten inches of carbon steel, sharpened and resharpened until it could cut through bone. The kettle started to boil, but he reached over and switched it off.

Cordelia turned to greet him as he entered the living room. Her eyes were challenging, but she stood with her arms by her sides, making no attempt to conceal herself. Her breasts were high and tight, almost like the breasts of a girl of sixteen, although the nipples were wide and crimson-tinted, as if she had taken a handful of strawberries and crushed them against each one. Her stomach was slightly rounded, which attested to at least one childbirth, but there were no other blemishes on her body whatever. She was strangely flawless, as if she had been moulded out of bisque.

'Bring the knife here,' Cordelia whispered. Edward approached her, hesitantly holding up the knife in his right hand. Her perfume seemed to be stronger than ever, and he found that he could hardly focus his eyes. Cordelia reached out and stroked his cheek, running her fingertips lightly across his lips, around his eyes, touching his forehead and his hair and the lobes of his ears. Edward could see her nipples rise.

'Now,' she murmured, 'you must cut the string that ties the prize.'

She lowered her hands, and held out the thin braided silk tie that kept her *cache-sex* in place. Edward at last understood; and without any further hesitation, he slid the cold blade in between her bare white thigh and the thin string of silk.

Cordelia half closed her eyes. 'Cut,' she instructed

him, so softly that he wasn't even sure that he had heard her. There was the very faintest sizzle of steel on silk, and then her *cache-sex* dropped away from her. She had only the faintest fan-shaped covering of dark hair on her vulva, as if she were an adolescent girl who had only just started to grow it. It did nothing at all to conceal her full outer lips, or the startlingly pink cleft between them, which was already glistening in the dim light of the afternoon. Edward felt himself hardening, and he knew now that there was nothing he could do to resist her. It was like an extraordinary dream; a blurred and grainy vision of a scene which he had once played out when he was sleeping, but which he had long forgotten. He felt Cordelia's fingers loosening the knot of his necktie; then the buttons of his shirt slowly, one by one; and when his shirt fell to the floor it seemed to float and whirl and crumple as if it were falling in slow-motion.

Naked, the time forgotten, the tea forgotten, he carried Cordelia through to his bedroom. She was so light that she was easier to carry than a child. He laid her down on the dark blue satin bedspread, and kissed her, tasting her perfume, tasting her skin, exploratively at first, but then with increasing urgency. She returned his kisses with a tongue so long that it seemed as if she were licking the back of his throat, and as she did so she gently scratched her long fingernails all the way down his stomach, stroking it tenderly but dangerously.

Making love to Cordelia Gray was unlike anything that Edward had ever experienced before. She was yielding but cruel to him, continually biting at his neck and his nipples, continually scratching him, but then parting her thighs widely and wantonly, so that he could thrust his fingers up inside her; or twisting around so that she could take him into her mouth, so deeply that he couldn't imagine how she didn't choke.

She led him further and further away from safety and reality, out into a black erotic ocean where she herself seemed to be able to swim with disturbing skill, but where Edward began to feel that he was drowning.

'Now, take me; now, have me; take everything that I can give you; take all of them,' Cordelia whispered hotly in his ear; and as he mounted her she clasped each of his testicles with her claw-like fingernails and pulled him towards her.

It seemed to Edward as if whole hours went by. All he could hear were murmurs, kisses, the accompaniments of sliding satin and slippery skin. The room grew darker and darker. He shuddered, lying on his back, with Cordelia sitting astride him, in the last possible climax that he could manage. Cordelia leaned forward, her nipples softly touching his chest, and whispered, 'Perhaps it's time for tea now.'

'Mmm,' he nodded. He rested his head on the pillow. He closed his eyes. In the living room, he could hear the radiator clanking, and Cordelia walking around. He had never felt so contented in his life. An excellent lunch, a whole afternoon spent in bed with the most demanding woman he had ever met in his life, and now peace and darkness and a chance to sleep.

He thought briefly of Cordelia, and of what they had done together. His body was satisfactorily sore. The sensations that she had given him had been stunning. There had been one moment, when she had reached her first orgasm, when the inside of her vagina had literally *seethed*. Edward had never felt anything like it in his life.

He heard her come back into the bedroom. She sat down on the edge of the bed next to him, and lightly touched his shoulder.

'Darling,' she whispered. 'Are you asleep?'

'Mmmph,' he replied, without opening his eyes. 'Not yet, but nearly.'

'You must sleep,' Cordelia told him, and touched his eyelids with her fingertips.

Edward slept, deeply and dreamlessly, sinking so far into unconsciousness that his breathing became shallow, and his pulse-rate slowed. Cordelia called 'Edward?' once or twice, but after five minutes she stood up and walked naked back into the living room.

Quickly, she dressed, not forgetting to pick up her discarded *cache-sex* and tuck it into her handbag. Before she left, however, she also picked up Edward's jacket, brushed it down, and then systematically searched through all his pockets. In the right-hand ticket-pocket, she found his keys: apartment key, car keys, gallery door keys and gallery alarm keys. In the left-hand side pocket, she found Edward's maroon leather address book. She leafed through it until she found '*Laura Kelly*', with what must have been her family address: '*2206 Maple Avenue, New Rochelle.*' Underneath, Edward had written, in far smaller letters, '*Mrs D. Monblat, 65 West 10th*'. Cordelia tore out the page, folded it once, and put it into her bag along with the keys.

She looked around to make sure that she had left nothing behind. Then she left, closing the apartment door tightly.

Edward half opened his eyes, raised from his sleep by the strange impression that he was alone now, that something had gone wrong. He knew that he should get up and entertain Cordelia, but somehow he felt paralysed with tiredness, and he simply couldn't summon up the energy to stir. He closed his eyes again, and slept. It was six o'clock now, on a dark December afternoon, and outside his window New York echoed and roared and bustled, ten days to go before

Christmas, and over on the opposite side of the park, children were clustered around the brightly lit windows of FAO Schwarz, looking at the glittering fairy castle and the toy railway and the smiling bear who flew around and around in his bright yellow helicopter.

Cordelia had taken Edward's keys, and a page from his address book. But she had left him with four or five souvenirs in return.

As Edward slept, a small off-white maggot emerged from the warm sweaty crevices around his testicles, and made its way slowly up his hairy thigh, its brown-tinged sightless head waving from side to side. Soon it reached the crest of his flaccid penis, where it rested against his leg. The maggot crawled over the top of it, and then underneath, until it instinctively found the crevice of his urethra. It waggled its way gradually inside, and disappeared.

The maggot was soon followed by another, and another. A fourth maggot worked its way into the sphincter of Edward's anus, into his lower bowel. Yet another began the long wriggling journey up his stomach and up his chest towards his slightly open mouth.

Still Edward didn't wake. The carriage-clock on his bedside table chimed seven. The last maggot finally reared itself up on Edward's lower lip, and dropped silently into his mouth.

Nine

'He's not here,' said Vincent, climbing back into the car and irritably slamming the door.

'What do you mean, he's not here?' asked Charlotte. 'It's only seven-thirty in the morning. Where else could he be?'

'Maybe he went to the gallery.'

'At seven-thirty in the morning? Anyway, you told him you were going to call around to his apartment to collect the keys. Are you sure he wasn't in?'

'I rang the doorbell about two hundred times; and then I went down to the lobby and had the concierge call him on the telephone. Nothing.'

'Maybe he went to an all-night party,' Charlotte suggested. 'People do still have them, you know, even if old fogies like us can't stay awake until eleven o'clock.'

Vincent steered out into the rainy early morning traffic. His windscreen wipers shuddered and squeaked. 'Believe me, Charlotte, I don't care what the boy does, just so long as it doesn't inconvenience me. And right now, I've been inconvenienced.'

'Oh, don't be so pompous,' Charlotte prodded him.

'All right, I'm being pompous. Now and again, a man has a right to be pompous. Especially at seven-thirty in the morning when he's pushed for time and he's trying to get hold of the keys to his own goddamned art gallery.'

He U-turned, incurring at once the one-fingered annoyance of a cab-driver who had been following close behind him, and a moose-like blast on the horn from a truck which was ploughing northwards on Eighth Avenue.

'Get us killed,' Charlotte remarked airily. 'Just because you have a right to be pompous.'

'I'm sorry, all right?' Vincent told her.

He drove back across Central Park South, and with every minute the rain grew heavier, until it was thundering on the Bentley's leather-lined roof, and the windscreen wipers were tossing themselves frantically from one side to the other, just to keep up with the downpour.

'This is all I need,' said Vincent.

'You don't want the trees and flowers to grow?' Charlotte teased him.

'Trees and flowers, for God's sake.'

They arrived outside the gallery nearly twenty minutes later. Vincent said, 'Wait there,' and climbed out of the car. His head bowed down against the rain, his collar turned up, he hurried across the pavement to the gallery doorway, and peered inside. Only the display lights in the window were on, and they were controlled by a time-switch. There was no sign of Edward at all. Vincent shaded his eyes so that he could see right to the back of the gallery, but there was nobody there.

He hurried back to the car.

'No luck?' asked Charlotte.

Vincent shook his head. He brushed rain from the shoulders of his four-hundred-and-fifty-dollar Jupiter raincoat. 'That boy is going to get scalped when I find him. I'm going to hang him out to dry.'

'He's not usually unreliable, is he?' said Charlotte.

'Once is enough,' Vincent fumed.

'Maybe he's on his way here, and got held up in traffic,' Charlotte suggested. 'Maybe he couldn't get a taxi, and had to walk.'

'He couldn't have taken any longer to get from Eighth Avenue to here than we did. Even if he *was* walking.'

'Does he have family?' asked Charlotte.

'What does that have to do with it?'

'Well, maybe something went wrong at home, and he had to leave urgently.'

'Without calling me? He knows my number at Candlemas. And he knows damned well that I don't have any keys.'

'What are you going to do?' Charlotte asked him.

Vincent splayed his fingers on the steering-wheel. 'To be totally honest with you, I haven't the faintest idea. I have four dozen paintings to catalogue. I have a representative from Sotheby Parke Bernet calling; I have three meetings with dealers and two with artists; as well as about twenty pages of accounts. And I can't even open the door.'

'Are you sure he's not there?' asked Charlotte.

'Go look for yourself.'

Charlotte hesitated for a moment, and then opened the door. The rain had eased off a little now, and the pavement was bright and wet. She crossed over to the gallery on very high heels and looked inside. Vincent let down the passenger window and heard her knocking with the flat of her green-gloved hand.

Vincent called, ' "Is there anybody there, said the traveller, knocking at the moonlit door." '

Charlotte, undeterred, knocked again, and then she twisted the door handle.

'It's open,' she said.

'What?' Vincent demanded. He had just turned on the Bentley's motor, ready to leave; now he turned it off again.

'It's open,' Charlotte told him. And with a flourish, she opened the gallery door wide.

Vincent, under his breath, said, 'My God. There is thirteen million dollars' worth of other people's paintings in there.' He climbed out of the car again, and hurried to join Charlotte at the gallery entrance. She was right. The door was unalarmed, unlocked; and anybody who had accidentally or curiously tried the handle, as Charlotte had, would have had unrestricted and undisturbed access to one of the finest private collections of Pre-Raphaelite paintings that New York had ever seen.

'Edward!' shouted Vincent, stalking across the floor. 'Edward!'

There was no answer. Vincent opened the office door, and then came back into the middle of the gallery and stood with his hands on his hips, his coat-tails cocked, looking around him with baffled disbelief.

'There's nobody here,' he said.

'Is there anything missing?' Charlotte asked him.

Vincent shook his head. 'Not from this collection here. Not unless somebody's taken one of the pictures, and substituted a perfect fake.'

'What about the storeroom?'

'The storeroom has a combination lock. Edward doesn't know the code.'

'Still,' Charlotte suggested, 'perhaps you ought to look.'

Vincent walked along the corridor to the storeroom, switching on lights as he went. Charlotte looked the opposite way while he unlocked the door: she respected his security. But she came up close behind him as he stepped into the storeroom and switched on the fluorescent lights.

'I can't imagine Edward leaving the gallery unlocked,' she said. 'He's so conscientious; it just isn't like him at all.'

It was cool and dry in the storeroom, compared with the stuffy, sinus-drying heat of the gallery itself. The fluorescent lights flickered for a moment and then sternly illuminated the long rows of grey steel shelving: each row labelled with its school and its year. Vincent listened, his head raised, and then called out, 'Edward? Are you in here?'

Charlotte reached across and caught hold of Vincent's wrist, and said, '*Ssshh!*' But there was no reply, no muffled cry from a gagged Edward tied up by art thieves, nothing. Only the dull whirring of the air-conditioning plant, and the occasional click of the thermostat.

'Maybe he's been here already this morning,' said Charlotte. 'Maybe he just stepped out for a sandwich or something.'

Vincent shook his head. 'He knew that I would meet him at his apartment; I made that clear. And even if he was only stepping out for a couple of minutes, he would never leave the gallery unlocked. At least, I sincerely hope not.'

Vincent paced down one of the aisles, running his hand along the edge of the stored pictures. 'I suppose it's conceivable that somebody mugged him, and took his keys. But what for? They didn't take anything. Not from the main gallery, at least. Obviously I'll have to check through the inventory in here, but I can't see how anybody could have cracked that combination. That's a Heustadt lock, the best there is.'

'Perhaps the mugger didn't like Pre-Raphaelites.'

'Well, that's a possibility. A video-recorder is usually a darned sight easier to get rid of than a Holman Hunt; especially in Harlem.'

They were about to leave the storeroom when the telephone rang. Vincent picked it up off the hook by the door and said, 'Pearson Fine Art. How can I help you?'

He listened for a while, and then he said, 'Okay, thank you,' and hung up.

'What was that?' asked Charlotte. She couldn't help noticing his frown.

'The daytime concierge at Wentworth Apartments. He just arrived on duty. I left him a message to call me.'

'And?'

'He said that Edward arrived back home yesterday afternoon, with a woman, and that the woman left about six o'clock, on her own.'

'So what does that mean?'

'It means that neither the daytime nor the night-time concierge have seen Edward leave his apartment. As far as they're concerned, he's still there.'

'But he didn't answer his doorbell.'

'That's what worries me,' said Vincent.

He went into the office and checked quickly through his diary. 'The first dealer won't get here until ten-thirty, so that's okay; and I'll have the message service take my calls.'

'How can you lock the door, without the keys?'

'I can lock it on the latch. I'll just have to pray that nobody tries breaking a window, and that I can find those keys before I get back.'

They went out into the rain again. Vincent slammed the gallery door, and silently cursed his luck at the same time. He climbed into his Bentley, and pulled away from the kerb with a squittering of tyres.

The traffic had eased off a little, so it didn't take them so long to get back to Wentworth Apartments. They crossed the echoing hallway to the small glassed-in office where the concierge sat, reading the *New York Post* through a large smeary magnifying glass, and smoking a King Edward cigar.

'I'm Mr Pearson,' said Vincent. 'You called me just a short while ago, about Mr Merriam.'

'That's right,' the concierge nodded. He coughed, a thick phlegmy cough, and took the cigar out of his mouth. 'Mr Merriam ain't been out since yesterday afternoon, and I can swear an oath to that.'

'Is there any other way out of the building, apart from this hallway?'

'A fellow could jump, I guess.'

'Well, I hope not,' said Vincent. 'Is it okay if I go on up and try knocking on his door again?'

'Be my guest,' said the concierge.

Vincent and Charlotte took the elevator up to the seventh floor. Charlotte said, 'I didn't realize Edward lived anywhere so grand.'

'It belongs to his family. His father's a broker, something like that. They filmed *Rosemary's Baby* in the apartments on the next block.'

Charlotte made a face. 'I thought there was something redolent about it.'

They reached Edward's door, and rang the bell. There was no answer, although they could hear the bell ringing clearly inside the apartment. They rang the bell again.

'Could be asleep,' said Charlotte.

Vincent hammered on the door with his fist, and called, 'Edward! Edward? It's Vincent!'

Still no answer.

Vincent said to Charlotte, 'Do me a favour, would

you, Venus, and ask the concierge to bring his passkey up here. I'll keep on knocking.'

Vincent knocked and knocked until the apartment door opposite opened up, and a silver-haired woman in a pink silk bathrobe snapped, 'Quieten down that noise, will you? My husband's not well, and he can't stand banging.'

'I'm sorry,' said Vincent. He wiped his forehead with the back of his hand. 'It's just that I can't seem to rouse my colleague here.'

'Sleeping the sleep of the unjust, shouldn't be surprised,' remarked the woman.

'I beg your pardon?'

'Well, it isn't like me to pry, nor to listen to business that isn't mine, but Mr Merriam had a lady up in his rooms yesterday afternoon, and from the sounds they were making, I would say it was hanky-panky.'

'Oh, you would?' asked Vincent sharply.

The woman folded her arms, not in the least abashed. 'She came out of there quickly enough; quickly and quietly like somebody guilty. She was down that corridor and into that elevator before you could say knife.'

'What was she like?' Vincent asked her.

The woman sniffed. 'Good class, I'd say; although you can't tell these days, can you? Even the hoo-ers dress finely. Thirty, maybe, going on forty. Pale face, high cheekbones; a well-looking woman. More to *your* taste and age, if you don't mind my saying so, than young Mr Merriam's. That Laura of his; now she was *such* a pleasant girl.'

'I'm surprised you saw her so clearly,' said Vincent.

'Oh, for sure,' the woman told him. 'I was just off to get Howard his tablets, and she came out of Mr Merriam's apartment at the same time.'

Just then, Charlotte returned with the concierge, who was jangling his keys vigorously as a non-verbal expression of his irritation at being disturbed, and puffing out smoke like an old-time locomotive.

'Good morning, Mrs Turzynski,' he snapped tautly, out of the corner of his mouth.

'Mr Maggs,' the old woman acknowledged, and retreated into her apartment like a Polynesian turtle withdrawing its head into its shell.

'Now then,' the concierge demanded, looking up at Vincent with one eye squinched closed against the smoke of his cigar.

'My friend isn't answering,' said Vincent. 'And that lady, as well as you, are both convinced that he must still be inside his apartment.'

'Well . . .' said the concierge. 'There's no ordinance that says he has to answer. No law.'

'All the same,' said Vincent, as encouragingly as he could, 'it does strike us as rather unusual that he shouldn't. We would appreciate it if you would use your passkey, simply to make sure that Mr Merriam is all right.'

'The agents will have my ears if they find me doing this,' the concierge protested. 'This is supposed to be a security building, you know? The residents pay for security.' This was concierge code-language for 'how much will you pay me to make it worth my while?'

Vincent said, 'We must be able to come to some kind of understanding.' He took out his wallet, and counted out five five-dollar bills.

'I learned about Abraham Lincoln at school,' said the concierge, irrelevantly, tucking the notes into his cardigan pocket. 'The Gettysburg Address, I used to know that by heart.'

'How nice,' Vincent replied tartly.

The concierge unlocked the door of Edward's apartment, and Vincent pushed the door wider and stepped tentatively inside. 'Edward?' he called again, but there was silence; and darkness, too. Vincent groped around for the lightswitch, and eventually found it. All the curtains in the living room were drawn tight; and there was an odd smell around, like perfume, only ashier. It reminded Vincent of his grandmother's apartment in the Beresford; a smell of long ago. In the far corner of the living room, the radiator clanked intermittently. Outside on Central Park West, a police siren briefly whooped.

'Edward?' Vincent repeated, more softly this time, as if he knew that he wouldn't be answered.

Charlotte held Vincent's arm. 'He's not here,' she said, cautiously. 'He'd answer, if he were here.'

'Let me try the bedroom,' said Vincent.

'I'll, ah, wait here,' Charlotte told him. 'Just in case he's – well, you know, not decent. Or something.'

Vincent walked through to the bedroom. The door was slightly ajar. He didn't know why, but he hesitated. He wasn't afraid. At least, he didn't think that he was afraid. But what if Edward were sick, or asleep? He wouldn't particularly want Vincent and Charlotte marching into his bedroom, would he?

You're making excuses, he told himself. *Get on in there.*

He slowly pushed open the bedroom door. It was utterly silent in there. He was about to call Edward again, but somehow the words dried up on the back of his tongue.

Edward was there. He was lying on the bed, with the satin bedcover drawn up to his neck. His eyes were closed; one hand was lying on the pillow next to him.

Vincent turned and whispered to Charlotte, 'He's asleep.'

'Asleep? Are you sure he isn't dead?'

'No, he can't be dead, look. The bedcovers are moving.'

Charlotte tiptoed a little closer. 'He looks dreadfully pale.'

'Maybe he's been sick.'

'Do you think we'd better wake him up?'

'Well, I guess so,' said Vincent. 'If he *has* been sick, we ought to call a doctor.'

Vincent went across to the window first, and drew back the curtains. The grey rainy daylight illuminated the room. Then he crossed back to the bed, and leaned over Edward, and said, 'Edward. Edward, it's Vincent. It's time to wake up.'

Edward remained silent, with his eyes closed.

'Edward!' called Vincent, more forcefully, and shook Edward's shoulder.

Charlotte stood back a little, and frowned. 'He hasn't gone into a coma, has he, or something like that?'

'I don't think so,' said Vincent. 'Look – you can see his eyes moving under his eyelids, the way they do when you dream.'

'Rapid eye-movement,' said Charlotte, abstractedly.

'Edward!' Vincent repeated. But still there was no response.

'Take a look at his eyes,' said Charlotte. 'Maybe he *is* in a coma.'

Vincent reached down and lifted Edward's right eyelid with his thumb. Instantly, with a horrified shout, he snatched his hand away, and almost stumbled over himself as he jumped away from the bed.

Charlotte shrieked.

For out of Edward's right eye-socket, a wriggling knot of off-white maggots dropped and fell on to the pillow, where they separated and writhed as they tried to seek shelter. One or two more wriggled their way out from under Edward's eyelid; and then more began to crawl from his nostrils.

Shaking with disgust and terror, deaf to everything except Charlotte's screaming, Vincent reached forward and took hold of the top of Edward's bedcover, the bedcover which had been moving as if Edward were still breathing underneath it. He hesitated for a moment, and then he whipped it back.

'Oh, my God,' he said, and felt a wash of bitter bile rising up into his mouth.

Edward's body was a rippling mass of white maggots – maggots which had already consumed the soft flesh of his stomach, and which were now feeding in blind and relentless greed on his bowels and his lungs and his liver. They crawled through his ribcage in waves, giving the obscene impression that his lungs were rising and falling, and that his bowels were contracting in peristalsis. They seethed around the muscles of his upper arms, and poured over his legs.

It was the writhing that disgusted Vincent more than anything else; he would never be able to erase it from his memory. The mindless twisting and turning of all of those thousands of semi-transparent bodies, and the way they glistened in the daylight. They were already burrowing into the bright red meat of Edward's thighs, and the white curves of his pelvic bones rose out of their teeming depths, completely stripped of flesh.

Vincent's arm jerked upwards in shock, as if he had been unexpectedly struck by a doctor's reflex hammer. He said, 'God,' and that was all he could manage. Then he took Charlotte by the arm, because she seemed too dazed by what she had seen to know what to do next, and he dragged her out of the room. He closed the door behind them; and then just stood there and stared at her in disbelief and horror.

Charlotte said, in a high, off-key voice, 'Vincent, what happened to him? How could that have happened?'

Vincent briefly shook his head. There was a grey, greasy taste in his mouth, and he found it impossible to speak.

Charlotte covered her face with her hands for a moment, and then she retched.

'Quick, the kitchen,' said Vincent, and took her through to the sink. She bent over, holding up her hair, and vomited up her breakfast. Vincent felt his own stomach tighten into knots, but he managed to swallow two or three times and control the urge to throw up.

'Are you okay?' Vincent asked Charlotte, after a while. 'I'd better call the police. And an ambulance, too, although I don't know what they can do, except carry him away.'

Charlotte nodded. Her face was bleached with disgust.

At that moment, the concierge came in, still jingling his keys. 'Are you people through yet? I have to get back downstairs.'

Vincent said, 'I have to call the police. Mr Merriam's dead.'

'Dead? What do you mean dead? What's this dead?'

'He's dead, that's all, in the bedroom.'

The concierge took the cigar out of his mouth, and peered hard at the bedroom door, as if he were attempting to see right through it. 'What, he kill himself, or something?'

'I don't know. I don't think so. Now, if you'll excuse me.'

Vincent picked up the phone and dialled 911. The concierge kept hovering around him, sucking noisily at his cigar.

'What is it, messy or something? He shoot himself, or what?'

'I don't know,' said Vincent. 'It's impossible to tell. Now, please. We've both had a severe shock and all I want to do is call the police.'

Charlotte came through to the living room and she was trembling. She scarcely made it across to the nearest armchair before she had to sit down. She took out a pack of More, and lit one for each of them. Vincent very rarely smoked cigarettes, but he took his gratefully, and drew down a deep lungful of smoke. Anything to fumigate the diseased air that he had breathed in that roomful of maggots.

The concierge sucked at his cigar and realized it had gone out. 'You know something?' he said. 'I get nothing but tragedy in these apartments. The things I seen, you know? The tragedy. You wouldn't credit it. All the lonesome lives that get lived out here, even the rich people, lonesome as all hell. And now this. Only a young guy, wasn't he? Mid-twenties?'

Vincent at last was connected through to the police. 'I wish to report a death,' he said, in a voice that didn't even sound like his own.

10

Laura was slicing zucchini in the Cuisinart when the door chimes rang. She wiped her hands on a tea-towel, and called out, 'Just a moment!' Then she switched off the processor, and walked across the polished floor in her flip-flapping Japanese mules, her scarlet-fingernailed hands held out on each side of her like little cherub's wings.

She reached the front door and frowned through the spyhole, her long eyelashes batting as she tried to focus. The two boys who lived downstairs were always 'borrowing' the lightbulbs in the hallway, so it was almost impossible for Laura to see who was out there. But she could distinguish a pale face, a face that looked like a woman, and that reassured her. Danny always told her that if the face was male, or black, or both, then she wasn't to open up the door, no matter *who* they said they were.

'Are you Mrs Laura Monblat?' the woman called. A high-pitched, well-educated voice.

Laura said, 'That's me. What do you want?'

'My name's Sybil Vane. I'm an old friend of your mother's. Can I come in? I'm afraid there's been an accident.'

'Accident? What kind of accident?'

'It's your father. Please. It's very difficult to talk through the door.'

'What's happened?' Laura insisted, worriedly.

'He's had rather a bad fall. He's in hospital. Please, if you open the door I can tell you properly.'

Laura slid back the bolts, top and bottom, then turned the key in the eight-lever deadlock. There had been two rapes and eight burglaries in this building in less than a year, and Danny Monblat wasn't going to go off to the office leaving his young wife unprotected.

The woman stepped into the apartment. She was slightly taller than Laura, although that could have been the effect of her high-heeled black shoes. She wore a long black winter coat, on which a scattering of melted snowflakes glistened like stars in a suffocating universe. She wore a black turban hat with a nodding grey feather. Her face was as white as milliner's tissue, and although she had obviously once been very beautiful, she looked tired, now, and deeply lined.

'When did this happen?' Laura asked her. 'Why didn't anybody phone?'

The woman tugged off her gloves. 'Your mother tried to call you from the clinic, but your line was busy. She called me instead, and asked me to come around. I have an apartment over on Gracie Square.'

'Is it really serious?' asked Laura.

'The doctors seemed to think that your father might have fractured one or two of his lower vertebrae. They're going to be running more tests on him tomorrow, and taking more X-rays. It could be very serious indeed, if there's any extensive spinal damage. I'm sorry.'

Laura was flustered and shocked. 'He won't – I mean, he's not in any danger of dying, is he?'

'I don't think so, my dear. But he may partially lose the use of his legs.'

'Oh, my God, that's awful. Can I call my mother? Do you have the clinic's telephone number? Which clinic is it?'

The woman called Sybil Vane touched Laura's arm and smiled sympathetically.

'Your mother was hoping that you could come straight up to New Rochelle. That's why she asked me to come around. My car's outside. I can drive you there.'

'Well, I don't know. I ought to call Danny.'

'Please do, by all means. But your mother wants you to come just as quickly as possible.'

Laura untied her apron, and went through to the kitchen.

'I was right in the middle of making zucchini bread,' she said, almost shamefully, as if somehow she should have been looking after her father instead.

The woman stayed in the living room. It was bright and well-lit and warm, with one wall cleaned back to its natural red brick. There were palms and ferns in big basketwork planters, and the furniture was all glass and chrome and natural beech. The woman's fingers touched the walls as if she wanted to sense the vibrations of the lives that were being lived here, as if she were tuning herself in to Laura's emotions.

Laura came out of the kitchen, and quickly brushed her hair.

'Do you know how it happened?' she asked.

'I'm not sure,' said the woman. 'Your mother said something about going to fetch a glass of water from the bathroom, and slipping over. She was very upset.'

Laura picked the phone off the wall and punched out the number of Danny's office. 'He's always been so *healthy*, my father,' she said, as she waited for the connection. 'Well, if you're a friend of Mother's, you probably know that already.'

'Your mother and I were at school together,' the woman told her. And smiled again as if that answered everything.

Laura sighed and punched out the number again. The woman watched her as she waited. A very pretty young girl indeed. Dark auburn hair, greenish eyes, an oval face; almost Irish-looking. Skin as fine and pale as orchid petals. Over made-up, of course, as most American women always are, but nothing that a little cold cream couldn't cure. And a trim figure, too. Narrow hips, well-proportioned legs, and not too extravagant in the bust. A very slight blemish on the left cheek, probably a childhood accident, but nothing too serious.

'Can't you get through?' asked the woman called Sybil Vane.

'The line seems to be dead.'

The woman smiled yet again. She had such a strangely sweet and indulgent smile; and despite herself Laura found it comforting. 'I have a telephone in my car,' the woman said. 'You can try calling Danny again while we drive.'

'Okay,' said Laura. 'Just let me get my coat.'

'Don't be too long,' the woman told her. 'My car's parked in the tow-away zone.'

Sybil Vane stood patiently studying a framed poster for *It Happened One Night* while Laura put on her coat, and switched off the lights, and spread out a fresh bagful of cat-litter.

'Have you seen my cat?' she asked the woman, frowning. 'She was here a moment ago.'

The woman shook her head. 'She's very probably asleep somewhere. You know what cats are like.'

Laura knelt down, still buttoning up her coat, and looked under the furniture. 'She's not here. Phoebe! Phoebe! Puss, puss!'

She went through to the bedroom, and looked in the bathroom, but there was no sign of the cat anywhere.

'I don't mean to rush you,' Sybil Vane said. 'But we really ought to be going.'

Laura gave Phoebe one last call, but there was no response. She followed Sybil Vane out into the hallway, and double-locked the door behind her. Together, they walked down the four flights of darkened stairs to the street. The woman's high heels clattered like nails being hammered into oak.

'The doctors couldn't say whether it might affect his walking or not?' Laura asked.

The woman shook her head. 'They weren't prepared to commit themselves to any specific prognosis at all. That's what your mother told me, anyway. We can give her a call, though, once we're in the car, and you can ask her for yourself.'

Laura said, 'Poor old Dad. He's always so active. He won the New Rochelle Amateur Golf Tournament the year before last.'

'Yes, I know,' said the woman. She took Laura's hand, and squeezed it, and smiled. 'Let's look on the bright side,' she said. 'He's probably done nothing worse than chip one of his bones.'

'Oh, God, I hope so,' said Laura.

The car was waiting by the kerb: a black Fleetwood limousine, at least ten years old, its polished hood beaded with raindrops.

'You drive this yourself?' asked Laura.

The woman opened the passenger door for her. There was a strong smell of leather, and ashes of roses. 'It's my only self-indulgence,' she said. 'It belonged to my brother. My brother used to say that no self-respecting American should ever drive a car that is less than twenty feet long.'

Laura climbed into the car and closed the door. The woman prised off her five-inch high heels, and slipped on a pair of black nylon socks. Then she twisted the key in the ignition, and the Fleetwood's engine started up with a squeak and a roar. The woman pulled out into the traffic without making a signal, and drove down to the end of the block, where she turned right into Sixth Avenue and headed uptown.

'Are you warm enough?' she asked. She drove with a kind of imperious inaccuracy, tutting and clicking her teeth impatiently whenever another vehicle cut in front of her, or slowed down, or signalled to turn left, or otherwise irritated her.

Laura said, 'It's very warm, thank you.' In fact, the inside of the car was stifling, and Laura had already unbuttoned her coat.

'I can't bear the cold, you see,' the woman said. Her diamond rings glittered as she turned the steering-wheel. 'The cold makes my head ache.'

They passed Radio City, and its red lights were garishly reflected on the Fleetwood's long black bonnet.

It was still snowing, and the pavements were clustered with umbrellas. Laura said, 'Did you say you met Mother at school?'

'That's right. We were the closest of friends; and after that we always kept in touch.'

'You should have come to the wedding.'

The woman smiled. 'I wanted to. Your mother invited me. But, unfortunately, I was in Europe at the time. Family business, it couldn't be helped.'

'I'm just surprised you never came to the house.'

The woman turned and looked at her. 'Of course I came to the house! I used to visit regularly, until my poor husband fell so ill. I can remember when you were just a little girl.'

Laura half expected the woman to elaborate on her reminiscences, but she didn't. They sat in silence until they reached Central Park South, where the woman turned right. The Fleetwood's worn suspension clonked loudly over the potholes and drain-covers, and the windscreen wipers shuddered and protested with every stroke. Laura found the car so perfumed and stuffy that she let down her window an inch or two. The chilly evening air eddied in, and for a while she felt refreshed; but then the woman said, 'If you don't mind keeping the window closed. The cold does so disturb me, you know.'

'Oh, I'm sorry,' said Laura, and closed up the window again.

They headed north. As they reached 125th Street, it began to snow more furiously, and the woman was almost in collision with the back of a bus. She didn't sound her horn, but tutted menacingly, and made an elaborate fuss of driving around the side of the bus, causing even more disruption, and provoking a volley of horns from cars and taxis all around her. Laura could hardly see through the Fleetwood's windows. At the back and the sides they were all steamed up. She was beginning to regret very much that she hadn't waited for Danny to come home, to drive her up to New Rochelle himself, and she found herself gripping the doorhandle and the worn-out leather of her seat, and praying that the woman wouldn't get herself involved in an accident.

'No courtesy these days,' the woman remarked. 'You should see how they drive in Europe. With *style*, and supreme politeness. Here, these hogs – well, that's the only word for them. Hogs.'

'Are you really sure this isn't too much trouble?' Laura asked her.

'Trouble?' asked the woman called Sybil Vane, as if it were a foreign word she had never encountered before.

'Well, it's a pretty bad night, and New Rochelle's a long way from Gracie Square. I could always take a taxi instead. I mean, you could let me out and I could go the rest of the way by taxi.'

The woman laughed sharply. 'Let you out? Here? In Harlem? On a snowy night, with your father lying sick in the clinic? What on earth do you think your mother would say to me, if I did a thing like that? Now, just look at this lunatic, slowing down right in front of me.'

'Please be careful,' said Laura. 'The roads are really slippery.'

'My dear,' the woman replied, 'I've been driving for more years than – *look* at that fool, just look at him!'

Laura could do nothing but sit where she was, and swallow back her nervousness. The woman called Sybil Vane was right: she could hardly get out of the car here, in the teeming snow, in the middle of Harlem, in the dark. Her chances of finding a taxi were practically nil. Her chances of being mugged or worse were appreciable.

'My brother always used to *adore* driving in the snow,' said the woman airily. 'It separates the tigers from the oxen, that's what he used to tell me. In the snow, you have to drive like a tiger!'

Laura said, 'You told me there was a phone in the car.'

'Yes, there is,' the woman replied. 'My brother always made sure that we had a phone in the car. He used to drive so much! A regular Wolf Barnato.'

'May I use it?' asked Laura, anxiously.

'What?' frowned the woman.

'The phone. May I use it?'

'Of course. It's in the glove compartment.'

Laura opened up the glove compartment. There was a cellular phone neatly packed inside, as well as a pack of mint imperials from Taylor's of Bond Street. Laura picked up the phone and switched it on. The red pilot light flickered, but all she could hear in the receiver was a long, slow, fizzling sound.

'I don't think it's working,' she said.

'Probably the snow,' the woman remarked. 'It never seems to work in the snow. Nor in the rain, either, for that matter.'

'I have to call Danny,' Laura insisted. 'He's going to be worried about me.'

'Well, that's all right,' said the woman, quite pleasantly. 'As soon as we reach a gas station, we'll stop; and then you can get out and phone him.'

'Oh, please, if you don't mind,' said Laura.

They were crossing into the Bronx now. The traffic was thinning out, and the woman was driving more steadily. Laura watched the melted snow trembling on the windowpane beside her, and the blurry lights of Queens, and listened to the ceaseless sizzling of the tyres on the concrete roadway; and although she still regretted having accepted Sybil Vane's offer of a ride to New Rochelle, she began to feel safer now, and she reassured herself that her parents would be pleased to see her, and that everything was going to be fine. She hadn't been to see her mother since the wedding, and she found that she was quite looking forward to it.

The woman, as she drove, began to talk. She started off by telling Laura about what she had been doing in Europe. Then she went on to discuss fashion, and shoes, and how badly they were cut these days, and how a woman had to watch out for callouses on her feet. It was an extraordinary monologue, about everything and nothing, and the woman recited it in a remarkably repetitive voice, emphasizing the same patterns of syllables again and again, so that Laura felt as if she were listening to a long monotonous piece of music, rather than a woman's voice. Everything the woman said was rhetorical, giving Laura neither the opportunity nor the incentive to answer, or even to think very clearly about what she was hearing. The Fleetwood swept on through the night, the windscreen wipers skidded regularly from side to side, and the woman talked on and on in the same mesmerizing tone, until Laura closed her eyes for a moment, and then for a longer moment; and then slept.

She dreamed, as she slept, that she was flying through the night on the back of a black scaly creature, a creature whose huge wings shed fragments of flesh and bone with every downward sweep. She dreamed that she was lost in a maze of black cindered hedges, burned and shrunken; a maze in which voices could be heard around every corner, but nobody else could be seen. She dreamed that she was alone in a rainswept house, a house that everybody had forgotten, and which was about to be demolished around her ears. She wept in her dreams, and talked, and wrung her hands; and when suddenly the Fleetwood swung around in a semi-circle, and there was a crunching of tyres on shingle, and the engine abruptly stopped, she woke up to find that her cheeks were wet with tears.

She stared at the woman, who was still sitting next to her. Then she stared out of the window. It was dark outside, apart from a single old-fashioned lamp standard. The snow had eased off, and now it was raining.

'Are we here?' she asked in bewilderment. 'I must have dropped off for a while.'

'We're here,' the woman replied. She turned and

smiled at Laura; and Laura suddenly realized how shrunken and wrinkled the woman appeared. She seemed to have aged ten years since this afternoon. Also, there was a different look in her eyes. Not kindly at all, but cold and scrutinizing, as if she were peering at Laura through the torn-open apertures in a mask of white skin.

'Is this the clinic?' asked Laura. She rubbed her eyes with both hands. Her head felt thick and muzzy, as if she were suffering from a hangover. She peered out of the Fleetwood's rain-freckled window. 'This isn't the clinic.'

'No, of course not. This is my home. Since you fell asleep for so long, I thought you might like to come in and freshen up a little first, before we drive down there. Also, I have one or two things I promised to take to your mother.'

'What's the time?' Laura asked her. Her watch seemed to have stopped.

'Ten after seven,' the woman told her.

'Ten after seven? But that means I've been sleeping for two hours! Why didn't you wake me? We were supposed to stop at a gas station and call Danny.'

'Don't worry,' the woman smiled, although her smile was hardly a smile, more of a grimace. She patted Laura on the hand. 'You can telephone from here, if you wish. Look, here's my brother Maurice.'

A tall grey-haired man appeared out of the rainy darkness, wearing a black raincoat. He bent forward and looked into the interior of the car, then smiled, and opened Laura's door. 'Well, well,' he said. 'You must be Laura. Cordelia has told me so much about you. Please, climb out, and I'll show you into the house. I'm sure you could use a cup of tea after your journey.'

Laura eased herself out of the Fleetwood, and

buttoned up her coat. It was chilly and damp here, and smelled woodsy. It was impossible to see very much, since the woman had switched off the Fleetwood's headlights, and there was no other illumination but the old-fashioned lamp standard. The man's black raincoat rustled, just like the wings of the black scaly creature in her dream had rustled. Somewhere, not too far away, a dog was barking.

'The dogs can always scent strangers,' Maurice Gray remarked happily. 'Come now, follow me, the pathway is rather dark, and you'll find that the bricks are slippery. We haven't had time yet to scour off the moss. Cordelia, my dear, you be careful, too.'

'Cordelia?' asked Laura. 'I thought you said that your name was Sybil.'

The woman came up and took hold of Laura's arm, quite tightly. There was the clinging, familiar smell of ashes of roses, even through the rain. 'Calling myself Sybil Vane is just one of my little eccentricities,' she said. 'It used to be my stage name, many years ago. I was a theatrical actress, you know. A very good one, in my way. I was a marvellous Magda.'

They made their way cautiously along the darkened path. At length they reached a high red-brick wall, heavily overgrown with *Clematis tangutica*, bare and brown now, and dripping with rain; and Maurice opened a rusted iron gate, which squeaked dolefully. Beyond the gate was a brick-laid yard and then the dark outline of a huge house. There were no lights at any of the windows, and as Laura followed Maurice towards the front porch, she could smell freshly turned earth, and drains, and damp.

Maurice opened the peeling, grey-painted front door. 'It's all rather decrepit at the moment, I'm afraid. Cordelia probably told you that we've been away in

Europe for rather a long time. We came back only two weeks ago; so we haven't been able to do much.'

Laura said nothing as Maurice shuffled around inside the darkened porch for the lightswitch. She couldn't imagine why he hadn't left the light on when he came out to greet them. But at least he found it, and a bulb burned brightly in a cobweb-covered lamp suspended over the steps, and Maurice ushered them in.

'I'd like to use the phone straight away, please,' said Laura.

'Of course,' said Maurice. 'Come with me, and I'll show you where it is.'

'Are we far from the clinic here?' asked Laura. 'Falling asleep has made me lose my sense of direction. I mean, this is New Rochelle, isn't it?'

'The telephone is this way,' said Maurice. He switched on the main chandelier in the hall, and lit up high, half-panelled walls, a curving oak staircase and a boarded floor without any rugs. The house was very cold, which surprised Laura since Sybil or Cordelia or whatever her name was had made such a fuss about the cold. It was so cold, in fact, that their breath appeared as little embryo ghosts.

'This *is* New Rochelle?' Laura repeated, suddenly uncertain. There was something about the way in which Maurice was standing at the far end of the hallway, his hands clasped together like a retired thespian, and about the way in which Cordelia had turned away from the lights; something unnatural about it, something staged and tense and disturbing.

'This is *close* to New Rochelle,' Cordelia assured her.

'Close? How close? Come on, I've come all the way out here on trust. I want to know exactly where I am, and where the clinic is, and what the clinic's telephone number is, so that I can call my mother.'

There was a lengthy and difficult silence. Maurice looked past Laura at Cordelia, and shrugged, as if to say, what's the use? Laura said, unevenly, angry and frightened now, 'I *have* to know.'

Cordelia stepped forward, her heels clicking like a metronome on the boarded floor. She held out her hand, although she obviously didn't expect Laura to take it.

'My dear,' she said, 'I have to tell you that your father is perfectly well, at least as far as I know. You are not in New Rochelle; in fact you are in Darien, Connecticut.'

Laura stared at her. 'This is incredible,' she said. 'This is absolutely incredible. But why? What on earth do you want *me* for? What have I ever done to you?'

'Nothing at all,' said Cordelia, 'apart from coming to our attention.'

'I want to phone my husband,' Laura demanded.

'I'm sorry,' said Maurice, quite gently. 'That won't be possible.'

'You were going to let me phone him just now.'

'No, no, my dear, of course I wasn't. I was simply going to lock you in the library. In fact, I am *still* going to lock you in the library.'

Laura felt her breath tightening, and her heart beating in deep, painful thumps. 'I'm going,' she said. 'You can't stop me. I'm going.'

'You mustn't be frightened,' said Maurice.

'I'm going,' Laura shouted at him. 'I'm going, and that's all there is to it!'

Laura turned round and strode towards the front door. She tugged it open, and there he was. A tall and handsome young man with dark curly hair, wearing a well-tailored grey suit and smoking a cigarette. There was a carnation in his lapel, and Laura suddenly felt that the whole hallway was dense with the fragrance of carnations. The young man didn't move, but drew in a leisurely way at his cigarette, and smiled at Laura with amusement and pleasure. 'Well, well,' he said, in a sharp English voice. 'Is this the young lady you were speaking of, Cordelia?'

'Have you been out?' Cordelia asked him, and it was plain that she was displeased.

The young man stepped into the hallway and closed the front door firmly behind him. He nodded his head just a fraction, as if he acknowledged Laura's fear and desperation. 'I walked around the rose-garden, that's all. I needed some air. I took my large black umbrella, the one that Frank gave me. It was rather pleasant. Rather perverse, too, I suppose; but rather pleasant.'

Maurice came forward now and touched Laura's shoulder with a gentle, appreciative hand. Laura recoiled, and stared from one of her abductors to the other, scarcely able to believe that what was happening to her was real. She was half convinced that she was still in the passenger seat of the Fleetwood, driving towards New Rochelle through the snow, and that she was still asleep and dreaming.

'This is Henry,' said Maurice. 'Henry is our *older* cousin; the son of our father's brother John. Henry, this is Laura. Cordelia collected her today.'

'Well, she's very pretty,' said Henry, walking around her. 'Is she for Aunt Isobel, Cordelia, or are you keeping her for yourself?'

Cordelia said stiffly, 'Whoever has the greater need.'

'She's your mother,' said Henry, with feigned off-handedness. 'Whether you want her to survive or not, well, that's up to you, naturally. I must say the roses are in a terrible state.'

Laura swallowed dryly, and announced, 'I'm going. Will you please let me pass?'

'Going?' Henry asked her, in surprise, tapping his

cigarette-ash on the floor. 'My delightful young lady, you can't be serious. Why, you have arrived by luck amongst the most hospitable and amusing people in the whole of Connecticut. Surely you can stay for a drink? Surely you can stay for one of dear Aunt Isobel's tiny cakes, with pink sugar-frosting on top? Why, you must stay for Christmas.'

Cordelia grasped Laura's wrist; and her grasp was bony, and relentless, and surprisingly strong.

'Christmas, *chez* Gray, is always a wonderful occasion,' she said, in a sing-song tone. 'You must stay, if only in spirit.'

She kissed Laura's cheek with lips that were as cold as refrigerated liver; and it was then that Laura felt the first slow drenching of utter dread. She thought she might have screamed, but she wasn't sure.

Eleven

New York, 17 December

'You can understand, sir, why your story doesn't altogether add up,' said the black detective in the smart new tan raincoat, his hands clutched tight behind his back.

'Yes,' said Vincent. 'But I can't tell you anything more than the truth.'

'Your man was in the kind of condition we normally expect to find after ten days of decomposition in summer weather,' the detective said. 'Yet, what you're trying to insist on here is that you saw him alive on Friday evening, round about five.'

'That's correct,' said Vincent. He shuffled together all the sheets of his latest inventory, and methodically blocked them straight. Then he fastidiously clipped them together with a gold Gucci stapler. 'I'm sure that plenty of other people must have seen him, too, if you'd care to make enquiries up and down the street.'

'Well, we've done that, sir, and nobody remembers too well.'

'Isn't that what they call selective amnesia, brought on by a chronic fear of being subpoena'd as a witness?'

'That's conceivable,' said the detective. 'What's *more* conceivable, however, is that Edward Merriam wasn't here at all on Friday, but was already lying dead and decomposing in his apartment, a situation well known to you, and possibly known to Ms Greene, too.'

'Detective Clark,' said Vincent, as patiently as he could, 'Mr Merriam's concierge remembers him returning to his apartment on Sunday, along with a middle-aged woman. If he was still walking around on Sunday, how could he possibly have been dead and decomposing on Friday?'

Detective Clark tugged at his thin Little Richard moustache. 'We do have a theory that the man whom the concierge claims to have seen wasn't Mr Merriam at all, but a look-alike. That concierge couldn't see too well; he wore the thickest eyeglasses; and sitting in that office of his, he could easily have been mistaken.'

'I have invoices signed by Mr Merriam on the Thursday and the Friday,' Vincent insisted, trying not to sound irritable. 'Good God, man, he sold two water-colours on Thursday morning. I can contact the buyer and have him confirm it for you!'

Detective Clark let out a testy breath. 'Any of these invoices could have been altered. All you had to do was change the date. And if you had happened to have somebody here who looked like Mr Merriam, well, that would be quite sufficient to delude any customer, wouldn't it, into making a positive identification, especially when the remains that we have in the morgue don't have very much of a face left to make comparisons with!'

Vincent stood up straight, and lifted one steady finger. 'Let me tell you something, Detective. I appreciate your difficulties, and believe me I am just as anxious as you are to find out what happened to Edward on Sunday. But Edward was here on Friday; I believe that he was still alive on Sunday; and I take grave exception to these unsubstantiated accusations

162

you are attempting to make that either I or Ms Greene had anything to do with killing him.'

Detective Clark spread his hands. *'Killing?* Did I say *killing?'*

'You didn't have to. The implication was enough.'

'Well, all right, then, if it's cards on the table. Whatever you say about Mr Merriam being here in this store on Friday afternoon –'

'Gallery,' Vincent winced. *'Gallery,* please.'

'– here in this here *gallery* on Friday afternoon – the categorical fact remains that the condition of his body was consistent with ten days of decomposition and that is in the *summer,* and this is the *winter,* and there is no possible *way* according to the medical examiner that Mr Merriam could have been alive on Sunday, not decomposed to such an extent, and that's it.'

Vincent let out a long and patient breath. 'Very well, Detective, I take your point. Something appears to have happened here which defies the normal laws of medical science.'

'Either that, or you and Ms Greene are not being as accurate in your recollections as you might be.'

'Yes,' Vincent agreed. 'You have to consider, of course, what possible motive either of us could have had for killing Mr Merriam; or, even if we *didn't* kill him, what possible motive either of us could have had for failing to report his death at the time when your medical examiners seem to believe that it happened.'

'There's always the famous love triangle,' suggested Detective Clark.

Vincent shook his head in subdued exasperation. 'Ms Greene and I are friends, not lovers; and Mr Merriam certainly had no interest in either of us. So that rules out any possibilities of a love triangle, straight or gay.'

'So *you* say.'

'Well, yes. So I say.'

Detective Clark looked pugnaciously this way and that, nodding his head as he did so as if to make a silent and continuing comment about the gallery and about Vincent and about everything he saw in here: paintings, hunh, old-time pictures worth millions of dollars, when there were families just about destitute this Christmastime, and filthy old derelicts sleeping in cardboard boxes in the side-entrances to Macy's, and it was cold out there and people were killing each other.

'I'll be back,' he told Vincent, and there was a challenge in his eyes.

Vincent said, 'I'm sure you will.'

After the police had left, Vincent went into his office, took a bottle of Jameson's whiskey out of the desk, and poured himself a small glassful, which he knocked straight back. He firmly screwed the top back on the bottle, closed the desk and then went back to his inventory. He was still haunted by those off-white, wriggling maggots. He had thought about them so much that he was beginning to feel that they had actually penetrated his skull, and that they would soon be dropping out of his ears, the way they had dropped so sickeningly out of Edward's eyes.

Detective Clark was quite right. It was impossible for Edward's body to have been eaten away so dramatically by maggots in such a short space of time. At the very longest – even if Edward had died soon after Vincent had last seen him – he could only have been lying there for two days and two nights. Under normal circumstances, his body would scarcely have started to give off any odour by then; and certainly no maggots would have yet appeared. All the medical books talked about was a 'greenish tinge' around the abdominal area.

Vincent sat at his desk and went through his inventory once again. The gallery may have been broken into some time over the weekend, but nothing had been taken, not even the petty cash. Vincent was convinced that the mysterious woman who had been seen with Edward at his apartment was responsible for taking his keys and letting herself in here. Who else could it have been? She might even be responsible for Edward's death. But Detective Clark had not been amused. None of Vincent's pictures had been stolen, and Mrs Turzynski had not only failed to remember what the woman had looked like, but even if the woman had come out of Edward's apartment at all. The gallery keys had disappeared, and Vincent had been obliged to have a new set cut, but what did that prove? Nothing, except that Edward might have been careless.

Vincent was going through the list for the third time when the gallery door opened, and a stocky dark-haired man walked in, wearing a creased blue three-piece suit. His face was sallow, and he didn't look as if he had washed or shaved that morning. There were heavy gold rings on his fingers, so he couldn't have been impoverished.

'Can I help you?' Vincent asked him. 'Or would you just like to look around?'

The dark-haired man came straight to the point. 'I'm looking for a guy called Edward Merriam. He work here?'

Vincent eyed the man with care, and thoughtfully drummed his fingertips on the desk. 'He *did* work here. May I ask who wants to know?'

'You mean he's gone?' the dark-haired man demanded.

'In a manner of speaking, yes.'

'Where did he go? Did you see him go? Did he have a

165

girl with him? Twenty-three years old, slim, reddish hair? Did you see them?'

Vincent said, 'I would like to know who you are, please?'

The dark-haired man said, 'All I need to know is where they went. If they took off, where did they go? That's all.'

Vincent walked around the desk. 'Were you a friend of his? Edward's?'

'I know him. Why? Not too well. We aren't exactly compatible, if you know what I mean.'

'He's dead,' said Vincent.

The dark-haired man looked even more sallow. 'He's *dead*? He didn't – not Laura – he didn't touch Laura, did he?'

'Laura?' frowned Vincent.

'Laura's my wife. Laura Monblat. My name's Danny Monblat. Laura used to live with Edward Merriam before I met her; before we got married. I got home yesterday afternoon and Laura wasn't there, and I kind of assumed that she might have gone back to Edward. She was always talking about what a decent guy he was, that kind of thing. I just assumed.'

'I'm sorry,' said Vincent. 'But Edward was found dead yesterday morning round at his apartment on Central Park West. There was nobody with him when he was found.'

Danny wiped his hand across his mouth. 'That's terrible. Was it natural, or did somebody kill him or something? Jesus.'

Vincent nodded towards the doorway. 'That was the police, just leaving. They don't yet know what could have happened to him. Apparently there was a woman with him, shortly before he died – but no, wait a minute, before you get upset – this woman was middle-aged,

166

with a black coat and a black hat with a feather in it.'

'Well, that wasn't Laura,' said Danny, with relief. 'Least, it doesn't *sound* like Laura, unless she's taken to wearing disguises. The trouble is, I still don't know where Laura could be.'

'You've told the police?'

'Oh, sure, and they just stared at me like I was an idiot even for bothering to tell them about it. Do you know how many people go missing every single day? In New York alone? Thousands, they said. Not hundreds. Thousands. Can you imagine that? And one of those thousands is Laura. But they don't care. They *can't* care. You can't even *expect* them to care.'

Vincent looked soberly down at his inventory. Then he said, 'You've called her parents, I guess?'

'Sure. They were the first.'

'And?'

'They were as upset as me. They didn't have any idea what could have happened.'

Danny Monblat unhappily ran his hands through his hair. 'I just can't imagine where she might have gone. The funny thing was, I was supposed to be going home early; she was making a special dinner for me. Then I had this call from Farrar & Bibbie, or at least it was supposed to have come from Farrar & Bibbie, they're special clients of ours, and I had to go all the way across town. The trouble was, when I got there, nobody at Farrar & Bibbie had any idea what I was talking about. It was then that I went home, and found that she was gone. The dinner was still there, everything. The Cuisinart was full of sliced zucchini.'

Danny had to take a breath, to steady himself. He lifted his hands helplessly, then dropped them again. 'She didn't leave a note, nothing. It wasn't like there was any kind of explanation. I mean, I could cope with that.

I'd know what to do. But when somebody just disappears, how the hell do you go about finding them?'

Vincent said, 'Did you tell the police about that call you had from – what was their name?'

'Farrar & Bibbie.'

'That's right, Farrar & Bibbie. Did you tell them about that?'

'I mentioned it in passing, but they didn't seem to be particularly interested.'

'You realize that it might have been a diversion, of a kind. A way to keep you out of the office while – well, while your wife disappeared.'

Danny Monblat stared at Vincent narrowly. 'What are you saying? That somebody dragged me halfway across town on purpose? You mean like Laura was kidnapped, or something?'

'I don't know, Mr Monblat, it's only a supposition. I don't want to alarm you. There's probably a very simple explanation, and tomorrow you'll find you're both laughing at how worried you were. Maybe she had to go help somebody who was sick; somebody who had a crisis on their hands.'

'She didn't take the car,' said Danny Monblat, slowly shaking his head. 'And, besides, she still would have found time to write me a note. She's that kind of a girl. She knows how much I care about her. Like she always locks the door properly, chains, bolts, everything, and never lets nobody suspicious in, not for nothing.'

'That only strengthens my theory,' said Vincent. 'If she wasn't in the habit of opening the door to suspicious strangers, then she probably went out of her own accord. You may even find that she's back home now. Do you want to call?'

Danny Monblat said, 'I've been calling all day. But – sure, okay. Thanks.'

He picked up Vincent's phone and dialled his home number. He waited and waited, but there was no reply. At last, he hung up again.

'Would you like a drink?' Vincent asked him.

He shook his head. 'I want to keep a clear head. Listen, I think I'll go on home, and wait to see if she comes back. That's probably best.'

Vincent laid a hand on his shoulder. 'You can call me if there's anything you want.'

'Well, it's not really your problem,' said Danny Monblat. 'But, thanks, anyway.'

Danny Monblat left, and Vincent sat down behind his desk and rubbed his eyes tiredly. He had the unsettling feeling that as winter was drawing itself darkly all around him, so strange and inexplicable forces were beginning to stir and flicker in the shadows of his life. What puzzled him the most was the feeling that somehow he was personally responsible for Edward's death, and even in a tangential way for Laura's disappearance. Well, maybe not actually responsible, but certainly *involved.* He knew there was no logic behind the idea, no sensible or reasonable way in which he could have had any connection with Ben Miller's catatonia or Edward's hideously rapid decay, but he seemed to have found himself in the eye of such a black and silent hurricane that the feeling was impossible to shake.

Some invisible but insistent hand was tugging at his sleeve. Some unheard but persistent voice was speaking in his ear. The world had tilted into a different kind of winter this year; and Vincent felt an apprehension that was quite unlike anything he had ever experienced before.

'*They're back,*' Ben Miller had insisted. '*They're back.*'

The phone warbled, and Vincent jerked in involuntary shock. Then he picked it up and said, with reassembled smoothness, 'Pearson Gallery, how can I help you?'

It was Margot, Vincent's not-so-recent ex-wife. She sounded aloof and harassed, as if she were just about to run out of the door to do something more important, but recognized her duty to let Vincent know what was going on.

'About Christmas,' said Margot. 'I wonder if you'd mind if I brought Thomas over in the afternoon, rather than the morning.' The implication in her voice was that he had better *not* mind.

'I think that should be okay,' said Vincent. 'Is there any particular reason?'

'Well, it's just that Bruce is coming up from Baltimore that Wednesday, and I do want Thomas to get to know Bruce better.'

'Bruce, hm?' Vincent replied.

'You don't have to say "Bruce, hm" like that,' Margot protested, her aloofness beginning to crack a little. 'Bruce is a fine, dedicated and very intelligent man.'

'Did I once say that he wasn't?'

'At least Bruce doesn't go around expecting everybody to be supernaturally perfect.'

It had been Vincent's neatness and tidiness and sense of perfection that had finally brought their marriage to a painful but inevitable finish. Whereas Margot was scattered and erratic and never minded if anybody else was, Vincent had always wanted his life to be ordered and meticulous. It may have been a hidden fear that if he didn't regulate his personality, he would end up as forgetful and disorganized as his father (well-loved, but always tangled up in the messiest of legal and financial and personal problems). Or it may simply have been that, as much as he liked her, as charming and as witty as she could be, he had mistaken a potential friend for a potential lover, and only realized it after Thomas was born and it was far too late.

Vincent said, 'All right, don't let's get into an argument. Bring Thomas over after lunch. But not too late, please. We're having a few neighbours round for drinks, and then we're going carol-singing.'

Margot said, 'You still haven't told me what you want for Christmas.'

Vincent smiled. 'I don't know. Whatever I ask for, you always buy me something different. Anything, as long as it's not another one of those Mexican ashtrays.'

'What Mexican ashtrays?'

'The red and blue and yellow thing, with pictures of chickens on it.'

'Vincent, that wasn't a Mexican ashtray. That was a Portuguese spatchcock press, for cooking chicken in.'

'Oh, I'm sorry. But it did make a very good ashtray, too.'

'I'll see you Sunday,' said Margot, not altogether warmly.

Vincent put down the phone. It was about twelve o'clock now, and he decided to close up the gallery for lunch, and see if Meggsy wouldn't be interested in joining him in the Oak Bar at the Plaza for two or three of their excellent martinis. The shock of Edward's death was just beginning to make itself felt: a coldness of the nervous system, an urge to do something spontaneous and irrational, to show that Edward's sudden disappearance from the world hadn't gone completely unnoticed.

He was about to put on his coat when a rotund Greek couple came in, wearing curly-haired fur coats. They wanted to look at anything with a classical Greek subject, preferably with plenty of marble pillars and diaphanously draped nymphs. They were building a new villa on the island of Nisiros, and were interested in a painting 'one hundred forty-two centimetres by one hundred eighty-seven centimetres' for the downstairs half-bathroom.

It was over an hour before Vincent was able to satisfy them with a painting, *The Gardens of the Cyclades*, by Leonard Pym, an eccentric American painter who had lived in Delaware for most of his life. It was too late now for Meggsy's lunch-break, so he would just have to go and drink on his own. He switched on the alarm, and was halfway to the door when the phone rang again.

'God damnit,' he muttered. That would be Margot again, with some sharp retort to his using her Portuguese spatchcock press as an ashtray. Margot, like most people, could never think of a smart reply until it was too late; but unlike most people, Margot would pursue you when she had thought of a put-down, and make sure she told you later. Occasionally, three months later.

'*Margot –*' he began; but it wasn't Margot.

'Mr Pearson? I'm sorry to trouble you again. This is Danny Monblat. You said I could call if I needed anything.'

'Of course. How can I help?'

'Would it be too much to ask you to come down to the Village?'

Vincent frowned at his watch. 'Well . . . I'm a little pushed for time.'

'I know I'm out of line, asking you this. But you're the only person I could think of who might understand.'

Vincent thought: I don't really feel like sitting here all afternoon anyway, and I certainly don't relish the idea of drinking martinis on my own. So, what do I have to lose? Besides, I've made an offer of help, and it would be churlish not to honour it, only an hour later.

'Give me your address,' he told Danny Monblat.

Outside in the street, it was bright and noisy and wickedly cold. Vincent managed to hail a taxi on the corner of Fifth Avenue, heading south, and in spite of the traffic he was down on 10th Street within twenty minutes. His driver was Chinese, and carried a baseball bat on top of the dashboard, signed by the entire South Korean baseball team.

Vincent walked the last half-block to the Monblats' apartment building. When he rang the bell, Danny answered the door almost immediately, without asking who it was. He looked grey, and his necktie had been dragged loose, as if he might have been sick.

'Come in,' he said. 'Thanks for coming.'

'What's the problem?' Vincent asked him, stepping into the apartment. His expensive shoes sounded precise on the boarded floor.

'Come and take a look in here. I didn't find it, the first time I came back. I was looking for Laura, that was all. But when I came back this afternoon, well, I suddenly realized the cat wasn't there, either, so I started hunting around. Well, and this is it.'

He led Vincent along the hallway, which was lined on one side by white-painted louvred doors. He opened up the end door and said tersely, 'Look.'

The top shelves inside the cupboard were stacked with sheets and blankets and towels. At the bottom, there was a cluster of large glass bottles as well as two or three boxes of wine-making equipment, corks and labels and glass tubing. Vincent didn't understand what he was supposed to be looking at to begin with, but then

Danny Monblat repeated, '*Look*,' and pointed towards one of the jars at the back of the cupboard.

Vincent leaned forward, straining his eyes into the shadows. What he could see was so extraordinary that it took him a second or two to realize what it was. Then, when he began to make out the shape of it, he took one and then another step back. He stared at Danny Monblat, feeling chilled and alarmed and frightened, and he didn't know what to say.

'I haven't touched it,' said Danny Monblat. 'I didn't have the courage.'

'But how could it – that's your cat?'

Danny Monblat nodded. 'That's my cat. I haven't looked too close, but I can tell.'

Vincent hesitated for a moment, and then reached into the cupboard and moved aside three of the large glass bottles that were standing in the way. Carefully, he eased out the bottle at the very back of the cupboard and lifted it into the daylight. He could have retched; but he held his breath, and took out his handkerchief, and pressed it against his mouth, and after a while the feeling of nausea subsided.

Somehow, the Monblats' cat had managed to squeeze itself into the empty glass wine-bottle, even though the open neck was no wider than three inches in diameter. Once inside, the cat appeared to have tried to bite and tear itself to pieces. The bottom of the bottle was an inch deep in dark crimson blood. The cat had ripped at its own fur, clawed its own eyes out and chewed its way through the muscle of its left hind leg. The inside of the bottle was all blood and congealed fur and strings of feline sinew. It looked like an exhibition in a Victorian museum of animal horrors.

'Nobody could have done that, except the cat itself,' Danny Monblat said, in an unsteady whisper.

Vincent said, 'If I hadn't seen it for myself, I wouldn't have believed it. For Christ's sake. How wide is the neck of that bottle? How could it have gotten its head through there? And *why*? Cats aren't that stupid. They may get stuck up trees, but they don't generally get themselves caught in places they know they can't get themselves out of. *Look* at that thing.'

Danny Monblat turned away, his hands in his pockets. 'I guess it went crazy, that's all.'

'You saw the cat yesterday morning? It was all right then?'

'Sure. It was sweet as pie.'

'Then what made it do anything as terrible as this?'

'It reminds me of something,' said Danny Monblat.

'Well, I'm glad it doesn't remind *me* of anything,' Vincent told him, shaking his head. 'I never saw an animal destroy itself, not like this. I don't know what to say.'

'You know what it reminds me of?' Danny Monblat persisted. 'It reminds me of a picture that was in a book about *Life* magazine. It showed some prisoner who was trying to get away from the Germans, because the Germans were going to burn him alive, and this guy somehow had managed to force his head and half of his shoulders through this tiny space underneath the walls of this wooden hut. They killed him all the same; but you should have seen the tiny space he managed to get through.'

Vincent looked at him. 'What does that mean?' he wanted to know. 'I mean, what kind of a conclusion are you drawing from that?'

'I don't know,' said Danny Monblat. 'I just think that the only thing that could have made that cat force itself into that bottle was the will to live.'

'You mean it was trying to get away from something? Trying to hide, where it couldn't be reached?'

Danny Monblat nodded.

Vincent turned round and walked back into the living room. His stomach still felt unsettled, from the sight of the Monblats' self-sacrificed cat. He stood by the window for a very long time, looking out over 10th Street, at the tarred rooftops and the water-barrels and the rusted air-conditioning vents, and then he said, 'If that cat was trying so desperately to hide, then somebody must have been here, that it wanted to hide from, apart from Laura.'

'That's why I called you,' said Danny Monblat. He was on the very edge of tears.

Vincent said, 'I only wish I could help you. I only wish I could think of something sensible. I'm sorry. We'd better call the police. At least they can go through the proper investigative procedures. I mean, once they've seen that cat, I don't think they'll treat Laura's disappearance just like one more missing person.'

Danny Monblat stood in the corridor next to the bloody bottled remains of his cat, and asked Vincent plaintively, 'Do you think she's dead? Do you think somebody killed her?'

Vincent said, 'You have to have hope, Danny. For Laura's sake, as well as your own.'

'Hope?' asked Danny. 'Hope? That's my wife you're talking about. That's my *life*.'

Twelve

Jack woke up and it was snowing. The bedroom was full of that lilac unnatural light that snowfields reflect in the early hours of the morning; and he could hear the softest kissing of snowflakes against the windowpane. He lay there for a while, knowing that he ought to get up, but allowing himself just five minutes of peace. In a week, it would be Christmas. He had made a special effort this year, and bought his presents for Nancy a month early: a bottle of Cartier perfume and a French cookery book and three pairs of sexy black panties. Nancy was still asleep, her hand raised to her face like a child. It was 7.21. Jack decided that it was probably time to get up.

He was down in the kitchen, his bare feet freezing on the blue-tiled floor, when the telephone rang. He poured himself a freshly perked cup of black coffee with one hand, and answered the telephone with the other.

'Smith,' he said, harshly.

'Sheriff? This is Norman Goldberg. I'm sorry to trouble you so early, but we may have found ourselves a lead in the Nepaug murder.'

'What kind of a lead? When?'

'Early hours of this morning, Sheriff, round about two a.m. Dunkley picked up a twenty-nine-year-old white Cauc hitch-hiker on the Goshen Road, not far from Dog Pond. The hitch-hiker said he was lucky to be alive. Apparently some man had picked him up, then tried to persuade him to stay the night with him. When the hitch-hiker refused, the man attempted to inject him with a hypodermic. The hitch-hiker twisted the wheel, the car stopped, and after a struggle the hitch-hiker was able to get out of the car and make an escape. According to the hitch-hiker, the man kept talking about his skin; and what a miraculous thing skin was; and stuff like that.'

'Where is the hitch-hiker now?' asked Jack.

'Still here, sir. Sleeping, the last I looked.'

'Don't let him leave. I'll be right with you.'

'Yes, sir.'

Jack hurriedly dressed, finished his coffee, then went upstairs to kiss Nancy on the cheek before battling his way out into the snow. He cursed his laziness for not putting the car into the garage last night: the Volkswagen was almost completely buried in thick soft snow. He spent an exasperated ten minutes scraping the snow off the windscreen and the side windows with the torn-off flap of a cardboard box. When at last the car was reasonably clear, it took six or seven whinnying attempts at the starter before the engine abruptly clattered into life.

It was a skiddy, dangerous, frustrating drive up to Torrington. The snow whirled down, thick and furious as burst pillows. Several times, Jack's windscreen wipers clogged up, and he had to stop and clear them with his bare hands. Twice, the car slid inelegantly sideways in the middle of the highway, and once he collided with a fence-post. He asked God out loud what the hell he was doing out here in this blinding white wilderness when anybody with any sense at all would be sitting home by the fire and calling their boss to plead that they were snowed in.

At last he reached Torrington. There were scarcely any other vehicles around, except for a parked snow-plough and a couple of four-wheel-drives with snow-chains. Jack parked next to a huge sloping drift, and crunched his way across the car park, furiously rubbing his hands to warm them up. The sky was the colour of corroded zinc, and the town was so hushed that he could easily have believed that its 34,000 inhabitants had died in the night.

Inside the modern glass-fronted sheriff's head-quarters, it was overheated and bright, and there was a brisk clattering of typewriters and a shrilling of tele-phones. Jack went straight through to his office, and flung his wet leather gloves into his OUT-tray. Norman Goldberg appeared almost immediately, fat and gentle-mannered and beaky-nosed, a Jewish deputy who took considerable pride in the even-handed way in which he policed a wealthy enclave of Anglo-Saxon Protestants.

'The guy's waiting for you downstairs,' said Norman.

'In the cells?'

'We also have him on a vagrancy charge. He says the man who picked him up must have stolen his wallet; but he has several priors for vagrancy and hitch-hiking and petty theft.'

'I want to see him right away,' said Jack. 'Have Jenny bring some coffee down, would you? One for the hitch-hiker, one for me. And a couple of doughnuts, too. That drive from Harwinton was hell on ice.'

'You should have let Bradley come down for you with the Cherokee.'

'Bradley's dangerous when he's walking along the pavement. You don't actually think that I'd let him *drive* me?'

*

The hitch-hiker was lying on his bunk in the end cell of three. His eyes were closed but Jack knew that he wasn't asleep. There was too much tension in him. He was thin and young, with dark scraggly hair and the kind of unwashed, unshaved good looks that had characterized the youthful American bum from pioneering days to the Great Depression to the beat generation. He wore a green checkered work shirt, and very faded Levi's.

Norman unlocked the cell and Jack stepped inside.

'There'll be coffee and doughnuts in a short while,' he said, without waiting for the hitch-hiker to open his eyes.

The hitch-hiker didn't move for a while, but then he opened his eyes and looked at Jack, and then swung his legs round so that he was sitting up.

'Are you going to let me out of here?' he asked, in a distinct Southern accent. He didn't have to ask who Jack was; the Litchfield County Sheriff's badge said it all.

'It's more than likely,' said Jack. 'It really depends on how much assistance you're prepared to give me.'

The boy shrugged. 'You name it. I'm no lawbreaker. I was just hitch-hiking, that's all.'

'Hitch-hiking is against the law in the state of Connecticut, and almost every other state, come to that.'

'Well, I wasn't doing what you could call any *serious* hitch-hiking. It was just to save some money, that's all.'

Jack looked at the boy steadily. The boy held his stare for a moment, then dropped his eyes down and tightly folded his arms.

Jack said, 'I want to know what your name is.'

'Elmer John Tweed.'

'Where are you from, Elmer?'

'Moultrie, Georgia, originally.'

'What are you doing here in Connecticut?'

'I was here to see some friends, that's all. A couple I used to hitch-hike around with, four or five years ago. You can check up on them if you like. Nathan and Carla Prescott, they live on a farm at Canaan, making pottery and stuff.'

'So why were you thumbing for rides in the middle of the night on the Litchfield road?'

Elmer made a face. 'I don't know. I spent two nights at Canaan, and then I guess I just got claustrophobic. Nathan and Carla were so darn home-made, all the time kissing and cuddling each other and putting logs on the fire and baking this wheatmeal bread. In the end I just had to get out of there, before I died of wholesomeness. Well, I'd been drinking, too. Nathan's home-distilled pear brandy. We had what you might describe as a forceful difference of opinion. That's strong stuff, that pear brandy. It can make you disagree with just about everything.'

Jack reached into his shirt pocket and took out a pack of Big Red chewing-gum. He offered some to Elmer, but Elmer declined. 'I'll wait for the doughnut, thanks.'

Jack said, 'Tell me what happened last night. Right from the start.'

'You mean right from when I was picked up?'

Jack nodded.

'Well . . . I'd been walking along the road for quite a while. There isn't too much traffic on that road at that time of night, must have been twenty after one in the morning, and even when a car does pass you by, they don't like to stop on account of you're probably a criminal or a lunatic, trying to hitch a ride in the dark. I was getting desperate, as a matter of fact, because the pear brandy had all wore off, and it was freezing cold, and then it started to snow, and I was beginning to think that they were going to find my body lying by the side of the road stiff solid in the morning, dead of exposure, and I've seen a few of those.'

Jack said nothing, but waited for Elmer to continue.

Elmer began to look nervous now, and his narrative became more discursive, as if he were afraid to describe what had happened with any great particularity, in case he invoked again too sharply the terrors of the previous night.

'All of a sudden, a large black Cadillac drew up beside me. Fleetwood, maybe fifteen years old. I hadn't even heard it coming; the snow must have muffled it, I guess. I couldn't believe my luck. Well, would you, on a freezing highway in the middle of the night? I couldn't see the driver's face, but he reached across the car and opened the passenger door for me, and I slung my hiking bag in the back and climbed in. He said, "Where are you headed?" and I told him anywhere at all, as long as I could get myself warm and maybe buy some breakfast. So off we went.'

Jack said, 'What was he like, this man?'

Elmer shrugged. 'Middle-aged. Hard to say.'

'Well-dressed?'

'Sure. What would you expect, from someone driving a Cadillac? I don't know, grey suit, white shirt, neat but kind of old-fashioned. I remember the way he smelled, though, like lavender-water.'

'Lavender-water? What does somebody like you know about lavender-water?'

Elmer looked down at his hands. 'My grandmother always wore it, back in Moultrie. She was a real old-style Southern lady. *Her* grandmother used to have twenty slaves; or so she said. She said that lavender-water – *that* was the mark of a lady of quality.'

'So you took this man who picked you up and gave you a lift to be a person of quality?'

'He spoke like it, and dressed like it, too.'

'What did he talk about?'

'This and that, not much, not to begin with. But then he told me he was fresh back from Europe, and glad to be home in Connecticut; and then, after maybe ten minutes or so, he said that he was driving back home to Darien, and would I like to come along all the way?'

Jack said, 'What was your response to that?'

'I said that Darien was fine. Darien was better than no place at all.'

'When did you start to get suspicious about what was going on?'

Elmer rubbed his hands together and kept on rubbing them, around and around. 'Pretty much straight after. He said that if I was going to ride with him all the way to Darien, well, then, perhaps it wouldn't be such a bad idea if I spent the night at his family house. Well, I've got to tell you, the number of faggots that stop on the road these days, when you're hitch-hiking, and start laying their hands on your knee when they're driving along, and ask you to come home with them, or back to some motel or other, you get pretty damned wary whenever some guy starts coming on about spending the night, even if it's perfectly innocent. So I said no, thanks all the same, I'd find myself some place to sleep, I didn't want to impose on him or nothing. But then *he* said that he insisted, and that he could give me a comfortable bed and a good breakfast; and I thought, sure, and a poke up the ass, too, if I wasn't careful.'

'You told my deputy something about skin. He mentioned skin.'

'That's right. That was a little later. By that time, I thought he'd kind of forgotten about inviting me home, he was just driving and listening to the radio, some classical music or other, but then all of a sudden he said, "It's real hard to find boys of your age with excellent skin. Do you know that?" Well, that confirmed it, so far as I was concerned. The guy was a gay. But then he said something that didn't sound gay at all. He said, "Do you know something, if you were to remove all of your skin from your body, and lay it out flat, it would cover an area of four and a half square yards. Just enough to upholster the driving seat of a Rolls-Royce." And then he touched my wrist, and said, "If you knew the qualities of the human skin, you would never take yourself for granted again." I could smell his breath then, he was leaning over so close, and it smelled like peppermints or something, as if he had bad breath and wanted to hide it.'

Jack folded another stick of gum into his mouth. 'Is that when you told him you wanted out?'

'Not straight away. But then he started saying how good-looking I was, and all kinds of creepy stuff I can't even remember, and I said, "Listen, this'll do, just drop me off here."'

'What happened then?'

'I tried to open the door, but it was locked. I guessed, well, it was snowing outside, so I wouldn't do myself too much harm if I rolled into a snowdrift. I told him to unlock the door. I said, "Will you please unlock the door, I want to get out." But he kept on driving and didn't say nothing at all. So I asked him again. I said, "Will you please let me out?" But he said, "You're not going anyplace. Now, sit still, and keep quiet, and behave yourself." I said, "You can't take me nowhere, not unless I want to, that's kidnap." But he didn't say nothing; and I waited a while, until the road was pretty long and straight, and then I seized hold of the wheel, and the car slid around on the snow, and we ended up facing back the way we'd come, up against the rocks at the side of the road.'

Jack had been watching Elmer's face all this while; and he couldn't remember any other witness who had been so consistently agitated; who had wrung his hands so much as he told what had happened to him; whose eyes had flicked from side to side, as if they were following fragments of frightening memory around the room. Even assault victims; or rape victims; or witnesses to terrible highway accidents.

'Go on,' Jack encouraged him, very gently this time. 'What happened then?'

'I don't, I don't recall for sure; not exactly for sure. It couldn't have lasted more than a second or two. I get clear pictures; then it seems like I can't remember nothing at all; only dark and fighting; and that noise he made.'

'Try,' said Jack. Flatly, not insistently; no more demanding than a small-town optician coaxing an eye-patient to read the smallest line of letters.

Elmer took a long time to reply. Jack waited, without saying anything else, steadily chewing gum. At last Elmer said, in an oddly muffled voice, 'He took hold of my wrist, and he was much stronger than he looked, strong like a mad person, you know, or somebody having a fit. And all the time he was struggling around in his coat pocket with the other hand, and he managed to take out something that shone, I saw it shining, and I thought, Jesus, he's going to stab me, but when I wrestled myself around I saw him biting a plastic cap off of the end of it, and I realized that it was a hypodermic. I hit him with my left hand, the flat of my left hand, twice, once across the face, although it wasn't much of a blow because the car was too cramped inside, and he was still holding on to my other wrist. But the second time I hit him, the hypodermic dropped on to the floor.'

Elmer was perspiring now, even though the cell was far from warm.

'Go on,' said Jack.

'He ducked down, bent forward – I guess to pick the hypodermic up. I managed to pull my wrist free and shove up against him, and he kind of caught his head against the steering-wheel. I reached around behind him and released the door locks, and then I was out of that car so damned fast it wasn't even real. I caught my elbow on the way out; you can see the bruise.'

Jack said, 'There's something else, isn't there? Something you saw?'

Elmer nodded.

'You can tell me,' Jack encouraged him.

'I was standing in the snow, and the door of the car was open, and he lifted his head and turned around and stared at me, and I never saw anybody's eyes look like that, they could've been molten lead, and he stretched open his mouth and he roared at me. And, Jesus, it was like twelve men roaring at once, the sound it made, and my hair stood up like icicles, and something came blasting out of his mouth, I thought it was foam at first, you know like mad dogs, but it was white and it splattered everywhere, almost as if he was puking with rage. That was when I ran. I ran and I ran and I kept on running until I saw the police car.'

Jack eased a small Sesame Street notebook out of his shirt pocket, and made a few notes next to a smiling picture of Ernie and Bert. Then he sniffed, and said, 'You'd been drinking, hadn't you? You sure you couldn't have imagined any of this? Maybe not all of it, but part of it?'

'No, sir,' said Elmer. He looked quite white now, and

he couldn't seem to stop himself from wringing and rubbing his hands. 'No, sir, everything I told you happened for real.'

'And the man in the car said he was going to take you to Darien, and that was where he lived?'

'Yes, sir, Darien.'

Jack jotted down a few more notes, and then he tucked his book away and said, 'You just get yourself some rest, Elmer. If you need anything, all you have to do is call. We won't be keeping you here long; but it's thick snow outside, and I need you around for a couple of hours while I do myself a little checking around.'

Just then, Jenny came down with a cardboard tray of hot coffee and doughnuts. Jack took his coffee off the tray, and nodded to Jenny to leave Elmer's on his folding table. 'See that this gentleman gets everything he needs,' he told Jenny, with exaggerated courtesy; and then he carried his coffee back to his office.

'Well?' asked Norman, who had been waiting for him.

Jack shrugged. 'Hard to say. Could be hysteria. Could be drugs. Could be nothing more than too much home-distilled liquor and two or three hours in sub-zero temperatures.'

'But you're going to check it out?'

'Sure I'm going to check it out. This mysterious well-dressed middle-aged man claimed that he lived in Darien, after all, and how far is Darien from New Haven? Or even from Nepaug, for that matter. And the way that he talked about skin . . . well, that would indicate to me somebody with a slightly unusual turn of mind, to say the least.'

Outside the window, the snow continued to fall with felty softness. Jack knew that he probably wouldn't get home tonight, and so he punched out his home number on the telephone, and told Nancy not to wait up for him this evening, and could she remember to call Freeman the plumber and have that yard tap fixed, before it turned the back of the house into a skating rink.

Nancy said, 'I love you,' and Jack said, 'I love you, too.'

While Norman ate half of Jack's doughnut, Jack called his friend at Darien police headquarters, George Kelly. George was the kind of officer who believed in traditional community policing; in getting to know everybody from the most influential Rotarians to the boy who wiped the windscreens at the Ocean Street gas station; and everything about them. He was popular in Darien because he fitted the *Saturday Evening Post* image of a small-town policeman who rescued lost dogs and returned small boys who had run away from home and upheld all those straightforward 1950s values of honour and decency and American fair play. Only a few of his brother officers knew that he had been relocated from Manhattan's 17th Precinct fifteen years ago after a particularly questionable shooting incident, although all of them knew that when the occasion called for it, he could be hard and quick, and that his vocabulary could be as harsh as glasspaper.

'George?' said Jack. 'I need a little help here.'

'You want a shovel to dig yourself out?' George returned. 'I hear you've got it pretty bad up there.'

'George, I'm looking for a well-dressed middle-aged man who drives a black Fleetwood, maybe '70 or '71 model. He says he lives in the Darien locality, although he returned there only recently from Europe. Do you have any ideas?'

George said, 'You want to hold him?'

'I want to question him first. We have a hitch-hiker who claims this man assaulted him last night, after he gave him a ride; and there may possibly be some connection with the Nepaug Reservoir homicide.'

'Well,' said George slowly, 'I know your man. One of the Grays.'

'You *know* him?' asked Jack. Norman blinked, and stopped chewing Jack's doughnut.

George said, 'For sure. Everybody in Darien knows about the Grays. They came back from France or Belgium or someplace, about a month or so back. They're a real old Darien family, dating way back before Independence. They've always kept up a house here, The Wilderlings, out on the New Canaan road. They hadn't been living there, though, for fifty or sixty years, maybe longer. The house was looked after by trustees, for most of the time, although from what I've seen of it, they didn't look after it too good. It's pretty run-down.'

'How come they suddenly decided to come back?' asked Jack.

'Who knows?' said George. 'Fred Archer, he's the president of the First Darien Bank, he said it was something about European taxes being too high for them. He wasn't too clear. He said they were wealthy, though. Just to keep up a house like The Wilderlings for half a century without even living in it, that takes some pretty heavy inherited lettuce.'

Jack sipped his coffee. It had come out of the beverage machine in the police station lobby, and the styrofoam cup tasted of chicken soup. 'So who's my suspect?' he asked George. 'And who else is in the family?'

'Your suspect sounds like Maurice Gray, he's just about the only member of the family who's seen around town, although he sometimes has a lady with him. Once or twice I've seen them together at the post office, and they had dinner one time at the Steppan House, but that's about all. You could say they were recluses.

Young Bill Farkas, though, he delivers groceries for the Colonial Supermarket, he's been up to The Wilderlings twice a week since the Grays came back, and he's seen a young man round about twenty or twenty-two years old, and two women walking in the garden, and a wheelchair, although there wasn't anybody in it.'

Jack said, 'Tell me more about Maurice Gray. He drives a Fleetwood?'

'Black Fleetwood limousine, that's correct.'

'Do you have any idea what he does for a living?'

'I don't think any of the Gray family do anything for a living. People of leisure, so to speak.'

'Do you know where they got their money from, originally?'

'I guess I could find out.'

Jack smiled. 'I guess you could.'

George said, 'What do you want me to do about Maurice Gray? Do you want me to haul him in for you?'

Jack sipped more coffee, then wiped his mouth with a Kleenex. 'I don't think so, not yet. I've only got myself one uncorroborated witness, and the way he talks about Gray – if it really was Gray – he wouldn't stand up against a good defence lawyer for five minutes. Just keep your eyes open, if you don't mind, and find out what you can about the Grays, on top of what you know already. I'll come down myself later today and see if I can't get to talk to them.'

'Whatever you say, my friend. But have a care in the snow, okay?'

'All the best, George. And thanks.'

Jack put down the phone. Norman brushed sugar off his shirt, and said, 'You've found him? Just like that?'

'Just like that,' said Jack. 'His name's Maurice Gray, and he lives just outside of Darien. Rich and eccentric, from what George says.'

'You're not going down to Darien today?' asked Norman.

'I think I have to. Supposing there *is* a connection with the Nepaug Reservoir death. Supposing Gray was trying the same kind of assault on our friend downstairs. He's done it twice, maybe he attempted it a third time. If so, he could easily do it again.'

Norman wrote down the name *Maurice Gray*. Then he said, 'You want me to run this through the FBI?'

'No harm. And put it through Interpol, too. Maurice Gray's been living in France or Belgium for most of his life; maybe for *all* of his life. The Grays left Connecticut fifty or sixty years ago, according to George, and this is the first time they've been back.'

Norman asked, 'Any indication why they should come back now?'

'George said something about European taxes being too high. But who knows. The only way I'm going to find out for sure is by asking them.'

Norman turned towards the window. 'It's snowing real bad out there, Sheriff.'

'I'll take the Cherokee. And if I get myself stuck, I'll call in.'

'Okay,' said Norman. Jack knew that Norman's real concern was at being left in charge of the office in the middle of a blizzard, with cars and trucks sliding everywhere, and motorists trapped in snowdrifts; with pipes freezing and families imprisoned in their houses. It was the nightmare season in Connecticut, if you were a policeman; in the same way that mid-summer was the nightmare season for police forces in Phoenix and Dallas and downtown Los Angeles.

Jack said, 'Listen, I won't be long. All I have to do is talk to Gray; size him up; and find out what the hell is going on.'

'Sure you do,' said Norman, and picked up the remaining half of Jack's doughnut. He devoured it quickly, chewing noisily, but without relish.

Jack sat back in his chair and wished just as much as Norman that he didn't have to drive down to Darien; but a killing was a killing, and he began to believe that he might have almost solved it.

Thirteen

New Milford, 18 December

It had been snowing so thickly that Dr Serling had to leave his car at the junction with the New Preston road, where the snowplough had already been through, and walk the rest of the way to the Miller house. It was four o'clock, already twilight, but the snow lent a strange luminosity to everything around him, as if he were walking through a nuclear winter.

He reached the Miller house, and banged at the door. Mrs Miller opened up almost immediately, and fussily hurried him in. 'I was worried you wouldn't come,' she told him, brushing the snowflakes off his lapels. 'I was afraid the snow was too bad. But, you've come, God bless you. Would you like a cup of coffee? Or some soup?'

'I'm fine for now, thank you,' said Dr Serling, and handed Mrs Miller his coat. He was a large, slow-moving, big-nosed man, with the kind of reassuring weatherbeaten face that made him one of Litchfield's most popular country doctors. He rubbed his hands briskly, to stimulate the circulation, then he picked up his bag and said, 'How's that son of yours today? Any better?'

'He still talks, still rambles,' said Mrs Miller. 'He hasn't said one word of sense since the last time you was here.'

Mrs Miller led the way into Ben's bedroom. The television was on, tuned to *Love, American Style*, but Ben wasn't watching it. He was lying back in bed, looking shrunken and pallid, like a beansprout that somebody had left on a damp cloth to germinate. He kept on muttering and twitching and feinting at imaginary assailants, and even when Dr Serling leaned over him, and grasped his shoulder, and shook him, he paid no attention to Dr Serling at all.

'He doesn't talk to me any more,' said Mrs Miller. 'He mumbles, and mutters, and waves his fists around, but that's all. I feel like I've lost him.'

Dr Serling sat on the end of the bed, with a squeak of springs. He leaned forward and lifted one of Ben's eyelids. Then he reached into his waistcoat pocket for his pencil flashlight, and shone it directly into Ben's eye. 'Hm, pupils not dilated. How's his appetite?'

'He's been off his food; at least since the last time you came. I can't barely get him to eat nothing more than porridge.'

'Any vomiting? Diarrhoea?'

'Well, his bowels have been a little loose, but nothing too serious.'

Dr Serling let Ben rest back on his pillow, and sat up straight. 'I'm going to have to take some blood and urine samples, to check, but my first guess is that he's started to suffer from uraemia. That means a failure of his kidneys to get rid of everything they ought to get rid of; a condition that unfortunately isn't uncommon amongst paraplegics like Ben. Has his urine been dark? Darker than usual?'

Mrs Miller shook her head. 'It's been just regular. It seems to me like he's more frightened than sick.'

'Well, uraemia frequently brings on convulsions and fits, and all the hallucinations that go with them. I think that I'm probably going to have to take Ben into hospital for a day or two, for observation. The trouble is, you see, May, that a really severe attack may cripple him even more severely, or even kill him.'

Mrs Miller looked down at her son as he lay softly gibbering on the bed. Dr Serling, with his hand resting on Ben Miller's wrist, said nothing. He had already recognized that fleeting glimmer in Mrs Miller's eye, a glimmer that he was quite used to. It was the tiny, guilty light of private hope: perhaps, after all these years of bad temper and incontinence and mutual suffering, the Lord at last will take him away. Oh, please, dear Lord, take him away.

Dr Serling opened his large black executive-style medical case. It was his only concession to the twentieth century. His daughter had given it to him for his last birthday, to replace his old Victorian doctor's bag, the one that babies used to come out of. He took out a syringe and a bottle of sedative and a bottle of alcohol to clean Ben's arm.

'I'll put on the coffee,' said Mrs Miller. 'I never could abide the sight of blood.'

'This is only a sedative,' Dr Serling told her. 'I want him to sleep, and get some real rest; and then we'll see what he's like in the morning.'

Mrs Miller was just opening the bedroom door when Ben suddenly shrieked out, *'Back!* They're back! Oh, God, don't let them get me! Oh, God, *don't let them get me!'*

He violently jerked and heaved beneath the blankets. Dr Serling's executive case tilted, and then went tumbling on to the floor, spilling syringes, sticking-plasters, bottles, tongue-depressors, scissors, pills. Dr Serling made a grab for Ben's wrist, to hold him still, but Ben twisted around and threw himself right off the opposite side of the bed, hitting the floor with a harsh, jarring thump.

'*Ben!*' shouted Dr Serling.

But Ben seemed to be deaf to everything except what was happening inside his own head: the dreams, the nightmares, the shapes that came in the darkness. He screamed and babbled and threw himself wildly around the floor, knocking his face against the legs of the bed, crashing his shoulder against the edge of his closet, scratching and scuffling at the floor until his bitten fingernails bled. Dr Serling was forced to struggle into a kneeling position beside him and pin his wrists, but somehow Ben still managed to twist and writhe from side to side, as if somebody were torturing him.

'Ben, listen to me!' Dr Serling commanded. 'Ben, this is Dr Serling! Listen to me! Listen! You've got to pull yourself out of this! Do you hear me? You've got to pull yourself out of this, and you've got to do it now! Right now, Ben, right this minute!'

Ben screamed a hideous, ululating scream, and stared up at Dr Serling with eyes that were blood-crimson from broken capillaries. In between his screams and his garbled rushes of unintelligible speech, he took in deep, painful breaths of air; breaths that made his whole crippled body shudder, like a live caterpillar dropped on to a hotplate.

'Listen, Ben, you have to calm yourself down,' Dr Serling told him. 'If you don't settle down, I'm going to have to have you restrained, and taken away; and you know that would break your mother's heart. Now, please, try to get a grip on yourself.'

'They're close,' Ben moaned in sheer desperation. 'Please don't let them get me. You won't, will you? Please don't let them. Promise me, won't you? Please!'

'Ben, listen to me. *Who's* back?' Dr Serling asked him.

Ben stopped twitching, and suddenly stared directly into Dr Serling's face, fierce and agonized and scared beyond anything that Dr Serling could imagine. *'Who?'* he demanded.

'You keep insisting they're back,' Dr Serling replied, trying to remain steady. 'But you haven't told me *who's* back. Who is it, that frightens you so much?'

'They're just the same,' Ben murmured. His eyes drooped, although his pupils began to dart rapidly from side to side. 'They're just the same as they were before. It isn't possible. And you know what they're going to do, don't you? You know what they're going to do! They have to! They have to! They can't live without it! Oh, God, don't let them! Oh, please, God, don't let them!'

Ben fell into another convulsive sleep. Dr Serling lifted him up; and then, with Mrs Miller's help, lifted him back on to the bed and tucked him in. There was a long and difficult silence between them as they both looked down at him, the mother and the doctor; mainly because the doctor knew what he was going to have to say, and the mother knew that she didn't want to hear it.

'I'm sorry, May,' said Dr Serling.

Mrs Miller said, 'You're going to have to take him in, aren't you?'

Dr Serling nodded. 'I can't see what else I can possibly do. This could be chronic uraemia. It could be something else, worse. Some kind of pressure on the brain. But, either way, I think he needs to be someplace safe, under constant supervision.'

'What about the cost?' asked Mrs Miller unsteadily.

'Well, it depends. But we'll try to keep it down.'

Mrs Miller hesitated. On the bed, with his shrunken legs drawn up under him, Ben Miller was muttering and worrying, shaking his head from time to time as if he were arguing with somebody, or trying to brush away a troublesome horsefly. He had told his mother after the accident that he was only half a man, and it was true; mostly because he had allowed himself to be. He had become corrosively testy, endlessly critical and cruelly vexatious, and he hardly ever gave his mother a word of thanks, or a single compliment; nor even told her once that he loved her.

What price could Mrs Miller put on a life like that? She thought of her savings, $7,350 in the New Milford Savings Bank. It had taken her eleven years to save that money, mainly out of her wages from cleaning the Pearson house. Was Ben going to take all that away from her, too?

She turned away. Dr Serling watched her, saying nothing. In the end, under her breath, she said, 'You'd better do what's best, Doctor. I can't say any more than that.'

Dr Serling cleared his throat, as if he were about to say something very personal, but then he changed his mind, and shrugged, and said, 'I'd better call the ambulance. I don't really see any alternative.'

He straightened Ben's blankets, and waited for a moment, to give Mrs Miller a last opportunity to change her mind; but Mrs Miller said, 'It's all for the best. I know. It's the Lord's choice, not mine.'

But Ben suddenly hissed, *'Don't you come anywhere near.'*

'What?' asked Dr Serling.

'Don't you come anywhere near,' Ben repeated. *'Don't you touch me. Don't touch my skin.'*

'Ben?' asked Dr Serling softly.

Ben gargled and made a choking sound, but then he stared at Dr Serling and whispered, 'Don't you dare to touch my skin. Don't you dare. I've seen you looking at me. I know what you want. You just take your eyes off me. Don't touch me! Don't look at me! I know what you're going to do! God Almighty, I know what you're going to do!'

Dr Serling sat down on the edge of the bed, and gently but authoritatively prised Ben's fingers away from the bed-rail. Ben kept throwing him odd sideways looks, like a beaten dog, as if he were frightened of him but angry with him, too. 'Don't you dare to touch my skin,' he breathed harshly. 'Don't you dare.'

At length, Ben dropped into a shallow sleep. Dr Serling straightened his bedcovers again, and tiredly stood up. 'He's hallucinating badly,' he told Mrs Miller. 'I don't know why. Maybe it's a side-effect from all that albumen in his system. That's what happens with renal failure. The body backs up like a blocked drain, and the blockage can affect the mind.'

'He seems *so frightened*,' said Mrs Miller, in a distracted voice.

Dr Serling picked up the last of his scattered bottles, and closed up his medical case. 'I've seen worse. Do you remember old man Burack, who used to live across at Boardman's Bridge? He was convinced that FBI men kept coming into his bedroom at night and beating him with rubber hoses. And, I mean, he *believed* it, to the point where he started coming up in bruises. That was renal failure, too.'

'What did Ben mean about not touching his skin?' asked Mrs Miller.

Dr Serling shook his head. 'I don't know. When the human mind hallucinates, it doesn't usually follow any kind of logical pattern. It just erupts like a volcano, and all the things that have been scaring and worrying us the most just come bursting out.'

'He never said anything like that before,' said Mrs Miller. She was almost in tears.

Dr Serling laid his hand comfortingly around Mrs Miller's shoulders. 'How about a good hot cup of coffee? I'm still only half thawed out.'

Mrs Miller looked back at her son. 'Do you think it's all right to leave him? Supposing he wakes up again, and has another of those fits?'

'We'll leave the door open,' Dr Serling suggested.

They left the bedroom, as Ben slept a disturbed and murmuring sleep. Mrs Miller went through to the kitchen to put on the percolator, while Dr Serling, with the familiarity of somebody who knew the house well, went into the parlour, and took out his spectacles, and picked up the telephone.

Mrs Miller came back into the parlour just as Dr Serling got through to the Litchfield County Hospital. She stood in the doorway with her hands clasped over her flowered apron, watching him with sadness and resignation.

Dr Serling was saying, 'That's right. Good. Well – the sooner you can get him into dialysis, the better.'

'Coffee won't be long,' said Mrs Miller.

It was only five minutes later, while Dr Serling and Mrs Miller talked in the kitchen, and the percolator popped and bubbled, that Ben suddenly opened his eyes. He lay back on his pillow for a while, his lips silently shaping unfamiliar words; listening to the chinking of cups, as his mother set out the coffee-tray; the banging of the kitchen cupboard doors; the murmur of conversation.

Mrs Miller was saying, '. . . ever since that time he nearly died . . . the nightmares he's had . . . but not like this . . .'

With a shuddering grunt of effort, Ben raised his head and looked across at his bedside table. Beside the base of his bedside lamp, his digital clock flickered to 4.33, and the surface of his glass of water gleamed, an ellipse of silver as bright as mercury.

'Not my skin,' he whispered hoarsely. And he reached over to the table, groping around with his half-paralysed hand until he managed to grasp the water-glass tightly and bring it back towards him, so that it was resting on his chest.

With a convulsive tremble, he emptied the water all over his blankets, and then raised the glass up towards his face.

'Not my skin,' he repeated. 'You're not going to touch my skin.'

He gripped the rim of the glass between his teeth, clenched his jaws for a moment and then bit the glass so that it broke, with a sharp snap. A curved crescent of glass glittered in his mouth, like fangs.

Carefully, he picked out the crescent from between his teeth and let the rest of the glass roll on to the floor. 'Skin,' he murmured, and there was a curious sensuality in his voice.

Holding the piece of glass between finger and thumb, he slowly but unhesitatingly drew a deep cut on his right cheek, close to his nose. A line of dark red blood ran immediately down to his chin, and slithered down his neck, forming a pool at the base of his throat. Ben held the curve of glass up to the light. Its tip was tinged with red, and he murmured to himself, 'Stained glass. Like a church. That's the secret. That's the secret. Holy, holy glass.'

He sliced at his face again, lifting a large bloody flap of skin and flesh right away from his cheekbone. He felt the edge of the glass run coldly against the bone itself, and it made him quake. But then he cut again, across the same cheek, in a criss-cross, so that the diagonal wound became two pale triangles.

Systematically, with his hand as bloody as a red plastic glove, he cut up his forehead, his chin and both cheeks. One slice went halfway through his left ear, right across his cheek, and penetrated through to the inside of his mouth, so that he cut his tongue, as well.

Blood smothered his face and splattered all over the blankets. His pillow was crimson. He cut his lower lip vertically, right through to his bare gums. He poked the point of the glass up inside his right nostril, and then quickly sliced sideways, so that his nose was opened out.

The pain was now beginning to penetrate his nerve-centres. Sharp, cold, jangling pain. But as a final gory gesture against the spirits who were pursuing him so relentlessly, he pinched his left eyelid out as far as he could, and sliced it right off.

It was only then that he let out a blood-spraying screech of agony, and hurled aside the broken glass, and dug his fingers deep into the terrible cuts in his cheeks as if he wanted to wrench his entire face away from its roots and hurl that away from him too, so that he was no longer human at all.

Dr Serling came bursting into the bedroom as violently as a buffalo. Mrs Miller was right behind him, but Dr Serling took one look at Ben and immediately swung round, forcing her back out of the room and across the hallway, knocking two pictures awry.

'I saw blood!' screamed Mrs Miller. 'What's happened? God in Heaven, what's happened?'

Dr Serling held her wrist tightly. His face was wild. 'Mrs Miller, May, listen to me. The ambulance is already on its way. There's been an accident. I don't know what.

But stay away, please. Stay out, and let me deal with it alone.'

'Accident?' asked Mrs Miller, distracted. 'Accident?'

Dr Serling refused to let go of her wrist. 'Go back into the parlour,' he told her. 'Stay there, keep calm and call me when the ambulance arrives. Now, please, I beg you. Let me deal with Ben. It's probably far less serious than it looks.'

Ben roared out again, a terrible bubbling roar, as if he were choking on his own blood. *'Please,'* Dr Serling insisted; and at last, quivering, Mrs Miller returned to the parlour, pausing for a moment halfway to stare at Dr Serling with an expression which he hoped he would never have to see again.

It was the most frightening experience he could ever recall: witnessing total fear on somebody else's face.

Dr Serling pressed his hand against his mouth for a moment, summoning up strength and courage, and trying to suppress his heartbeat. He took a long, steadying breath, and then he stepped back into Ben's bedroom.

God Almighty, there was blood everywhere.

'Ben,' he said softly. He stared at Ben Miller in complete horror, and Ben Miller stared back at him like a creature from the bottom of the ocean, a bloody squid, hooked and dying, with one lidless eye rolling around inside a gory socket.

'Ben, for God's sake,' Dr Serling whispered.

Ben said nothing while Dr Serling tore up the sheets from his bed and used them to staunch the flow of blood that poured out of his face. It was a miracle that Ben hadn't severed any arteries, but Dr Serling had never seen anyone before who had mutilated themselves as severely as this – even in Litchfield, where bored and isolated wives were occasionally moved to burn the backs of their hands with lighted cigarettes, or stick barbecue skewers into themselves.

'Ben,' said Dr Serling thickly. 'Ben, what happened?'

Ben turned his bandaged head, and slowly nodded. The sheets were already dark with blood, and Ben's face was so ghastly that Dr Serling could scarcely bear to look at it. Raw sinews, shreds of bright-red flesh, gleaming cheekbones and, as Ben panted for breath, a stream of bloody saliva and bubbles, running down his neck.

'*Why*, Ben?' Dr Serling asked him, holding his arm, although he didn't really expect an answer.

Ben nodded, and to Dr Serling's horror, almost managed to smile. 'Won't want me now,' he gurgled. 'Won't want me now, not like this. I'm safe.'

'*Who* won't want you? What are you talking about?'

'All twelve,' Ben choked. 'All twelve. Won't want me now.'

Ben's naked eye rolled upwards, and he suddenly lapsed into shock. Dr Serling shook him and called his name again and again, but couldn't rouse him. Almost immediately, he heard the whooping of the ambulance siren and the barking of Mr Dunfey's dog, and red lights flashed against the smeary bedroom windows.

Mrs Miller had already opened the door for the two ambulance medics when Dr Serling came out to greet them. They stamped the snow from their boots, and clapped their hands together like performing seals. One was Irish, ginger-haired and freckle-faced; the other was black, an Eddie Murphy look-alike. Randy and Wellington, Dr Serling knew them both well.

'What's up, Doc?' asked Randy, his familiar greeting.

Dr Serling beckoned him without speaking across the hallway; and at the same time nodded to Wellington to take care of Mrs Miller.

'It's Ben Miller,' he said, in a low voice. 'He's cut himself up pretty bad.'

'Attempted suicide?' asked Randy.

'Worse than that.'

'*Worse?*' asked Randy, raising his gingery eyebrows.

'Go in and see for yourself. But make sure that Mrs Miller doesn't get even a glimpse. There are some sights that no mother should ever have to see.'

Randy stared at Dr Serling for a moment, and then said, 'I'm beginning to think that I shouldn't have bolted that hot dog.'

While Randy and Wellington brought in their stretcher and their first-aid packs, and dealt with Ben, Dr Serling took Mrs Miller back into the parlour. She wouldn't sit down, but stood under the cheap brass-and-teak light-fitting, looking old and defeated, a woman who had been condemned by the world to suffer.

'Will he die?' she asked Dr Serling.

'He's badly hurt,' Dr Serling told her. 'But he's in good hands.'

'I saw blood,' said Mrs Miller.

Dr Serling nodded. 'For some reason, Ben cut himself. I'm not sure why. He broke his water-glass, and cut his face.'

'It's the nightmares,' she said, as if that explained everything.

They heard Randy and Wellington rolling the stretcher across the hallway, but neither of them went out to take a look. A sharp wintry draught blew into the house; the medics had left the door open behind them. Mrs Miller's grey hair rose up, as if by some strange electromagnetic force.

Randy came in and said, 'We're off now, Doc. Will we see you later?'

'Give me a couple of hours,' said Dr Serling.

'Sure thing,' Randy told him, and then, 'Goodnight, ma'am. Don't worry. They're really going to take good care of your boy.'

Dr Serling listened to the four-wheel-drive ambulance whooping its way back towards the main highway, then took Mrs Miller's hand.

'My boy,' said Mrs Miller, and in those words there was everything that Ben had ever meant to her, as a newborn baby, as a grade-school kid, in summers and winters, in laughter and Christmases and sunny afternoons gone by; until that last afternoon when he had dived from the roof, dived as if in a dream, into solid concrete, and ended Mrs Miller's happiness for ever.

'I'm sorry, May,' said Dr Serling. 'I'm more sorry than I can tell you.'

Fourteen

New Milford, 18 December

Aaron had called him and said, 'You have to come up. I'm sorry. You have to.'

Vincent had retorted, 'Aaron, I'm coming up for Christmas in any case. Margot's bringing Thomas over, and Charlotte's probably coming up too. So what's the panic? You only have five days to wait.'

'Vincent,' Aaron had told him, 'I hardly ever ask you a favour. When was the last time I asked you a favour?'

'You asked me to bring back fifty-six pounds of Italian plaster from Milan. That was a favour, believe me.'

'This is serious, Vincent. Something's happened to Van Gogh.'

Vincent had been right on the edge of making a sharp witticism about Aaron and his overindulged cat, when he suddenly thought of Danny Monblat's cat, bloody and dead in its bottle.

'Aaron?' he had asked cautiously. 'You don't mean something bad? Like, an accident?'

'I can't describe it,' Aaron had told him, and there had been a sudden surge of grief in his voice. 'Vincent, will you please come up here?'

Vincent had been obliged to break another date with Meggsy, although this time he had gone around to her office on 47th Street, where she was sitting in her tight white angora sweater and her tight black mini-skirt in a fluorescently lit partitioned office with plastic cacti and acrylic paper-clips in the shape of copulating couples, under a calendar depicting Michelangelo's *David*. Vincent had given her a sword plant in a pot, a half-bottle of Moët champagne and a kiss.

'I'm sorry,' he had told her. 'But Aaron's really upset. I'll make it up to you.'

Meggsy had taken off her tinted spectacles and looked up at him with that myopic blue-eyed stare which always aroused him; especially since her huge warm angora-coddled breasts were pressed against his chest.

'If I didn't *revere* you so much,' she had whispered, 'I would hate you to death.'

He had kissed her, tasted Givenchy perfume, and smiled the smile of a man who is fully aware that when girls start to revere him, he is growing a little too old.

Now he was driving back to New Milford, to have the house opened up, so that after he had visited Aaron he could spend the night in his own bed. It had stopped snowing, but some of the narrower roads were still icy, and gleamed in his headlamps like the spines of petrified whales. He had been playing Vivaldi on his car stereo, but as the roads grew skiddier, he switched it off, so that he could concentrate on driving. The tyres made a hollow crunching sound as they crushed the lumps of ice and slush which were scattered across the highway, and pattered furiously against the wheel-arches.

He reached Mrs Miller's house shortly after six. He parked outside and tiptoed his way inelegantly through the uncleared snow towards the front door, wishing that he had been blessed with the presence of mind to bring his galoshes with him. Strangely, the Miller house was in darkness. He rang at the doorbell, and then banged on the door with his fist.

It began to snow again, very lightly, no more than a dusting. It wetly prickled Vincent's face.

'Mrs Miller!' he called. 'Mrs Miller, it's Mr Pearson!'

He walked round to the side of the house, the seams of his Bally shoes already letting in chilly water. Mr Dunfey's dog started to yap at him, tugging at the chain that held it close to its kennel; and then Mr Dunfey appeared, thin and weasel-eyed, and wearing a brown zip-up cardigan over overalls.

'Yell as loud as you like,' he said, leaning laconically against the rail that ran down the side of his steps. Vincent saw the scarlet glow of his cigarette.

'Isn't she in?' asked Vincent.

'Went out just about 'n hour ago. Ambulance came and took poor Ben; then Mrs Miller follered.'

'What happened to Ben?' Vincent wanted to know.

'Didn't see; the medics had him covered up. Dead, I thought, to begin with, but Dr Serling said it was just routine. One of them fits of his, more than likely.'

'Do you know which hospital?'

'Litchfield County, that's my guess.'

'Well, thanks,' said Vincent.

'Don't mention it,' said Mr Dunfey, still leaning on his stair-rail, as if he intended to stay there all night.

Vincent walked back to his car. Mr Dunfey called, 'Wouldn't go that way, it's all snowed up. Go back the way you come, and make a detour through South Kent, if I was you.'

'Thanks,' said Vincent. It was very dark now, and bitterly cold. The wind-chill factor was at least fifteen. He climbed into his car and started up the engine, and perversely drove by the shortest route, in the opposite direction to that suggested by Mr Dunfey, following the tracks left in the hardened snow by the four-wheel-drive ambulance. Mr Dunfey watched him go, and spat his cigarette butt into the darkness.

'Can't tell the bastards nothing.'

The drive was jolting and uncomfortable, but after ten minutes Vincent was out on clear highway again, and heading north-eastwards. He decided to drive straight to Bantam, to see Aaron. If the snow grew any thicker, he could always ask Aaron for the use of one of his dilapidated sofas to pass the night. He switched on Vivaldi once more and began to hum along, although after a minute or two he switched it off again, to think what might have happened to Ben Miller.

There was so much fear in the air. Ben had talked about somebody or something coming back; Laura Monblat had disappeared; Edward had died in a mass of maggots. Now Aaron had called for help. Vincent glanced at his reflection in the rear-view mirror and wondered if he were some kind of plague-carrier, some kind of albatross, who had brought bad fortune and alarm.

He reached Bantam, parked in the shadow of Aaron's giant oak and stiffly climbed out of the car. Nobody came out to greet him. He stood in the porch chafing his hands and waiting for somebody to answer the doorbell. At last Marcia appeared, looking pale. She said, 'Oh, Vincent. I'm glad you could make it. Come on in.'

The house was unusually quiet and cold. 'Can I take your coat?' Marcia asked him, and Vincent smiled as cheerfully as he could, and said, 'Sure. Thank you. Is Aaron around?'

'In the studio,' said Marcia. She helped him out of his coat, and then she said, 'He's very upset, Vincent. He loved that cat. Whenever he was working, Van

Gogh was always sitting there, right beside him. Not only that, it happened so suddenly. And the *way* it happened –'

'The *way* it happened?' Vincent frowned. 'What do you mean?'

'I'm sorry. You'll have to go see for yourself.'

'Marcia –' Vincent began, but Marcia held his hand and squeezed it, and there were tears glistening in the corners of her eyes, which meant: I'm hurt, we're all hurt, and we're frightened, so please treat us gently.

'Okay,' said Vincent, taking a breath.

He went through to the studio. Only a single electric bulb was alight in there, way down at the far end, and at first Vincent didn't think that Aaron was anywhere around. The light cast huge shadows, transforming canvases and easels into hunchbacks and trolls and prong-horned devils, and changing Aaron's half-squeezed tubes of oil-paint into mountains of wriggling metal maggots. Vincent slowly walked the length of the work-table until he found Aaron sitting on a small painter's stool, with a half-empty bottle of Bantam Beaujolais beside him, his ginger-bearded head resting in his hands.

'Well,' said Vincent. 'You called me, maestro; and here I am.'

Aaron didn't look up, but poured himself another glass of wine.

Vincent waited for a very long time, his hands in his pockets, trying to be restrained, trying to be patient; but when Aaron still refused to acknowledge him, he said, 'I'm here, Aaron. But unless you say hello, I don't think I'm going to stay here for very much longer.'

Aaron glanced up, then glanced away again. 'I'm sorry,' he said. 'I guess that I'm shocked, that's all.'

'Are you going to tell me what happened?'

Aaron made a face, and then nodded. 'I don't have to tell you. I can show you.'

'All right, then. *Show* me what happened.'

Aaron said, 'You're going to have to forgive me, Vincent. I can't look at it myself. And when I first saw it, I blamed you. You and your family anyway. You and your grandfather and that goddamned . . . good-luck painting.'

'The Waldegrave?' asked Vincent.

'See for yourself,' said Aaron. With a dismissive and inaccurate wave, he directed Vincent towards the easel at the far end of the studio, still draped in its bedspread.

Vincent took two or three steps towards the easel and then hesitated. 'What is it?' he asked Aaron, feeling suddenly unsettled. 'It hasn't – *changed*, has it?'

'See for yourself,' Aaron repeated unsteadily.

Vincent took hold of the bedspread and gradually drew it away from the dark-painted canvas. He was secretly prepared for some kind of gruesome shock, but on first glance the painting appeared just the same as usual. The same group of white-faced people, clothed in black. The same red room. The same sense of arrested decay. A fashionable leper colony in a long-forgotten drawing room, doomed by Walter Waldegrave's talents slowly to rot for ever and ever.

Vincent turned round and said as brusquely as he could, 'There's no difference. Aaron. There's no difference! It's old, yes, I'll give you that; and it hasn't been very well preserved; but there's nothing else.'

Aaron fixed Vincent with a long-sighted look of annoyance. 'You saw this painting time and time again when you were a boy.'

'Yes. What of it?'

'Don't turn around,' said Aaron, 'but tell me what the woman seated third from the left is holding on her lap.'

Vincent stared at him.

'Tell me,' Aaron demanded, gently but insistently.

'We never knew what it was,' said Vincent, in a cardboardy voice.

'All right, you didn't know what it was,' agreed Aaron. 'But *describe* it.'

'It was a – well, what could you call it? A fuzz of black fur. A monkey, a cat, a spider. I don't know.'

Aaron said, 'Look at it now.'

Vincent slowly turned and looked, and he was amazed that he hadn't noticed it before. Yet, there it was; its paws tucked in, its eyes closed sitting contentedly on the lap of the faceless woman in black, while her hand hovered just an inch above its head, about to stroke it. A marmalade cat, exactly like Van Gogh. In fact, so much like Van Gogh, that it could only *be* Van Gogh.

Vincent tentatively touched the portrait of the coat with his fingertips, and his fingertips came away sticky with treacle-coloured paint.

'I'm sorry,' he said. 'I didn't realize it was still wet. I've smudged it.'

'It doesn't matter,' said Aaron, easing himself out of his broken-down chair. 'I didn't paint it.'

'That new assistant of yours? The girl from Gaylordsville?'

Aaron shook his head.

'Then what you're trying to tell me is that somebody broke in here and painted Van Gogh on one of your canvases? Just for a joke?' Vincent leaned forward and screwed up his eyes and examined the canvas even more closely. 'A very fine painter, too. Quite like Waldegrave himself.'

'Nobody broke in here, and nobody was playing jokes,' said Aaron. He lost his balance a little, as he came around the end of the work-table, and jarred his thigh. 'What you see there, Vincent my friend, is reality. That – that smudge which you have just smudged even more – that smudge *is* Van Gogh. That's all that's left of him, anyway.'

'Aaron,' said Vincent, trying to be conciliatory, trying to be calm. 'Aaron, that's just a painting. That isn't Van Gogh.'

'That's Van Gogh himself,' Aaron insisted, his voice slurring from the effects of two bottles of home-made red wine on an empty stomach.

'Aaron, what the hell are you talking about?' Vincent demanded. Then he said, 'You're drunk, for Christ's sake.'

'Yes,' said Aaron. 'I'm drunk. But not for Christ's sake. I'm drunk because my cat has been killed and now he's turned up in that goddamned painting of yours, alive, in that painting, as if nothing had happened, except that he's only paint now, and not flesh, and not fur.'

Vincent licked his lips, because they felt dry. Then he took out his embroidered Irish-linen handkerchief and wiped his mouth. In Aaron's presence, he felt incongruously citified and overdressed. 'I don't understand,' he said. He didn't. He couldn't decide whether Aaron was playing some kind of elaborate practical joke on him, or whether too much of the Bantam Beaujolais had finally sent him over the edge.

Yet Danny Monblat's cat had died an agonizing death in a bottle, trying to escape a nemesis too frightening even to think about; and here was Van Gogh, captured in paint, on a canvas that was characterized only by its decay and its deep sense of mid-Victorian doom.

'Well, you don't understand, and neither do I,' said

Aaron. He looked away for a moment, trying to collect himself, trying not to cry. 'I don't understand it one goddamned bit. But there it is.'

Vincent took hold of Aaron's arm and looked at him closely and anxiously, and said, 'Aaron, this is only a painting.'

Aaron drew his arm away. 'My dear friend, this is not "only a painting". I only wish that it were.'

'But it's not as if Van Gogh has been *hurt*, simply by having his portrait painted. That doesn't prove anything. He probably got himself lost in the snow, that's all, and someone's keeping a hold of him until the weather clears up.'

Aaron stared at Vincent for a moment, watery-eyed. 'I found Van Gogh,' he said. 'That's the trouble. I *found* him.'

'Was he hurt?'

'I'll show you. You want to see? I'll show you.'

Aaron walked along to the far end of the studio and took down a large flashlight that was hanging up there. 'Come on,' he said. 'I'll show you.'

Hesitantly, Vincent followed Aaron out of the studio door and into the snowy night. A bitter north-west wind was slicing across from Mount Prospect, which stood 1,350 feet high in the wintry darkness, separating the village of Bantam from Nepaug Reservoir. 'Should I get my coat?' asked Vincent. 'It's as cold as a polar bear's packed lunch out here.'

'This won't take long,' said Aaron. Vincent had never known him so evasive and so mysterious and so unfriendly. He stalked ahead of Vincent through the garden, the beam of his torch freckled with sudden whirls of dry snow. Vincent followed, his shoes soaked, his collar turned up against the wind, his hands thrust into his pockets.

They reached the base of the giant oak which dominated Aaron's house. In the torchlight, the trunk looked even more deeply furrowed and gnarled than it usually did, like some hideous creation by Arthur Rackham. Aaron stood beside it, his eyes rimmed with scarlet, his beard sparkling with snow, and pointed the torch upwards, so that it illuminated some of the lower branches.

'What am I supposed to be looking at?' asked Vincent. He was shuddering with cold already.

'Follow the light,' said Aaron flatly. 'Follow the light and tell me what you can see.'

Vincent squinted upwards, his cheeks wet with tears because of the wind. At last, he could make something out, something that dangled from one of the tree-limbs close to the studio roof. It was red, and ragged, and very long, like a twisted scarf. It spun slowly in the freezing wind, around and around, and then spun back the other way.

Vincent took out his handkerchief and wiped his eyes, and then peered at the scarf again. This time, however, he could see that it wasn't a scarf at all. It was the skinned body of an animal, strung up by the neck with wire. Its apparent length was caused by the way in which it had been disembowelled, so that its intestines hung below it, adding two or three feet.

Vincent stared at it for one chilled and disbelieving second, and then turned back to look at Aaron. Aaron switched off the torch.

'That's Van Gogh?' asked Vincent, in horror.

Aaron nodded.

'But how do you know?'

Aaron fumbled around in his jacket pocket, and at last produced a small red cat-collar. 'I found this on the ground, just over there.'

'I can't imagine that anyone would want to *do* such a disgusting thing.'

'Well, me neither, but they did.'

'Did you call the police?'

'I called Sheriff Smith. They said that he was down in Darien today, and that the rest of the officers were all tied up with traffic problems, on account of the snow. But they can send somebody round in the morning. That's why I had to leave him strung up like that. They didn't want the scene of the crime disturbed.'

'We're not treading on any valuable footprints, are we?' asked Vincent, looking around.

Aaron shook his head. 'Whoever killed him must have done it before the fresh snow started. When I came out here looking for him, there wasn't a footprint anywhere.'

Vincent glanced up into the darkness of the tree, and then followed Aaron back into the studio. Briskly rubbing his hands, he approached the Waldegrave portrait again and examined it closely. It still gave off that pungent odour of decay; it was still as gloomy and scaly as ever. Yet here in the front was Van Gogh, the marmalade cat, painted fresh and bright and in scrupulously accurate style.

'This doesn't make any sense at all,' said Vincent.

'It doesn't make the kind of sense that we usually like to think of as sense,' Aaron remarked. 'But the facts speak for themselves. Van Gogh disappeared, and was skinned, and then he showed up in the portrait.'

'I have to ask myself whether you might have painted him into the portrait yourself,' said Vincent gently.

'Vincent,' Aaron retorted, 'I've asked myself the very same question. Whether I might have done it while I was drunk; or whether I found Van Gogh's body, hanging up in the tree, and did it kind of automatically, or hysterically, out of shock. But look at it. It's beautifully painted. It's painted in Waldegrave's idiom, in Waldegrave's colour-range, and it's incredibly detailed. I couldn't have painted anything like that in a week, let alone a couple of hours. And that's quite apart from the fact that up until now, I haven't been able to get any fresh paint to stick on to this goddamned portrait at all.'

He paused, with one fist clenched and trembling, and then said, very quietly, 'I didn't do it, Vincent. I swear to God. It simply appeared.'

'Are you going to mention it to Sheriff Smith? The painting, I mean?'

'I don't know yet. I haven't been able to think straight. He'll probably tell me I'm out of my head.'

Vincent drew up a chair splattered with hundreds of different hues of dried paint, and sat down on it, so that he could look at the Waldegrave portrait more closely. 'Something is happening,' he said.

'Well, you *bet* that something is happening,' Aaron expostulated. 'Goddamned bloody cat murder.'

Vincent shook his head. 'No, no, it's like . . . I don't know . . . it's like a party. You know when you go to a party and everybody's laughing and chatting and having a good time, and then suddenly somebody walks in and that one person has such an atmosphere about them that the whole place falls silent and nobody feels comfortable any more. Well, that's the same feeling I get. It's like somebody's walked into our lives, and made us all feel awkward and tense and uncomfortable.'

Aaron said, 'Who? *Who's* walked into our lives, and made us feel awkward and uncomfortable?'

'I don't know. But some things have been happening that don't seem at all connected; and yet they do.'

Aaron tugged morosely at his beard. 'Have some wine,' he said. 'I don't think I understand you any more than I can understand what's happened to Van Gogh.'

Vincent said, 'Listen . . . first of all Edward died . . . in an incredibly terrible way. Then Mrs Miller's son Ben had some kind of psychic fit. From what I hear, they've taken him into hospital. Then Edward's previous girlfriend disappeared . . . and her cat jammed itself into a bottle and ripped itself to pieces. Now, Van Gogh has been skinned.'

'I don't see any connection at all,' said Aaron.

'The connection, Aaron, is *me*. All of these incidents have happened to people that *I* know.'

'You can't blame yourself. That isn't any kind of connection.'

'I don't know. What you said earlier . . . about this portrait . . . well, that may have something to do with it. My grandfather wasn't just protective about this portrait, he was almost obsessive about it. There were whole clauses in his will about it: how my father had to keep it safe; how it was never supposed to be sold; how it should never be lent to any outside gallery, or sent abroad, or put on public display. And here it is, right in the centre of everything that's been going on. It's falling to pieces, sure. It's almost beyond restoration. And yet I can't help feeling it has some kind of life of its own. In fact, I have the feeling that it has *more* life now than when I used to look at it when I was a boy. As if it's woken up, somehow.'

Aaron poured himself a large goblet of wine and drank almost half of it straight off. 'I have to tell you, Vincent, I don't understand what the hell you're trying to say. But you're right. That portrait has a life of its own; including the life of my cat.'

Vincent said, 'I'll take it off your hands. Don't worry. I'll take it straight home with me tonight.'

'Well, I wish you would,' said Aaron. 'I can't stand the sight of it and I can't stand the *smell* of it. I don't ever want to hear the name of Walter Waldegrave again, as long as I live.'

'If you do decide to tell Sheriff Smith about it, refer him to me,' said Vincent.

'I don't think I will tell him,' Aaron replied. He finished the rest of his wine and wiped his mouth with the back of his hand. 'He'd probably lock me up. And you, too, unless you're careful.'

They had very little else to say to each other. They had both been badly disturbed by what had happened to Van Gogh, and by the thought that the portrait somehow contained a key to all the horrifying events of the past few days. Aaron wrapped the painting up in brown packing-paper, more carefully than was necessary, and Vincent carried it on his shoulder out to his car and locked it into the boot. They stood together in the light of Aaron's porch, their breath smoking in the wind.

'I'll tell you what the sheriff said, once he's visited,' said Aaron. He clasped Vincent's hand.

'Thanks,' said Vincent. 'And, believe me, I'm sorry about the picture.'

'Well, we're probably letting our imagination run away with us,' Aaron replied, scuffling his foot in the snow. 'It'll all seem ridiculous in the morning.'

'Sure,' said Vincent.

Aaron hesitated for a moment, then clasped Vincent's shoulder and told him, 'Take care, won't you? I mean, you never know.' And he inclined his head towards the boot of Vincent's car.

*

Vincent drove back to Candlemas feeling unhappy and unsettled. The house was in darkness when he arrived, and fresh snow was beginning to twist and tumble out of the sky. He drove the Bentley all the way round to the side of the house, where the garages and the stables were, and left the engine running while he climbed out and opened up the old-fashioned green-painted garage doors. He parked the car inside, killed the headlights and switched off the engine. As he did so, however, he was sure that he heard a screeching noise.

He sat listening for a short while. There was no sound now but the gradual ticking of cooling metal and the digestive gurgling of the air-conditioning system. Perhaps the screech had been nothing more than a slipping fanbelt. He shrugged to himself, took out the keys and climbed out of the car.

It was then that he heard it again, high and chilling. He stood where he was, but it had faded, and there was no indication where it might have come from, or what it might have been. A dog, maybe; or a child playing games. A cat, in pain.

He lifted the Waldegrave portrait out of the back of the car and carried it round to the front of the house. He unlocked the front door and stepped inside, groping for the light-switch. The hallway was chilly and musty, and smelled of dead log-fires and neglect. He propped the portrait against the panelled wall, and went through to the kitchen to switch off the burglar alarm and switch on some more lights.

It took him an hour to stoke up the boiler in the cellar and get it rumbling, and then light log-fires in three of the downstairs rooms and in his bedroom, too. But soon the house was beginning to feel more warm and cheerful, and he rewarded himself by pouring out a large glass of Irish whiskey, and searching out a sirloin steak from the freezer, so that he could microwave himself a decent supper.

He was selecting a record to play – Beethoven's Pastoral? or Tchaikovsky's Serenade for Strings in C Major? – when the telephone rang. He reached over and picked it up, and said, 'Pearson.'

'Oh, it's you, Vincent,' said a dry, elderly voice. 'This is Gary Spellecy, from across the way. I saw your house-lights on, and I wanted to make sure it wasn't an intruder.'

'Thanks, Gary,' said Vincent. 'I came up unexpectedly. I did go round to Mrs Miller's to see if she could open up the house for me, but she wasn't around.'

'Well, she won't be, for a while. She's gone to stay with the Guthries.'

'I heard that Ben had been taken to hospital. Is it anything serious?'

'Not sure that it's my place to tell you,' said Gary Spellecy.

'Gary, what's happened?' Vincent wanted to know. The logs in the fireplace popped noisily, and a sudden downdraught blew smoke back into the room.

'Well, Ben disfigured himself, that was the word I heard.'

'*Disfigured* himself? How?'

'Cut his face to pieces with a broken drinking-glass. Worst case of self-mutilation he'd ever seen, that's what Dr Serling said.'

Vincent felt as if his brain were suddenly swelling and threatening to burst out beyond the confines of his skull. His forehead pounded, and he had an aching sensation all around his lower jaw that penetrated right down to the roots of his wisdom teeth. It was the effect of cold, and tension, and sudden shock.

'You okay?' Gary Spellecy asked him.

'Yes, sure, I'm fine.'

'You don't *sound* okay.'

'I'm tired, that's all. Listen, do you have the Guthrie number? I think I ought to give Mrs Miller a call.'

'She was back down at the hospital, last I heard.'

Vincent put down the phone. He stared at his glass of whiskey for a while, as if it were the fatal draught of hemlock, but then he swallowed it in three larynx-bobbing gulps. It burned his tongue and stung the corners of his mouth.

He knew that his intuition was right. Something or somebody had arrived in his life and was affecting everything around him. It might not be anybody he knew. The only clue he had so far was the vague description given to him by the old woman at the Wentworth Apartments, of a black-dressed, white-faced lady in her mid-thirties.

Vincent went out into the hallway and stood looking at the wrapped-up Waldegrave. He was still not completely sure that Aaron hadn't been suffering under the influence of too much home-made wine. Aaron was the most skilful in-painter that Vincent knew, and if anybody could have created that portrait of Van Gogh, it was him. It seemed incredible that the cat had appeared on the canvas by some sinister magical force, as if it had been painted there by the spirit of Walter Waldegrave himself.

The most rational explanation was that Aaron had painted it himself, perhaps in remorse for having killed Van Gogh in a burst of drunken temper. But then, Vincent had never known Aaron to lose his temper, at least not violently, not even when he was pickled beyond redemption.

And there was no doubt that something was wrong. The cold winds of Christmas were bringing frightening sounds and strange voices and terrible events, and no matter how logically he tried to think about it, Vincent was growing increasingly convinced that they were all stirred up by *him*.

Fifteen

They had locked her in a small upstairs bedroom, with bolted and shuttered windows, so that even when the sun burned brightly for a few minutes just before twilight, all she could see were narrow cracks of orange light as fine as overheated wires. She cupped her hand up to the shutter, and the sunlight crossed her palm like a glowing lifeline. She whispered to herself, 'Please, God, don't let them kill me.'

The room was woolly with dust. The walls must once have been eggshell blue, but now they were faded grey and blotched with damp. There was a single iron bed, with a sagging horsehair mattress, but no sheets or blankets. The only other furniture was a wooden chair with a broken back, and a small Victorian bureau with chipped walnut veneer.

In spite of her discomfort, Laura had slept for two or three hours during Tuesday morning, and when she had woken up, she had found that a tray had been left for her on top of the bureau. Under a tarnished silver dish-cover, she had discovered a salad of smoked chicken, coleslaw and pickled beetroot. A freshly baked bread-roll had been set on a clean but unstarched napkin. There was also a glass of white wine, but it had tasted sharp and vinegary, as if it had aged past its prime.

Laura hadn't wanted to touch the food at first, but during the afternoon she had grown hungry and tasted a few mouthfuls. It reminded her for some reason of the food that her grandmother used to prepare.

Tuesday night had been silent and sleepless. She had heard nothing in the house but the north-easterly wind blowing across the mouths of the chimneys, and the regular chiming of a clock. But when she had woken this morning, her tray had been taken away and replaced with a fresh tray, bearing exactly the same meal.

The afternoon had crawled across further tracts of silence. Now it was dark, and she sat on the edge of the bed, waiting, listening, unsure if her captors had forgotten her or not.

The clock in the hallway downstairs chimed eight.

Laura had never experienced anything like this before. She had never in her life before been frightened, or threatened, or locked up. Her parents had always taken care of her and Edward had always taken care of her, and Danny treated her as if she was actually fragile. It hadn't occurred to her to shout out and bang on the door and demand that Cordelia Gray should let her free. All she could think of was to sit and wait for something to happen; for someone to come and tell her that her imprisonment was at an end. Or that they were going to kill her.

At half past eight, she heard footsteps on the uncarpeted stairs, and voices. Two people were arguing on the landing outside, and they sounded like Maurice and Cordelia Gray. Maurice kept saying something about 'Selfishness, selfishness', and in return Cordelia was snapping, 'You're always so judgemental. How can *you* decide what's best?'

'Because I have the experience,' Maurice told Cordelia. He was standing almost directly outside Laura's door now, and so she could hear him distinctly. 'Besides, Father has always left such decisions to me, and if you're challenging me, well, you're challenging Father, too.'

'Father is not the Lord Almighty, Maurice. He never has been and he never will be. The only reason he left *you* to decide who should benefit and who should not is because he could never bear to make such decisions himself; and you are the oldest surviving male. His weakness and Albert's accident aren't exactly what I call credentials for family authority.'

'Nevertheless,' Maurice insisted, 'you will not have the girl.'

'Which is more important?' Cordelia demanded. '*My* appearance, or Mother's? It's been seven years since Mother was fit to come out in public. What difference will another year make? Or even another two years? Look at my face. Look at it! You can see for yourself what's happening to me. How can I get hold of the picture unless I can go wherever I please – unless I'm charming. Unless I'm *more* than charming.'

'God, you're so vain,' said Maurice. 'That's all that really matters to you, isn't it? The admiring looks of handsome young men. I can't think of a better name for you to have taken than that of Sybil Vane.'

'You never knew Sybil,' Cordelia replied, and there was a haughty kind of pain in her voice. 'I loved Sybil dearly.'

'It was certainly a very dear love as far as *she* was concerned,' said Maurice. 'In fact, the most expensive love she was ever to have.'

'Don't speak of her,' said Cordelia.

There was a pause, and then Cordelia said something indistinct. After a while, Maurice said, 'I will wait until Christmas, but that is all I am prepared to do. It is only fair that Mother has her. You haven't even been up to *see* Mother since we got back here; you don't know how ill she is. All that travelling, and now to come back to The Wilderlings. She had her greatest triumphs here, and her greatest tragedies. It's all been a terrible strain. She wouldn't have come, you know, if you hadn't persuaded her that you could find the picture.'

'Well, I've *found* the picture, haven't I?' said Cordelia.

'Yes, and I congratulate you on your persistence. Unfortunately, we don't yet have the picture *here*.'

'We'll get it, don't worry. It was far too risky yesterday. There are still people in Litchfield County who would kill us all, if they knew we were back.'

'You're talking like Mother now. Nobody remembers.'

Cordelia said nothing for a moment or two, but then remarked, 'We have to get the picture without anyone knowing where it has gone, or why. That was Father's fatal mistake, the last time, letting those people know.'

There was more muttered conversation which Laura was unable to hear; but then Maurice said, '. . . that cat.'

'Well, what of it? It was so like Firework. And have *you* ever thought about Firework, or doing for Firework what all the rest of us have been so vainly doing for ourselves?'

'Firework is dead, Cordelia. There was no earthly point in Henry taking all of that risk. Once one of us is gone, there is no restitution, you know that for yourself. That is why you must think of Mother.'

Maurice walked a little way down the corridor, and then added with disgust, 'Besides, Henry is so clumsy. Henry is a pork-butcher.'

'I was thinking of giving the girl to Henry,' said Cordelia calmly.

'Not to –?'

Cordelia laughed that high glassy laugh of hers. 'Of course not. Do you think I'd let him ruin her?'

'She's not for you, Cordelia. I hope I've made myself clear.'

'Well, we can wait until Christmas Day, can't we, before we make up our minds about that? Perhaps Mother and I should play rummy for her, don't you think that's a good idea?'

'You curdle my blood sometimes, Cordelia.'

'But you don't mind if Henry has the girl for now?'

'Is it so important to you?'

Cordelia said archly, 'I enjoy it, when Henry has his girls. I think it arouses a certain sort of *fin-de-siècle* corruptness in me. He does it with such panache. It brings back those days in Berlin. Do you remember the Dodo Club?'

'I remember you getting drunk on *crème de menthe* and dizzy with cocaine, both at the same time.'

'You're the stuffiest brother that anyone could have, Maurice.'

'And *you*, Cordelia, are the most relentless of sisters.'

Without warning, Cordelia suddenly turned the key in the lock of Laura's door, and opened it. Laura stepped back, alarmed that Cordelia might realize that she had been listening; but Cordelia stalked into the tiny bedroom with glacial elegance and smiled at Laura indulgently, as if Laura were a between-stairs maid who happened to have polished the firedogs rather well. Laura couldn't help feeling that there was something desperately *old-fashioned* about the Grays which went deeper than the usual WASPish conservatism of Darien and Westport and all parts east.

Cordelia wore a striking black off-the-shoulder evening dress, sewn with darkly sparkling black sequins. There were diamond combs in her hair, and a diamond choker around her neck. Her make-up was deathly white, and although she was still beautiful, she looked as if she had been completely drained of blood. Even her lips were white.

She glanced at the lunch-tray, and smiled. 'I'm pleased that you've eaten,' she said. 'Sophonisba hasn't used the kitchen for years and years; but she'll improve.' She paused, and then she added, 'We were so spoiled in Europe, you know.'

Laura said tightly, 'I want to call my husband.'

'You shall, my dear. Shan't she, Maurice?'

Maurice appeared, immaculately dressed in a black tuxedo, with a high collar, and nodded in a vague, unhelpful, James Masonish kind of way. 'Of course she shall; all in good time.'

Laura said, 'Are you going to kill me?'

'Kill you?' asked Cordelia, pressing her hand incredulously against her white bosom. 'What on earth has given you that idea?'

'You keep saying that you're going to *give* me . . . either to your mother, or to Henry, or . . .' Laura's voice trailed off.

'Well, you mustn't get the wrong idea,' said Cordelia, linking her arm through Laura's. 'Come, you must come downstairs with us and meet some of the rest of the family. Then I'm sure that you and Henry should get better acquainted.'

'Please . . .' said Laura. 'Please, all I want to do is go home.'

She knew very urgently and strongly that she *did* want to go home, that she *did* want to talk to Danny; that the very last place in the whole world that she wanted to be was here, with all these strange and frightening people. Yet somehow she couldn't bring herself to speak with any conviction. It was more like the urgency she might have felt in a dream, slow and glutinous and complicated. She began to feel that if she did what she was told, and smiled, and behaved herself, then everything was going to be all right. She looked into Cordelia's mirror-like eyes, and she saw for certain that everything was going to be all right.

'I mustn't stay too long, though,' she said, allowing Cordelia to lead her through the door and along the landing. From somewhere downstairs, she could hear piano music, an odd melody that almost sounded as if someone were playing it backwards.

'Of course not,' Cordelia reassured her. Maurice, a little way behind them, grunted in what might have been approbation; or not.

They descended the stairs to the hallway. On their left, the double mahogany doors to the music room were opened, and without hesitation Cordelia led Laura by the arm straight into the room. There, for the first time, she saw the Gray family.

There were nine more of them. They were gathered around the huge grand piano, which was draped in a brown shawl-like piano-cover, and all of them were in evening dress. The three men, including Henry, had stiff upright collars, and the six women were variously dressed in green and black and crimson gowns that seemed to have borrowed their styles from every period from late Victorian times to the heyday of Princess Grace.

Henry was seated at the piano. He stopped playing and rose to bow to Laura as Cordelia brought her in. 'I have been waiting to see you again with the same anticipation that the Lappish people look forward to the coming of spring,' he said.

'Henry can be obscure,' remarked Cordelia, out of the side of her mouth, as Henry kissed Laura's hand.

'This is my Uncle John,' Cordelia said, as a tall white-haired man came forward and inclined his head in welcome. Uncle John looked as pale and dry-skinned as the rest of the Grays, and there was a noticeable *collapsed* appearance about his face, like the hull of a boat whose fashion-pieces have rotted away. He mouthed the word, 'Charmed,' and retreated.

In turn, Cordelia took Laura around to her Uncle Belvedere, her mother's brother, a slight, small man, with the constant nodding of Parkinson's disease; her Aunt Willa, a stout woman in a green silk dress that was far too tight under the arms; her cousins Emily, Ermintrude and Nora, three fussy lisping little girls with ringlets whom Laura found it difficult to tell apart; and in the background, Cordelia's sister Alicia, who looked younger than Cordelia but far more stricken, with a larger nose; and her second cousin Netty, who was paralysed, and sat in an incongruously modern wheelchair, her knees covered with a pink blanket.

'We were singing,' said Henry. 'At least, I was playing, and we were about to sing.'

'Aunt Alicia says that we have nothing to sing about,' said Ermintrude, giggling. 'Aunt Alicia says that life is a tragedy.'

'Well, then,' said Henry, 'we shall sing that life is a tragedy.'

He began to play the same backwards-sounding music, the rings on his fingers glittering as his hands wandered over the keyboard. Laura stood where she was, in dread of this extraordinary company in which she had found herself, yet hypnotized by the melody, and by a feeling that if she tried to leave now, she would be missing the most important event of her entire life.

Something was going to happen to her. She couldn't think what, and it didn't occur to her to ask. But she knew that it was fearfully important.

> *The kiss of death is on our lips.*
> *The day of mourning dawns.*
> *The marble angels cast their shade*
> *Across the frosty lawns.*

Henry sang with robustness, as if it were a marching-song, and then immediately broke into 'The Boers Have Got My Daddy'.

> *The Boers have got my Daddy,*
> *My soldier Dad.*
> *I don't like to hear my Mammy sigh.*
> *I don't like to hear my Mammy cry . . .*

At this, however, Uncle Belvedere banged the flat of his hand loudly on top of the piano, and Henry stopped. Everybody looked at each other in embarrassment. Cordelia moved around behind Henry, and said, 'That wasn't quite the thing, was it, Henry?'

Henry stood up. He pressed one key, middle C, waited until the tone had died away, and then closed the piano lid.

'My apologies, Uncle,' he said. 'I would have thought that all happened rather a long time ago.'

'To *you*, perhaps,' Belvedere replied. His voice was reedy and hoarse. 'But there are some of us who will remember to the very end of time.'

'You already have my apologies,' Henry repeated, and walked quickly out of the music room into the hallway, where he stood with his hands on his hips, his head raised in temper. Cordelia followed him, and beckoned to Laura to join her. Laura was rather relieved to be excused from the midst of the Gray family, and came after her as quickly as she could.

'How long before we can get hold of the painting?' Henry was saying testily. 'Uncle Belvedere grows more damnably irritating with every day that passes.'

'We're going to try again on Sunday,' Cordelia reassured him. 'If we're lucky, Mr Halperin will be out for brunch.'

'You're absolutely sure that he has it?'

'No question at all,' said Cordelia. 'Mr Astengo said that he had seen it in Halperin's studio himself.'

Henry took hold of Cordelia's shoulder. 'Well,' he said, 'I have to admire your intelligence. I don't think that *I* would have thought of tracking down all the picture restorers in the north-eastern United States, let alone phoning them all up.'

Cordelia smiled. 'Meanwhile, Maurice is quite agreeable to your having this young lady to amuse you; at least until we decide what to do with her.'

'Well, well, that's excellent,' said Henry. He turned to Laura and looked her up and down, with undisguised pleasure. 'And when will you decide? You and the estimable Maurice?'

'Christmas,' said Cordelia. 'So you have a few days.'

'Thank you,' Henry told her. Thank you very much indeed.'

'Only one thing to remember,' warned Cordelia.

Henry made a smirking face. 'Very well. I'll try. *That* would rather ruin things for you and Aunt Isobel, wouldn't it? You wouldn't have very much left to fight over. Still, she's very pretty. I hope I'm not tempted.'

Laura kept on thinking over and over: *I must call Danny, I must get away.* But the more she repeated the words inside her mind, the less meaning they seemed to have; and, as she stood next to Cordelia and Henry Gray in the hallway of The Wilderlings, she felt no real urge now to escape. She was caught by the aura of the Gray family as helplessly as if she were an insect surrounded by liquid sap.

'Come,' said Henry, and beckoned Laura across the hallway to the staircase. She followed him obediently. The patterns on the floor appeared to lean away from her at all the wrong angle. She mounted the stairs, which seemed to slope. She told herself for the very last time, *I must tell Danny where I am*, but then she couldn't even think who Danny was.

Henry led her the length of the landing to a large bedroom with double doors. He opened up the doors with a flourish, and indicated with a nod of his head that she should step inside. She hesitated for a second, trying to see by his eyes what he was thinking, what he was feeling, what he was going to do to her; but his eye-sockets might just as well have contained polished ball-bearings for all the expression she could see. His eyes were bright and alive, but gave nothing away.

Inside the bedroom, there was a wide bed with an elaborately carved headboard of dark and dusty oak. The curtains were half drawn, but Laura could just make out the pale radiance of snow outside the window, in the garden. There was an uncomfortable-looking ottoman, a heavy wardrobe and a rococo bureau in the French style.

Henry closed the doors and turned the key. 'You must forgive my family sometimes,' he said. 'Over the years, they have become obsessed by their memories.'

'Why was your uncle so upset by that song?' asked Laura.

'Well,' smiled Henry, casually taking off his tuxedo and hanging it over the arm of the ottoman. 'It always reminds him of Albert.'

'Albert?'

'My cousin. He was killed, you know.'

'But not in the Boer War.'

Henry was unlinking his cuffs. He looked at Laura in surprise, and then laughed. 'Please,' he said, 'you must make yourself comfortable.'

'I don't understand.'

Henry came over and took hold of Laura's shoulders. He stared into her eyes for a very long time. She couldn't imagine how long it actually was, although she thought she heard the clock chiming again. All she could remember afterwards was looking at Henry's beautifully curved lips, as they softly told her what she had to do.

'You are mine, now. Do you understand that? You belong to me. You are my servant, and you will do everything that I ask of you, without question. Your will is completely subjugated to mine. There is nothing that you will not do for me.'

Laura said nothing, but at last lowered her head.

Henry told her, with even greater gentleness, 'I will be kind to you, you can be sure of that, unless you try to disobey me; in which case I shall have to punish you severely. You will always ask for your punishment when you have distressed me. Punishments will not be given unless requested; but by the same token, you will not be absolved from your guilt unless you have been punished.'

At last, Henry turned away and walked across the bedroom and into a dressing room at the side. He returned with a Hasselblad camera, rather an old one, and a tripod, which he set up at the foot of the bed.

Laura watched him dully. She felt as if she had no energy either to move or to speak.

'You can undress now,' said Henry. 'I want you completely naked.'

He went back to the dressing room, and came out with a photo-flood lamp on a stand, and a silver photographer's umbrella. He set these up on either side of the bed, and plugged the lamp in, switching it on momentarily to test that it was working.

'But you're not undressed,' he said. 'Let me help you.'

Laura could see a bright green after-image of the photo-flood's element dancing in front of her eyes. Behind it, Henry appeared, and stood close to her, and with cool hands and an expressionless face, he began to unbutton her blouse. 'I am the most fortunate and at the same time the most unfortunate of men,' he said. 'I have met some of the most entrancing women in the world, from child-women to those ladies who are in the full sensual flare of their maturity. I have photographed hundreds of them. But that is all I can do. I cannot take them. I am prevented by the unnatural strictures of my existence from ever satisfying my desires. Thus I have to satisfy myself with film; with negatives and trans-parencies. How right those descriptions are! Negatives and transparencies. And those are all that I am able to love. A company of ghosts.'

Laura hardly heard these words. Her eyes were half closed now, and she felt as if she were falling into a kind of waking sleep. She felt Henry's fingers unbutton her cuffs, and then draw the blouse off her shoulders. She felt his cold breath on her shoulder as he leaned forward and reached around to unclasp her bra. She smelled his cologne. Then he bared her breasts, and with the lightest of touches, his fingertips traced around the curves of each of them, cupping their heaviness for a moment, and then caressing each nipple until it crinkled and stiffened.

Now his hands ran down each side and made her shudder. He unfastened the waistband of her skirt and let it fall to the floor. Without any apparent effort, he lifted her up in his arms and carried her over to the bed.

She opened her eyes and stared up at him. In the lamplight, he was remarkably handsome. She could have believed that she was in a Regency romance, being carried to bed by a good-looking swain. Yet there was something infinitely corrupt and cold about Henry: some crucial lack of humanity that was erotic and at the same time frightening. She feared him, but she also desired him. There was no whisper of Danny in her mind, no whisper of home or safety or getting away.

Henry laid her on the bed. Then he knelt beside her and leaned over her and kissed her on the mouth; a strange chaste kiss with his lips closed.

'You don't know how much I long for you,' he said.

He bent his head and kissed each of her breasts, his lips brushing her nipples and arousing them again. His cool fingers traced their way down her stomach again, and around her thighs. His knuckles trailed between her legs.

'*Henry,*' she said, in a voice that didn't sound at all like her own.

But Henry didn't reply. He gently tugged down her white cotton panties and drew them over her ankles. For a fleeting second, his middle finger ran down the neatly closed line of her vulva; but even as she shuddered again, he stood up, and smiled at her, and turned away from the bed.

'You tempt me as much as the very best of them,' he said. His hand was clasped over his mouth, so that she couldn't hear what he was saying very distinctly.

238

'What do you *want*?' she asked him. It seemed very important to know.

Henry went across to the photo-flood and switched it on, drowning the bed in dazzling white light.

'I want to take pictures of you,' he said. 'I want to add you to my collection.'

He bent over his Hasselblad and adjusted it. Then he said, 'I don't want you to pose. All I want you to do is to listen to what I say, and try to conjure up a picture of it in your mind. You are mine, remember. You have no soul of your own. Whatever I want you to be, you will be, without question. You are a servant, who must fear her master.'

Laura lay back naked on the bed, staring up at the ceiling. The bright light from the photo-flood made her feel somehow as if scores of people were watching her out of the darkness. Defensively, she crossed her hands over her breasts and strained her eyes to see beyond the circle of light. All she could distinguish, however, was Henry's hunchbacked silhouette as he bent over his camera, and the reflected glint of its lens.

'You are a Swedish girl, blonde and blue-eyed, who has been abducted whilst on vacation in Egypt by an Arabian slave-trader. You have been chained by the ankles and led far across the desert in a coffle of black slave-girls, your white skin protected from the sun by a white flowing burnous. At last you arrive at an oasis, far out in the desert, and here you are to be sold.'

Laura closed her eyes. She hardly heard the discreet chirring sound of Henry's camera. But she could hear the soft and abrasive whisper of sand blowing across the dunes, and she could hear the snorting of camels and the billowing of tent-flaps; and she could almost see the sun's red reflection setting in the oasis.

She was led into the tent. There was a red woven

carpet on the floor, and smoky torches burned all around her. By the swivelling light of the torches, she could make out a circle of Arabian faces, hook-nosed men in black robes; Nubians in pale djellabas; Tuaregs, with faces wrapped up to the eyes, displaying curved daggers in jewelled sheaths. There was a smell of charcoal and lamb-fat and spices, mingled with the sharper odour of sweat. Somebody clapped, and a springy-sounding drum started up, and some of the men began to clap and tap their feet in time to its complicated rhythm.

'She will dance for you!' a voice declared, quite close to her. And with a single tug, her white robes were pulled away from her, so that she stood suddenly nude in front of the greedy and lascivious faces of her would-be owners.

The drum played, and Laura danced, elegantly and slowly at first, running her fingers through her hair, swaying her hips. But as the music grew faster, she began to run her hands down her body and caress her breasts, squeezing them so that her pale pink nipples protruded from between her fingers. The watching Arabs shouted out to her and cheered her, and one of them let loose a white cockatoo, which fluttered in panic around the tent.

She twisted and turned her body as provocatively as she could, sometimes approaching the Arabs so closely that she could smell the lamb and licorice on their breath. Her body was glossy with sweat, and she shone in the torchlight, her hair clinging damply to her head. At the very back of the tent, a stark-naked boy of no more than fourteen watched her with calm and sensuous eyes, his penis half erect.

Now she knelt on the carpeted floor, arching her body back, opening her thighs. The drumming speeded up to a fierce and arousing patter. The Arabs shouted and clapped and grew restless, never once taking their eyes away from her body. She reached down between her legs with both hands, and opened herself out for them, glistening pink, wider and wider, giving them everything they wanted: her privacy, her pride, her sexuality, her soul.

She could feel a climax rising up within her, tightening the muscles of her pelvis, and she ground her teeth and shook her head from side to side. But right on the very brink, the bright light suddenly died. The tent collapsed, the desert blew away, the oasis dried up; and she was lying naked on a strange dusty bed in a gloomy room, panting and perspiring and shocked.

The drumming resolved itself into a persistent knocking at the bedroom door. Henry went to answer it, while Laura lay back stunned on the bed, unable to understand where she was or what had happened.

Henry opened the door. 'What is it, Maurice?' he asked irritably. 'You must have known that I was busy.'

Maurice said, 'I simply wish to advise you, dear boy, to remain as quiet as possible. The police are here.'

Henry said, 'Very well,' and came back to the bed. He held out his hands to Laura and smiled. 'You did very well, my love. You have far more imagination than I expected.'

Laura couldn't find the words to answer, but took his hand and shakily stood up.

'You may dress now,' said Henry. 'If you look in the wardrobe, on the left-hand side, you will find a number of dresses. They are all black, but then you are a servant and must wear black. There are some shoes there, too. You will wear no underwear. I forbid it.'

Laura nodded. Henry took her arm and kissed her on the forehead. 'We have until Christmas,' he said. 'That will be plenty of time for some of my finest adventures. Have you ever been to Berlin, to the Salambo Club, where men can dance with naked women? Have you ever been to Thailand, to the brothels?'

'No,' whispered Laura.

'You shall,' Henry promised her, kissing her again.

Sixteen

Darien, 18 December

George Kelly showed his badge, and said, 'Are you Maurice Gray?'

Uncle John smiled thinly. 'I'm sorry,' he replied. 'I regret not.'

'Is Maurice Gray here?'

'Not that I am aware of.'

Jack, who was standing next to George with the collar of his sheepskin coat turned up, pointed to the side of the house. 'That Cadillac parked there. Does that belong to Maurice Gray?'

Uncle John shook his head. Although the snow was beginning to fall quite thickly now, and George and Jack were shuffling their feet on the doorstep to keep themselves warm, he showed no inclination to invite them inside.

'If it doesn't belong to Maurice Gray, who does it belong to?' asked Jack.

'I'm afraid that I really don't know.'

George sniffed and patiently massaged his leather-gloved hands together, and said, 'We want to talk to Maurice Gray in connection with a homicide inquiry. It's very important, do you understand that? Some people have been killed. It's important that we talk to

Maurice Gray so that we can eliminate him from our investigation.'

'I see,' nodded Uncle John unhelpfully.

Jack said, 'If he's not here now, can you tell me when you're expecting him back?'

'I'm not expecting him back.'

'Then do you happen to know where we could find him?'

'I'm sorry, I regret not.'

At that moment, Cordelia appeared, gliding across the hallway in her striking black evening gown. 'John,' she said, 'do you have to leave the door open? Netty's complaining of the draught.'

She took one look at George and Jack, and smiled vaguely, her eyes already moving on to something else. 'I'm Cordelia Gray; Maurice Gray's sister. Who, pray, are you?'

Jack stared at her in fascination. He tried to look away from her, but found that he couldn't. He tried to think conventional thoughts about her: procedural, sheriff-like thoughts, but found that he couldn't do that, either. She was so glacially self-assured; so haughtily erotic; so contemptuous. She stood with her head slightly tilted upwards, her eyes narrowed as if she found it difficult to focus on tradesmen and uninvited callers, one hand perched in a mannered fashion on her left hip. There was something about the way in which her jet-black gown was stretched between the twin blades of her pelvis, with just the slightest suggestion that it clung briefly to her swelling mound of Venus, that made Jack feel irritable and unsure of himself, off-balance, itchy.

And yet, if Elmer Tweed's story had any truth in it, and George's suspicions were correct, this woman was closely related to a psychopathic killer. It was even possible that she was implicated in the homicides herself.

Jack usually found that people who killed other people were boring and clumsy. They were never startling, like Cordelia Gray. They never made him feel socially inferior, the way that she did. Nor did they ever make him feel like prey.

Jack tried to introduce himself as clearly and as confidently as possible. 'My name's Jack Smith, ma'am. Sheriff Jack Smith, from Litchfield County. This is George Kelly, from the Darien police department.'

Cordelia's eyes returned to them briefly, but the smile didn't. 'What are you looking for?' she asked.

'We're looking for somebody called Maurice Gray.'

'Has he done anything wrong?'

'We don't know that yet, ma'am. But it's vital that we talk to him.'

Cordelia thought for a moment, and then she said, 'You can't.'

'Any good reason?' asked Jack. He was beginning to find these people very baffling and frustrating. What was more, his toes had already disappeared, and he was sure that the rest of his feet were soon going to follow. It was eight below, and still dropping.

Cordelia said, 'My dear man, you can have any reason you want. He isn't here. He *is* here but he isn't well enough to talk to strangers. He won't talk to anybody from the police without his lawyer being present. He died last year. He didn't die but he feels as if he might.'

George gave another, more vigorous sniff. 'If you'll pardon me, ma'am, none of this is very constructive. We're only trying to carry out our duty to the community.'

'Do you have a warrant for Maurice Gray's detention?' asked Cordelia coldly.

'No, ma'am, we don't.'

'Do you have a subpoena for him to appear before a judge or a jury?'

'No, ma'am, that neither.'

'What about a search warrant?'

George shook his head.

'In that case,' Cordelia told him, 'you may go. Come back only if you have the necessary papers. We have been away in Europe for a very long time, but now that we have returned to the United States, we expect to be able to enjoy all of our constitutional guarantees.'

Jack was about to say something, but George firmly squeezed his elbow and said, 'Come on, Jack. This lady's quite right. We shouldn't go making a nuisance of ourselves, not without warrants.'

Jack glanced at him, but George remained affable and avuncular. 'Here, ma'am,' he said, slipping a card out of his coat pocket and handing it to Cordelia. 'That's my number, down at headquarters. If Maurice Gray decides he might like to have a chat with us purely out of public service, then we'll be glad to hear from him. Meanwhile, we'll see what we can do to roust out some warrants.'

Cordelia refused to take the card, keeping her hands by her sides. But George was unfazed. He tucked the card back in his pocket, and beamed, and said, 'You can find me in the phone book, under *Cops*.'

There was an instant when Jack found himself locked with Cordelia in an exchange of stares as complicated and as hostile as barbed wire. Usually, Jack found it easy to read other people's eyes. The kind of people who found their way into police cells never found it necessary to conceal their feelings. If they hated your guts, it showed. But Cordelia's eyes transmitted evil of peculiar complexity; an evil that may have been no more serious than arrogance and vanity, but which could have encompassed sadistic acts of unimaginable terror.

'Let's go, Jack,' said George, and for the first time Jack understood that for all his offhandedness, George was as cautious of Cordelia as he was. 'Let's go find some coffee, before our butts fall off.'

Jack and George walked away from the house and back down the snowy drive. Jack turned round as the front doors slammed shut behind them, but George grabbed his arm again, and pulled him along beside him.

'Now that is a lady who could make a man's toes curl,' Jack remarked. George raised his fingers to his lips, and indicated that they wait until they got to the car before they discussed it.

'Morticia isn't in it,' he agreed.

They reached George's Chevy Silverado, and climbed aboard. The windscreen was already dense with freshly fallen snow.

'I'll bet you two months' salary that was Maurice Gray's Cadillac parked outside there and another two months' salary that Maurice Gray was home,' said Jack, as George started up the engine, switched on the windscreen wipers and pulled away from The Wilderlings in a tight, crunching circle.

'Sure it was, and sure he is. You don't have to bet me money,' said George.

'Then why did we beat the retreat so easily?'

George said, 'Hand me those cigarettes, will you?' He shook one out of the packet with his right hand, and propped it between his thick, comfortable lips. 'We beat the retreat because those people are very wealthy and because they're not stupid, and also because we won't get a search warrant out for all the snow on Stratford Street.'

'We have Elmer Tweed's testimony.'

'That won't count for chickenshit, not when we're trying to get a warrant against the Gray family.'

George lit up his cigarette, and jostled it from one side of his mouth to the other, using only his lips. 'The Grays may have been living in Europe for seventy-odd years, but they still have plenty of influence here. They own a lot of land and a lot of property and there are quite a few families around Darien who still count them as their friends.'

'Did you find out *why* they went to live in Europe?' asked Jack.

George blew smoke, and coughed. 'Nobody knows for sure. I looked it up in the newspaper morgue, but there wasn't even a mention that they'd left. One week the Grays were being regularly reported as a leading local family, the next thing, they were gone.'

'Does anybody remember them personally? Any old-timers?'

'I managed to find one, Mrs Elizabeth Cartwright. She lives in Stamford now, but in the old days she and her family used to live right next door to The Wilderlings, in a house they used to call The Juggs. She used to play in the Grays' orchard when she was a girl, and she says she remembers some of the ladies of the family promenading through the apple trees in August. Beautiful women they were, that's what Mrs Cartwright says. Beautiful women. And she remembers the father of the family, Algernon Gray, and his wife Isobel. She remembers some cousins, too. She played with them once, with hoops, even though they didn't visit The Wilderlings too often. A girl called Ermintrude; she doesn't recall the rest of the names. But anyway, she went to play there one day and all the trunks were packed and waiting outside in the drive, and the whole family just took off, cousins and all, and she never saw them again. She remembers the family seemed very upset, though, the day they left. Isobel Gray was wearing a black veil over her hat, and she was crying.'

Jack sat back in his seat, his right foot resting against the wheel-arch, and blew out his cheeks in tiredness and frustration. 'How about immigration? Did you have any luck with them?'

'Not a thing. The Gray family flew into Boston on 18 November on a Sabena flight direct from Brussels. All their passports and customs documents were in order. None of the family have any criminal record in Europe, none of them belongs to the Communist Party, none of them is known to be affiliated with any subversive or illegal group. They weren't carrying dope, guns, knives or pornography.'

Jack said, 'Maybe I'm just kidding myself. Maybe Maurice Gray doesn't have anything to do with these skinning murders at all.'

'Maybe he doesn't,' George agreed. 'But I don't think we should let this one go until we find out a little bit more about the Gray family.'

'George, this isn't your problem.'

'I know it isn't my problem. But I'm curious, that's all. Those people looked interesting to me. Didn't they look interesting to you? You don't see people like that every day, even in Darien. Very chic, did you notice? Evening dress, expensive perfume, yet the house is still looking pretty run-down. Do you know what they remind me of? The Addams Family. I wouldn't be surprised if they had a butler called Lurch.'

'You're up to something,' said Jack.

'I'm just satisfying my natural and desirable interest in local affairs,' George told him. 'I'm supposed to police this district, right? In that case, I need to know everything that's going on. Who lives here, what kind of people they are.'

'So what are you proposing?'

They could see a garage ahead, its pale light blurry in the evening snow. 'You want a coffee?' asked George, and Jack said, 'Sure.'

They pulled up outside the small diner that was attached to the garage, and climbed down from the car. As they walked across the untrodden snow to the doorway, George laid his arm around Jack's shoulder and said, 'Listen, go back to Litchfield for a few days, at least until Christmas is over. I need a little more time, that's all, to see if I can't pull together enough evidence for you to go for a warrant.'

'How come you're so interested?' said Jack, his hand on the diner doorhandle.

George smiled. 'I'm just interested, that's all. That woman told me no dice today, and in my book no dice is a challenge.'

'So what are you going to do?'

'I'm going to make believe that the Judge of Natural Justice has just issued me with a valid warrant to search The Wilderlings from attic to basement, and all stops in between.'

'What happens if somebody finds out what you're up to?'

'They won't. I wasn't trained in midtown Manhattan for nothing.'

'Well, I'm not sure that I like the idea of your taking the risk. Besides which, any evidence you find will be inadmissible. Illegal search.'

'There are ways of making it admissible, believe me.'

Jack half opened the diner door, and somebody inside called out, 'Are you coming in, asshole, or are you going out?'

Jack said to George, 'Let's get that coffee. But two words of warning. One, don't do it. Two, don't get *caught* doing it.'

George playfully slapped his cheeks. 'You're talking to a pro here, Jack my boy. Believe me. We'll get our own back on those haughty-talking Grays, fair and square. Well, square, if not fair.'

They said very little to each other on the way back to George's headquarters. They shook hands and wished each other a happy Christmas, and then Jack collected his car from the car park and headed back to Torrington. The snow had died away again now, and he found that he could drive quite fast, although he was alone on the highway, a single car in a world of deathly white.

He knew that he should have insisted that George stay away from The Wilderlings. He almost felt like calling him up when he got back to Torrington. His worst fear was that George would find clear-cut evidence that linked Maurice Gray with the skinning murders, but that it would be thrown out of court because George had obtained it by subterfuge, violating Maurice Gray's legal and constitutional rights. On the other hand, he knew that Elmer Tweed was an unreliable witness with a shaky past, and that no judge would grant them a warrant of any kind on the basis of Tweed's half-hysterical ramblings about hypodermic needles and roaring noises, and inconclusive third-party conversations about the beauty of skin.

They needed more, much more; and he simply prayed that George would be able to dig it up.

It was ten minutes past eleven when he arrived back at headquarters. He eased himself stiffly out of the driving seat, and walked with a weary limp into the reception area. Norman Goldberg was sitting behind the desk, talking to somebody on the telephone; but he raised his hand as Jack came in, to indicate that he wanted to talk to him.

'Yes, ma'am,' Norman was saying. 'Well, I'm sorry, ma'am. No, it's not, I'm afraid. No. You'll have to take it up with your husband. Well, yes, you could wake him up now, but why don't you wait until morning?'

Jack leaned on the desk and dry-washed his face with his hands.

'What's cooking?' he asked.

'That lady wanted to know if we could arrest her husband.'

'Why should she want to have us arrest her husband?'

'He came home from an Elks meeting, skidded on his own front driveway and rear-ended her brand-new Topaz.'

Jack grunted in amusement. 'I wonder whether that comes under domestic disturbance or traffic accident. Anything else?'

'Yes. You had a message from Dr Serling, out at New Milford. He says that he wants to talk to you about some kind of medical incident that happened this afternoon.'

'Was it urgent?'

'He said soonest, if you could spare the time. He's at Litchfield County, extension 422.'

Jack yawned. 'Okay, then. Can you put me through?'

Norman punched out the number. While he waited to be connected, he said, 'How did it go with Maurice Gray?'

'It didn't. We went to the house, but his family said that he wasn't home, and that even if he was, he wasn't going to talk to us.'

'Well, you guessed that they might be awkward, didn't you?'

Jack took out his chewing-gum and unwrapped a

stick. 'I guess so. It was the way they did it, though, that rubbed my fur up all the wrong way. George and I might just as well have been a couple of Fuller brush salesmen, for all the respect they showed us.'

'Crime is a buyer's market these days, Sheriff.'

Norman got through to the hospital, and after a short delay he was transferred to Dr Serling. He handed the phone to Jack, and then sat back with his hands clasped over his pot-belly.

'Dr Serling? Sheriff Jack Smith, from Torrington.'

'Ah, thank you for calling, Sheriff. We've met a few times, you and I. Remember the Cancer Research Cook-out at Kent Furnace? We had quite a talk there about post-mortems.'

'Yes, Doctor. I remember. What seems to be the problem?'

'Well,' said Dr Serling, 'I've had to deal with a serious case of self-mutilation here today. A young paraplegic patient of mine called Ben Miller. He was paralysed from the waist down a few years back when he fell off a roof, and ever since then he's been depressed and occasionally hysterical – understandably, of course, since his whole future was taken away from him.'

'So what's happened?' Jack asked impatiently.

'What's happened is that he's cut up his own face, so seriously that the surgeons thought earlier on this evening that he might not live. He's lost a whole lot of blood, and his nervous system is traumatized, and he's still in a state of psychological and physiological crisis.'

Jack rubbed his forehead. He could feel the deep-seated beginnings of a bad headache. 'I'm sorry to hear that, Doctor. I'm not quite sure what I can do about it.'

'Well – I hope this doesn't sound ridiculous –'

'No, no, Doctor, believe me –'

'I heard, you see, that you were involved in trying to

solve these terrible murders in which people were skinned alive –'

'That's correct.'

'Well, Ben Miller, before he committed this act of self-mutilation, had been growing increasingly anxious for several days – first of all that somebody or something had come back, somebody or something which was threatening him; and then this afternoon that they wanted his skin, and that whatever happened they weren't going to get it.'

Jack slowly stood up straight. Norman sensed that he was suddenly interested in what Dr Serling was saying, and straightened up, too.

'What did he say, precisely?' Jack asked.

'He said, "Don't come anywhere near." He said, "Whatever you do, don't touch my skin."'

Jack was silent for a moment, then he said, 'Was Miller physically or mentally ill in any way before he mutilated himself?'

'I thought that he might be. It was my suspicion that he was suffering from the side-effects of a renal breakdown. But when they operated on him this evening, the surgeons discovered that his kidneys were functioning extremely well, given his paralysed condition.'

'Was he very suggestible?'

'He wasn't particularly stable, if that's what you're trying to ask me. He could occasionally fly off into terrible tempers; but then many chairbound people do.'

Jack tried to make himself clearer. 'What I'm actually suggesting is that he might have read about the skinning murders in the news, and taken it into his head that the killer was after him, too. That does happen pretty often, even amongst completely sane people.'

Dr Serling said stiffly, 'Ben Miller isn't insane, Sheriff.'

'I'm sorry,' Jack replied. 'I didn't mean to say that he was. I'm simply saying that when a series of murders is highly publicized, it isn't uncommon for certain susceptible people to have – what shall we call it? – an exaggerated fear of being the next on the list.'

'You're quite a psychiatrist, Sheriff.'

'I have to be,' Jack retorted. He was too tired for sarcasm.

Dr Serling said, 'I'm sorry. I accept your point. And, after all, what I'm trying to suggest isn't particularly logical. I accept that too. But Ben Miller, after the accident in which he broke his spine, was very close to the point of death. Clinically, for a very short period of time, he was actually dead.'

'I'm not sure that I'm following you, Doctor.'

'Well,' said Dr Serling, 'it isn't easy to explain. But those accident victims who have technically died almost always emerge from their experience with a sharply heightened sensitivity to death and danger. There are many recorded instances of it. There was a woman in Seattle only last year who managed to save her child by pulling him away from a new construction site, just seconds before the scaffolding collapsed. She claimed afterwards that she had actually *seen* the disaster before it had started to happen.'

'Doctor, this is very interesting stuff, but –'

'Listen to me, please,' Dr Serling interrupted. 'I'm as sceptical as you are; probably more so. But I've been talking to Ben Miller's mother all evening while the surgeons have been operating on Ben, and I believe that Ben's case is at least worth a look. Ben may possibly have been able to sense something or work something out in his mind that you, with your usual police procedures, may have missed.'

'Doctor,' said Jack, 'I'll tell you what I'll do. I'll come

around to the hospital tomorrow morning, round about eleven o'clock, and talk with you some more. Maybe I can get to see Ben Miller, too. Don't think that I don't appreciate your call. I do. I'm a little pooped, that's all. I'm always interested in theories that come off the wall. I'm even a little bit interested in the occult myself. My wife has a friend who tells a mean fortune. Tea-leaves, cards, even the way the hairs grow out of your nose.'

'Very well,' said Dr Serling. 'Make it ten-thirty, and I can be there. Room 454, at Litchfield County.'

Jack put down the phone. Norman said, 'What was all that about?'

'I don't know. Dr Serling thinks one of his patients may be psychic or something; and that he might have picked up some kind of – what do you call it? – *aura*.'

'Aura?'

'Oh, search me. I think I'm going to go home to bed.'

'There was one more thing,' said Norman, leafing through the pad of telephone messages.

Jack waited, halfway across the reception area, his car keys raised in the palm of his hand.

'Here it is,' said Norman. 'Two telephone calls from Aaron Halperin – you know him, that picture restorer guy out at Bantam, the one we keep pulling in for drunk-driving. The first message to say that somebody had stolen his cat. The second to say that he had found the cat in his garden.'

Jack could hardly believe what he was hearing. 'You're preventing me from going home to my wife because a drunken picture restorer lost his cat and then he found it again?'

'Unh-hunh,' said Norman, shaking his head. 'He found it hanging in a tree. It was skinned.'

Jack stopped jingling his keys.

'Something's going down here,' he said. 'Something

very, very unpleasant is going down here. Get me some coffee. Black, no sugar. I'm just going to call home to tell Nancy that I'm okay. Then I'm going to drive over to Litchfield County.'

'You're going now? Tonight?'

'Do you think I'm going to be able to sleep if I don't?'

Seventeen

Litchfield, 18 December

Dr Serling was hurrying out of the hospital as Jack arrived. He was crossing the brightly lit reception area, tugging on his brown tweed coat and jamming his crumpled brown fisherman's hat on to his head. They almost collided in the swing-doors, and Dr Serling's case caught Jack a sharp knock on the left knee.

'Sheriff Smith!' Dr Serling exclaimed. Then he frowned and peered at Jack more narrowly. 'It *is* Sheriff Smith, isn't it?'

Jack rubbed his knee. 'Yes. I'm glad I caught you.'

'I didn't expect you until the morning,' said Dr Serling, extending his hand. 'You've changed, haven't you, since the last time we met? Didn't you used to sport a moustache?'

'I've lost about twenty pounds in weight,' said Jack. 'I gave up beer, and maple syrup, and corn chips, and I started coaching a kids' football team. Would you believe the Harwinton Hackers?'

'Tonight, I think I'm pretty much ready to believe anything,' said Dr Serling. He checked his watch and said, 'Look, it's late. If you want to see Ben Miller tonight, you'd better come up and meet Dr Schuhmacher right away. He's the surgeon who did the operation. He was washing up to go home the last I saw him.'

Dr Serling ushered Jack over to the shiny glass-fronted lifts and pushed the red-lighted button for UP. Jack looked around while they waited. Litchfield County was one of the most modern medical facilities in New England, with gleaming white-tiled floors and a huge abstract statue of twisted bronze in the centre of the reception area, entitled *Healing.* Dr Serling thought that it looked like a bay horse with a chronic case of the staggers, but he had never said so.

There was a strong aroma of synthetic apple-blossom around, and a constant *a cappella* chorus of dissonant squeaks from the nurses' vinyl-soled shoes.

'This case has upset me,' Dr Serling told Jack, leaning back against the rear wall of the lift as they rose up to the fourth floor.

'Believe me, this case has upset me, too,' Jack responded, unwrapping another stick of gum.

Dr Serling nodded, and kept on nodding, as if to say that he knew, he knew. 'I never believed much in psychic phenomena,' he remarked. 'You know, levitation, ectoplasm, that kind of thing. What I really believe in is the human spirit. I believe that our minds and our bodies have extraordinary powers, which in everyday life are only half understood. When you run a country practice like mine, you come across all kinds of wild and wonderful things, and most of the time you can only guess how they might have occurred. Do you know something, last year, out in South Kent, an elderly woman patient of mine claimed she had dug a tumour out of her own stomach with nothing more than a wooden spoon? She showed me the spoon, and she showed me the tumour in a pickle jar, and she showed me her stomach, too, with a small red scar that was perfectly healed.'

The lift reached the fourth floor, and they stepped

out. It was quieter up here, although the smell of synthetic apple-blossom was just as distinctive. Jack sniffed, and Dr Serling said, 'The hospital administrators believe that people would rather suffer in an orchard than in a public toilet.'

He walked in front, swinging his medical bag. 'I was always aware that Ben Miller had been mentally affected by what he had experienced, that time he almost died. And there are dozens of recorded cases where people who have been brought back right from the very brink of clinical death claim to have acquired what you might describe as "second sight". But I never would have believed any of it, not for certain – if I hadn't talked to Ben this afternoon, and heard what his mother had to say.'

'And what *did* his mother have to say?' asked Jack.

Dr Serling stopped halfway along the corridor and looked at Jack with a face as grave as a country undertaker. 'She told me that ever since his accident Ben had been able to forecast storms, and to tell her in advance whenever one of her friends was going to get sick, or die; and that he had predicted auto wrecks, out on the highway, and fires, and all kinds of disasters.'

'And you believed her?'

'Not at first. I asked her why she had never told me about it before, and she said that she had always been afraid to, in case I thought Ben was crazy and had him committed.'

'I suppose that's a plausible explanation,' said Jack. 'But it's still no reason to believe that it was true.'

Dr Serling said, in a quiet and measured voice, 'Mrs Miller also told me that Ben had felt sorry for me, the day my daughter died.'

'Your daughter isn't dead though, is she? Didn't I read something about her last week in the *Litchfield*

Sentinel? She was organizing some fair or something, wasn't she, for cancer research?'

Dr Serling nodded. 'That's the daughter that everybody knows. But, years ago, when I was still at medical school, I conceived another daughter. I never saw her, scarcely ever heard from her. Her name was Fay, and she lived in Gainesville, Florida. She died about a year ago from multiple sclerosis.'

'Is there any possible way that Ben Miller could have found that out?'

Dr Serling shook his head. 'Nobody knew; except for Fay, and her mother, and me. Now you know, too, but you're the only other person who does.'

'So you genuinely believe that Ben Miller may be psychic, and that he's been picking up threatening feelings from this killer?'

'I don't know,' said Dr Serling. 'I may be making a fool of myself. I may be acting overemotional about Fay. I didn't really allow myself to grieve for her, and believing in Ben Miller's psychic abilities may be a way of expressing my grief.'

Jack pushed his gum from one side of his mouth to the other. 'Physician, stop trying to heal thyself,' he said. 'If Ben Miller knew something about you which it was impossible for him to know, then what you're trying to suggest about his psychic abilities may not be as wacky as you think.'

'Do you think he might be able to help you to catch the killer?' asked Dr Serling.

Jack shrugged. 'Right now, I'm just about ready to try anything.'

'Come along and take a look at him, then,' said Dr Serling. 'Dr Schuhmacher has him in intensive care.'

They walked side by side down to the end of the corridor. There was a waiting area there, with potted yuccas and a coffee-table and leather-covered sofas, and an original print on the wall of Geoffrey Callender's *Sunflowers and Cats*. The two cats in the picture were both marmalade cats, with intense green eyes. Mrs Miller was sitting right beneath the picture, looking white and distraught, while a grey-haired woman in a plaid overcoat and spectacles sat close beside her, holding her hands to comfort her.

'This is Mrs Miller,' said Dr Serling. 'I've allowed her to stay for a while, at least until Dr Kellstrom comes on duty.'

'Mrs Miller,' said Jack, nodding sympathetically. 'I'm Sheriff Jack Smith. I'm real sorry to hear what happened to your son. It must have been a bad shock.'

Mrs Miller looked back at Jack distractedly, but didn't reply. The woman next to her said, 'She's been sedated, Sheriff. I'll be taking her home in just a moment, as soon as Dr Schuhmacher has made his last examination.'

'This is Mrs Guthrie,' said Dr Serling. 'She and her husband will be taking care of Mrs Miller while Ben's in hospital.'

Just then, Dr Schuhmacher appeared; a small blackbearded man with spectacles as strong as magnifying-glasses. His black hair was neatly and systematically combed over a widening bald patch.

'Dr Serling?' he said in surprise. 'I thought you'd gone.'

'I was about to, but then I met my friend the sheriff here. He decided that he'd very much like to take a look at Ben Miller tonight, if that's agreeable.'

Dr Schuhmacher glanced towards Mrs Miller, and then said, 'I don't see why not. Listen – let me talk to the mother, give her some reassurance and get her off home. Then I'll take you in.'

Whatever the surgeon said to Mrs Miller, she and Mrs Guthrie soon left, and Dr Schuhmacher came back to Jack and Dr Serling, busily cleaning his spectacles on his green jacket.

'She needs to rest,' he said. 'She's had a really traumatic day. In fact, I'm more worried about her than I am about her son.'

He led the way further along the corridor, and then smartly turned right through a pair of swing-doors marked *Intensive Care*. Jack said, 'How's the son shaping up?'

Dr Schuhmacher said, 'Badly. He was making progress for a while, but in the past hour or so he's started to show signs of serious deterioration. Dr Ahuja's with him now, as well as the cardiac crisis team, but to be honest I don't think that his system is going to be able to stand the shock. He's a paraplegic, remember, and his heart and kidneys are already in a bad way. Now he's suffering from every kind of physiological emergency you can think of. His lungs collapsed twice during the operation, and that almost finished him off.'

'What do you give him?' asked Jack.

Dr Schuhmacher stared short-sightedly at Jack through his fishbowl glasses. 'It isn't up to me to *give* him anything,' he replied. 'It's all down to good medical care, and the survivability of his own system.'

Jack was unfazed by Dr Schuhmacher's attitude. He had never yet come across a surgeon who liked policemen. 'Give me an educated guess,' he said.

Dr Schuhmacher looked at Dr Serling, obviously displeased, but Dr Serling gave him an encouraging nod.

'Very well then,' he said. 'Six or seven hours, at the outside.'

'Is he conscious?'

Dr Schuhmacher shook his head.

'Is he likely to regain consciousness?'

'I don't think so. And, even if he did, he wouldn't be able to talk to you. His mouth was very severely cut up, and at the moment he's unable to move his lips.'

Jack tiredly massaged the back of his neck. The Cherokee's passenger window didn't fit properly, and a cold draught had been blowing down his back all the way from Darien. 'All right,' he said. 'Let's take a look at him.'

Dr Schuhmacher led the way through to the observation room, next to the intensive care unit where Ben Miller was now struggling to stay alive. Jack walked up to the window and stared at Ben Miller in silence. Ben was surrounded by doctors and nurses and blue-coated medics from Litchfield County's cardio-vascular crisis team. All that Jack could see of him behind the gleaming complexities of equipment was a head, bandaged up like the Invisible Man, with two dark and impenetrable eyeholes.

'He *felt* something,' Jack said, more to himself than to Dr Serling. 'He *felt* something, the same way that I felt something.'

'You felt something, too?' asked Dr Serling.

'About a couple of days ago, after I had my fortune read. The cards were full of bad luck, you know? Beware of strangers, and stuff like that. Then I cut my hand on one of the cards, and practically bled to death all over my wife's new rug. And I just had this *feeling*, you know –'

Dr Serling raised an eyebrow and turned to Dr Schuhmacher; but all Dr Schuhmacher could say was, 'Excuse me, I have to get home now. I have a mastectomy at nine in the morning.'

When he had gone, leaving the door swinging behind him, Jack said to Dr Serling, 'I have an idea. If you're really serious about Ben Miller – if you really believe that he has some supernatural sense – then I want you to back me up.'

'I'll go along with anything, within reason.'

Jack inclined his head towards Ben Miller. 'He's only got six or seven hours, right? And if you ask me, Dr Schuhmacher was being optimistic. He's not going to regain consciousness, so we won't be able to ask him exactly what he felt, or what he saw, or what it is that made him so scared.'

'Go on,' said Dr Serling suspiciously.

'All I'm thinking is this: that if his psychic senses are as strong as you seem to believe they could be, we might be able to talk to him while he's still out for the count.'

'I'm not sure that I understand.'

Jack said, 'I'm a well-balanced, well-trained, non-superstitious, normality-oriented person. I don't believe in magic and I don't believe in ghosts. But I'm beginning to convince myself that there *are* powers and there *are* auras and there *are* weird influences that make themselves felt from right outside of our normal experience. And why not, you know? They may be happening all around us, all the time, and most of us would never notice. You ought to try interviewing seven different witnesses to the same auto accident. You wouldn't even think the accident happened to the same cars on the same day, on the same goddamned street.'

'Well, I'm inclined to agree with you,' said Dr Serling. 'But the point is, how do we communicate with Ben Miller while he's still completely unconscious?'

Jack thrust his hands into his back trouser pockets. Then, as diffidently as if he were suggesting that they go across the street for a late-night cup of coffee, he said, 'We call my wife's friend Pat down here, the one who does the tea-leaves and everything, and we hold a what-do-you-call-it. A séance.'

'A séance? In Litchfield County Hospital? Are you kidding me? Dr Schuhmacher would haemorrhage!'

'Does Dr Schuhmacher have to know?'

'I don't see how we could possibly arrange it *without* him knowing.'

'Could he be convinced?'

Dr Serling pressed his hand against his forehead and thought for a moment, and then said decisively, 'No. There isn't a chance. He has his professional reputation to think of, not to mention the reputation of Litchfield County.'

'You have a professional reputation, too; and so do I.'

Dr Serling said, 'Yes. But we're the kind of men to whom practical results are more important than reputations. That's not to say that Jerry Schuhmacher isn't a very fine surgeon; he is. But the kind of clients he has to deal with wouldn't take particularly kindly to the idea that he believed in black magic.'

'Nobody said this was black magic.'

'Nobody said that it wasn't.'

'Listen,' said Jack, 'I was reading about this just last week. Police forces all over the world have been using psychics to track down criminals and turn up missing children, and who knows what else. They even had a seminar on it last year, in Phoenix.'

'Well, I really don't know,' said Dr Serling. 'I mean – quite apart from the ethics of it – do you think that it could work?'

'We don't have any other way of talking to Ben, do we? Maybe it won't work. But I know that Pat's pretty good at it. There isn't any harm in trying.'

They were about to leave the observation room and go back to the waiting area when there was a quick knock at the door, and Vincent appeared, his expensive black overcoat sparkling with melted snowflakes.

'Ah, Dr Serling. The surgical sister said that you might be here.'

'How are you, Mr Pearson?' asked Dr Serling, and shook his hand. 'This is Sheriff Jack Smith.'

'I believe we've met, briefly,' said Vincent, and nodded to Jack in greeting.

Jack acknowledged Vincent's nod but didn't particularly care for the lord-of-the-manor way in which Vincent had walked into the observation room and taken over the situation as if he had some kind of royal authority.

'I guess you came to visit Ben,' said Dr Serling.

'Have you seen Mrs Miller?' asked Vincent, tugging off his gloves.

'She's still in shock, but Martha Guthrie's taken her home.'

Vincent peered through the glass at Ben Miller, at the tangle of life-support machinery, and at the doctors and nurses who were clustered around him. He remained silent for a long time, and then he turned away.

Dr Serling said, 'Ben's already had his entire blood supply replaced three times.'

Vincent unbuttoned his overcoat and looked at Dr Serling with a serious face. 'They don't hold out much hope, then?'

'Six or seven hours,' Jack told him. Then, 'We're a little pushed here, if you really don't mind.'

Vincent nodded, not understanding that (in the politest way that Jack knew how) he was being asked to leave. Jack was anxious to call Pat, and to get her down to the hospital to start a séance, but he wasn't at all sure what Vincent's reaction would be, if Vincent found out what they wanted to do; and apart from that he wasn't at all sure that he wanted Vincent to become involved. To Jack, Vincent represented New York, and money, and all the people whose wealth Jack was paid to protect, even though they visited Connecticut only rarely and made about as much contribution to the life of the rural community as the Pope did to little-league baseball.

'You know, it probably sounds absurd,' said Vincent. 'But I feel partly responsible for what's happened to Ben.'

'How could *you* be responsible?' Jack asked, impatiently. 'The man disfigured himself.'

'Well, it doesn't have very much to do with logic, or scientific reasoning, or police procedure for that matter. But – over the past week or so – well, I find it very difficult to explain it – but all kinds of very unpleasant and tragic things have been happening, not only here in Connecticut but in New York, as well. I mean truly bizarre and inexplicable things, and frightening, too, and somehow they all seem to centre around me.'

He paused, and then he said expressively, 'I feel as if I'm at the eye of a storm; as if I'm surrounded by a great and quickening whirl of unnaturally bad fortune. Almost as if I've attracted it.'

'Bad fortune?' asked Jack. The question wasn't meant as cynically as it sounded. Bad fortune was exactly how *he* would have described the feeling that was rising in the air. Vincent, however, interpreted the query as the natural scepticism of a small-town law-enforcement officer.

'Perhaps I'm imagining it,' he said. 'But when you look at what's happened to Ben here . . .'

'What exactly do you define as bad fortune?' Jack asked him.

'Well,' said Vincent carefully, smoothing the palms of his hands together. 'My assistant in New York died at the weekend. He was quite young; in his twenties. No history of illness. But when I went to call on him on Monday morning, he was dead. Not only that, but . . . well, he had badly decomposed.'

Jack raised an eyebrow. Vincent, remembering Edward's body with a slow spasm of greasy internal disgust, said, in a low and hurried voice, 'He was almost completely devoured by maggots.'

'After being dead for how long?' asked Jack.

'No more than forty-eight hours. Probably less.'

'So what did the New York police have to say about it?'

Vincent ran his hand through his hair. 'I think they wanted to believe that I killed him myself, several days before. Unfortunately for them, too many people had seen him alive, right up until a couple of days before I found him.'

Jack said, 'Any clues? Any witnesses? Anything at all?' He was trying to assert himself over Vincent's suaveness by being abrasive and professional.

'A woman was seen leaving Edward's apartment. A very beautiful woman, apparently, dressed in black, very pale in the face. But that was all.'

'You said there were other incidents,' Jack reminded him.

Vincent said hoarsely, 'Yes,' and told Jack and Dr Serling about Van Gogh, the cat; and about the Waldegrave portrait. 'The cat was dangling in the tree, it had been hideously mutilated.'

'How, mutilated?'

'Well, somebody had – skinned it.'

269

Jack watched Vincent intently. He was looking for any flicker of insincerity; any hint at all that Vincent might be lying, or joking, or centre-staging. But Vincent's fear of what was happening was genuine and just as strong as Jack's, although he was expressing it in a different way. Unlike Jack, he felt himself to be responsible for it; and perhaps he was. But Jack could tell a liar, and he could tell a fraud, and he could tell a florid eccentric, too, and Vincent Pearson was none of these.

He said in a level tone, 'If it's any consolation, Mr Pearson, I believe you.'

Vincent looked up. 'You believe everything? Even the way that Edward died?'

'Why should you lie?' Jack asked him.

'To conceal the fact that I killed Edward myself,' Vincent suggested.

Jack shook his head. For a long while, he stood with his arms folded and looked at Vincent and said nothing. Then he said, 'Tell me something – that woman who was seen leaving Edward Merriam's apartment – mid-thirties, is that right? Dressed in black? Very pale complexion, but outstanding in appearance?'

'That was the first description I was given; although the lady denied it later. I guess she just didn't want trouble.'

Jack said, 'I think I've seen her.'

'You think you've *seen* her?' Vincent repeated. 'Where, for goodness' sakes?'

'Today. Well, yesterday now. I drove down to Darien to interview a man named Maurice Gray in connection with these skinning murders we've been having around here. I didn't get to see Maurice Gray himself, but I did get to see the lady of the house, Ms

Cordelia Gray, and she answers that description pretty well exactly.'

Thoughtfully, Vincent said, 'There's a connection here, isn't there? I mean, sure, it takes quite a sideways leap of the imagination. But when you add them up – all of these individual incidents – they seem like they're part of the same jigsaw.'

Jack remarked, 'I'm interested in what you said about Ben Miller shouting "They're back". The Gray family have only just returned from seventy years in Europe.'

'He said more,' Dr Serling added. 'He said, *Don't touch my skin.* He was frantic about it. *Don't touch my skin.* Then – when I asked him who he was frightened of – he said *all twelve.*'

'All twelve?' frowned Jack. 'What do you think he meant by that?'

Vincent felt another piece of the same sinister jigsaw slot silently into place. 'There are twelve people in the Waldegrave portrait,' he said.

'The Grays,' said Dr Serling; although he needn't have voiced it out loud.

'I'd like to take a look at that portrait,' Jack told Vincent. 'Maybe I can call by your house sometime during the morning. Meanwhile –'

Vincent said, 'That sounds like you're trying to get rid of me, that "meanwhile –"'

'Well, no, but –'

'Tell him, Sheriff,' Dr Serling put in. 'From what he's said to us here tonight, I think he's more likely to help us than stand in our way.'

Jack hesitated. He felt rural and unsophisticated in front of Vincent, apart from being dog-tired, and he would rather have kept the idea of holding a séance to himself. Vincent looked like the kind of man who might have friends in influential places; the kind of man who probably played golf with the mayor and went to cocktail parties with district attorneys. Still, what the hell. If the séance didn't work, nobody would be any the wiser; and if it did, the ends could well justify the means.

'We've been thinking of holding an impromptu séance,' he said, trying to sound as level and as matter-of-fact as possible. 'Well, not exactly a séance, but a kind of a telepathy session to see if we can communicate with Ben before he dies. Ben knows something, for sure, and if there's any chance that we can tap into his mind and find out what it is . . .'

Vincent stared at Jack in silence.

'Well, the point is,' Jack went on, embarrassed, 'whatever we find out – that's if we *do* find anything out – won't be usable as evidence in a court of law. I mean, can you imagine presenting a judge with a transcript of a séance? But it may give us a lead. It may give us enough to turn up some concrete evidence; and once we've got that, we're on our way.'

Vincent said, 'Forgive me for being obtuse, but how are you planning to hold a séance in a hospital? Especially when the person you're trying to contact isn't even dead yet, and happens to be surrounded by medical staff?'

'It's a shot in the dark,' Jack told him. 'Maybe it won't work, maybe it will. But police forces all over the world use psychics to help them out.'

'Well,' said Vincent. 'I don't think it's up to me to be sceptical.'

They returned to the waiting area. Jack went to call Pat, while Vincent and Dr Serling found a drinks machine outside on the staircase, and bought themselves a root beer each, which was all that it had to offer.

'Do you know something, I always hated root beer,' Dr Serling remarked. Vincent couldn't keep his eyes off the two marmalade cats in the picture on the wall. He knew that it was just a coincidence, and not much of a coincidence at that; but they still made him feel uneasy. It was as if the world he lived in were suddenly revealing itself to be crowded with secret and threatening signs, which he had never noticed before. He could understand how people became paranoid; how they could interpret everyday events and everyday objects as warnings that something disastrous was about to happen.

Jack came back from the phone. He was red in the face from the embarrassing and difficult task of having persuaded Pat to leave her bed in the middle of a freezing cold December night and drive over to Litchfield County Hospital.

'Believe me, Pat honey, if this wasn't a matter of life and death, I wouldn't ask you.'

'Believe me, Jack honey, if this turns out to be a wild turkey shoot, you're going to regret that you asked me for the rest of your natural life.'

Jack went to buy himself a root beer while they waited. It was 2.07 in the morning, and outside the windows of Litchfield County Hospital, the snow was tumbling thickly and silently on to a sleeping world.

'Do you really think that a séance is a good idea?' Vincent asked Jack. He remembered his grandmother with her ouija board and her Tarot cards, and the way she whispered to herself whenever she was telling her own fortune.

Jack stuck his hands in his back trouser pockets and looked at Vincent belligerently. 'Sure it's a good idea. Do you have a better idea?'

He paused, and then he said, 'Besides, I've seen Pat work. I've seen her talk to dead people's relatives. If anyone can get Ben Miller to talk to us, she can.'

Vincent said, 'Very well. As long as you think that we can bear to hear what he's got to say.'

Eighteen

George Kelly arrived outside the gates of The
Wilderlings at a little after three o'clock in
the morning, and killed the engine of his Silverado with
a twist of his wrist. The snow was lighter and wetter in
Darien than it was in Litchfield, and it formed dewy
droplets on his windscreen. George crushed out his
cigarette and noisily cleared his throat.

He had picked his time carefully. At three o'clock in
the morning, even insomniacs started to nod off. It
was the deadest and coldest hour of the night, eleven
hours since darkness had fallen, and still another four
and a half hours to go before it grew light. George eased
himself out of the driver's seat and stepped down into
the snow. He was equipped with a flashlight, a small
black leather case of lock-picking instruments, and a
ten-inch screwdriver. Wedged between his podgy back
and his broad leather belt, he carried a hefty .357 Python
revolver, its muzzle nestling in the cleavage of his
considerable buttocks. He felt calm and peaceful and
confident. He liked it when he was challenged. He knew
that he was professional enough to be able to get his
own back and still come up smelling like lavender. Even
after that shooting in New York, when he had gunned
down the Loretta brothers, all four of them, for no

particular reason other than to save himself the nuisance of having to arrest them next time they held up a grocery store, nobody had been able to establish anything for certain. George had been too careful.

Because of the snow, the Grays had left their wrought-iron gates open. The curlicues of elaborately decorated metal were picked out in semicircular crusts of ice. George walked between the gates, and straight up the drive, although he kept himself close to the shadowy cypress trees which bordered it, just in case somebody happened to be looking out of a front window. His breath smoked in the darkness, and his boots made felty squeaking noises on the snow.

As he approached the front of the house, he left the drive and crossed the lawn on the left-hand side, passing a wide flight of stone steps, and a pair of carved stone urns heaped with snow. Soon he was skirting around the back, crouching behind the low brick wall which bordered the patio. Not far away, in the centre of the lawn, there was a circular ornamental pond; its surface frozen as blind as a leper's eye. There were no lights in the house anywhere; every window was black. Leafless creeper trailed down the southern wall like a tangle of witch's hair. He coughed once, a high dry bark, and then suppressed another.

It took him only a few moments to find what he was looking for: a stone staircase which led down behind the kitchen to the cellar door. He stopped and listened for a moment, but the silence of the night was quite complete.

Propping his flashlight between the stair-railings opposite, so that its beam shone directly on to the corroded bronze doorplate, George took out his lock-picks and began to work on the lock. He smiled as he did so; the lock was Victorian and very simple, although it was stiff from years of disuse. It took him three minutes of concentrated picking before the levers at last relented. George coughed, and turned the handle, and the door swung open.

Taking down his flashlight, he advanced cautiously into the first room of the cellar, closing the door behind him. The circular beam illuminated whitewashed walls, and cobwebs as thick as ladies' summer scarves, and an old-fashioned sink with a wooden draining-board, on which, inexplicably, a saddle rested, its leather cracked and dry. George crossed the room and came to a second door, which was unlocked. He opened it, pausing for a moment or two when its hinges grated, listening; but there was no sound at all from the house up above him, no footsteps, no shuffling, no squeaking of stairs. He opened the door wider and shone his flashlight ahead of him down a long whitewashed corridor.

George walked as quietly and as gracefully as his bulk allowed. On either side of the corridor, there were separate storerooms with iron-barred doors, in which George could make out stacks of packing-cases and tangles of old dining-room chairs and thick bundles of folded-up curtains. There was dust everywhere: it clung like a grey and unshakable memory of times gone by. There was a smell, too: a strange suffocating smell like dying summer flowers, or pot-pourri.

In one of the storerooms, there were racks and racks of wine-bottles, most of them with crusted corks and labels illegible from years of damp and dust. He picked up one bottle, however, wiped the dust off with his hand and examined it. The label read: *Château Duhart-Milon, 1905.* George put the bottle back again. He didn't know much about wine, but he did know that anything that was over eighty years old was probably undrink-able. He rubbed two or three more labels clean, but he was unable to find a single bottle that was later than 1912.

George continued his search, poking and probing, opening up old linen chests and trunks, moving from storeroom to storeroom until he came to the very end of the corridor, where there was yet another door, locked this time, and sheeted in lead, presumably to keep out the damp.

It took him a difficult ten minutes to open the lock, but when he did so, the door opened easily, as if the hinges had recently been oiled. George stepped into the next storeroom, which was as large as all the other storerooms put together, and quickly shone his torch around.

It was drier in here, although the spiders had taken advantage of the dryness to spin their webs and nests so thickly that it was almost impossible to make out what was stacked beneath them. It was only after he had twisted a rope of spider's web around the blade of his screwdriver and dragged it stickily away that George saw the dull gleaming of gilt, and realized that this was where the Gray family had stored its pictures.

He cleared cobwebs away from two or three of them. The first showed a Bacchanalian scene in the style of Rubens, crowded with fat pink nudes and welterweight cherubs. The second showed a severe forest, dark and uncompromising, on the side of a looming mountain. The third depicted a dead child, lying in its cradle, while its distraught mother buried her face in her hands. Behind the mother, his skeletal face barely visible inside his shadowy hood, stood the Grim Reaper, with his scythe over his shoulder.

George looked all around the storeroom, but there was nothing incriminating, only scores and scores of Victorian paintings. George had never seen so many paintings in his life. He clenched his flashlight between his thighs and took out his handkerchief to wipe the sweat and dust away from his face. He coughed again, twice; and then blew his nose. It was time to search upstairs, and he didn't want to be coughing and sneezing while he was going through the bedrooms.

It took him quite a while to find the staircase that led upstairs. It was concealed behind a plain wooden door which looked just the same as every other plain wooden door in the cellar. But he mounted it at last (making sure that he closed the door behind him) and made his way up to the door at the top, which was carved oak, with a brass handle, and which presumably led out to the hallway. Taking a deep and suppressive breath, George grasped the handle and turned it. To his relief, the door was unlocked.

No goddamned security, he thought to himself. If I was a professional yegg, I could empty this whole goddamned house before breakfast, and these people would never even know.

The door from the cellar opened out right beneath the main staircase. George eased his way through it, closing it behind him, but making sure that he could open it again if he had to. Then he padded softly across the hallway, until he reached the double doors of the music room.

He had just taken hold of the handles when he thought he heard the faintest of sounds. He froze, holding his breath, his ears aching to pick up any further noises. But almost half a minute went by and he heard nothing else. The Wilderlings was the most silent of houses. Even in the snow, nothing stirred, nothing moved. The house was like a mausoleum, sealed away from the outside world, dreaming its own impenetrable dreams of times that would never return.

George maintained his sweaty grasp on the door-handles, but some extraordinary reluctance prevented him from opening the doors straight away. He had never felt like this before, and he couldn't wholly understand what the feeling was. He was cold, but there were swathes of sweat under his armpits, and the handle of his revolver was beginning to dig into the flesh of his back. He began to think for the first time that here was a challenge he would have been wiser not to accept. In fact, without knowing it, he was frightened.

He hesitated a second longer, but then he said under his breath, 'Ah, bullshit,' and swung open both of the music-room doors.

Simultaneously, with a plangent and echoing chord, the grand piano struck up the first few bars of Beethoven's Symphony No 2. in D. George stood where he was, speechless, his mouth wide open, unable to move, while gradually the music room's electric chandeliers brightened from dull orange to glittering white, tier upon tier of sparkling crystal, shining on mirrors and pictures and ornaments.

At the piano sat a middle-aged man in evening dress, very upright on the piano-stool. Beside him stood a younger man, also in evening dress, with one hand in his trouser-pocket, the other raised lightly to his chin. Next to the younger man, a little way behind him, was a young woman, quite pretty but oddly expressionless, wearing a white lace maid's cap, and what – as far down as the waist – was a black long-sleeved dress of impeccable modesty. Below the waist, however, the front of her dress had been drawn right up and tucked into her thin black leather belt, baring for anyone to see her ivory-white thighs, in black silk stockings and garters, and the dark furry triangle of her pubic hair.

Neither of the two men in evening dress appeared to think that there was anything startling or unusual about the way in which the young woman was dressed. In fact, both of them ignored her. Their attention was undividedly fastened on George.

'Good evening,' said the middle-aged man, rising from the piano-stool. 'Or should I say good *morning*?'

George could think of nothing to say. For a taut split-second, he wondered if he ought to make a run for it back down to the cellar, or even through the front door. But if he tried to escape through the cellar, they would be able to catch him easily; and he didn't know if the front door was locked or not. Besides, to run would be a *prima facie* admission of guilt. He was a police officer. He was searching the house of a suspected murderer. He might not be doing it by the book, but at least he had a good reason for being here.

The middle-aged man walked slowly towards him, his hands clasped behind his back. 'My name is Maurice Gray,' he said courteously. 'You must be one of the officers who was seeking to talk to me yesterday afternoon.'

'That's correct, sir,' stumbled George, although he could have bitten his tongue off for calling a homicide suspect 'sir'.

Maurice Gray smiled in a tight, thoughtful, displeased kind of way, and walked all the way round George, inspecting him as if he were an unsatisfactory used car.

'You won't, of course, need this,' he said, and abruptly lifted up George's anorak to tug out his revolver.

George was scratched on the small of the back by the Python's forward sights. He whipped around in pain and irritation, and snapped, 'Give me that gun back!

That's police property! You hear me? Give me that gun!'

Maurice turned the revolver this way and that, peering at it closely. 'I really don't think that I should. It strikes me as dangerous, to say the least. It also gives you a very unfair advantage.'

'I'm a police officer,' George blustered. 'If you don't return that weapon to me right now, then I'm going to have to arrest you.'

Maurice handed the Python to Henry. 'You may be a police officer when you are patrolling the streets. You may be a police officer when you are searching the houses of suspected criminals, armed with an appropriate warrant. But this morning, my dear fellow, you are nothing more than an armed intruder; and as such you have very few rights. You depend more on my personal mercy now than you do on the law. I hope you realize that.'

George said, 'I'm leaving. I'm going to turn around and I'm going to walk straight out of that door. I'll be back for the gun, with all the warrants you like.'

He turned his back on Maurice and walked smartly across the hall until he reached the front door. Maurice and Henry remained where they were, watching George with restrained amusement as he tried to open the bolts and the locks. Laura came forward and touched Henry's arm, and Henry took hold of her hand and kissed it with ice-cold lips.

After a minute of sweating and struggling, George knew that he wasn't going to be able to get out. He walked back across the hall and stood in front of Maurice Gray with his fists on his hips.

'All right,' he said, 'I admit that I was wrong to intrude. But there isn't any future in keeping me here, is there?'

Maurice inclined his head benignly. 'Not for you, I have to admit. Well, not for all of you, let me put it that way. A part of you will find its way into the scheme of immortality.'

'What are you, crazy?' George demanded. Then he looked at Laura. 'And what's this? This girl walking around showing off everything she's got. What's this? Some kind of perversion or something?'

'Perversion is only in the mind of the perverse,' remarked Henry. He deliberately let his hand stray down between Laura's thighs; and even though George tried hard not to look, he couldn't help seeing that Henry's middle finger momentarily disappeared. All the time this was happening, Henry continued to smile at him, and Laura registered nothing on her face at all, as if she were asleep with her eyes open.

'She will permit you to do the same,' said Henry. 'Whatever you ask of her, provided that I approve, she will do. Would you like her to bend over a chair, so that you can have sex with her?' He paused, and then he said, 'I don't really think that "making love" is an appropriate term for anyone dressed in a dirty wind-breaker and size 42 denims, do you?'

George said, 'You people are out of your minds. Now, you let me out of here. My wagon's outside. If it's still there by daylight, people are going to start wondering; and then they're going to come right up here, asking where I am.'

Maurice laid an arm around George's shoulders. 'The thing is, old fellow, we've already taken care of your wagon. While you were down in the cellars, we drove it around the back and put it under shelter. Nobody will ever find it, you know. By tomorrow evening, it will be completely dismantled.'

George wrenched himself away from Maurice's

embrace. He was panicky now, and crimson-faced. 'You listen to me!' he shouted. 'That vehicle is police property! You lay one finger on that vehicle, and that's an offence! The same goes for the weapon; and the same goes for me! I'm an officer of the law, and I'm warning you! I'm warning you here and now!'

Maurice looked almost embarrassed by George's outburst, but when George had finished, he said, 'We are quite aware of that, my dear chap, but we really can't let you go. Apart from the fact that you have been intruding in our house without a warrant, we need you. You are a godsend, as well as a nuisance. You see, you're not what we call *quality*; but there is so much of you.'

'What the fuck are you talking about?' George demanded, frightened and defensive. 'You're nuts, both of you; and her too, standing there showing her box like that.'

Maurice turned his back on George and looked at Henry, his forehead creased in sophisticated indecision. 'I don't really want to puncture the back in any way,' he told Henry. 'So, what do you think?'

Henry made the slightest of resigned shrugs. 'The eyes, I suppose. Not very satisfactory, but there you are.'

'I want to know what's going on here,' George butted in. 'You – Gray – what in hell goes on here?'

He reached out and grasped Maurice's shoulder, trying to pull him round. Maurice was only too delighted to oblige. Spinning round deftly on the ball of his left foot in a remarkably Fred Astaire-like movement, he turned and faced George with his right hand upraised. George snarled, 'Now, you hear this –' and in his pugnacity he didn't even see what Maurice was holding.

With malicious accuracy, Maurice pierced George's left eye with the sharp point of his silver pipe-cleaner.

There was an audible pop, and optic fluid burst out bright and jellyish.

George's hands rose protectively to his face, but Maurice was too practised and too quick for him. The second jab penetrated George's right eyelid, and stuck deep into his optic nerve.

George roared out loud in agony and terror, and collapsed to his knees on to the floor, clutching his hands over his eyes. Maurice stepped back and shook out his pocket handkerchief, so that he could wipe his pipe-cleaner. Henry clapped his hands and said, *'Toro! Toro!* You would have made a first-rate matador, Maurice!'

'I'm blind! Oh, Jesus Christ, I'm blind!' screamed George. *'You've blinded me, you bastard, you've blinded me! Oh, God!'*

He lost his balance and fell heavily on his back on to the floor, where he twisted and rolled and writhed, not only in pain but in abject fear. Maurice watched him for a while dispassionately, and then said to Henry, 'We'd better have him upstairs, then, hadn't we?'

Henry said to Laura, 'Will you go to the room at the far end of the landing, my dear? Here's the key. On the second shelf down, you will find a clear glass bottle labelled *chloroform.* Bring me that bottle, please, and some clean cotton.'

While Laura went to fetch the chloroform, Maurice returned to the piano, and began to play, accurately but rather heartlessly, a selection of Chopin's polonaises. All this time, George stumbled and groped around the hall, shuddering and crouching and whimpering to himself, with blood and fluid smeared across his cheeks. Henry stood with his hand resting on the back of a chair, his ankles carelessly crossed, watching George with a smile.

Eventually, Laura returned, her white thighs shining, her black stockings slippery and perfectly seamed. Henry took the bottle from her and kissed her on the cheek. 'You are an angel,' he told her. 'If only I could keep you for ever.'

Maurice and Henry now cornered the weeping George. 'I'm here,' Maurice told him, in a tone of voice that was almost kind. 'I'm holding out my hands for you. Take them, and I shall guide you.'

George blubbered, 'I'm blind, I'm blind, I'm totally blind.' But Maurice said, 'Don't worry, old man, there are far worse things than being blind,' and gave him his hands. George eagerly grasped them, and tried to pull Maurice towards him as if he wanted to embrace him; but now Henry stepped forward from behind and pressed a large pad of chloroform-soaked cotton over George's nose and mouth.

George struggled, but Maurice kept a tight grip on his hands; and the more desperately George fought, the more stertoriously he breathed in the chloroform. It was only a matter of seconds before he staggered and dropped on to one knee, and then fell face-down on to the floor. Maurice said, 'How *are* the mighty fallen,' and then fastidiously inspected his wrist, to make sure that George hadn't scratched him in the struggle.

Between them, Maurice and Henry carried George upstairs. They took him along the landing to Maurice's operating room, which was bare and high-ceilinged, and decorated in two drab shades of green, like an Edwardian hospital. In the centre of the room, underneath a large metal-shaded lamp, there was a marble-topped table, with grooves all around it, into which the blood and fluids could flow. Against the side wall, there was a high veneered sideboard, on which a copper sterilizing kettle was already simmering and all the surgical instruments which Maurice would require were laid out on clean white cotton towels.

There was a steamy smell in the room from the sterilizer, and a smell of carbolic. But underlying them both, there was that persistent and nauseating odour of open human bodies, of bile and blood and faeces. Maurice was accustomed to it; in fact he found it quite exhilarating, in the same way that soldiers who fought in Normandy after D-Day found, in later years, the smell of apples exhilarating. It reminded them forever of blood, and fear, and orchards.

George was laid out on the marble table, on his back. Henry undressed him, struggling with his heavy-duty jeans. Underneath, George wore large boxer shorts with pictures of palm trees and deckchairs on them. Henry removed these too.

Naked, George was white and hairy and huge, a human walrus. Maurice examined him with distaste. All that could be said for him was that his skin was in good condition, unusually supple and fine, and that there was plenty of it. Maurice took off his evening coat, unfastened his cufflinks and rolled up his shirtsleeves. Henry said, 'Shall Laura get you a drink?'

'Later, thank you,' Maurice replied. 'I think I'm going to require a very steady hand for this one.'

The operation started at 4.35 and continued for nearly six hours. Outside, the ink-black sky faded into light snowy grey, and Henry could see the leafless trees down at the far end of the paddock; or what had once been the paddock, when The Wilderlings had been crowded with laughter and parties, and the Gray family had kept a full complement of horses. Henry had rather hoped when he returned to The Wilderlings that just a little of that gaiety would still be here, but the world was no longer effervescent, not in the way it had been then.

Where were the Goulds and the Vanderbilts and the Zimmermanns? Where were the parasols and the boating parties and the pink champagne? Where were the Gibson girls? In those days, seduction had been flavourful and corruption had been a dizzying cup drunk deep. But now, what was there? A life of averages, without extremes; a life in which the wealthy were shy of flaunting their wealth, and forbidden love-affairs were internationally publicized and uniformly tiresome.

Henry had once ridden in a dog-cart drawn by six naked girls, all of them society belles, and he had whipped them mercilessly until they had taken him all the way round the grounds of The Wilderlings and back. After that, he had taken all six of them to his bed.

As Henry stared out of the window and peeled back the pages of his memories, so Maurice conscientiously peeled away George Kelly's skin. Even as he separated the layers on George's back, Maurice knew that this was one of his most accomplished operations. There was scarcely any bleeding, and he skilfully exposed the sheets of white fat beneath George's epidermis as if he were opening a tissue-wrapped parcel of glistening tripes.

George recovered consciousness after two hours, but by then the skinning was so far advanced that his nervous system became overloaded, and he lapsed almost at once into silent shock. Now he lay trembling and raw on the marble table, stripped of his skin to the waist down, and close to death.

Henry said, 'A hundred dollars says you'll lose him before you're through.'

'No, no,' Maurice replied, his scalpel delving under the transparent skin on George's thighs. 'He'll rally at the last, you'll see.'

And Maurice's prediction was correct, for just as he was tearing the tubular sheath of skin from George's left leg, George suddenly quaked and cried out, *'Mother of God! Mother of God! Mother of God!'*

When the skinning was complete, they wrapped the blotchy scarlet bulk of George's body in a green vinyl bag and carried it downstairs again. They walked across the snowy yard with it and lifted it into the boot of Maurice's Cadillac.

They stood in the cold for a while, rubbing their hands together, enjoying the freshness of the winter morning.

'Uncle Algernon will be reasonably satisfied with that night's work, don't you think?' asked Henry.

Maurice looked tired. 'I hope so. It's the best that I can do. I just wish to God that Cordelia would hurry up and get hold of the portrait. We can't go on at this rate for very much longer.'

Henry said, 'I'll get rid of him, if you like.' He nodded towards the open boot of the Cadillac.

But Maurice shook his head. 'I feel like a drive. The house is becoming rather oppressive. I have nothing against your father, but it's Belvedere, and those sickly girls of his. Besides, Father and Mother aren't exactly easy.'

Henry said, 'Will you buy some oysters while you're out? I have a craving for oysters.'

They were about to walk back to the house when they heard the faintest mewling sound. Maurice said, 'That sounds like a cat,' and almost as he said it, a marmalade tom jumped down from the snowy roof of the garages and curled itself affectionately around his leg. Maurice lifted the cat up and peered at it with fascination. Its eyes were not green, but as dark as mirrors.

'Do you know something, Henry?' he said. 'This is

Firework. I can't believe it, after all these years. This is actually Firework.'

'What did I tell you?' smiled Henry. 'It seems as if the day of true revival is at hand.'

Nineteen

Litchfield, 19 December

Pat was not particularly amused when she reached the hospital and heard what Jack had to say.

'A séance?' she said. Her eyes were still puffy from sleeping, and her lime-green plastic curlers were only half concealed by a pink nylon headscarf.

'It's the last possible chance we've got of finding out what Ben was actually frightened of,' Jack told her. 'He's not going to make the morning, Pat. The doctor said that he was going pretty fast.'

Pat said, 'I don't believe what I'm hearing. It's three o'clock in the morning, and I've just driven fifteen miles in the snow, because my friend's husband wants me to hold a séance.'

'I thought that *I* was your friend, too.'

'You were, Jack – until tonight.'

Jack rubbed the back of his neck. 'Listen, Pat, you know that I'll make it up to you. But, as of now, I don't see any other alternative.'

'He doesn't see any other alternative,' Pat informed the ceiling. 'He's the sheriff of Litchfield County; the man on whom a hundred and fifty-five thousand people depend for their safety and their security; and he doesn't see any other alternative. Jack – what happened to good old-fashioned detection? Don't they do that any more?'

Jack glanced across to the waiting area, where Vincent and Dr Serling were holding a subdued conversation while they waited for him to persuade Pat that a séance in Litchfield County Hospital at three o'clock in the morning was a red-hot first-rate idea. 'Pat,' said Jack, 'the thing is that this isn't quite your normal kind of case. It has some very bizarre aspects to it.'

'Do you want to tell me about it?' Pat demanded. 'As long as I'm here, I might as well know why. I want to hear what it is that makes a shrewd and sensible police officer ask for the help of a tea-leaf reader.'

Haltingly, trying to make it all sound believable, Jack told her what had happened to Ben Miller; and about Aaron Halperin's cat; and Edward; and about his abortive attempt to talk to Maurice Gray; and about his belief that all of these incidents were somehow connected with the skinning murders.

When he had finished, Pat opened her handbag and took out a cigarette. Vincent came over and lit it for her, and asked Jack, 'Any luck?'

'This is out of my league,' Pat told him. 'It may be a whole lot of baloney, but if it isn't, then I don't want to get involved.'

'But why?' asked Vincent. 'All we're asking you to do here is get in touch with a perfectly ordinary young man.'

'Oh, yes?' Pat challenged him. 'He's ordinary, he's cut his face off. What do you think it's like, inside of his mind? Anybody who could cut their face off, they must be crazy, or half crazy, or scared to death. And what you're asking me to do is get right inside of that craziness, get right inside of that fear, no matter what caused it. That's what happens in a séance, my friend.

The medium, who in this instance happens to be *me*, has to experience first-hand the feelings inside of the person she's trying to get in touch with. Now, I've contacted dead people, and that isn't too bad; because you kind of experience it faintly, like feeling something through the wrong end of a telescope. But even so, you can get upset sometimes, particularly if the person's angry, or frightened, or hurt. Here, though – *here* you want me to feel exactly what that guy's feeling, first-hand, while he's still alive. I can't take it, I'm sorry. I don't need it.'

Jack was silent for a moment, then he raised a hand in resignation. 'Okay, Pat, I'm sorry. I should have thought about it more carefully. It was just an idea, and I guess it was a pretty rotten idea. You go on home. I can have someone drive you, if you're too tired.'

Pat said, 'You really have nothing else to go on?'

Jack counted off on his fingers. 'I have a hitch-hiker from Moultrie, Georgia, with a far-fetched story and a criminal record. I have two skinned humans and one skinned cat. I have a hundred-year-old painting that's falling to pieces. Then I have a dead art-dealer who decomposed even before he was buried, and a missing wife, and a white-faced woman in a black dress who might be one of the Gray family, but in fact could be anyone at all.'

Pat said, 'I see your problem. But, what can I say?'

'Well, don't worry about it,' said Jack. 'I'll manage. There has to be an answer somewhere. It's just a question of finding it.'

At that moment, sensing that Jack was having difficulty, Dr Serling came up. 'Have you decided how you're going to arrange it?' he asked Pat paternally.

'Arrange what?' Pat replied.

'Well, the séance. We *are* going to have a séance, aren't we?'

Pat hesitated for a moment, looking at Jack in helpless sympathy. With all the expertise of someone who knew from years of professional experience how to make other people feel guilty, Jack shook his head; as if to tell Pat that she shouldn't do it, not unless she really wanted to, not unless she wanted to help out a friend who needed her badly, and didn't know who else to turn to.

Pat said cagily, 'I don't see what *good* it would do, holding a séance. All you're going to get from the guy is pain, and fear.'

'It's all right,' said Jack, and laid his hand on her shoulder. 'Just go home, Pat, and get back to bed.'

Pat shook her head, and turned from Jack to Dr Serling and back again. 'Okay,' she said, 'you win. We'll do it. But I want one thing clearly understood – if it gets too upsetting, if it gets too heavy, then it's finished straight away. No arguments.'

'You're sure this is what you want?' asked Jack. 'I mean, I don't want you to think that I'm blackmailing you into it.'

'What I think is my business,' said Pat.

'Do we have to hold the séance in Ben Miller's room?' asked Dr Serling.

Pat said, 'No. Anyplace close will do. All this mumbo-jumbo about holding hands and sitting in circles just isn't necessary. Spirits are everywhere, and nowhere at all, both at once.'

Dr Serling looked at Jack and said, 'Well, Sheriff, shall we do it now?'

Jack nodded. There was nothing to be said. He felt desperately awkward and unsure of what he was doing, and if he tried to justify it, he would probably talk himself out of it. He knew that it was unusual but acceptable police procedure to enlist the help of psychics; and that he would probably be able to convince the county authorities that holding a séance had been worth attempting. What really concerned him, though, was that the idea had come to him so readily, and had seemed at the time so logical. He had discovered, to his own surprise, that he believed in the supernatural.

Vincent didn't need convincing that there were other influences in the world apart from the visible influences of flesh and blood. His grandfather had always sworn that he believed in ghosts, and that Candlemas was haunted by the spirit of a young Puritan woman who had been strangled on her wedding-night. Quite apart from that, any natural scepticism that he might have had had been completely overwhelmed in the past week by the horrors of Edward's death, and by the skinning of Aaron's cat. He had seen for himself the painting of Van Gogh on the Waldegrave portrait, and that was evidence enough.

He felt distinctly reassured by Sheriff Smith's response to everything that he had told him, particularly after the suspicious cynicism of Detective Clark in New York; and he was gratified that an officer of the law should accept the presence of occult forces without turning a hair.

Dr Serling stepped forward now. 'Are we ready?' he asked. There were plum-coloured circles under his eyes, and he was looking very weary.

Vincent said, 'Is there a room we can use? Somewhere quiet, where we won't be disturbed?'

Dr Serling said, 'There's an office upstairs for the use of outside doctors. Nobody's likely to interrupt us there, particularly at this time of the morning.'

They went upstairs in the lift. They hardly spoke to each other, out of tiredness and tension and apprehensiveness. Jack took out his gum, which his colleagues at headquarters always took as a sign that he was getting serious.

The doctor's office was wood-panelled, with a low sofa, three large armchairs and a glass-topped coffee-table, on which there was an arrangement of dried flowers and a stack of recent issues of *World Medicine*. Dr Serling closed the door behind them, and Pat said, 'Will everybody sit down, please? It doesn't matter where.'

Jack asked, 'Would you like the table cleared?' and Pat nodded yes.

'How about the lights?' asked Dr Serling.

Pat said, 'You can leave the lights. None of the spirits that I've been in contact with have worried much about lights.'

Vincent said, 'This won't be dangerous, will it?'

'I don't know,' Pat told him. 'I've never tried to get in touch with a living person before. It may not work at all.' She gave a sardonic, unfunny laugh. 'Who knows, it might even kill me.'

'That's not a joke, Pat,' Jack told her.

She sat down in the centre armchair, between Vincent and Dr Serling. 'You're telling me?'

She sat up straight in her chair, clasped her hands together and closed her eyes. 'I want you to think about Ben Miller,' she said, matter-of-factly. 'If Ben Miller's spirit is able to get in touch with us, then the more deeply we think about him, the quicker he's likely to come. It's like fishing in a pool of spirits. He's out there somewhere, just like we all are, floating.'

Vincent glanced at Jack, and then closed his eyes and thought of Ben. He tried to picture Ben's face; he tried to remember that day when Ben had gone berserk. He also tried to think of Ben before he had fallen from the roof; Ben as a teenager, coming around to Candlemas in his white Ford pick-up to collect his mother from work.

'Concentrate,' Pat repeated. 'Try to imagine that Ben is in the room with us, sitting close. Try to believe that he's here; he's actually here; because we can really bring him here if we try hard enough.'

With his eyes tightly shut, Vincent did his best to imagine that Ben was sitting on the sofa opposite him.

Pat whispered, 'Ben Miller, Ben Miller, I know that you're near. Ben Miller, I'm calling you, Ben. I want you to come to me, Ben, and talk to me.'

Vincent opened his eyes for a moment, and saw that Jack was staring at Pat with deep uncertainty. Jack saw that he was looking, and quickly closed his eyes.

'Ben Miller,' Pat murmured, 'where are you, Ben Miller? I want to talk to you, that's all. I don't want to hurt you. I don't want to frighten you. I just want to talk.'

'Do you think this is really going to work?' asked Dr Serling. 'I can't feel anything at all.'

'Quiet,' Pat told him. 'All you have to do is concentrate. All you have to do is think of Ben.'

They sat in silence for longer than a minute. The office was well-insulated from the corridor outside, and all they could hear was their own steady breathing, and the very distant ringing of a telephone.

They thought of Ben. Vincent tried to imagine Ben's mind, something like a transparent jellyfish, swimming around in a silent shoal of other transparent minds. He closed his eyes tighter and tighter, until he felt that the darkness inside his head was folding in on itself like a black sea-anemone, and that he was falling deeper and deeper into his own subconscious.

'Ben Miller, I know you're there,' Pat repeated; but this time her voice sounded peculiarly blurry, as if she were speaking through muslin. 'Ben Miller, come close. We want to talk to you, Ben. We're friends.'

Vincent was suddenly aware of a soft crackling sound, as if something was alight. He immediately opened his eyes, but the room was in total darkness.

'The lights have gone,' he said, and his own voice sounded strange and slurred.

'The lights are still on,' Pat replied. 'What has happened is that the darkness inside of our minds has filled the room. Now, quiet. I think that Ben is quite close. I think I can feel him coming nearer.'

'I can't see,' Jack protested.

'You haven't lost your sight,' Pat reassured him. 'Your perception has turned inwards, that's all. What you can see in front of your eyes now is the inside of your own mind.'

Dr Serling said, 'This is quite amazing. I've never experienced anything like it.'

Pat shushed him. 'Ben Miller,' she called, softly and encouragingly, 'Ben Miller, are you there, Ben Miller?'

Vincent strained his eyes, yet the darkness was seamless, and the harder he stared, the more impenetrable it seemed to become. He felt as if time had somehow wound down, as if they were travelling through each second of each minute with infinite slowness: a caravan of imperceptibly moving figures making their way through the endless desert of the days. He wasn't afraid. He felt a sense of calmness rather than fear, as if he had been drugged. He could feel the others close to him, too: Pat on his left, Jack just opposite, Dr Serling on the far side. Their personalities were as real to him as their physical presence; their minds were as tangible as their bodies.

The crackling noise altered and became a low fizzing, like static electricity. Vincent suddenly became aware that somebody else was in the room, somebody different. He could hear Pat calling, but her voice was so slow and attenuated that it was impossible to make out what she was saying.

But then he heard a man's voice mumbling, '. . . *Leave me alone . . . leave me alone . . .*'

Pat's words became more distinct, although they continued to rise and fall; as if she were speaking to them on a short-wave radio.

'. . . Ben Miller . . . is that you, Ben Miller . . . ?'

'Leave me alone,' the man replied. Vincent couldn't be sure that it was Ben.

'Are you Ben Miller?' persisted Pat.

'Leave me alone, they'll find me if you don't leave me alone. They'll find me.'

'Tell me who you are,' Pat demanded. 'Tell me what your name is.'

There was a long pause, and then Vincent heard the words, *'Bennnn . . . Millerrr . . .'*

'Ben,' said Pat, 'I want you to show yourself, I want to see you, Ben, so that I know that it's you.'

'. . . *Leave . . . alone . . .*'

'Ben, listen to me. We're friends here, people who know you, people who care about you. You can help us to protect you. You can help us to stop those people from coming after you. Please, Ben, this is your only chance.'

There was another long pause. Vincent thought he saw a flickering of light in the darkness, but it must have been his imagination, or something floating across the surface of his eye. Pat called again, but there was still no sign of Ben Miller; nothing but the blackness, crowded with thoughts and hopes and strange terrors.

'Ben, if you don't show yourself, we're going to leave you,' said Pat. 'Do you want us to leave you, so that *they* can get you? Do you want us to do that? Listen to me, Ben. This is your very last hope.'

Almost immediately, the static sound grew more intense, and the darkness appeared to clot itself together, like blood. Then, silently, a shower of brilliant white specks slid through the air, a meteorite shower in slow motion, and assembled itself over the centre of the glass-topped table into a negative image of Ben Miller. The image wavered and broke up from time to time, like the picture on a black-and-white television tube, but it was clearly Ben, even though his eyes gleamed white from a face as black as graphite. The room remained in darkness, but Vincent could tell that the apparition was suspended above the glass table because its reflection wavered upside-down beneath it, another dark face with albino-white eyes, drowning in a pool of glass.

'Ben,' coaxed Pat, 'you have to help us. We have to know who you're frightened of.'

At once, Ben's image opened its mouth impossibly wide and let out a sharp and chilling howl of anguish. Vincent wasn't sure that he had heard the sound aloud. It seemed to have been transmitted through the bones of his face, rather than through his ears. It was a hideous, horrifying howl: a howl of panic and pain and utter desperation. It was the howl of a man being crushed to death by his own total fear.

Pat screamed too, just as piercingly. Vincent couldn't see her, but he could sense that she had doubled up and that she was clenching her fists in anguish. He heard Dr Serling say, 'Let go! Pat, if it's hurting you, *let go*!'

But Pat either couldn't or wouldn't let go. Ben screeched and roared, and Pat screeched with him, the two of them intertangled in terror and pain.

'Pat!' Jack shouted; and Vincent could feel that he was trying to get up off the sofa but somehow found it impossible. The darkness they perceived in front of them was the darkness of their mental landscape, their souls externalized; and while they were collectively joined in it, they were physically unable to move. It was as if they had been turned inside out, and their minds were all around them, and the material world had been shrunk within their heads, so that the doctor's office existed only in what had previously been their imagination.

But the screaming and the roaring went on and on, and none of them could do anything but sit where they were and pray that it would stop.

Vincent began to feel a sharp pain in the sides of his jaw, just below his ears. He winced, and bent his head forward, in an effort to relieve it. Pat was still screaming; but as the pain in his jaw grew more and more unbearable, Vincent found that he could no longer hear her, because he was shouting himself.

The negative image of Ben Miller became insanely distorted, so that his face stretched diagonally and his body was drawn out across the room. He began to flicker and fade, and Vincent realized, not without relief, that they were probably going to lose him.

'He's going!' Jack shouted. He, too, sounded as if he were in pain. 'Pat! Pat! For Christ's sake stop him! *Stop him, Pat! He's going!*'

Pat suddenly screamed, 'Don't you realize why? He's *dying*! I can't stop him! He's dying!'

'Pat! I have to know who it is! I have to know who's been after him!'

'No, Jack! Let him go! If you don't let him go, he'll suffer terrible pain! His spirit may not even survive!'

Vincent could feel Jack thrashing around on the sofa, trying to get up and seize Ben Miller's image before it finally died away.

'God damn you, Ben Miller!' Jack yelled at him. 'God damn you to hell, Ben Miller! Who were you frightened of? Who was it scared you? Do you hear me, Ben Miller? Who was it scared you so much? Who was it wanted your skin?'

'. . . can't say . . .' Ben murmured. 'They'll kill me . . . if I tell . . . even after I'm dead . . .'

'Ben!' roared Jack. 'Ben, risk it! We'll get them for you, I promise! Ben, for God's sake, tell us who it is!'

There was some indistinct muttering, but then Vincent clearly heard the words '. . . Litchfield Cemetery . . . Johnson's . . . next to the oak . . .'

There was a sound then like no sound that Vincent had ever heard before: a kind of warping, twisting, tearing sound. Ben Miller's image shrank and shrivelled, and for a fraction of a second Vincent saw something that looked like a human embryo, only strangely slippery and transparent. Then the lights abruptly appeared, and the doctor's office reassembled itself around them, and they were sitting there staring at each other in disbelief.

Pat was trembling. Jack came across and bent over her, and said, 'Are you okay?'

Pat nodded. 'I could use a glass of water,' she said.

Dr Serling went through to the small kitchen that adjoined the office, and brought Pat a glass of water and a mild sedative powder. 'If I were you, I'd have one of Sheriff Smith's people take you home. You're not in any condition to drive.'

'I'm all right,' said Pat. 'The pain's gone now.'

'All the same,' Dr Serling insisted.

Vincent said, 'Is Ben really dead? What I saw just now – was that Ben dying?'

Pat unsteadily drank her water, and then said, 'I've never seen that before, but I could feel it. He wanted to go. He was desperate to go. He wanted to go so much that I was almost tempted to go with him. Can you understand that? He was *aching* for it.'

Jack turned to Dr Serling. 'Do you want to call down to intensive care, to see what's happened?'

Dr Serling picked up the phone, and asked the switchboard operator to put him through to Dr Kellstrom. While they waited, Jack unwrapped his last stick of chewing-gum and pushed it into his mouth in three measured bites.

'Seems as if I made a fool of myself, doesn't it?' Jack remarked, chewing with his mouth open.

'I wouldn't say that,' Vincent reassured him. 'It was worth taking a shot at it.'

'We've almost certainly killed Ben Miller before he was due to go,' said Pat.

'He only had a couple of hours, if that.'

Pat finished her water. 'We still killed him. He was in a coma, and that coma was protecting his mind from whatever it was that frightened him so much. The coma was giving his nervous system a chance to recover. What we did was to dive deep down underneath that coma and drag him out of it. He wasn't ready for it. His system couldn't stand the stress.'

Dr Serling had been talking to Dr Kellstrom. Eventually, he put down the phone, turned round and said, 'He's dead, all right. Shock, loss of blood, renal failure. You name it, he had it.'

'And we're still none the wiser about what frightened him,' said Jack.

'I'd lay money that what scared him was those twelve people in the portrait,' Vincent commented.

'Well, you could be right,' Jack told him. 'But "all twelve" could have meant anything at all. He was pretty religious, especially after his accident: maybe he was talking about the Twelve Disciples. Maybe he was talking about twelve-card poker. Maybe he didn't say "all twelve" at all, but something which sounded like it.'

Pat put in, 'Stop inventing complications, Jack.' She turned to Vincent, and explained, 'He's always creating complications. If the snow started to melt tomorrow, Jack would give you a dozen reasons why it shouldn't.'

'What did he mean about Litchfield Cemetery?' asked Vincent.

'He was rambling,' Jack replied. 'He was frightened out of his mind.'

'But he mentioned a name, Johnson's. And a place, too – "next to the oak".'

'I must confess I didn't hear that,' said Dr Serling. He wiped his glasses and then very loudly blew his nose. 'I think I'm allergic to the supernatural.'

'I heard it,' said Pat.

'Maybe that's where he wants to be buried,' Jack suggested.

Vincent said, 'Maybe we should go take a look.'

'It's still dark,' Jack pointed out.

'You have a flashlight, don't you?' Vincent asked him.

'Sure, but what are we supposed to be looking for?'

'I don't know. But you specifically asked him what he was frightened of, and he said that he couldn't tell you, because they'd kill him, whoever they are, even after he was dead.'

'That doesn't sound very logical,' Dr Serling remarked.

'It does to me,' said Pat.

'How come?' Jack asked her. He felt irritable; not only because the séance had been so inconclusive, but because he knew that it had been rash of him to urge Ben Miller to stay longer, when Pat had been suffering such agony.

Neither Vincent nor Dr Serling had criticized him openly about it, but all of them were conscious that his action could have cost her her sanity; or even her life.

As a sheriff who had been elected for his traditional down-home views on law enforcement, it had been risky and unorthodox for him to decide on holding a séance. He had been convinced that it would be a success; and to the extent that Pat had managed to raise Ben Miller's spirit, it had been. But Jack needed very much more. He needed evidence, and his failure to get it made him feel sharply diminished.

Vincent said encouragingly to Pat, 'You sound as if you've come across this kind of thing before.'

Pat said, 'I have. Some of the spirits I've been in touch with, even though they're dead, still say that they're frightened of dying.'

'Well, what could that mean?' asked Dr Serling.

'I'm never quite sure. At first I used to think they said it because they didn't realize that they were actually dead. Then I thought, well, if I'm talking to them, if they're talking to me, if we're having constructive conversations, then they *can't* be dead. So maybe people live much longer than we think, but in different forms, like butterflies. Maybe we go through five or six different stages before we finally cease to exist. Maybe *this* part of our lives, the flesh-and-blood part, is like stage two or three in the whole process. Maybe there are ghostlike people living around us who are terrified of "dying" and turning into solid creatures like us. Like – they believe that *we're* the ghosts, and *they're* alive.'

Vincent said, 'That's an interesting theory. I don't know how you could ever prove it.'

'But you saw Ben Miller for yourself,' said Pat. 'When he died, he turned into something like an embryo. A baby spirit, if you want to call it that, just about to be born again.'

'None of this makes any sense of what Ben said about the cemetery,' Jack put in.

'Well, maybe it does,' Vincent told him thoughtfully. 'If Pat's right, and we *do* live four or five lives, then Ben's fear of being killed could have been genuine. In which case, what he told us could have been some kind of clue – you know, like a crossword-puzzle clue. He wanted to tell us who was after him, he wanted to tell us who was frightening him so much, but he didn't dare to say it straight out.'

'I think we ought to try the cemetery,' said Dr Serling.

Jack checked his watch. 'It's five after four,' he said, trying to sound brisk. 'I vote we leave it until it gets light. I could do with a wash and a cup of coffee.'

'I think we all could,' said Dr Serling. 'It's been a strain, this séance, and I don't mind admitting it.'

They went to Bonnie's All-Nite Drugstore, on the other side of the snow-covered green, and huddled in their overcoats and tiredly drank coffee. They were too tense to eat, but Jack bought himself two more packs of gum and a Mounds bar. They talked for a while about the séance, and what had happened, although as dawn gradually broke over Litchfield Hospital, they found it increasingly difficult to believe that any of it had been real.

Snowclouds were hanging over the town like grey chiffon veils by the time they drove out to the cemetery in Jack's Cherokee. The houses and stores lay closed and silent, as if a plague had silently swept through Litchfield during the night and left all of its population dead in their beds. Vincent, in the back seat, yawned and covered his mouth with his hand. In spite of the coffee, he was beginning to feel very jaded, and to wonder what on earth he was doing, driving out to Litchfield Cemetery at first light, after a night without sleep, in the highly assorted company of the county sheriff, a country doctor, and a Jewish lady spiritualist in plastic hair-curlers.

They reached the cemetery shortly after seven. The wide iron gates were open, and Jack drove straight in and parked next to the House of Remembrance – a scaled-down version of the Charles Clapp dwelling in Portland, Maine: all Ionic columns and pilasters and oval windows. Smoke was blowing out of the building's chimney and mingling with the early morning mist, which showed that the cemetery caretaker had already arrived.

They walked through the chilly marble hall. Jack knocked on the caretaker's door, and then opened it. The caretaker was a severe, dry-voiced, haughty man, with a pinched mouth, pale disapproving eyes, and shiny black hair which looked as if it had been painted on to his narrow skull with varnish.

'We're looking for the Johnson tomb,' said Jack, without any introductions. He had attended dozens of funerals here: friends, relatives, homicide victims, suicides, sudden deaths – and so he and the caretaker knew each other well. They didn't like each other. The caretaker believed that once the dead were buried here, they were his, and he resented further investigation into the causes of death. He particularly objected to exhumations, which disturbed the peace of his sleeping charges and ruined the lawns.

'There are three Johnson tombs,' he said coldly. 'Which is the one you want?'

'Is there one close to an oak tree?' asked Jack.

The caretaker regarded him suspiciously. 'The

Frederick E. Johnson tomb. Frederick E. Johnson, Mrs Philomena Johnson, and their two children Charles F. Johnson aged eight years and Henrietta Johnson, spinster, aged seventy-nine years.'

Dr Serling said, 'Strange, isn't it, what death does to people? A sister of seventy-nine and a brother of eight.'

The caretaker peered at Dr Serling over his spectacles. 'They grow not old, Doctor, as we who are left grow old.'

He gave Jack a Xerox copy of the cemetery map, and they walked between the rows of graves under a lemon-yellow sun. Marble angels with snow on their wings regarded them with expressionless eyes. Flowers sprawled dead in frozen vases. The shingle paths had been salted to clear them of snow, but the shingle itself was crunchy with ice, and as they progressed up the hill, their footsteps echoed across the cemetery, the living walking amongst the dead.

The oak tree stood close to the edge of the cemetery, amongst the older graves. It was only ten or eleven years old, so it was little more than a sapling; but the plan had been to plant scores of shade trees between the graves, so that eventually the cemetery would take on the appearance of a garden. The Johnson tomb was only a few yards away, a dark granite catafalque with the names of the Johnson family deeply engraved on it. There was white gravel around the foot of the catafalque, and then a low granite wall, heavy with moss.

Dr Serling pointed to another grave nearby. 'You can see why Ben Miller knew this place. Look.' The grave's headstone read, *Zachariah Miller, 1862–1903*. 'Must have been his great-grandfather.'

Vincent clapped his hands to warm himself up. 'I don't understand this at all. There's nothing here.'

Jack sniffed, 'I told you. Ben was frightened out of his

mind. What he said just didn't make any sense. Come on – he just happened to think about dying, and for some reason he remembered this tomb.'

Pat said, 'There has to be more to it than that. I know he was frightened; I know he was hurting; but I really got the impression that he was trying to tell me something.'

Jack shook his head. 'I'm sorry. The whole ridiculous thing went wrong. It was my fault. I never should have tried it, and I never should have exposed you to any of that pain.'

'Jack – he was desperately trying to communicate with us. Why do you think he appeared at all? Spirits only manifest themselves when they want to; not because we call them.'

'Well, maybe you're right,' Jack told her, 'but he didn't manage it, did he? All I've got now is egg on my face.'

Vincent meanwhile was frowning at the Johnson tomb. If Ben really *had* been trying to tell them something, why had he picked this particular grave? Why hadn't he picked his own great-grandfather's grave, or any of the other graves in the cemetery? There was nothing special about the Johnson tomb. There was no special epitaph carved on it; there was no decoration, except for the hammered granite; and there was no statue. Vincent even tried to work out anagrams and acrostics from the Johnson family's names, but that produced nothing but nonsense.

'I'm for calling it a day,' said Dr Serling. 'Let's all go home and have a long think about it, and then maybe we'll be able to come up with an answer when our brains are refreshed.'

Jack said, 'It looks like snow. I'd better get myself back to headquarters.'

They left the cemetery in silence. The caretaker stood in the doorway of the House of Remembrance and smiled at them tartly, enjoying their obvious dejection.

'Everything was satisfactory, I hope?' he asked Jack.

'Fine,' Jack told him. 'You've got yourself a fine body of people here.'

Jack drove them back to the hospital, where they collected their cars. 'If anyone comes up with even half an idea, let me know,' Jack told them.

They promised they would. Jack hesitated for a moment, and then said, 'I'm not at all sure that séance was a good idea. I don't think I handled it very well, either. If I caused you any grief, well, I just want to say that I'm sorry. You especially, Pat. I feel like I used you.'

Pat took his hand and kissed him on the cheek. 'Don't start feeling bad about it. I did it of my own free will. Maybe I learned something, too.'

Vincent gave Jack a wave, and walked back across the car park with Dr Serling.

'An interesting man, our sheriff,' he remarked.

'He took a chance, I'll give you that,' Dr Serling replied. 'It's a pity he didn't have more courage in his convictions. That could be dangerous one day; if not for him, then for somebody else.'

Vincent cleared his throat. 'Did you ever go to a séance before?'

Dr Serling said, 'One.'

'Was it successful?'

'Do you think I would have gone along with last night's performance if it hadn't have been?'

'Then you're a believer, too.'

Dr Serling smiled. 'I suppose I am; although I don't quite know what it is that I believe in.'

Vincent said, 'About Ben –'

Dr Serling had reached his car, and now he was

digging in his coat pocket for his keys. He looked at Vincent keenly. 'What you're going to ask me about Ben is whether we killed him, by holding that séance. Well, the answer is probably yes – a few hours earlier than he was expected to die in any event. And if your next unspoken question is whether I feel guilty about it, especially since I happen to be a doctor, and morally charged with doing everything I can to prolong his life; well, the answer to that is also yes.'

Vincent didn't know how to answer that; but after a moment or two, Dr Serling said, 'They give you the power of life and death, when they make you a doctor. There are no two ways about it. I have to exercise that power day in and day out; and last night wasn't any different. I can accept the guilt. If I couldn't, I'd hang up my stethoscope and retire to Florida. I'll be judged, when the time comes for judgement, and if I've done wrong, then I'll be punished for it. That's all.'

It was snowing yet again as Vincent drove back to Candlemas, but the snow was dry and flaky and didn't settle. He kept on thinking about what Dr Serling had said, and about the séance, and about the Johnson tomb up on the hill, underneath the oak.

Ben Miller must have had a reason for mentioning that particular tomb; but why *that* tomb instead of any of the others? The only distinctive feature it possessed, the only thing that made it at all different from any of the other tombs, was the low granite wall that ran around it.

Vincent was usually excellent when it came to solving puzzles. His mind was both educated and quirky. He could see the Johnson tomb as an intellectual problem, and yet his brain just didn't know where to begin.

Perhaps he was trying to be too complicated about it. Ben Miller, after all, had been a pretty simple-minded young man, with very little more than a grade-school education. If a simple-minded person were setting a problem, how would he go about it? Not with words, perhaps; certainly not with academic references; probably not with numbers. No – the puzzle would more than likely be very simple and very *visual*. Ben Miller had been a television watcher, one of Marshall McLuhan's audio-visual generation; and if somebody like that had thought about the Johnson tomb he would have seen a mental image of a –

Vincent said, 'God *damn* it,' out loud.

The Johnson tomb was a grave with a wall. The *only* grave with a wall. The walled grave. And that was what Ben had been so frightened of.

The Waldegrave.

Twenty

When Vincent arrived back at Candlemas, he saw Charlotte's bright red Datsun sports car parked outside, and the lights shining in the living room. Charlotte came to open the door for him, wearing a maroon wool dressing-gown Vincent had bought in London, at Harrod's.

'I've been waiting for you all night,' she said, kissing him. 'Where on earth have you been?'

He took off his overcoat and hung it up. 'If I told you, I don't think that you'd believe me. But I'm all right. In fact, I'm a little *better* than all right. I think I'm beginning to understand what's going on. Or half understand it, anyway.'

'For goodness' sakes, come and have some hot coffee,' Charlotte told him. 'You look absolutely beat.'

'I'm okay,' Vincent insisted. 'What time did you get here?'

Charlotte led the way into the living room. She had already raked out the fire and stacked it up with fresh logs, and it was happily starting to crackle. 'I got here just after midnight. I guess I missed you, that's all.'

Vincent stripped off his tie and his sports jacket. 'That doesn't sound like the whole story.'

'Well, it isn't,' she said. 'I went out to dinner with Dick, and we had a fight.'

'Do I know Dick?'

'Dick Cortabitarte. He works for Artprint.'

'Oh, *that* Dick. Well, it doesn't surprise me. Dick Cortabitarte has a very obnoxious personality indeed, as far as I remember. In fact, I seem to remember that even his *hair* was obnoxious.'

'That's the man. Dick, with the obnoxious hair.'

Charlotte made coffee while Vincent went upstairs. As he sat on the end of the bed, unbuttoning his shirt, he lifted the receiver off his bedroom telephone and punched out Jack Smith's number. After a long pause, one of Jack's deputies answered. 'He's not here right now. Can I take a message?'

'Yes, please. Tell him that the Johnson tomb was a walled grave, like a grave with a wall. Then spell out the name W-a-l-d-e-g-r-a-v-e for him.'

'Will he understand what you mean?'

'About as much and about as little as I do.'

'Okay, sir. I'll see that he gets the message.'

Vincent took a shower. When he came downstairs, dressed in a black wool suit and a cream-coloured silk shirt, Charlotte said, 'You're going out again? I was going to cook you lunch.'

'I have to go out. You can come with me, if you like.'

'Where are you going?'

'Only over to Litchfield. I have to look up some papers.'

'Vincent,' Charlotte protested, 'something's going on here, and I think I'd like to know what it is.'

Vincent went out into the hall and came back with the Waldegrave portrait. He took the brown-paper wrapping off it and propped it up on a chair. Charlotte examined it closely, and then turned to Vincent with her nose wrinkled up.

'It's awful,' she said. 'It *smells*. It smells like rotting meat.'

Vincent said, 'My grandfather said this picture was the Pearson family's good-luck charm. He thought it was so important that we kept hold of it that he even had a special clause written about it in his will.'

'And your father?' asked Charlotte. 'He thought that, too?'

'My father was more ambiguous about it. But he did what my grandfather had told him, and kept it safe, the same way that I did. Not because we understood *why*; but simply because we were told to. And the Pearson family have always been very obedient to their elders. My father told me not to buy any painting that I didn't understand, and I never did, and that's why the Pearson gallery has always flourished.'

Charlotte said tartly, 'Apart from acquiring a peerless reputation for stuffiness.'

'Is that what you think of me?' asked Vincent.

'You've never tried to seduce me. What else should I think?'

Vincent gave her a long, considered look. 'Is this a backlash from Dick Cortabitarte?'

Charlotte very slowly and deliberately shook her head from side to side. 'No,' she said.

Vincent finished his coffee and put down the cup. 'I hope you realize that this is going to spoil everything.'

'Why should it?'

'I don't know. But I don't want to lose you. I don't want to lose your friendship. And the very first thing that gets laid on the line when you decide to be lovers is friendship. If we love, and fall out of love, then bang goes everything. The walks, the talks, the theatre, the meals, the weekends up here in Connecticut.'

Charlotte reached across and held his wrist. 'Sometimes, you have to take risks. You can't go through your entire lifetime not taking risks. I'm in love with you, and you're in love with me, so why are we wearing these invisible chastity belts? Just in case we happen to lose our friendship? One second of true love is worth five years of friendship.'

'Not always.'

Charlotte knelt forward and kissed his cheek, then his lips. The kiss began innocently, lips closed, but then Charlotte probed into his mouth with the tip of her tongue, and after a moment or two they were kissing passionately and deeply. Vincent at last felt all the long-stored affection for Charlotte welling up in him, irresistibly; and both of them knew that before the hour was out they would be lovers.

It happened with dignity and grace. Up in the master bedroom, among the grainy violet shadows; on the bed which had witnessed the intimate history of the Pearson family for the past hundred years. Naked, Charlotte lay between the sheets, and as Vincent climbed into the bed with her, she reached up and touched his cheek and kissed him. His fingers traced her nerve-endings, in tingling and anticipatory whorls: from her neck to her shoulders to the curve of her breasts, so that her nipples knurled like the tight buds of Mme Grégoire roses.

She grasped his hardened penis in her hand, and guided it between her parted thighs. He slid quickly inside her, as deep as he could go, and she shuddered with the pleasure of it; and with the emotional release of having at last consummated their relationship. They held each other very tight as the rhythm of their thrusting steadily increased. Vincent said, 'You're murdering me,' and laughed; and then Charlotte felt the irresistible spasms of an oncoming orgasm; and there was nothing at all that she could do to hold it back any longer. She quaked, and cried out loud, and the rippling of her vagina brought Vincent to his climax, too, and as she cried he flooded her with warmth . . .

They made love once more before they left the bed, more slowly this time, savouring the feeling of their bodies together, their fingers lingering between their legs, touching each other, feeling with wonder and satisfaction their physical joining-together.

Vincent said, 'If this never ever happens again, believe me, it will have been worth it. You're beautiful.'

Charlotte propped herself up on her elbows and watched him with mischievous eyes. 'We should have done this years ago.'

'No, I don't think so. This is the right time for it. I never like to make love to a stranger.'

'What about Meggsy?'

'That was lust, not love.'

'Was?'

Vincent reached across to the bedside table and checked the time on his watch. 'You don't think I'd two-time a nice sweet girl like that?'

'What about a nice sweet girl like me?'

'I wouldn't two-time you, either.'

They dressed, and had a drink together beside the fire, and then Vincent said, 'We have to go. I promised Mr Morris that we would be down at his office before lunch.'

'Mr Morris?'

'The family lawyer.'

The drove over to Litchfield under a sun that was no longer yellow but deathly white. The countryside around them was like a silvery dream: misty hills and pearl-grey distances. Charlotte sat close to Vincent as he drove, one hand resting on his thigh, not possessively,

317

but with the warm reassurance of shared experience. Loving friendship had bloomed into love. Riskier, perhaps; but very much sweeter, and much more intense.

'Do you have to go back to MOMA before Christmas?' Vincent asked her.

'I was supposed to call in on Monday.'

'That sounds like you've changed your mind.'

'It depends. Are *you* going back to the city?'

'I don't think so.'

'Well, then, I'll stay with you.'

Vincent glanced at her, and smiled. Charlotte kissed the tips of her fingers, and pressed them against his lips.

The offices of Morris, McClure & Winterman were situated just outside of Litchfield in a large eighteenth-century building that had once been a farmhouse. The roof was covered in thick white snow, beneath which the dark weatherboarded walls looked even darker, and the small leaded windows looked even smaller, and the overhanging porch looked even more sinister. It was the kind of house in which Vincent could have easily believed that witches had once lived; one of those suffocating colonial mansions riddled with narrow corridors and musty cupboards and crazily angled staircases. Mr Morris occupied an eyrie in the eaves, an untidy nest that had been lined with heaps of legal documents and sprawling files. He was white-haired and big-nosed, with horn-rimmed spectacles heavily obscured with thumbprints, and when he sat down and crossed his knees, the leg of his long Johns was exposed above his sock. He was always glad to see Vincent. He shook his hand, and beamed, and offered Vincent and Charlotte a glass of his English-bottled sherry, Harvey's Bristol Milk. Charlotte sat down in an old leather-covered chair as deep as a bathtub, and became aware with private pleasure that her pants were wet: a sensation that made her feel closer to Vincent than any words of affection could have done. She smiled at him; and he smiled back; although he didn't know why she was smiling.

'Your great-grandfather was a copious diary-keeper,' said Mr Morris, untying the ribbons that had held together a box-file marked *Pearson, 1891–1913* for more than seventy years. 'He was not a communicative man, not to speak to; but he wrote everything down, from the sale of the smallest and most insignificant painting, and to whom it was sold, and why, and whether he believed that the new owner was worthy of it; to his own marital affairs, and the arguments he used to have with your great-grandmother, and some of his more personal adventures.'

'It's the Grays that I'm interested in,' said Vincent.

'Well, indeed, as you said on the telephone. I've heard the name, of course. They were a mainstay of Connecticut society, from the 1870s through to the 1900s, when they suddenly decamped and left for Europe. The departure of the Grays caused a tremendous stir at the time, and left local society bereft. Just imagine what would have happened to Newport if the Vanderbilts had suddenly disappeared. There are many older people in Darien today who believe that Darien could have been the jewel of American society if the Grays hadn't left. In their day, they were as wealthy and as popular as any Astor or Frick or Havemeyer.'

'The Grays are mentioned in my great-grandfather's papers?' Vincent asked him.

Mr Morris nodded. 'Several times. I did as you asked, and tried to find as many references to them as possible.

Unfortunately, I've been rather pressed this morning; I've been dealing with the Hartley case, for all of my sins; and so I've only managed to get halfway through. If you'd like to examine the papers for yourself, of course . . .'

'I'd be delighted,' Vincent told him. 'Is there an office we can use?'

'Use this one. I have to be in court in twenty minutes. You won't disturb me, except if you drink too much of my sherry. My cousin brings it over, you know. Don't you think it's rather fine?'

Vincent sipped a little more, and lifted the glass. 'Thank you, Mr Morris; it's very fine.'

Vincent and Charlotte took the bulky box-file and crowded together at a small side-desk, while Mr Morris shuffled papers and repeatedly cleared his throat and picked up his telephone from time to time and spoke in baffling terms to his secretary, who sat just outside his office door in a cable-knit twinset and upswept spectacles that always reminded Vincent of the rear end of a '59 Buick Le Sabre.

The Pearson file contained page after page of feint-ruled quarto paper, softened and yellowed with age and filled on both sides with tiny handwriting in purple ink. It began in the summer of 1891, when Vincent's great-grandfather was twenty-seven, and his grandfather was five. There were pages about Candlemas, and how it was being redecorated and altered, and how the family had spent the summer riding and boating and going on picnics. Mr Morris had left strips of torn blotting-paper in between the pages on which the Grays were mentioned, as markers. Vincent's great-grandfather had obviously met the Grays some years before, because the first reference, on 12 August 1891, said:

Algernon Gray came up this weekend from Darien, bringing his wife Isobel and his daughter Cordelia. He seemed as sprightly as ever; in fact he has scarcely changed since I was first introduced to him at the age of nineteen, at the Darien Independence Day Ball, and Cordelia appeared as youthful and as blooming as she was on that day, although she must have attained her twenty-eighth year by now. Mr Gray was much interested in some paintings of Rouen Cathedral which Jean Laplage recently sent me from Paris, and I agreed to consider a purchase price of $150 each for two of the best of them, although I have never thought that the Grays were the kind of family to whom sensitive paintings should be sold. There is something altogether too *feral* about them; as if they are meat-eaters with a vengeance.

The next mention of the Grays was in 1893, when Vincent's great-grandfather met Belvedere and Willa Gray at the theatre, in New York.

They were not their usual selves, although they looked well enough. They spoke a great deal of Oscar Wilde, and what a great playwright he was, and of Tree's production of *A Woman of No Importance*, which has just opened in London. I am growing curious about the Gray family. Whenever I see them, they seem to be possessed of such unnatural joyfulness, and they have confidence in the future which far outweighs the normal optimism with which one usually regards one's remaining years. Belvedere spoke of the turn of the twentieth century, and how different it would be from the turn of the nineteenth century, almost as if he expected that he would be there to witness it. Most odd!

There were further mentions of social meetings with the Gray family, all the way through to 1905. In February 1905, Vincent's great-grandfather wrote,

I am almost persuaded now that the Gray family have formed some pact with the Devil himself. They remain, all of them, as youthful as they were more than twenty years ago. Cordelia cannot be younger than forty now, and yet she happily remains unmarried and looks quite half that age. The last time I spoke to her, at the Newport regatta, she said that she was thinking of marrying 'soon', but she wanted to be sure that her husband-to-be was suitable for her. 'There is, after all, no hurry.' For a woman of forty to say that there is no hurry when she is considering the question of marriage is quite startling; but no less startling is Cordelia herself, whose neck remains smooth, whose eyes remain unwrinkled, whose hair remains as glossy and as lustrous as ever. Her older brother Maurice is equally well-preserved. And what can I say of Algernon and Isobel, whose freshness is remarkable? I myself grow older and greyer by the month; yet Algernon, who is some years older than me, remains as well-preserved as if he were in amber.

There were two or three gaps in the diary, until 1911; but it was then that Vincent's great-grandfather became completely convinced that the Grays were no ordinary family, and set out to find out how, and why. In June 1911, he dressed himself 'in a nondescript linen suit' and travelled to Darien to talk to some of the Grays' neighbours, and 'those of the townsfolk of Darien who had their wits about them, which were not as many as I would have liked.'

Suddenly, Vincent pointed to a lengthy paragraph, denser than the rest, as if it had been copied out from notes. '*This* is what we've been looking for!' he told Charlotte. 'This is the proof. The family in the Waldegrave portrait *are* the Grays; without a shadow of doubt.'

The paragraph was a deposition that Vincent's great-grandfather had taken from a woman called Nora Cartwright, who used to run the domestic staff at The Wilderlings. Apparently she had found it almost impossible to find regular employment after she had left the Grays; even in those days, they already had a sinister reputation; and she had gladly spoken to Vincent's great-grandfather in exchange for a boiled ham and $10.

In December of 1882, after a tour of America which had included San Francisco, Leadville, Denver and Savannah, the celebrated Irish aesthete Oscar Wilde visited Newport, RI, and there became acquainted with Algernon and Isobel Gray at a supper party given by the Goelets. Algernon and Isobel Gray were both enthusiastic collectors of modern art, and were delighted when Wilde introduced them some days later to Walter Waldegrave, a fashionable British painter who had accompanied Mrs Lily Langtry to the United States when she visited New York just after Christmas, 1882. Waldegrave was a realist of the Pre-Raphaelite school, and Algernon was very keen for him to paint a family portrait of the Grays, at their home in Darien. Unfortunately, Waldegrave contracted pneumonia during his visit to New York and returned to England prematurely in February, 1883, still too weak to undertake any commissions. The Grays, however, travelled to London during the summer of 1883, specifically to visit Walter Waldegrave at his house in Norbury, in south London, and to have their portrait painted. They returned to Darien in October, but their behaviour was 'much changed'. They began to treat their staff very cruelly, and both Maurice and Henry Gray were guilty of taking improper advantage of the family's maids; so much so that local families refused to let their daughters work at The Wilderlings. There were stories of riotous parties; of narcotics; and of unusual sexual practices, particularly whipping and bondage; and although many of these were undoubtedly exaggerated by fear and superstition, there was no doubt that some strange influence had taken possession of the Grays, and that they seemed to believe that they were beyond the law; both the law of man, and the law of heaven. They did not lose their position in society, for in the company of their friends they always behaved impeccably. But the young children of Darien were warned by their parents not to venture too close to The Wilderlings, for fear of being consumed alive, and whenever the Grays walked abroad, they were always given the widest of berths.

Just as Vincent and Charlotte finished reading this entry, Mr Morris rose from his desk, took Vincent by the hand and said, 'I wish I could stay, and take you to lunch. But you know how it is. *Hartley vs Hartley*. The most complicated custody case in Connecticut's legal history. Except *O'Connell vs O'Connell,* but that, of course, was an epic. An epic, my God! And the best legal fees since the *Matter of Vanderbilt.*'

Vincent said, 'You've been a great help. You don't mind if we stay here for a while, and finish up reading these papers?'

'Well, help yourself,' said Mr Morris, trying to wink. 'I'm not really supposed to let you do it, under the terms of the will, but since you're the only surviving member of the family, I can't see that we're at very much risk, legally, can you?'

He uttered the oddest of laughs: as if someone had suddenly seized hold of his throat and waggled his head from side to side, choking him.

They sat in the claustrophobic silence of Mr Morris's room, in that house built for witches, and read through the rest of the file; far beyond the pages that Mr Morris had marked, carefully running their fingers down the columns for any sign of the word *Gray,* or any mention of *Waldegrave* or *Darien,* or *Oscar Wilde.*

The purple ink ran out, and abruptly, in 1912, they were reading pages written in black Indian ink, on a different quality of paper, in far more energetic writing. Writing with loops under the *y*s and squiggles under the *g*s and thunderbolts under the *q*s. Writing with brisk crosses on every *t* and diamond-shaped dots on every *i*. This was the diary of Vincent's grandfather, who had taken over the pursuit of the Grays, and seemed determined to hunt them down and to prove their venality beyond reasonable doubt.

I have talked now to scores of servants, friends, and acquaintances, and I have become convinced *in spite of the apparent absurdity of it* that the

Grays underwent some extraordinary trans-
mogrification when they visited England in 1883.
The writings of Mr Oscar Wilde appear to bear me
out; and although he has been dead these past ten
years, I have been fortunate in being able to
interview several of those who met him when he
visited New England in 1882, and their opinion
seems to be that the Grays were much taken with
Wilde, and also with Walter Waldegrave, and that
during the Christmas of 1882 they could speak of
nothing else. In fact, the entire Gray family seem
to have been on tenterhooks until they had word
from England in the summer of 1883 that Mr
Waldegrave was now quite well, and willing to
paint their portrait.

There was a long gap in the diary, and then a heavily
underlined entry for May 1912:

My correspondent in England, Mr Frederick
Rickwood, has now informed me that Walter
Waldegrave, before his suicide in 1885, was under
suspicion for blasphemy and witchcraft, and that
he was a member of that infamous coven known as
the Norbury Nine, many of whom were
prosecuted in 1884 for unnatural acts, and for the
pagan sacrificing of sheep. Waldegrave had
apparently discovered the formula by which those
who promised to live a life of corruption and
devilry could survive for ever, without growing
old. Mr Rickwood says that a competent artist had
only to paint the supplicants' portrait; and that the
words of the exorcism had only to be said over
them, backwards, and immortality would be
assured. Their portrait would age, as they might

have done; but they themselves would remain young.

And here, Vincent's grandfather quoted the exorcism, in reverse:

Nos audi, rogamus te, digneris humiliare Ecclesiae sanctae inimicos ut; nos audi, rogamus te, seruire libertate facias tibi secura tuam Ecclesiam ut; Domine nos libera, diabolii insidiis ab.

The diary went on:

I talked about the Grays with Father Summers, from the College of Jesuits, and during July he agreed at last to travel to Darien with me, and to pay them an uninvited visit. Both of us, I think, were apprehensive.

Charlotte said, hesitantly, 'You don't think that Maurice Gray – I mean the Maurice Gray that your Sheriff Smith was talking about – you don't think that he was the *same* Maurice Gray, do you? I mean, this Maurice Gray was over forty years old in 1882. He couldn't have –'

Vincent read through the pages again. ' "*Waldegrave had apparently discovered the formula by which those who promised to live a life of corruption and devilry could survive for ever.*" '

'But you don't believe that? If you *believed* that, Maurice Gray would be more than a hundred years old. And, I mean – well over a hundred years old?'

Vincent said, 'Yesterday morning, I would have said that it wasn't possible.'

'But the séance has changed your mind, is that it?'

Vincent raised both hands, to show that he understood just as little as she did. 'I saw the spirit of a dying man, floating in the air; I heard voices, when there was nobody talking. Right at this moment, I think I could well believe anything – even a hundred-and-twenty-year-old art connoisseur.'

'You were tired. What did you really see?'

Vincent looked at Charlotte narrowly. 'You don't believe me? I saw Ben Miller, the same way that everybody else at that séance saw Ben Miller. He was there, for real. There's no denying it.'

Charlotte touched the back of his hand. 'These Gray people – if this is true –'

'You mean they frighten you?'

'Yes,' said Charlotte, 'of course they do.'

'Well, if it's any consolation, they frighten me too.'

Vincent went back to the diary and read out the next entry, slowly and dogmatically, as if they were the operating instructions for a dishwashing machine.

Father Summers and I went to The Wilderlings and found the Gray family outside in the garden, taking tea. It was a perfect afternoon. The Grays were the picture of elegant politeness. They seemed to be oblivious to the fact that this was now 1912, almost thirty years after their portrait had been painted by Walter Waldegrave, and that none of them had aged even one whit since that time. Algernon Gray should have been seventy-five by now, and yet he looked like a man in early middle age. His wife Isobel looked almost as young as her own daughter, Cordelia, who should now have reached her forty-sixth year; and yet was as fresh and pale as a seventeen-year-old. They had the same cat that I remembered as a child: a marmalade cat with a kink in his ear, called Firework. Yet this cat should have been dead by now, three times over. Father Summers and I said nothing to the Grays, not directly; but on the way out, while we waited for our hats, I showed Father Summers the Waldegrave portrait in the hall, and it was plain what had happened. The portrait showed the Gray family as we might have expected to see them, with Algernon white-haired and aged, and Isobel wrinkled; and Cordelia looking like a middle-aged matron. The cat Firework was gone, and in its place was nothing more than a furry black shadow. Maurice was grey-haired, still stylish, but showing his years; and Henry was lined with worry. It seemed to us then that the people sitting out in the garden were like the characters out of a dream, and that this portrait showed their waking selves, as they really were. Father Summers crossed himself, and said a prayer, but he was interrupted by the sudden appearance of Maurice Gray, who courteously but firmly escorted us away from the house and down to the driveway, where our motor-vehicle was waiting. Maurice Gray said very little, but made it clear to us that the Gray family would not welcome any further unsolicited visits; and that we should stay away from The Wilderlings in future.

During the summer of 1912, Vincent's grandfather recorded the deaths of seven young women in the Darien area, all of them unexplained, and he became increasingly convinced that they were the work of the Gray family; particularly since most of the bodies showed signs of having been whipped and tied up, and he had heard reports that Henry Gray had talked to his friends incessantly of the pleasures of bondage, and how much he appreciated the 'less acceptable' work of Swinburne. When Henry Gray was charged with culpable homicide in September 1912, but quickly released because of 'insufficient evidence', Vincent's grandfather decided that it was time for him to act. He paid a professional thief to enter The Wilderlings at night and steal the Waldegrave portrait. He then wrote to Algernon Gray, inviting him to meet him at Candlemas, 'if he should wish to know where the Waldegrave portrait might have been spirited away'.

The meeting, apparently, was acrimonious. Algernon Gray accused Vincent's grandfather of theft and conspiracy, and said that he would have him hanged. But Vincent's grandfather quite calmly explained that he intended to hold on to the Waldegrave portrait, and that he would keep it safe, provided the Grays left Connecticut immediately and never came back. If they returned, he said, or if they attempted to steal the portrait, he would burn it.

It was a dangerous gamble, of course: for Vincent's grandfather had no way of knowing for sure whether the stories about Waldegrave had any foundation in fact. It was conceivable that the Grays had remained so young-looking because of their excellent health. But when Algernon Gray grudgingly agreed to leave the country, on the sure and certain guarantee that the Waldegrave portrait would not be harmed, then Vincent's grandfather knew that everything he had heard about the Grays had been true.

The very life-essence of the Gray family was contained within the painting; and whatever marks the years made upon them, the painting reflected each and every one; although the faces of the Grays themselves remained smooth. Every debauch, every drug-riddled party, every perversion; each appeared on the portrait as if by some magical hand, a hand that kept count of every second, a hand that recorded every corrupt and self-indulgent pleasure. For time and corruption must always make their marks somewhere, just as surely as a man must make his mark when he walks across the snow.

There were very few entries in the journal at the time when the Grays actually packed up and left Connecticut, although one line read, *Algernon has tried again to bribe me; and then, when that failed, to threaten me!* Vincent's grandfather must have been bullied and cajoled by the Grays far more than he admitted. After all, the painting was not just a painting. It was not just a family heirloom. The painting was *them*: the Grays themselves, their living identities; and the moment that it ceased to exist, so would they. Their fear when they left Connecticut must have been enormous, and they must have continued to live in fear for every single second of every single day, ever since. It would have taken nothing more than a fire, or a flood, or an over-enthusiastic vandal, and 'all twelve' would instantly have perished.

Now, however, the Grays were back in Connecticut, and they had roosted again at The Wilderlings, and they were looking for their portrait. Without saying it out loud, Vincent thought to himself, *That's why Edward died.* The woman in black hadn't wanted his body; she probably hadn't even wanted to kill him. She had wanted his keys, nothing more, so that she could search the gallery. And what had she taken? Nothing; because the Waldegrave portrait hadn't been there. In fact, it was the only painting which an outsider might reasonably have expected to be there, but wasn't; and that was only because Aaron Halperin had been trying to restore it, up in Bantam, Connecticut.

She had left Edward with a corrupt and terrible gift: the maggots out of the grave – the maggots which should have devoured *her*, forty years ago.

Charlotte said, in an awed whisper, 'Vincent – does this mean what I think it means?'

Vincent nodded. 'The Grays found a way of living for ever; or at least what they believed would be living for ever. The only trouble was, they took advantage of their immortality, and started to live completely debauched lives, without caring who they hurt, or even who they killed.'

'And your grandfather found out – and stopped them.'

Vincent breathed. 'If only he'd told us why we had to take care of that picture.'

'Do you think any of you would have believed him, if he had?'

'I don't know. I don't think my father would.'

'Well, then,' said Charlotte. 'Perhaps it was better that he kept silent.'

Vincent said, 'These skinning murders . . . Sheriff Smith seems to think that they might be connected with the Grays . . . maybe they're part and parcel of the same thing.'

'What do you mean?'

'Well, the portrait is decaying, because of Walter Waldegrave's poor technique. Perhaps, as the portrait falls apart, the Grays are falling apart, too. You see what it says here, in my grandfather's diary, "The very life-essence of the Gray family was contained within the painting." If the painting is flaking; then the Grays' life-essence must be falling to pieces, too. I mean – perhaps I'm being injust. The only evidence that Sheriff Smith has so far which connects the Grays to the skinning murders is the uncorroborated testimony of a notoriously unreliable hitch-hiker. But it all seems to fit together, doesn't it? The Grays have a reason for wanting fresh skin. Because you go back and smell that picture, and what you're smelling isn't egg-tempera, or damp canvas, or decomposing varnish. That's the smell of real people, rotting. That's human gangrene. And if they're rotting, what do the Grays need more than anything else, so that they can keep up a respectable front?'

Charlotte said, '*Skin*,' and stared at Vincent in horror.

Vincent said, 'Don't look so shocked. I think you're right. They want fresh, unpolluted skin, to cover themselves up. They want human masks, so that the rest of us can't see what's been happening to them. They've been rotting alive; but they've been keeping up a reasonable day-to-day appearance by stealing the skin of other people, and wearing it as naturally as if it were part of them, the same way that a clown puts on his slapstick. It's the Grays, all right. They've been murdering people for nothing, except their skin; and as that painting decomposes more and more – well, what do you think?'

'They'll want more skin?' asked Charlotte.

Vincent said, 'God, it seems like it, doesn't it? God. It's disgusting.'

'And they want the picture, too, just as badly?'

'At least I've left the house locked tight,' said Vincent. 'The Lord only knows what they could be capable of doing if they ever manage to lay their hands on that picture.'

'Can't you just go arrest them?' Charlotte demanded. 'If they're all that evil, if they're really murderers, why doesn't Sheriff Smith drive straight down to Darien and collar them, before they kill somebody else?'

'You can't arrest anybody without evidence, my love.' Vincent was acutely conscious of the fresh connotations that this morning's events had given to the words, 'my love'. 'And – no matter what we might *believe* – all the evidence we have so far is the unsubstantiated story of a hitch-hiker, which any half-decent defence attorney could have thrown out of court before the judge's bottom hit the chair.'

'But your great-grandfather's diaries. Your *grandfather's* diaries.'

'They don't prove anything, except that my great-grandfather and my grandfather had some trouble around the turn of the century with some people called Gray, all of whom should now be long dead. Come on, Charlotte, are you seriously asking this court to believe that Maurice Gray, who stands accused here today of homicide in the first degree, is the *same* Maurice Gray with whom my great-grandfather was acquainted, in the year 1891? The very idea of it is preposterous. Immediate acquittal, and costs against the county.'

'Then what can we do?' asked Charlotte.

Vincent finished his glass of Bristol Milk sherry, and then said, 'We could destroy the portrait. Then the Grays would be destroyed, too – according to what my grandfather says, at least.'

'You really think that we could deliberately kill twelve people?' asked Charlotte. Her eyes in the mid-morning sunlight were green as onyxes, and twice as bright.

Vincent said, 'It wouldn't be the same as shooting them, would it? It would be execution, by remote control. I wouldn't even have to go anywhere near them: I could torch the painting, and read in the Darien newspapers the very next day that the Grays were dead.'

'I'm not talking about the *method*,' said Charlotte. 'I'm talking about the morality.'

'Well, let's put it this way,' Vincent told her, 'there's nothing intrinsically immoral about destroying a rotten old Victorian painting that long ago lost any artistic or financial value, is there? And if the Grays *do* happen to die, at the same time that I burn the painting, then all I can say is that what my grandfather said about them was true, and that it was time they were dead, anyway. But if they *don't* die, then no harm has been done, to anybody.'

'I'm not sure about the logic of that,' said Charlotte doubtfully.

'I'm not sure about the logic of *any* of this,' Vincent told her. He stood up, and closed his grandfather's file. 'But let's go back to Candlemas and burn that painting, anyway.'

They left the offices of Morris, McClure & Winterman and trudged across the snowy car park. Charlotte said, 'Why didn't your grandfather destroy the painting, if he believed that the Grays were so evil?'

Vincent shrugged. 'The one thing that you can say about my grandfather is that he was always a man of honour; a man who kept his word, and stuck to it, no matter what. If he had promised Algernon Gray that he would keep the painting safe, then he would have kept the painting safe.'

'And you're prepared to break his word of honour?'

Vincent unlocked his car door. 'I don't think my grandfather had any inkling that the Grays would take to skinning people alive.'

They drove back to Candlemas in silence, although Charlotte stayed close to him. Vincent parked the car and opened the front door. His telephone answering-machine was blinking, which indicated that somebody had called him; but he ignored it for the moment and walked through to the living room, where he had left the Waldegrave portrait. The fire in the living-room grate had sunk low; and the wind was blowing softly down the chimney-stack, scattering the ashes across the rug, but the room was still warm. Vincent lifted up the portrait and said to Charlotte, as she came in the door, 'Are you going to watch?'

Charlotte stared at him. 'It's changed,' she said. Her voice was as dry as cardboard.

Vincent frowned, and turned the portrait around, so that he could see it more clearly. 'Changed? How?'

'There,' said Charlotte. 'She wasn't there before, surely?'

And it was true; she hadn't been there before. In the very front row of the portrait, where the ladies of the family were posed, sat a girl in a black maid's dress, severe and prim; except that the hem in the front had been drawn up high to reveal her thighs and even a smudgy suggestion of pubic hair. The girl's expression was calm and blank, unlike everybody else in the portrait, who had originally been smiling, before the rot set in. She looked quite modern, too. Her hairstyle was 1980s, and so was her make-up.

'Laura Monblat,' said Vincent. He touched her image with his fingers, but if any fresh paint had been applied to the canvas, it was quite dry.

'Laura Monblat?' asked Charlotte. 'You mean, Edward's ex-girlfriend?'

Vincent sat down, with the painting on his knees.

'That's Laura, all right. Edward brought her into the gallery once, the second or third day he worked for me. Now the whole damned thing is beginning to make some sense.'

'*Sense*? It's sense that Edward's ex-girlfriend mysteriously turns up in the middle of a Victorian painting? She wasn't there before, was she – before we went out? So somebody must have broken into the house and painted her there, in two hours, in oil-paint, and the paint's perfectly dry?'

'I don't think anybody broke in,' said Vincent. 'I think Laura has appeared on this portrait because she's actually there, down at The Wilderlings, along with the Grays. In some strange way, they've made her part of the family; the same way that Aaron's cat has appeared, in the place of the Grays' original ginger cat, Firework.'

'So they kidnapped her? Is that what you're saying?' Charlotte asked him.

'That's the assumption I'm making; admittedly, with not very much in the way of evidence.'

'I can't believe this,' said Charlotte. 'The very first day that we decide to be lovers instead of friends, and it's crazy and weird from start to finish.'

Vincent said, 'They must have done it on purpose.'

'They must have done *what* on purpose?'

'They may have included Laura in the painting, so that I wouldn't be able to burn it.'

'I don't understand you,' said Charlotte.

'It's dreadfully simple. I wish it weren't. But anybody who appears in this portrait has their life-essence inextricably caught up in it. The painting grows old, while *they* stay young. So right from the very second they first appear in it, their very survival depends on the survival of the painting.'

Charlotte stared at the portrait for a very long time, without speaking. 'That poor girl,' she said.

'Yes,' agreed Vincent. 'That poor girl. If I burn the picture, the chances are that I will burn her, too.'

Twenty-one

Housatonic Meadows, 20 December

'They found him by chance,' said Norman Goldberg, the collar of his sheepskin coat turned up against the driving snow. 'They were looking for their gun dog; still ain't whistled it up yet; but there he was, face down. They thought he was a hog, at first, or a dead moose. But, well, when they looked closer . . .'

Jack could see the hideous redness of George Kelly's body, even from twenty yards away, through wind and snow. George was lying half submerged in a frozen puddle, with crusts of ice in between his skinned fingers, naked, raw, and stripped of his skin. Wallace Greenstreet was crouching over him, wearing a wide-brimmed hat and fastidiously lifting up layers of skin and muscle with a scalpel.

'Any tyre-tracks?' asked Jack. 'They couldn't have carried him here on foot.'

'No tyre-tracks worth casting,' said Norman.

'How about footprints?'

'It's snowed and frozen over since they left him here.'

Jack thrust his hands into his anorak pockets and chewed warm gum for a while, and then said, 'Shit.'

Norman said, 'You think it's those Grays, don't you?'

Jack nodded emphatically. 'Of course I think it's those Grays. Elmer Tweed put the finger on Maurice Gray, and George was trying to prove it.' He walked forward, until he was standing only a dozen yards away from the body and the bent back of Wallace Greenstreet. 'Wallace?'

Without turning around, Wallace said, 'I hear you, Jack.'

Jack asked, 'How long do you think he's been here, Wallace? He looks to me like he's frozen pretty solid.'

Wallace adjusted his hat and laid his hands on his thighs, contemplating George Kelly's body with professional glumness. 'You'd need a chain-saw, to cut him up.'

'Do your best, anyway,' Jack told him. 'Look for drugs in the bloodstream, especially. Elmer Tweed said that Gray tried to inject him with a hypodermic.'

'I'll call you,' Wallace assured him.

Jack walked back to his Cherokee, and Norman Goldberg caught up with him. 'What are you going to do?' Norman asked.

'I'm going to go talk to Vincent Pearson, that's what I'm going to do. Then I'm going to drive down to Darien, and I'm going to get myself a warrant to search the Gray house. I'm going to bust the whole damned family, on suspicion of kidnap, attempted kidnap, and as many counts of first-degree homicide as I think I can prove.'

'Maybe you should wait awhile,' Norman suggested. 'You know, gather a little more evidence.'

Jack retorted, 'George Kelly was murdered, trying to gather evidence. I'm not risking any more lives, especially my own. With any luck, the Grays will resist arrest, and I'll be able to shoot them all. They're vermin, Norman. They're totally corrupt. People like the Grays, you don't give them second chances. You shoot them first and then you worry about the consequences afterwards.'

Norman looked unhappy. He clung on to the Cherokee's door, the snow blowing in his face, and said, 'You're the best sheriff that Litchfield County had in a long time, you know that? I wouldn't like to see any drastic changes; not just yet.'

Jack said, 'You want to stand here and have a long debate about a sheriff's duty to protect the public? I didn't put myself up for this job because I thought it was safe, Norman. I put myself up for this job because there are so many people who don't think that personal safety matters a damn, so long as everybody enjoys their rights under the Constitution. Well – as far as I'm concerned – blacks have rights, and women have rights, and gays have rights, and even goddamned New Yorkers have rights. But homicidal lunatics like the Gray family *don't* have rights, and all I'm going to do is point that out to them, in person.'

'Jack –' Norman warned him, 'don't get too mad.'

'Just watch me,' said Jack, and drove the Cherokee off through the snow, bumping over tussocks and ditches and rutted tracks, his teeth clenched with anger and grief. God knows what George must have suffered, before he died, he thought. God knows who else was going to have to suffer, before the Grays were finally caught.

Jack drove directly down to New Milford, and over to Vincent's house. Vincent and Charlotte were just finishing a late lunch of microwaved pizza and lightly chilled Corvo. The log fires were burning, and the house was comfortable and warm. Charlotte took Jack's coat and poured him a crystal glass of wine, and

Jack sat down in the big brocade-covered armchair next to the living-room hearth, and began to feel human again.

Vincent said, 'I've been trying to get in touch with you since yesterday. I called your office about a hundred times.'

Jack told him, 'I've been out. I just came back from Housatonic Meadows. You remember my friend George Kelly, down in Darien – the one who was trying to roust out a little more solid evidence about the Grays? Well, two duck-shooters found him this morning, dead, not too far from Cornwall Bridge. They thought that he was a slaughtered hog, at first, that somebody had shot and skinned, and left to rot.'

'You mean they skinned him, too?' asked Vincent.

'That's about it.' Jack didn't want to say very much more, in case he started to sound hysterical, or vengeful. 'They killed him, and they skinned him. Not necessarily in that order.'

Charlotte came over and sat beside him and laid her hand on top of his. 'I don't know what to say. I'm so sorry.'

Jack swallowed hard, to suppress his feelings. Then shrugged and looked away.

Vincent sipped a little more wine, and then said, 'We've found out some more.'

'About the Grays, you mean?'

Vincent nodded. 'It isn't evidence; not in the sense that you could present it to a judge and jury, and hope to get a conviction. But it may help us to combat the Grays on their own terms.'

Vincent explained about their visit to the family lawyers in Litchfield, and about Walter Waldegrave and his unnatural portrait. He also explained about Laura; and as he did so, he lifted the portrait out from behind

342

the sofa, and took off the wrapping paper, and presented it to Jack for closer inspection.

Jack studied it in silence. Then he glanced at Vincent and said, 'This is for real, isn't it? I mean, this isn't a dream, or any kind of collective hallucination. This is for real.'

Vincent said quietly, 'Yes. I believe it is.'

'Then I'm driving down to Darien right now, and I'm going to arrest them, on suspicion of kidnap and homicide in the first degree. Either that, or I'm going to blow them away.'

'You think your friend George Kelly would have approved of that?'

'George would have relished it. George was always in favour of blowing criminals away. And who are you to criticize? You were just about to set fire to the whole damned painting and the Gray family with it. And you *would* have done, too, if it hadn't have been for Mrs Monblat being there.'

'If you kill the Grays,' said Vincent, 'the chances are that we may never get Mrs Monblat back. Not as her normal self, anyway.'

'What do you mean?'

'I mean that Laura Monblat has turned up in this painting for a very good reason. The Grays have somehow gotten her in there to protect themselves. Like saying, "You can't destroy this painting, because if you do, you'll destroy Mrs Monblat, too." Besides, the Grays are the only people who know how to get her off the canvas and back into real life. Back into normal, mortal life – the kind of life that ends when it's supposed to end. Well, I'm *hoping* they know, anyway, because if they don't, she's going to be trapped in that picture for ever.'

Jack didn't quite know what to say to that. His belief

in the supernatural was beginning to waver slightly, in spite of everything that had happened. Vincent was very persuasive, very sophisticated, and yet Jack wasn't entirely sure if he ought to believe him.

'Do you think Mrs Monblat is in any immediate danger?' he asked Vincent.

Vincent lit up a cigarette and puffed at it without inhaling: the last self-indulgence of a reformed smoker. 'I think that we have to assume that she is – although it's quite unusual, isn't it, for any of the Grays' victims to have been kept alive for so long? The young man you found in the Nepaug Reservoir had been killed and skinned almost straight away; so had that other body you discovered down at West Haven; so was George Kelly. I can't do anything except guess, but it seems to me that Laura Monblat may have been taken into the family as some kind of maid or servant. Take a look at that dress. I know that it's been pulled right up, to expose her; but it's a maid's dress, isn't it? It reminds me of those bondage drawings of Sweet Gwendoline; and we know from my grandfather's papers that Henry Gray was very interested in bondage.'

Jack said, 'You don't think that Laura Monblat is dead already? Maybe they put her into the portrait just to confuse us.'

'I don't think so,' Vincent told him. 'It seems to me that the picture and the people in it are inextricably tied up together. It's just as if the picture is some kind of life-support machine, keeping the Grays alive long past the time when they were supposed to be dead. I thought at first that Laura Monblat might have been killed, but then I looked at the cat. You see that cat? My great-grandfather knew that cat: when it was still alive, he mentioned it, and it appeared in the portrait when it was first painted. But when I was a boy, the cat was gone. There was only a black fuzz, nothing more than a shadow – like an empty hole in the canvas.'

'I don't follow,' said Jack.

'Well, look at it this way,' Vincent explained. 'When the Grays reached the age when they *should* have died, when they all reached the end of their normal and natural life-span, the picture slowly began to decompose, and I think that *they* did, too. Maybe Waldegrave's technique wasn't sufficiently polished. Maybe his magic wasn't up to it, if it really was magic. But the portrait and the family began gradually and simultaneously to fall to pieces, that's my opinion. That's why they keep murdering people, and taking their skins. They have to keep themselves looking young, they have to keep themselves together, or else they'll die.'

'And the cat?' asked Jack.

'They were probably so worried about themselves, it didn't occur to them to think about the cat. The cat died, leaving nothing on the canvas but a black empty outline where once it had sat; and it was only this week, when one of the Grays killed Aaron Halperin's cat and skinned it, that Firework reappeared. Miraculously, as if it had been reborn.'

Jack said nothing. Vincent's interpretation of what was happening was bizarre, to say the least, but it did have some peculiar kind of logic – and he could think of no better explanation. The trouble was, Jack had never handled a case before that was even remotely similar; and for all he knew, he was being taken for a sucker. What if Vincent were in collusion with the Grays, for example? What if the Grays had paid off Pat? What if Nancy knew something about it, and wasn't telling? And how come Dr Serling had been so ready to join a séance – him, the down-to-earth country doctor?

Jack had accepted the séance and the appearance of Ben Miller's spirit because it had been his own idea – at least he *thought* that it had been his own idea. But supposing Dr Serling had set up some kind of projector, in the doctor's office, and faked the séance? And supposing this story about Laura Monblat were nothing at all but nonsense? After all, Jack had never seen the Waldegrave portrait *before* Laura Monblat had appeared on it. How was he to know that the portrait was genuine?

Vincent was watching Jack closely. He sold paintings; he was a good judge of doubt. 'You're having second thoughts, aren't you?' he asked. Jack shot him a quick, defensive look, and then turned away again.

'Don't think that *I* don't have doubts,' said Vincent. 'I change my opinion about what's going on here from one minute to the next. But – no matter which way I twist and turn it – the matter has only one basic explanation, and that is that the Waldegrave portrait has in some way been keeping the Gray family alive. Don't ask me precisely how, because I couldn't tell you, and besides, I don't think that it's scientifically possible. After that, everything is guesswork, everything is sup- position. But what I've been trying to do is rationalize as much as I can, based on everything we know – right from the diaries that my great-grandfather wrote, back in the 1890s, up to Elmer Tweed's evidence of last week.'

Jack finished his glass of Corvo, but kept his hand over the glass when Charlotte tried to pour him another one. 'What do you think we ought to do now?' he asked Vincent.

Vincent said, 'I've been thinking about that. The key to this whole situation, as far as I can make out, is the Waldegrave portrait. So, what we have to do is find out more about Walter Waldegrave. If we can even get half an inkling of how this was achieved – how the portrait stayed old, while the Grays stayed young – then maybe we stand a chance of fighting and defeating the Grays on their own territory.'

'You said something about reciting the exorcism, backwards.'

'Well, that's what my grandfather said. But I'm not at all sure that a couple of lines of Latin in reverse is really the answer, are you? Not in this day and age.'

Jack shrugged, and unwrapped a fresh packet of gum.

'What we have to find out,' Vincent told him, 'is how Waldegrave painted this portrait so that only the people on the canvas grew old, while the real people stayed just as they were. And – most important of all – how is it being done today? How could Laura Monblat have appeared on that canvas, painted in the same style as Walter Waldegrave's original picture, without anybody having touched the portrait at all? I mean, how the hell is that *done*?'

'More to the point, how the hell is it *un*done?' Jack added philosophically.

Charlotte, quite suddenly, said, 'I have an idea. Listen, do you remember that special exhibition we held at MOMA, round about eighteen months ago?'

'Not the Kandinsky,' said Vincent, baffled.

'No, no, no. The one we held in the fall. Modern allegorical art.'

'Yes, I remember,' Vincent told her. 'I hated it.'

'I know you did. But the man who organized it knew just about everything that anybody could ever want to know about art and magic. What was his name? Mac-Something. McKinley, I think it was. Do you mind if I call up David Smedley, and find out where we could get in touch with him?'

Vincent picked up the phone and handed it to her. 'Be my guest, if you think it will help.'

While Charlotte called her executive director, Vincent and Jack stood and examined the Waldegrave portrait. Vincent looked more closely at the portrait of Laura. There was something impassive yet infinitely sad about her; something that reminded him of J. M. Barrie's Wendy flying half asleep through a fairytale sky, calling as she flew, 'Poor Wendy; poor Wendy.' Jack remarked, 'The last time I saw anybody who looked like that, they were high on scopolamine.'

Vincent carefully touched the portrait's face. He brought his fingers away, and one of them was wet. He frowned at it. Jack asked, 'Is the paint still tacky?'

Vincent tentatively licked his finger. 'It's salt,' he said. 'It's like tears.'

'Now you're letting your imagination run away with you,' Jack told him.

'Yes, maybe,' Vincent agreed.

He regarded the faces of the twelve Grays. Algernon and Isobel, standing at the back. Belvedere and Willa, close beside them, on the left. John and Henry, on their right. Maurice, standing jealously close to Algernon, almost as if he were supporting him from behind. And in the front, seated on chairs, the ladies: Emily, Ermintrude and Nora; Cordelia, Alicia and the crippled Netty. On Netty's lap sat Firework, the marmalade cat. And beside her, just below Henry, sat Laura Monblat.

Twelve blurred and decomposing faces – faces which looked as if they had been photographed far away and long ago, with a hand-held camera that had been jogged at the crucial moment, so that they were all out of focus. Only Laura's face was clear; but then Laura

348

had not yet reached the age when she should have been dead.

Charlotte came off the phone. 'We're in luck,' she said. 'The man who organized the exhibition of modern allegorical art was called Percy McKinnon. He lives in Seekonk, Massachusetts. Here's his telephone number.'

'Go ahead, call him,' said Vincent.

Charlotte punched out the number, and waited. After a long while, she said, 'Hello? Is this Mr Percy McKinnon?'

'This is *Doctor* Percy McKinnon,' replied a sharp, professorial voice, so loudly that Vincent could hear it on the other side of the room.

Charlotte explained who she was and what she wanted. There was a short, asthmatic pause, and then Dr McKinnon said, 'You'd better come down and see me. This is not really the kind of question that one can discuss over the telephone. I need to see you, face-to-face. To be quite frank, I need to know if you're serious.'

Charlotte put her hand over the telephone and said to Vincent, 'Can we get down to Seekonk?'

'I guess,' said Jack. 'I could drive you down in the Cherokee. Norman Goldberg can take care of the store for me.'

Vincent checked his watch. 'We'd be running pretty late if we tried to drive there today. How about tomorrow, round about noon?'

Charlotte suggested the time to Dr McKinnon. Then she said, 'He can only make Monday.'

'That loses us the whole weekend,' said Jack. 'The Grays could have skinned somebody else by then.'

'Dr McKinnon has a sick sister; he has to visit her. I'm sorry – he won't change his mind.'

'Okay, then, Monday,' Jack agreed. 'Maybe we can dig up something in the way of solid evidence by then.'

'Maybe you could go home and get yourself some rest,' Vincent suggested. 'Your wife must think you're a stranger these days.'

Jack bit off some gum, and pushed it into the side of his cheek. 'Yes, maybe you're right. I can't remember the last time I slept at home. As a matter of fact, I can't remember the last time I slept.'

Charlotte found his coat, and Vincent escorted him to the door. Outside, the snow was falling thickly, and the draught that blew in through the open door was as sharp as the edge of a freshly opened tin.

Jack tugged on his cap and wriggled his fingers into his gloves. 'Listen,' he said, without looking directly at Vincent, 'this whole case is wacky beyond normal belief. So don't get upset if sometimes I find it difficult to credit what you're trying to suggest, like I did just now. For some reason, I guess I always believed in whatever-you-want-to-call-it, the supernatural, except that up until now there wasn't any need to. Now there *is* a need to; but that's not making it any easier. Just understand that we're both on the same side; and that we're going to nail those Grays, one way or another, whatever we have to believe in.'

Vincent grasped his elbow. 'You bet,' he said. 'Now, go home, before your wife decides that you're more turned on by police-work than you are by her.'

Vincent closed the door, and came back into the living room, chafing his hands to warm them up. 'It looks like it's working itself up to a blizzard out there. I just hope it eases off before Monday.'

350

Charlotte said, 'Do you want me to open another bottle of wine?'

'Why not?' asked Vincent, kissing her hair. 'And let's take it to bed.'

'Don't tell me you're tired already,' she teased him.

They were just about to go upstairs, carrying the bottle of wine and two large crystal goblets and a barrel of pretzels, when they heard a car drawing up outside. Vincent went across to the living-room window, held aside the curtains and peered out into the snow. 'Damn it,' he said, 'it's Margot.'

'But she's two days early,' Charlotte complained.

'Margot is a law unto Margot, and unto nobody else,' Vincent replied irritably.

He opened up the front door again. Margot had parked her red Mercedes at the usual awkward angle across the drive (how many times had he told her that when she parked it like that, it made turning round almost impossible, and nobody else could get into the drive?). She was struggling with armfuls of parcels, while Thomas was standing beside her with his suitcase and a new pair of snowshoes. Vincent was silently furious. A new pair of snowshoes was already waiting for Thomas up in his bedroom, as a Christmas surprise. Vincent had walked all the way over to the ski store on 58th Street on a freezing afternoon to buy them, and he had *told* Margot all about them.

'You're a little previous,' Vincent told Margot caustically, taking some of her parcels and closing the boot for her. 'I thought we said Sunday.' He smiled at Thomas, gave him a squeeze around the shoulders with his one free hand and said, 'Hi, Terror.'

Margot adjusted her red woolly bobble-hat. 'He doesn't like to be called Terror any more. He says it's childish, and I agree with him. He asked me to speak to you about it.'

Through the falling snowflakes, Vincent looked at his son, and said, 'That true?'

Thomas shrugged, embarrassed, unwilling to be used by one parent against the other. Vincent knew that he loved his mother; and that he loved his father equally. Neither of them should force any choices on him, one way or another, but of course they always did. 'Let's get inside,' said Vincent. 'The fire's burning up real well. We could toast some marshmallows.'

'I'm glad to hear that your Boy Scout days are not yet over,' Margot remarked. Then she caught sight of Charlotte, standing in the doorway in her blue and white silk bathrobe. 'Oh,' she said. 'Perhaps they are.'

Margot bustled her way into the house and through to the kitchen as if the place still belonged to her. She deposited her parcels on the kitchen counter, and then took off her hat and shook the melting snow off it. 'The forecast said blizzards tomorrow,' she said. 'Bruce said that if I couldn't get Thomas up here today, then I probably wouldn't be able to manage it at all, not before Christmas.'

Margot was physically and temperamentally the exact opposite of Charlotte. She was only just over five foot two, with short dark curly hair, and a heart-shaped face which Vincent had once described to his mother as 'almost unbearably sweet'. She wore 'directional clothing' these days, baggy khaki culotte suits with huge aggressive shoulders, the uniform of women who want to show everybody they meet that they no longer depend on men. Vincent thought that she looked like a pre-shrunk General Patton, but had always been polite enough not to tell her. Her perfume and her shoes were expensive, which was a sure sign that she didn't have as much money as she thought she ought to.

She was as untidy as ever, too. Her parcels sprawled everywhere. Her hat lay on the draining-board. She took off her shoes (descending in height by at least two inches) and left them kicked across the floor.

'It *is* Charlotte, isn't it?' she asked. 'Yes, I thought it was Charlotte. Is Charlotte cooking the Christmas lunch, Vincent?'

'No; we're going over to the Housatonic Hotel.'

'How awful for you. Doesn't Charlotte cook?'

'Why don't you ask her yourself, dear? She speaks English.'

Margot rustled through all of her parcels. 'Don't you cook, Charlotte? Thomas does enjoy his traditional holiday food, don't you, Thomas?'

Thomas said nothing, but stood there in his anorak with his snowshoes under his arm, looking exactly like his father: serious-faced, curly-haired, good-looking, and broad across the shoulders and very tall for his age – waiting for his mother to go.

Charlotte said, 'I shall be cooking on Christmas Eve. Carp, goose, sweet potatoes. Very traditional. Thomas won't go hungry.'

'Well – all of your Christmas gifts are here,' said Margot. 'I'm sorry that I didn't bring anything for Charlotte, but, well, I wasn't aware that she was going to be ensconced. Besides, what *does* one buy for the girl who has everything?'

Vincent said, 'I wouldn't stay, Margot, if I were you. The snow's thickening up and it's going to be dark soon. You wouldn't want to be stranded here for Christmas, would you?'

'No,' said Margot. 'I certainly wouldn't. Now, would you please make sure that Mrs Charlesworth gets this present here. It doesn't have her name on it, but you can remember it by the paper. And this one's for Jennie. And that's for the Ullmans. All the rest are marked.'

'Would you care for some coffee before you go?' Charlotte asked Margot.

Margot gave Charlotte her 350-calorie smile, and tossed her curls. 'Thank you all the same. Bruce will be wondering what's happened to me, if I'm late.'

'Sure he will,' said Vincent, and put his arm around her, when she had struggled back into her shoes, and guided her gently to the door.

Once they were there, Vincent handed over her woolly hat. 'You used to put it on for me,' she said.

'That was before,' said Vincent.

'Before, and never again?' Margot asked him.

He kissed her cheek. Her skin was as soft as ever, but now felt unfamiliar. 'Happy Christmas,' he told her. It was only their second Christmas apart.

'Happy Christmas,' she replied, very quietly. Then she kissed and hugged Thomas, and walked out into the snow. Vincent saw her out to her car, and guided her when she turned it. Backwards and forwards, backwards and forwards, eleven times. When they were married, he would have climbed into the driver's seat and turned the Mercedes for her. Eventually, however, she managed to manoeuvre herself round, and disappeared down the sloping drive with a brave toot of her horn.

Vincent came back inside and closed the door. 'You *really* don't want me to call you Terror?' he asked Thomas.

Thomas gave him a lopsided, embarrassed smile.

'I know, I know,' said Vincent. 'How about a glass of wine, to celebrate Christmas?'

'Yes, please,' said Thomas. His voice seemed to be deeper now than it had been three months ago. He was almost as tall as Vincent, and Vincent realized that it wasn't going to be long before his own son was looking down on him. The thought suddenly made him feel very old. The thought suddenly made him wonder: what if the Grays *can* live for ever? And what if I can find out how they do it? Presented with the choice of dying at the age of seventy or thereabouts, in less than twenty-five years' time, and living practically for ever, what would I do?

Thomas said, 'Mom bought me these snowshoes. Maybe we could try them out tomorrow.'

'Well, that's a very fine pair of snowshoes,' Vincent told him. He turned them over and inspected the webbing and the straps. 'They match your other pair.'

'What other pair?'

'The pair *I* bought you for Christmas, dummy.'

Thomas looked at Vincent in dismay; but Vincent simply laughed. 'Don't worry about it. You're nothing but the poor innocent victim of parental rivalry. As a matter of fact, now we have two pairs, you and I can go out together. How about trekking over to Gaylordsville tomorrow, and maybe calling on the Fosters, too? Susie Foster came back from school last week.'

Thomas didn't look too interested, but Vincent said, 'You haven't seen her. She's grown up. And when I say she's grown up, I mean she's really grown up.'

'I hope you're not putting unhealthy ideas into his head,' smiled Charlotte.

'When he sees Susie Foster, he won't need *me* to put any unhealthy ideas into his head.'

They went through to the living room and sat down

by the fire. Vincent unhooked the toasting forks, while Charlotte went to find the marshmallows.

Outside, the snow fell softly and densely on to the rooftops and chimneys, and the great silence of Christmas-about-to-be fell across the valley of the Housatonic River, from the Appalachian Trail to Painters Ridge; silence and snow.

At the foot of the drive which led up to Candlemas, its exhaust issuing smoke and its windscreen wipers intermittently clearing away the fine wool of the snowfall, a black Cadillac Fleetwood was parked. Inside it, wrapped in dark mink coats, sat Maurice and Cordelia Gray. The heating was set to *high*; and there was a stifling smell of fur and pot-pourri inside the car.

'You're quite sure now that the painting is here?' asked Maurice, without attempting to conceal the sarcasm in his voice.

They had suffered an embarrassing experience that afternoon at the Halperin house. Creeping around the outhouses, they had been surprised by the Halperins' gardener, who was chopping up logs just outside the studio. Aaron and the rest of the family were out Christmas shopping; and Cordelia hadn't imagined that there would be anybody around. But – as it turned out – the gardener had been quite a help. Once Cordelia had reassured him that they were friends of the family, he had told them, among erratic gossip, that the Halperins were out looking for a new cat.

'After what happened to the *last* one, poor dumb critcher. Mr Halperin said it was that painting he'd been working on. Bad luck, that painting, that's what he said. He gave it back to Mr Pearson just as quick as he could. Wouldn't work on nothing that was bad luck; that's what he said. Don't say that I blame him, neither. Mark you, he does like his sauce. A man who likes his sauce as much as that can make some misjudgements.'

So here they were at Candlemas – having at last tracked down the Gray family portrait.

'How much do you think that Pearson knows about the painting?' asked Maurice. As he spoke, the windscreen wipers cleared away the freshest fall of snow with a rubbery shudder.

'I think we have to assume that he knows at least as much as his grandfather did,' Cordelia replied. 'His *dear* grandfather.'

Maurice rubbed his eyes. 'Yes,' he said, 'I suppose you're right. We must be cautious. I'd hate anything to go wrong now. After everything that Father and Mother have suffered.'

Cordelia glanced at her watch, although the time was displayed on the Cadillac's instrument panel. 'It looks as though they've decided to stay in for the evening. Perhaps we ought to try tomorrow.'

'Indeed,' Maurice agreed, 'and there *is* something useful that we can do now.'

Cordelia turned to him, the reflected light from the snow making her skin look even whiter, her eyes as black as jets. 'Ah,' she said. 'You're referring to Mr Tweed.'

Maurice released the brake, shifted the Fleetwood into *drive* and pulled out on to the highway, heading towards Torrington. As he drove, he hummed under his breath one of the old songs, from days gone by, 'Hello, Central, Give Me Heaven'. Maurice had always considered himself 'sentimental'. There had once been a girl in his life: Pearl, and he had loved her with excruciating passion. His father, however, had refused to have Pearl included in the family portrait, and the last time that Maurice had seen Pearl, she had been grey-haired, married and almost old enough to be his mother.

Cordelia said, 'What are you thinking about?'

Maurice smiled. 'Nothing very much.'

Cordelia touched his arm. 'Don't think about the past,' she said. 'Think about the future. Very soon, we will have the painting back; and then all our years of worry will be over.'

Twenty-two

The snow died down during the night, and the following morning Vincent and Thomas snowshoed all the way through the woods to Gaylordsville. The sky was clear and pale; the trees were as dark as bears, wrapped up in cloaks of white. Their snowshoes made a continuous shushing sound across the drifts; their breath smoked.

Thomas was far fitter than Vincent, and he managed to keep ahead of his father for most of the way; but as they slid their way along the last mile, he slowed down, and they walked side by side together.

'I've formed an arts club at school,' said Thomas.

'Is that why you don't want me to call you Terror any more?'

Thomas smiled, and shook his head. 'We have this really decadent password, to get into meetings.'

'Are you going to tell me what it is, so that I can come to meetings?'

'Well, I hope I can pronounce it properly. It's *Les sanglots longs des violons de L'automne*.'

'Paul Verlaine,' Vincent nodded. 'The long sobs of the violins of autumn. You're right. It *is* decadent.'

Thomas said, 'How long is Charlotte staying?'

Vincent looked at his son sideways. 'She's staying

359

until New Year's, I guess. That's when we both have to get back to the city. You don't mind, do you?'

'No, not at all. I like her. I think she's beautiful.'

'Don't start getting ideas,' said Vincent. 'You stick to Susie Foster.'

They slid down a long white slope, which was marked only by the arrowheads of birds' footprints, until they reached the darker crevice of the Gaylord Branch. It was half frozen into knobs and columns and twisted curtains of ice, but running still, so that its tributaries spread into a finger-like pattern through the snow.

'When I was young, I used to call this the Amazon River,' said Vincent. 'Up there, right on top of that waterfall, that's where I used to fight crocodiles, and undiscovered tribes of headhunters. You see that shelf of rock back there, with all the icicles on it? That used to be my lookout post. I used to lie up there for hours in the summer – or what seemed like hours. Sometimes I took off all of my clothes, and pretended that I was the lost white chief of the Ugarugah tribe. I remember I was squatting up there stark naked when my cousin Tilda came looking for me. She was twelve and I was ten; and boy, was I embarrassed. I wouldn't come out of the woods until it was almost dark.'

Thomas said, 'Do you miss it?'

'What?' asked Vincent.

'Being young, being a boy. You sound like you miss it.'

Vincent stood still in the snowy woods, looking around at the silent trees. 'No,' he said, after a while. 'I don't think that I miss it. I sometimes wish that I'd made more of it; but then I guess that almost everybody does. You can't miss it. How can you? No matter what happens, there's always going to be a boy in these woods, playing the lost white chief of the Ugarugahs, even if that boy is only a memory.'

He laid his arm around Thomas's shoulders, and realized that this was one of the last times that he would be able to do it. 'You have to grow up, and you have to grow old. Nothing can ever prevent that. Not all the wishing in the whole damned world.'

They snowshoed their way up the opposite bank of the Gaylord Branch, until they reached the road. Charlotte was waiting for them there, as she had promised, in Vincent's Bentley, so that they could drive out to visit the Fosters; but Jack Smith's Cherokee was waiting there, too. As they crossed the hard-packed snow on the highway, Jack came over, accompanied by Charlotte, and said, 'Good morning, Mr Pearson. How was your walk?'

Vincent kissed Charlotte, partly because he felt like it, and partly to show Sheriff Smith that he had intruded on his private family morning. 'I think my calf muscles have started protesting already,' he said. 'Is there anything that I can do?'

Jack looked at Thomas and said, 'How're you doing?' and then said to Vincent, 'Can we talk alone?'

'Surely,' said Vincent. He followed Jack to the side of the car, and then said, 'Well? What seems to be the problem?'

Jack cleared his throat, and sniffed. 'Elmer Tweed was found dead in his cell, about five o'clock this morning.'

'You're joking.'

'I wish I were.'

'But Elmer Tweed was your only witness. Elmer Tweed was the only person who could have connected the skinning murders with Maurice Gray.'

'How right you are; but he's dead.'

Vincent took off his gloves and wiped the frost away from his mouth. 'How did he die? Is there any indication?'

'Apparently a man and a woman came in to visit him at about eleven o'clock last night. They claimed they were Mr and Mrs Lyndon H. Tweed, and that Elmer Tweed was their son. Norman Goldberg says that they spoke in distinctive Southern accents, and because of that, he believed them.'

'Jesus,' breathed Vincent.

Jack said, 'They were given five minutes to converse with Elmer Tweed. Tweed himself didn't say anything when they were brought into the interview room; and I can only presume that he wanted to wait and see who they were. Maybe he thought they came from one of those do-gooding groups who specialize in springing waifs and strays out of jail. Quite often, they gain admission to the suspect by masquerading as parents or relatives.'

'Then what happened?' asked Vincent, dryly.

'They talked, for three or four minutes. The woman kissed Tweed, right on the mouth; more like she was his lover than his mother. They left, saying they would call again to see Elmer soon.'

'And?'

Jack unfastened the pocket of his anorak, and took out three colour Polaroids. He passed them to Vincent without any comment.

Vincent had only to glance at one of them to know what had happened to Elmer Tweed. The photographs showed a police-station bunk, a collapsed body and a torrential mass of off-white maggots.

'The Grays,' said Vincent. He took a deep breath, just to feel the clean frosty Connecticut air drop deep into his lungs, and then he handed the Polaroids back to Jack, without even bothering to look at all of them.

'It sure looks like it,' said Jack.

'So where do we stand now, legally?'

'Flat on our *tochis*. We could pull Maurice and Cordelia Gray in for questioning, but all we have to go on is circumstantial evidence, identification by police witnesses, and the weirdest, most preposterous story that anybody ever heard in their whole lives.'

'Quite apart from which, I'm sure that the Grays have an immaculate alibi,' Vincent remarked.

'Don't doubt it.'

Vincent stood and thought for a moment, his left cheek burned by the icy wind. Then he said, 'How about this for a suggestion? How about we ask your friend Pat to hold another séance for us; only this time we use the Waldegrave portrait as our central focus, instead of poor Ben Miller. Perhaps we can rouse the spirits of the Waldegraves, and get them to tell us something which might incriminate them.'

Jack didn't look at all delighted with that idea. 'Pat's husband went crazy when he found out what she'd been doing the last time.'

'She wasn't hurt, was she? We could pay her this time.'

'The Litchfield sheriff's department doesn't have a budget that runs to séances.'

'I don't mind paying. Say, two hundred fifty dollars?'

Jack took out his handkerchief and busily blew his nose. 'I guess she might consider it, under those circumstances.'

'Say, four o'clock this afternoon then, round at Candlemas,' said Vincent.

Jack said, 'I'll try. Maybe Nancy can persuade her.'

Before he went, Vincent said, 'Let me take a look at those Polaroids.'

This time, his stomach was settled enough to examine all three pictures carefully. 'There isn't any question about it at all. This was the same thing that happened to Edward. As far as I'm concerned, this implicates the Grays absolutely in Edward's death.'

Jack stared at him narrowly, chewing gum. 'You'll be wanting your share of revenge, then, the same way that I do.'

'I don't know,' said Vincent. 'I'm not altogether sure that revenge is the right word.'

Jack drove off to see if he could organize another séance; Vincent and Charlotte and Thomas drove in the opposite direction to pay a Christmas call on the Foster family. The Fosters lived in a striking A-frame just north of Gaylordsville, down a narrow side-turning, and had been friends with Vincent for nearly ten years. They had supported him during his divorce from Margot with patience, equanimity and plenty of good whisky. Today, they had their huge log fire crackling, and plenty of hot cheese pastries and mulled punch. Everybody sat on large red-and-yellow Indian blankets, amid heaps of cushions, and laughed and talked of Christmas.

Thomas immediately took to Susie Foster; who had grown up spectacularly from a plain-looking thirteen-year-old beanpole into a curvy young woman. Thomas and Susie had a few drinks with their parents, and then they went out into the snow, with their snowshoes. Vincent stood by the French windows, watching them scuffle and play in the sloping snowy yard. Jan Foster came up and stood beside him, and said, 'You must be proud of him, Vince, he's looking just like you.'

Vincent put his arm around her. 'They seem to be hitting it off, don't they? That's some pretty young lady you've raised there, Jan. If I was ten years younger . . .'

Charlotte called, from her cushion beside the

fireplace, 'You mean if you were *thirty* years younger. Don't take any notice of him, Jan. He's going through the male menopause. Not only that, he's having his second childhood at the same time.'

'What do you mean?' Vincent demanded. 'I haven't even been bar-mitzvahed yet.'

Doug Foster roared with laughter. 'Vincent still believes that he's twelve years old, because he hasn't been bar-mitzvahed. His parents forgot to tell him he wasn't Jewish, and that he never would be. Oh, Vincent, you're crazy sometimes.'

'Yes,' said Vincent quietly, watching Thomas and Susie, but thinking about the Grays.

Jan noticed his sudden change of mood, and said, 'Is anything wrong?'

Vincent shook his head.

'Come on, Vincent,' she said. 'We've been through a lot together, you and I.'

Vincent kissed her. 'Sure we have. But this is something that goes way back; long before you and me. Long before *me*, as a matter of fact.'

'I don't know what you mean.'

'I'll tell you all about it, when I've sorted it out. It's all to do with heritage. *Delicta maiorum immeritus lues.* Even though you are guiltless, you must expiate the sins of your fathers. And your grandfathers. And your great-grandfathers.'

'You've got me foxed,' said Jan, cheerful on the outside but plainly concerned about him on the inside.

'I'm okay,' Vincent told her. 'How about some more of this hot Kool-Aid?'

Doug Foster laughed again. 'Jan spends two hours making Old Connecticut Spiced Punch, and he calls it hot Kool-Aid. Vincent, you kill me.'

*

Thomas was invited to lunch at the Fosters, and begged to stay, which suited Vincent very well. As they drove back to Candlemas, along snowy deserted highways, he told Charlotte what had happened to Elmer Tweed, and also that he planned to hold a séance.

Charlotte said, 'Is it really necessary? It frightens me. I mean, what frightens me about it is that you're so serious.'

'We have to find out more about the Grays somehow.'

'We're going to Seekonk on Monday, to talk to Dr McKinnon. He'll tell us everything we need to know.'

'That's what we're hoping. But he may tell us nothing at all.'

'Couldn't we wait, at least, until we've seen him?' asked Charlotte.

Vincent shrugged. 'We *could*. But those Grays are homicidal savages, as far as I'm concerned, and right at the moment they're holding Laura Monblat. If they haven't killed and skinned her already, they could very well be thinking of doing it soon.'

Charlotte watched the white-faced world turning past her window. 'Have you called her husband?'

'Danny Monblat? No, not yet.'

'Don't you think that he has a right to know where his wife might be?'

'Not just yet.'

'But surely the police can go right in there and arrest the Grays, if they're holding her against her will.'

Vincent shook his head. 'You heard what happened to Sheriff Smith's best buddy. And look what's happened to his best and only witness. Sheriff Smith would like nothing better than to burst in on the Grays and round them all up, but this isn't any ordinary police investigation, and the Grays aren't any ordinary suspects. They've managed to survive for decades after they were supposed to be dead. Anybody who's done what they did to cling on to life, well, you don't think they're going to give up easily, do you?'

Charlotte reached across and touched Vincent's shoulder. 'They've made it the worst winter ever, haven't they, those Grays? Your grandfather should have burned the portrait long ago.'

They reached Candlemas and pulled up into the drive. Vincent wearily climbed out of the car and hobbled around it with aching leg muscles to open the door for Charlotte.

'You look like Quasimodo,' she smiled. 'Go take a hot shower; then I'll give you a massage.'

'The local residents aren't too keen about massage parlours. They've only just accepted the idea of self-service gas stations.'

They spent a quiet and thoughtful afternoon. They spoke little, drank wine, and let the strains of Mozart ease their minds. Outside, although it was only mid-afternoon, darkness began to encroach on the woods and the gardens surrounding Candlemas, and sudden gusts of sub-zero wind made snow-devils dance on the pallid lawns; like omens of unlucky times to come.

Jack didn't telephone. He drove up a few minutes after four o'clock in his squad car, with Pat sitting beside him. Vincent opened the front door for them, and they came into the large hall, stamping the snow from their feet. Jack looked at Vincent behind Pat's back, and made a face that meant, *Don't argue about it, here she is.*

Pat took off her gloves and unwound her scarf. 'I didn't come for the money, I'd like you to know,' she said to Vincent.

'I didn't think that you had,' he told her.

She stared at him acutely. 'How did you know?'

'Because you struck me back at the hospital as the kind of lady who cares about other people. You have a very special gift, and you know it, but you also know that having a very special gift like that gives you certain responsibilities to the people around you, whether you like it or not.' Vincent paused, and then he added, 'You wouldn't have agreed to hold that séance at the hospital, otherwise. You didn't take very much convincing.'

Pat looked at Jack with her lips pursed. 'He's better than my analyst,' she told him. 'Motivations, senses of responsibility – he knows it all.'

They went through to the living room. Vincent had set up the Waldegrave portrait on an easel at the end of the room. He hadn't yet drawn the curtains, but apart from the firelight which skipped across the hearthrug, the room was almost in darkness.

Pat approached the portrait very slowly. After a while, she reached towards it with her hand.

'That's evil,' she whispered.

'Evil?' asked Jack. 'What do you mean by evil?'

Pat slowly shook her head from side to side. 'This picture has such an *atmosphere* about it.'

'It smells of decay,' said Vincent.

'I'm not just talking about physical things; I'm talking about psychic things. There is a spiritual atmosphere around this picture that's absolutely terrifying. I've never come up against anything like it.'

She reached closer. Her hand, as it neared the surface of the painting, began to tremble. 'This is just awful,' she said. 'It feels so cold. It's like sliding your hand into icy slush. You know, it has a sort of lumpy feeling about it, apart from being so cold.'

Vincent and Jack came closer; Charlotte stayed away, by the fire. Pat reached out her other hand towards the painting and closed her eyes.

'What can you feel?' asked Jack, chewing gum with rhythmic rapidity. 'Can you feel anything?'

Pat was silent at first, her eyes still shut, her hands gradually feeling their way around the portrait as if she were a blind person palpating the face of somebody she had just met, in order to familiarize herself with every feature.

After a while, she said, 'These spirits are dead, or *should* be dead.'

Vincent asked, 'How do you know that, Pat! How do you know that?'

'I can feel their bodies,' Pat replied, in a horrified murmur. 'I can actually feel their dead bodies. They're very cold, as if they're in ice, but it's like the ice has half melted, and they're kind of floating around rotting. Soft, cold, slimy flesh. That's the only way I know how to tell you what it feels like.'

There was another long silence. Pat remained where she was, but now she began to breathe deeply and regularly, as if she were falling asleep. Charlotte asked, 'Do you think she's all right?' But Vincent waved her to stay as quiet as she could.

For an instant, Vincent thought he saw something clinging around the portrait, like a glowing transparent veil of whitish gas, but then Pat immediately withdrew her hands and opened her eyes, and it vanished.

'What was that?' Vincent asked her.

'You actually saw it?'

'I'm not sure. Just for a blink of the eye. It was like a cloud.'

Pat nodded. 'What you saw was the soul of one of these people in the picture.'

'A soul that should be dead, but isn't?' asked Jack.

'A soul that should have passed on to the next part of its existence,' Pat corrected him.

'Then why hasn't it?' Vincent wanted to know.

'I'm not sure. It's a very vain soul; a very proud soul.

It thinks of nothing but how great its own physical beauty was, when it was properly alive. It has very little kindness or understanding, although I think that it might have had once, when it was young.'

'You can tell all of that, just from reaching out towards the picture?'

'There's a whole lot more,' said Pat, not once taking her eyes off the portrait. 'There seem to be hundreds of souls in there. There are twelve dominant spirits, but there are crowds and crowds of others, most of them mutilated and hurt.'

'Their victims,' Jack commented. 'The people they've skinned.'

'Probably, yes,' said Pat.

'You mean that when they kill people, the spirits of their victims don't pass on to the next life, either? They all stay trapped in here, inside of this portrait?'

Pat lifted her hand up again. She closed her eyes. 'The victims of violent or painful death often find it difficult to pass on to the next stage of their life – especially if they don't have the prayers and good thoughts of the people they left behind to carry them through. It's just like they're unborn babies, conceived in a moment of terrible trauma and then undernourished and ignored.'

'But why *didn't* anybody pray for them?' asked Charlotte. 'Surely their relatives, or their friends . . .'

Pat said, 'When somebody goes missing, the only thing that their friends and relatives pray for is that they're alive. They *will* them to be alive. But what they don't understand is that if the missing person is already dead, if they've been murdered, that very act of willing them to be alive can prevent their spirit from passing through. People don't have any idea what effect they have on each other; not just physically, but spiritually.

You can knock somebody down with your fist. But you can totally wipe them out with your spirit.'

Jack glanced at Vincent, as if seeking his support to believe in what Pat was saying. Vincent deliberately avoided his gaze. He didn't want in any way to be held responsible for anybody else's belief or disbelief.

The log fire flickered low and made an odd guttering sound. Pat raised her hands toward the Waldegrave portrait once more and whispered, 'Come out. I command you. Come out.'

For a long time, nothing happened. But – whether or not it was a draught blowing in from under the front door – Vincent felt a distinct chill. He shivered, and Charlotte took his hand and shivered, too. Jack shuffled his feet and sniffed and chewed gum, trying to show that he was broad-minded about the occult, but at the same time pragmatic about its potential usefulness; a believer, yes, but a *practical* kind of believer.

'I command you, come out,' Pat repeated. Her voice sounded harsh now, and imperative. 'Come out, or suffer whatever punishment I choose to give you.'

'You can punish a spirit?' asked Jack.

Pat opened her eyes for a moment and looked at him. 'The human spirit's most burning desire is to continue on its journey, from the previous life to this life; from this life to the next. Somebody like me, a spiritual sensitive, has the power to delay somebody from passing through; and, believe me, spirits will do absolutely anything to pass through. If you want it in adult terms, it's like stopping somebody from having a sexual climax, right at the very last moment when they were sure that it was happening.'

Vincent said, 'Let her get on, Sheriff; please.'

Pat closed her eyes and began to recite, 'Spirit, I

command you to come out. I command you to make yourself known to me. You have no choice, except that I will imprison you in limbo for ever and ever, while other souls come and go.'

The white gaseous cloud appeared to return, twisting and writhing around the portrait like gauze blown in the wind. The temperature in the room dropped again and again, until Vincent felt a cold ache in his back and his temples, and he was sure that his breath was beginning to smoke. He began to *hear* something, too, like a very deep organ note, *basso profundo*, which was so low that it was scarcely audible. The china ornaments over the fireplace began to rattle and buzz, until one of Vincent's favourite pieces, an eighteenth-century Staffordshire shepherdess, abruptly exploded in a shower of white porcelain.

Pat took two or three slow calculated steps back. She raised her hands upward and cried out loudly, 'Come out! I command you! Come out!'

Gradually, the twisting white cloud began to pour downwards, towards the floor. Then, in utter silence, it began to rise up into a column again, a wavering column of boiling fumes. A girl appeared, naked, her hands manacled behind her back, her ankles fastened with shackles. Her head was lowered, out of shame or exhaustion, and even when Pat commanded her to speak, she said nothing.

'It's Laura,' said Vincent. He took a step towards her. 'Laura! Can you hear me! It's Vincent Pearson! Edward used to work at my gallery! Laura! Just lift up your head and talk to me!'

Laura slowly lifted her head. Her image was transparent, as if she were nothing more than a hologram, but the way she looked at Vincent made him believe that part of her, if not *most* of her, was actually here. She opened her mouth and said something, but it was too slow and indistinct for Vincent to be able to make out what she was saying.

'Laura!' he shouted; but Pat, still with her eyes closed, swung out her left arm and grasped his sleeve tight, to prevent him from approaching the Waldegrave portrait any more closely.

'But, damn it, that's Laura Monblat,' Vincent protested.

Pat dismissively shook her head. 'That's not Laura Monblat; that's an illusion. They're testing us. The twelve spirits in the picture are testing us. They want to see how much we care about Laura Monblat; because if we don't care at all, then she won't be very much use to them as a hostage.'

'You mean that they'll kill her straight away?'

'How do I know, for God's sake? Jack – I'm cold! Jack, if you want to ask her any questions, ask them now! I can't hold on to this much longer!'

Jack approached the image of Laura Monblat. She was even more transparent now, as if she were composed of nothing more than the glassy heat-waves which rise in the winter from an outdoor brazier and ripple across the snow.

'Laura,' he said, as decisively as he could manage. 'Laura, do you want to tell us where you are? We could come and get you, Laura. Help you get free. Just tell us where you are, is all; and tell us if you're still alive. You know, seeing like you're a ghost, it's pretty hard for guys like me to know for sure.'

Laura turned towards Jack with large, liquid eyes. Then she began to dance, to some unheard music, some silent Arabic tablas, with dry tone and guttural rhythm, some sinuous desert flute. Jack could scarcely see her now: she flickered in and out of his vision, her hands snaking down the sides of her hips, circling around her breasts.

Just before she vanished, however, she suddenly opened her eyes wide and held out both her hands, just as Pat had held out her hands towards the portrait, and she mouthed almost inaudibly the two terrible words, *Save me.*

The gaseous white robe around the portrait turned in on itself, and began to disappear. The fire in the hearth burned brighter. Vincent turned away from the portrait and took out his neatly folded handkerchief, and dabbed the chilly sweat around his forehead.

Jack said, 'That performance was controlled by the Grays, from start to finish. They're keeping her hostage, no doubt about that. But they're making her do just what they want her to do. Even that phony *"save me"*! What's that supposed to do? Send us rushing around there like half-assed heroes, with no warrant and no shred of reasonable suspicion? That would blow our arrest from moment one.'

Just then, however, when they thought that everything was over, they heard Pat cry, 'Don't.'

She was still standing in front of the Waldegrave portrait, her head down, her fists clenched, shaking. Charlotte said, 'Pat – are you all right? Pat?'

Pat said, 'Don't – come – closer – don't –'

'Pat, what the hell's the matter?' Jack asked her, and took hold of her arm.

Pat jerked her head around and stared at Jack with bulging eyes, and teeth bitten together so tightly that blood was running out of the corner of her mouth. 'They – won't let go – they –'

'Vincent,' Jack asked him urgently. 'Come over here. We've got trouble.'

They took hold of Pat, but she continued to shudder

and twitch, and her arms were as tense as if she were being electrocuted.

'Jack,' Pat appealed, her head dropping sideways against her shoulders. The seizure was so intense now that she could scarcely speak. Vincent could feel an extraordinary galvanic tingling running through his nerves and his muscles; and even the front of his head began to feel numb. He was conscious that he was shouting at Jack at the top of his voice, but for some reason he didn't seem to be able to make himself heard.

'Back – take her back – away from the –'

He could see through jolted, unfocused eyeballs that Jack had understood him, that Jack too was trying to drag Pat away from the malevolent influence of the Waldegrave portrait. Vincent's first analogy had been remarkably accurate. Pat was quaking because of the power from the Waldegrave portrait, in the same way that electrocution victims quake until someone manages to pull them away from the source of voltage.

Jack was screaming, 'Don't let her go! Vincent, you hear me? Don't let her go! She's going! For Christ's sake she's –'

There was a huge echoing shout, like a subway train suddenly hurtling into a tunnel. Pat shuddered and shook in between them; but they were powerless to move, not that they could have helped Pat, even if they had. The whitish gas began to blossom out of the portrait, only it wasn't gas at all, it was twisted evanescent faces and grasping claw-like hands; it was a hideous tangle of arms and legs and twisted viscera. And then suddenly there was something sharp, like a huge triangular butcher's knife, and it flashed upwards into Pat's stomach, so that Vincent could see the point of it momentarily glinting next to her spine. It couldn't have been a real knife, but Pat collapsed between them and sprawled face-down on the floor, while the gaseous apparition suddenly shrank away and fled; and at last the living room was still.

'Call the medics,' Vincent told Jack.

But Pat, with her face against the rug, said, 'It's okay. Please. It's over now. It was only an illusion. Illusions can't hurt you.'

Charlotte knelt beside her. 'That knife –'

'Just another illusion. They're warning me off.'

'Well, you're sure you're okay?'

Pat sat up, took out her handkerchief and pressed it against her face. 'I'm okay. Don't fuss.'

Vincent squatted down beside her and put his arm around her shoulders. 'That didn't hurt you? I thought you were dead.'

Pat smiled wanly. 'I could use a drink. Brandy, maybe? My circulation feels like death, even if I am still alive.'

While Charlotte unstoppered the brandy decanter, Vincent said to Pat, 'You knew how dangerous this was, the moment you held out your hand in front of that painting. You knew what would happen, didn't you?'

Pat didn't answer, but accepted a large glass of Courvoisier from Charlotte with a nod and a slightly twisted smile.

Jack said, 'Jesus. I thought for a second that I was dealing with another homicide there.'

Pat didn't look as if she was arguing. She drained the whole glass of brandy in one, and then held it out for a refill. Charlotte took it from her without a word.

'That was a warning?' asked Jack.

Pat nodded.

'Jesus. If that's what they do for a warning, you can imagine what they're like when they're really upset.'

Pat said, 'That was only their psyche, reacting against intrusion.'

'What does that mean?' asked Vincent.

'It means that the flesh-and-blood Grays who are alive and well and living in Darien may not even know that we've been sticking our noses in here. This wasn't their doing. Well, let's put it this way – it was nothing to do with the physical people you want to arrest. This was their spirits, the spirits that occupy their painting.'

'I don't think I get the difference,' said Jack, not altogether patiently.

'Usually, there *isn't* a difference,' Pat told him. 'Usually, a person is a person and a portrait is a portrait. The soul stays with the person, not the portrait, even when they're dead. How many stories did you ever hear about a haunted portrait?'

Jack, who rarely had a chance to read, or to watch television, or to do anything else but run after one yee-hawing scofflaw after another, gave an indifferent shrug.

'That portrait,' Pat went on, stepping away from it as she did so, 'that portrait is possessed. Believe me.'

'So, what can we do about it?' asked Jack, impatiently.

'You can burn it, you can smash it with a hammer, you can take it out to Fire Island and commit it to the waves, or you can sell it to anybody who might be freaky enough to take it off your hands. But you really ought to get rid of it. And I mean, *permanently*. I don't know what's happened here. I don't know why this portrait should feel so evil. But it does, and it's dangerous, and I really recommend that you get rid of it.'

Vincent said, 'The girl, Laura, the one who appeared in front of you . . . ?'

'She's alive,' said Pat.

'You mean that?' asked Vincent. 'I mean, alive in the sense that –'

Pat said, 'Alive in the sense that they haven't killed her yet, that's all.'

Vincent looked towards Jack, who was regarding the portrait with serious eyes, his hand pressed against his mouth. Then he turned back to Pat and gave her his hand, so that he could help her on to her feet. Charlotte stoked the fire, and then suddenly went across and draped the Waldegrave in its bedspread.

Vincent said to Pat, 'What I mean is, if Laura's still alive, and if we destroy the portrait . . .'

Pat said, 'It depends what you want. As it is, the Grays own her completely, body and soul. They will kill her eventually; but the question you have to ask yourself is when.'

'You really believe that they'll kill her?'

'There isn't any doubt. You didn't feel the portrait, the way that I did.'

Vincent said, 'If we burn the portrait, then Laura will burn, too. Is that it?'

Pat tried to smile. 'I'm not an expert, Mr Pearson. I never said I was.'

'But that's what you believe?'

Pat nodded, and then turned away. Vincent had the impression that the séance had disturbed her more than she was willing to admit.

'Are you feeling okay?' Jack asked her. 'Maybe you should sit down. Ms Greene, do you have any tea? Or coffee, maybe?'

'Pat?' asked Charlotte. 'What would you like?'

Pat sat down on the very edge of one of the sofas by the fire. She stared at the shrouded Waldegrave portrait, and continually rubbed her arm, the way that a nervous child does. 'That painting is so evil,' she said. 'It's like a psychic morgue in there.'

'I'm sorry,' Vincent told her. 'When I suggested you come take a look at it, I didn't think that –'

'You must get rid of it,' Pat interrupted. 'You don't have any choice.'

'But what about Laura Monblat?'

Pat shivered, and rubbed her arm even more neurotically. 'Do you seriously think that you can save her? Did you see what they made her do? They won't let her live. They won't let anybody live: anybody who threatens them, or anybody they can make use of. They're determined that they're going to go on living, Mr Pearson, and they don't care what they do, or how they do it, or how many people they kill.'

She hesitated for a moment, and then she clasped her stomach with both hands. 'I think they've hurt me,' she said, swallowing a sudden mouthful of saliva.

Vincent sat down beside her and gently turned her face around, so that he could look into her eyes. 'She's going into shock,' he told Jack. 'You'd better call those medics, and call them quick. Try Dr Serling, too.'

Jack went immediately across to the telephone and punched out the emergency number for the Litchfield paramedics. Charlotte helped Vincent to lay Pat down on the sofa, and then she went to the bureau in the hall to fetch a warm plaid travelling-rug. Pat's face had turned very white now, and she was shuddering almost as badly as she had when the ectoplasm from the painting had reached out towards her.

'It's all right,' Charlotte reassured her, wrapping the blanket around her. 'It's only shock. You're going to be fine.'

Jack finished talking to Dr Serling, and then came

over and knelt down beside the sofa. Pat was perspiring copiously now; sweat was running down the sides of her neck, and she was twisting and turning and clawing at the blanket.

'Standard symptoms of shock,' said Jack. 'Charlotte – would you fetch me some water, please.'

'Don't – touch me –' Pat whispered. 'Whatever you do – don't –'

She coughed, bringing up saliva streaked with blood. Charlotte said, 'My God, Vincent, she really *is* hurt.'

'The medics are on their way,' Jack told her. 'Vincent – would you help me to keep her still. Charlotte, please, that water.'

Charlotte brought the water and Pat managed to sip a little. She was still sweating and shaking, but the water and the warmth of the blanket seemed to have calmed her down. 'I'm all right, really,' she whispered to Jack. 'Please, it's nothing to worry about.'

'Are you kidding?' Jack smiled, and used his handkerchief to mop the shining perspiration off her forehead. 'I'd worry about you if you so much as hiccuped.'

'You have to – destroy the picture –' Pat insisted.

'We've got it in mind,' said Jack, stroking her forehead. 'Don't you worry about it. Those Grays aren't going to get away with anything.'

Pat suddenly clutched Jack's arm, and squeezed her eyes tight shut.

'Oh, God!' she cried. 'Oh, God, it hurts!'

'Where does it hurt?' Jack asked her, 'Pat. please, tell me. *Where* does it hurt?'

Pat pushed him away and sat up, one hand against her throat, the other against her stomach. 'I'm going to be sick,' she said, in the quietest of voices. 'It must be that water – I –'

Without any further warning, she vomited up a basinful of bright red blood. It splashed all over her lap, and all down the leg of Jack's uniform pants. She stared at Jack in horror and fright, and then vomited up more blood, as violently as if it was being tossed out of her in buckets.

'Jack!' she gagged, spattering more blood. 'Jack! Save me! Jack, it hurts!'

Jack yelled at Vincent, 'Call those goddamned paramedics again! Ask them what in hell is holding them up!'

Vincent stood up; but as he did so, Pat let out a gargling scream, and brought up pints of blood and chopped-up flesh. It splashed everywhere, all over the rug, all over the walls, into the hearth. Blood and stomach-lining and liver and lungs, heaved up out of her throat and stringily puked all over the floor. Pat sat where she was, shaking, bibbed in blood, staring with glassy and disbelieving eyes at the heaps of viscera which lay steaming all around her feet and in her lap, knowing in the very few seconds that were left to her that she had no chance whatever of survival. Nobody could speak: the horror of what had happened had been too abrupt. Nobody could do anything but watch Pat slowly twist around and collapse sideways, falling face-down on the floor in her own grisly mess.

Vincent said, 'I – Charlotte, I –' but then he couldn't carry on, through shock and emotion. He turned away and stood with his hands clasping the sides of his head, trying to keep himself under control, trying to stop his mind from bursting. He could hear Charlotte sobbing, and that was what managed to bring him together; although for one brief moment of psychic vertigo, he felt that he could have gone mad.

It was then that he felt Jack's hand on his sleeve. Jack said, 'Vincent. Vincent, look!'

Vincent slowly turned around, keeping his eyes on Jack to begin with, but then slowly allowing his gaze to fall towards the floor, where Pat was lying. Charlotte, on the other side of the living room, was already staring at Pat in horror and fascination.

For the blood and flesh that were splattered in heaps all over the rug were gradually *fading*, as if they never existed. The lumps of flesh grew fainter, and less distinct, almost like jellyfish seen underneath the ocean at evening time; then the splashes of blood started to disappear. Within four or five minutes, all trace of Pat's terrible sickness had completely vanished, as if it had never happened.

Jack whispered, 'We're imagining this.'

'Either that, or somebody's *making* us imagine it,' Vincent replied.

'The Grays?'

'More than likely,' said Vincent unsteadily. 'Just remember that they've had over a hundred years to perfect their psychic abilities, which is well over what anybody else is ever allowed, forgive me, God.'

Pat lay where she was, white-faced. Charlotte knelt down beside her and checked her pulse. 'I can scarcely feel it,' she said, 'but it's very fast.'

'That's consistent with shock,' Jack told her. 'Fast, faint pulse. Shallow breathing. Let's get her back on the sofa and keep her warm.'

They lifted her gently back on to the sofa and covered her up. 'Charlotte, would you call her husband?' asked Jack. 'Nathan Lerner. You can find his number in the book.'

Pat opened her eyes. Her pupils were widely dilated and her voice was hoarse. 'I thought I was dying,' she whispered.

'You're all right,' said Vincent. 'It was just the Grays, fighting back.'

'I feel terrible,' Pat told him, although she attempted a smile.

They heard the warbling of a siren outside, and then the ambulance scrunched to a stop outside the front door. 'You're in luck,' said Jack, leaning over the sofa and kissing Pat on the forehead. 'They didn't take the scenic route today.'

Only a few minutes after the medics had carried Pat out across the snow, and the ambulance had whooped off again, its red lights flashing pink against the white-blanketed woods, Dr Serling arrived. Jack had interrupted Dr Serling's attendance at a tea-party for some of his wife's cousins, for which interruption the doctor was bluffly grateful.

'I'll follow the ambulance,' he said, out of his car window, through the falling flakes of snow. 'No need for you three to stand out there and freeze your butts off.'

'I want you to come inside for a moment,' Jack asked him.

Dr Serling frowned at him, and switched his engine off. He climbed out of his car like an artist's easel being folded up to get through an attic door, and then unfolded himself in front of Jack until he was standing a good two inches taller.

'What's wrong? I thought you said that Mrs Lerner had fainted.'

'She didn't faint,' said Vincent, and took hold of his arm. 'Come on in. Let me tell you what happened.'

As they walked side by side into the house, Vincent tried as graphically as he could to explain about the second séance; and about the intense feelings of evil that had emanated from the Waldegrave portrait; and the horrifying sensation which Pat had described, of plunging her hand into a pool of chilly, floating corpses, half-preserved in the quintessential liquors of their own gradual decay.

He told Dr Serling about the imaginary knife that had flashed into Pat's abdomen, and about the way in which she had vomited blood.

Dr Serling carefully filled his pipe and lit it. He inspected the rug, which Pat had covered with hallucinatory blood, and then he checked the sofa.

'You saw this, too?' he asked Charlotte.

Charlotte nodded.

Dr Serling puffed smoke for a while. 'This isn't for me,' he told them. 'This is for somebody who knows what they're doing. A qualified psychical medium, with powers to fight back.'

Jack said, 'That sounds like somebody who's going to be hard to locate.'

Dr Serling made a face which meant that it probably would be. 'You could always treat this as a police matter, of course, and nothing else. You don't *have* to fight fire with fire. After all, even though the Grays seem to be very much more adept at psychic jiggery-pokery than any of us, Mrs Lerner obviously didn't get hurt today, not seriously; which leads me to suspect that the Grays can't hurt anybody by spiritual powers alone. Maybe they could, if they were *completely* dead, if they were nothing but spirits. But they appear to be divided. Their spirits are here, their bodies are there. If they want to do anybody any real mischief, they seem to have to do it with their own hands.'

Vincent was pouring them all a drink. He looked up and said, 'You sound as if you've dealt with troublesome spirits before, Doctor.'

Dr Serling tried to be gruff. 'The first visible evidence of the human spirit that I ever saw was at Ben Miller's séance.'

'But you're a doctor. A country doctor, at that. Don't tell me you haven't come across possessions before; or imaginary possessions; or ghosts.'

Dr Serling accepted his glass of whisky. 'I'm trying to make educated guesses, that's all.'

Jack walked across to the Waldegrave portrait with his hand in his pocket, and lifted the bedspread, so that he could look again at the decomposing faces of the Gray family. 'Would you believe it?' he said. 'The worst case I ever had, and all the suspects are dead, before I've even started.'

Vincent came and stood beside him. 'Not dead enough, that's the trouble. Dead; but not dead enough.'

Twenty-three

Seekonk, 23 December

Dr Percy McKinnon was a short, heavily built man, with one of those potentially explosive faces that reminded Vincent of Teddy Roosevelt, and a similar line in overtight three-piece winter suits in ginger tweed.

He had lectured for twenty-three years at Brown University on the history of art. Now he was retired, and lived on County Street in one of those white-painted houses favoured by genteel ladies with reminiscent names. On Sundays he could be seen, stiff-backed, walking his white bull mastiff in Slater Memorial Park.

He made coffee for all of them, in a copper coffee-pot, which he carried through to his relentlessly old-fashioned library. Then he sat by his black pot-bellied stove, and crossed his ham-like thighs, and challenged them to tell him what they wanted.

Vincent said, 'My family happen to own a portrait by Walter Waldegrave.'

'Unhappily for them, then,' Dr McKinnon put it.

'What makes you say that?' asked Vincent.

'How many reasons do you want?' Dr McKinnon countered. He took off his steel-rimmed spectacles, and addressed himself to Vincent with pale blue bulging eyes.

'As many as you can think of,' Vincent told him.

'Very well,' said Dr McKinnon. 'Walter Waldegrave was mentally immature, intellectually obscure, easily compromised both in morals and artistic integrity, a poor strategist, a worse colourist and far too easily swayed by fads and fashions.'

'I don't think my family acquired the painting for its artistic merit,' said Vincent.

'Well, that's one consolation, I suppose,' said Dr McKinnon, sipping his coffee. 'The only thing that concerns me, however, is that if your family didn't acquire it for its artistic merit, why *did* they acquire it? I can think of only one possible reason; and believe me, I don't care for it at all. No, sir.'

'We don't have to beat around the bush,' said Vincent. 'My grandfather took the picture away from its owners because he feared that the owners were abusing it. He feared, in fact, that Walter Waldegrave had somehow arranged it so that the portrait grew old, while the family who sat for it remained young.'

Vincent couldn't have put it more directly. Charlotte squeezed his hand. If Dr McKinnon was one of those academics who would have no truck with the supernatural, then at least they would know from the very beginning.

Dr McKinnon, however, replaced his spectacles, and swung slowly around in his newspaper editor's chair, the kind of revolving wooden chair that used to feature in Hollywood interpretations of the *Tombstone Epitaph*, and peered up at his shelves for one of his leather-backed books.

'Let me tell you,' he said, as he tried to find the particular volume that he had in mind, 'Walter Waldegrave was mischief, with a capital *M*. He was a weak, surly, half-talented young man, and he would have remained completely unknown to the world of art if he hadn't have happened quite by accident to catch the eye of Oscar Wilde and Frank Miles.'

Jack, who was sitting in the corner with his legs crossed, trying to appear official and matter-of-fact, said, 'We know that Walter Waldegrave was into black magic, Dr McKinnon. We wouldn't have come here, otherwise.'

Dr McKinnon found the book he was looking for and opened it, but then he peered at Jack over his spectacles and said, 'You're a sheriff, aren't you? Don't tell me that *sheriffs* believe in black magic?'

'I've kept an open mind about it all my life, sir,' said Jack. 'Now, for better or for worse, I've had it proved to me.'

Dr McKinnon turned to Vincent, and suddenly said, 'The *Gray* portrait. That's it! You have the Gray portrait. Am I correct?'

Vincent nodded. 'My grandfather acquired it in 1911. There was a series of murders in that year which my grandfather believed had been committed by the Grays; and so, not to put too fine a point on it, he stole the portrait and told them that if they didn't leave the country, he would burn it.'

Dr McKinnon said emphatically, '*Ah* ... so *that's* what happened! I had always suspected something of the sort. But I hadn't realized that it was the Pearsons who got hold of it. This is quite a revelation! This almost deserves a brandy. A brandy with your coffee? Would that go down well?'

'I wouldn't say no,' Jack put in. It had been a long and difficult journey from Litchfield, with several detours.

Vincent said, 'Thank you. We'd all appreciate it.'

'Do you know something,' said Dr McKinnon, after he had given them each a less-than-generous glass of brandy, 'I always believed that the Waldegrave portrait would turn up, some day. Your family were very secretive about it, weren't they? They never displayed it, or wrote about it; nothing. The Pearsons! I should have guessed, I suppose, that it was you! Your grandfather was very religious, wasn't he? He wrote a monograph or something on inspirational art. Well, of course, the moral laxity that the Grays had always exhibited must have been anathema to him. But you still have it! It still exists! Waldegrave's portrait of the Grays!'

Vincent said, 'I was hoping that you could tell me how it was done.'

'I'm sorry,' blinked Dr McKinnon, 'how *what* was done?'

'How the portrait was made to grow old, while the people in it stayed young.'

'Do you have the portrait here?' asked Dr McKinnon, with sudden anxiety.

Vincent said, 'No. It's back in New Milford. Back at my house.'

'Well, that's a pity. I would very much like to see it for myself. Can you arrange that, do you think?'

'Of course,' Vincent told him, a little impatiently.

'The secret is this,' said Dr McKinnon, holding up his book. '*Any* effigy of *any* living person; *any* representation of *any* living person; can *always* be used to affect the course of that person's life. You've heard of voodoo dolls, of course. Primitive figures, into which pins are stuck, to discomfort or even kill somebody whom the witch-doctor's supplicant happens to dislike. Well, you may smile about those dolls, but I have documentary evidence here that voodoo dolls were used to very excellent effect during the coming-to-power of Jean-Claude Duvalier in Haiti; and I have even more startling evidence that certain parties considered the use of magical effigies during the closing stages of the Watergate fiasco.

'The history of magical effigies is fascinating. Fascinating! But it probably reached its peak during the late Victorian era, when photography became sufficiently widespread for images to be taken of almost anybody the necromancer chose, so that he could inflict whatever punishment he desired, sometimes with remarkable accuracy. It is said, for instance, that Ulysses S. Grant was given throat cancer by a political rival, but there you are. We have no way of proving such suggestions for certain.'

Dr McKinnon swallowed some brandy, folded up his spectacles and leaned forward conspiratorially towards Vincent. 'As far as art is concerned, the use of images and effigies came into flower with the Pre-Raphaelites: Rossetti and Holman Hunt and all of their followers and imitators. Their technique was so meticulous, their detail was so perfect and their likenesses were so accurate, that their portraits could be used in the same way that voodoo effigies had once been used, given that whoever owned the portrait happened to know the right incantations.'

He leaned even closer and said, in a hoarse whisper, 'I did hear it said that Millais' portrait of Lady Penelope Cleaver was used by her husband to destroy her looks, from face cancer, when she was having an affair with one of his secretaries.'

Vincent said, 'Tell me something about Walter Waldegrave.'

'Well,' Dr McKinnon expostulated, 'the whole point about Walter Waldegrave was that he wasn't just a painter whose portraits were used by other people to inflict pain on their enemies or adversaries. Walter

Waldegrave was interested in black magic and the power of symbols and effigies *himself*, even before he first put brush to canvas. So when he painted, he painted with the *specific intention* of having his paintings used for occult purposes. If you like, he was the chief religious artist for the anti-Christian movement of the nineteenth century, and that was one of the reasons why Oscar Wilde liked him so much. Oscar Wilde absolutely adored beautiful-looking young men, and Walter Waldegrave certainly qualified, although you wouldn't say so now, not from his photographs; and he absolutely adored *irreligious* young men.'

'So,' Vincent put in, 'when Walter Waldegrave came to the United States with Lily Langtry, and Oscar Wilde introduced him to the Grays . . .'

'The fusion of interests was both natural and historical,' said Dr McKinnon, snapping his short squat thumbs. 'The Grays were wealthy, charming and impossibly vain. They felt they had reached their social apogee, and wanted to stay that way. So, when Walter Waldegrave suggested that he should paint their family portrait, and that *certain rituals* should accompany the signing of the painting when it was finished – how could they deny his offer? There was a chance that they would live for ever. There was a chance that they would be able to mix in wealthy society for season after season: Palm Beach in the winter, Bar Harbor in the summer, London and Paris whenever the mood took them. Not just for this season; not just for next season; but *for ever*. Can you imagine that? To know, with complete certainty, with complete confidence, that you will still be alive in a hundred years' time? And not just alive, but *young*?'

Vincent said nothing, but looked across at Jack. They were learning more and more about the Grays, but still they had no ideas at all about how they could destroy them – either straightforwardly, by arresting them for homicide and kidnap, or psychically, by breaking their link with the Waldegrave portrait.

Vincent said, 'My grandfather mentioned something about reciting the exorcism backwards.'

Dr McKinnon leafed through his book. 'That's partly it,' he said, raising his hand. 'You have to have your portrait painted with great attention to detail by a competent artist. If possible, a magnificent artist. It has to be a full-length portrait, otherwise your legs will age long before the rest of you and you will become a cripple, a young man with very old legs.'

He found the page he was looking for, and then he said, 'This is the ritual. It is partly based on the exorcism, yes: because it seeks to separate your spirit and your fleshly body, without actually killing you. In other words, your spirit becomes entrapped in the painting, embedded in the molecules of paint that are assembled to look like you, while your body and your intellect walk free. If anybody had ever *done* this, of course, they would have been completely joyless and heartless, because they would have been surviving on this Earth without their souls; which as everybody knows include their conscience, their sense of communal responsibility, their kindness, their pity, and even their sense of humour. A very serious matter, not to have a sense of humour.'

Dr McKinnon sniffed, coughed and swallowed some more brandy. 'If you're after the Grays, my friends, then all I can say is, good luck, because you're going to need it. You say that they've committed homicides. They will go on killing people for as long as they want to, for as long as they need to, without any qualms or compunction. They have no souls, Mr Pearson, not in the way that you and I have a soul. You can sink down inside of yourself, and feel your personality swimming around inside of yourself like a trained dolphin. They can feel none of that. They're empty! And that's how they survive! They're immortal, but they're completely superficial. They're stuffed animals. They have skin, which is immaculate on the outside, but what that skin is covering, God alone can imagine.'

Vincent swirled the last of his coffee around the bottom of his cup. 'They keep trying to find out where the portrait is,' he said. 'They even attempted a burglary, round at my restorer's house, in Bantam.'

'Well, of course they did!' Dr McKinnon exclaimed. 'They want the portrait for themselves. They want to feel that they're secure, and that their existence, such as it is, will not suddenly fall into the hands of irresponsible or antipathetic people.'

'Is that all it amounts to?' asked Charlotte. She had a headache, and she very much felt like a cigarette.

Dr McKinnon frowned at her deeply. 'Young lady, this is elementary social psychology, book one, page one, not some lurid paperback about psychic manifestations.'

Jack said, 'They've already showed us they can use the portrait against us, even when we've got it safe. Is there anything more they could do if they were actually to lay their hands on it?'

Dr McKinnon made a face. 'I don't think that they would *need* to do anything to you, if they ever laid hands on the portrait, although they might be malevolent enough to want revenge against you, because of what your grandfather did to them. No, the real danger would be that they would be able to restore the painting to its original condition, and that they would continue to survive as youthful-looking as ever, for generation after generation. Remember that they have no conscience, remember that they have no pity. Your grandfather first acted against them when they began to murder people; and I am sure that they were guilty of many other debased and profane acts which, for their victims, were almost as damaging as murder. If they ever managed to get their portrait back, they would be virtually untouchable. They are an influential family in their local area, remember. They have old money, and plenty of it; and I suspect that their capacity for bribery and blackmail would rival that of the Mafia. They weren't always alone when they held their debauches in the 1890s, and how many upper-class Connecticut families would like it to be known that their grand-fathers took drugs, for instance; or fornicated with sheep and underage girls; or bred children out of wedlock?'

Dr McKinnon refilled his brandy glass, but didn't offer any around. 'Not only would they be immortal and untouchable,' he added, 'they would *always* have a means of escape, no matter what.'

'Means of escape? What are you talking about?' asked Jack.

'The *portrait*, my dear sir. The *portrait*!' Dr McKinnon responded. 'Here – look in this book. Oh, well, it won't mean very much to you, it's all in Latin. But what it says here is that those who have gained immortality by means of representation in a portrait can always leave their physical bodies and retreat into the picture itself. In other words, they can conceal their physical bodies in places where nobody would normally think of looking for somebody who was hiding – buried in a coffin, even – and they can rejoin their souls inside the painting. Or, indeed – and this is where it all becomes most interesting – inside *any* painting.'

Jack frowned. 'I don't get this. I don't get this at all.'

'Well, in police terms, let me put it this way,' said Dr McKinnon. 'If the Grays ever regain possession of their portrait, and let us all pray to whatever gods that guide us that they do not, they will be uncatchable. You may extradite a murderer from Indiana; but how do you extradite a murderer from an oil-painting? You will have lost them for ever, my dear sir, and they will be able to continue their murders and their debauches whenever it so pleases them; for time everlasting, amen.'

Twenty-four

New Milford, 23 December

Thomas arrived back at the house a little after two o'clock in the afternoon. His cheeks were rough and red, his toes were freezing, but he felt ineffably terrific. He and Susie had been playing and tumbling in the snow for most of the morning, and then Susie's mom had given them hamburgers for lunch, and Susie's dad had allowed him a glass of Miller, without even making a big issue out of it, and he had felt grown-up and confident and more than a little infatuated with Susie.

Before he had left for home, he had said goodbye to her by the mailbox, and kissed her; warm wet lips and dry cold noses; and then he had slalomed his way through the woods towards Candlemas, whistling and singing to himself.

He reached Candlemas, and came up through the whitened garden, where the trees stood as frigidly as ghosts, and where the pathways of summer were buried like memories that would never return. There was no smoke blowing from the chimneys, which meant that the fires had gone out. He would have to stack them and light them before Dad got home; but in the mood he was in after visiting Susie, he didn't mind at all.

He found the front-door keys in his anorak pocket, and walked around the side of the house, jingling them.

And there they were, darkly dressed and silent, in black overcoats and black gloves, standing beside their long black limousine, waiting for him with dispassion and absolute patience.

'Master Pearson, I presume?' the man called out, in a dry, clear voice.

Thomas stayed where he was. His father had warned him against visitors. *If you happen to get back home before I do sit tight, and don't let anyone in. Don't even answer the door.* But what was he supposed to do when the visitors were actually barring the way to the door, so that he couldn't get inside and lock himself safely behind it?

'I'm, uh, just delivering something,' said Thomas. 'Mr Pearson left something around at my parents' house, and I'm . . . just delivering it.'

'Come, come, Master Pearson,' the man smiled, in chilled amusement. 'We know your face quite well, my sister and I. We're friends of the family.'

Thomas cautiously approached the front door. They looked civilized enough, these two, the man and the woman in their expensive black coats. Their Cadillac was rather too reminiscent of a hearse for Thomas's liking, but they must be rich to run a car like that, and whoever heard of rich burglars?

'My father won't be back until late. Maybe you should call tomorrow.'

The man sighed, and drew back his leather glove so that he could inspect his wristwatch. 'If only it were possible, my dear young friend. Unfortunately, we have to be back in Darien later this afternoon, and after that . . . well, who knows *where* we might have to be after that?'

'You're such a good-looking boy,' said the woman, speaking for the first time. She came balancing through the snow on high black heels, one ungloved hand clutching a black mink wrap against her bosom. Thomas glimpsed the sharp white glitter of a massive diamond brooch. 'Isn't he just like Vincent? The very same eyes! And that sullen mouth!'

Thomas backed away a little as the woman approached, although it seemed rather ungracious to retreat from two people who obviously knew his father. The woman came close and lifted the smoky black veil that covered her face, so that Thomas could see how beautiful she was. She was smiling. Her eyes were so black that the sockets could have been empty.

'Didn't your father tell you that we were coming?' she cooed, in a peculiarly irritating voice, as if she were talking to a toddler.

'He must have done,' the man asserted, grunting jovially. 'We called Vincent from Darien, before we left.'

'He's in Seekonk today,' said Thomas.

'Seekonk, well, well,' the man replied. 'It's not like Vincent to forget his dear friends.'

'Maybe I should go inside and call him,' Thomas suggested. 'He left a number, in case anything happened. Can you wait for a little while?'

'Well,' smiled the woman, 'we'd rather step inside, if you wouldn't mind awfully. It *is* rather polar out here.'

Thomas hesitated for one last moment. There was something not quite real about this couple; something indescribably frightening. They were too polite, too formal, and somehow they never quite seemed to say anything straightforwardly. But his father would be furious if he turned away a couple of old friends; and equally angry if he were rude to them, and left them standing in the snow.

He knelt down in the porch and unfastened his snowshoes.

'Neat snowshoes,' the man said, standing so close

that all Thomas could see of him were the sharply creased legs of his trousers, and his well-polished black Oxfords. 'I could do with a pair of those myself.'

Thomas at last unlocked the front door of the house. The man and the woman followed him into the hall so closely that their eagerness appeared to Thomas almost to have a hint of indecency about it.

'I don't know your names,' he said, unzipping his anorak.

'Basil Hallward,' the man told him, taking off his hat and fastidiously brushing the snow from around the crown. 'And my sister, Mrs Vane.'

'Is this the living room?' asked the woman.

'I'm afraid the fires went out,' Thomas explained. 'The kitchen should be warmer, if you don't mind waiting there.'

'No, no, don't trouble,' the woman replied. She appeared to have seen something in the living room which had caught her attention. 'As long as I'm out of the wind.'

Thomas followed them into the living room. The fire had only just died, and the ashes were measled with orange sparks.

'This could well be revived,' the man said, crouching down in front of it and prodding it with a poker. 'A few sticks of kindling, a log or two, and we could soon have a merry blaze.'

The woman meanwhile had walked across to where the Waldegrave portrait was standing, covered up, on its easel. Her arms were held rigidly down by her sides, but her fingers seemed to squirm with anticipation. Her chest rose and fell beneath her black mink wrap as if she were having difficulty in breathing.

Thomas picked up the telephone, listened for the dialling tone and then pressed out the number which his father had written on the pad for him. The man continued to poke at the fire for a while, but then without saying a word he stood up, brushed down his coat, came over to Thomas's side, and placed his finger on the telephone cradle, cutting him off.

Thomas stared at him. The man said, 'It really isn't necessary to bother your father. I think that we've found what we came here for.'

Thomas said, 'You're thieves. That's it, isn't it? You're thieves! You don't know my father at all! Well, damn it, I'm going to call the police! And you can get out of here, because I've seen your faces, and don't think that I'm frightened!' His heart was pumping so madly that he found it difficult to speak.

The man laid a hand on his shoulder and squeezed it. 'My dear chap, you've got us quite wrong. We're not thieves at all. We've come here simply to collect a single item of property which has always belonged to us; and which the Pearsons have been keeping for us – how shall I put it? – on extended loan. Your father knows all about it. We're not going to pillage the house or make off with the cutlery. All we're going to do is take this single insignificant item, and leave.'

Thomas said hotly, 'You can't take anything. You're not allowed to.'

But he was silent then, for the woman had drawn off her fur wrap and laid it across the back of the sofa, and was approaching the shrouded portrait with the gliding step of an Egyptian handmaiden approaching the effigy of Thoth. She took hold of the edge of the sheet which covered the portrait, and waited for what seemed like minutes before summoning up the courage to drag it away.

At last she did so, and the portrait was revealed: decayed and glistening in the wintry afternoon light.

The woman stared at it, aghast; and as she stared at it she slowly raised her hands until she was clutching tightly at her own hair.

With a high screech of anguish, she threw herself down on to her knees and huddled on the floor, shuddering and trembling, and uttering extraordinary mewls and whimpers.

Even the man had turned white, and his pallor emphasized the plum-dark circles under his eyes.

'Look what they've done to us!' the woman cried. 'Look what they've done to us! Oh, God in heaven, Maurice, look what they've done!'

The man crossed the room and laid his hands gently on the woman's shoulders, at length encouraging her to rise. She stood staring at the portrait, encradled by his arms, but feeling no comfort. For the first time in over seventy years, she had seen her face not as she had managed to preserve it, not masked by paints or powders or by the sacrificed skin of others, but as it really was.

Thomas took a cautious step towards the door. If he could escape from the house while the man and the woman were so preoccupied with the portrait, then it would only need a fast run through the woods to reach the Waxmans' house, and then he could call the police. They were too old to run after him, these two, and they could never drive through the woods in their Cadillac.

One step; two; three. But then the edge of his anorak caught the small occasional table beside the door, and a glass ashtray nearly tumbled, and made a clonking noise against the wall. Thomas turned. The man turned, and with a voice like clashing cymbals, the man roared, 'Stop!'

Thomas stopped. He didn't know why he stopped. He didn't know why he didn't run. But he stopped, and he waited in the doorway, stiff with fright, while the man walked firmly across to take hold of his arm.

'You mustn't *go*,' the man said unctuously. 'It's far too soon for you to *go*. And besides, we rather enjoy your company. You are what I like to think of as a pleasant boy, and believe me there are few enough of those. Boys are mostly scrofulous and rude. You, on the other hand, are a pleasant boy.'

The woman had at last turned away from the portrait. She looked shocked, and her cheeks were still shining with tears.

'You must try to think of the future now, my dear,' the man told her. Thomas thought that he didn't sound very sympathetic, or even as if he were making any particular effort to be. 'Let us wrap the portrait and take the boy, and then let us leave. His unfortunate father may be back before we know it.'

The woman appeared still to be dazed, and she turned around hopelessly like someone who wishes they could faint, but can't.

Thomas said, in a small voice, 'I don't want to go with you. Please. I won't tell anyone who you are. I promise I won't tell anyone.'

'But we *like* you,' said the man. 'Come on, now, I won't hear of any argument. It's snowing, and we have quite a long way to go.'

'Did you see what they have done to us?' the woman demanded, shrilly, all of a sudden.

The man laid his arm around Thomas's shoulders. 'It's quite all right, my dear. You will soon have the opportunity to do very much worse to one of them.'

Twenty-five

Seekonk, 23 December

Dr McKinnon grew increasingly explosive the more he tried to explain. He kept appealing to Vincent and Charlotte, because he obviously felt that Jack was something of a half-wit. But the idea that a human being could actually enter their own portrait, that they could exist in three dimensions in a two-dimensional painting, was more than any of them could accept.

'It's perfectly simple, once you grasp the idea in your imagination,' Dr McKinnon protested. 'I'm not saying that it's easy to explain, either logically or scientifically, but it does have a logical and a scientific explanation.'

'Even if there is an explanation,' said Jack, 'I'm not sure that I want to know it.' He shook his watch, listened closely to it, and then asked, 'What's the time?'

'Five after,' said Vincent. 'We ought to be getting back soon. But first, I really want to try and understand this whole business of living people getting inside paintings.'

'I can only do my best,' said Dr McKinnon, in an offhand way which suggested that he was already tired of trying to lighten their darkness.

'Then, please, if you would,' asked Charlotte.

'Well,' sighed Dr McKinnon, 'there was a famous – or

rather *notorious* – paper written by Professor Jerome Franck, in 1948, for the Institute of Dimensional Research at Berkley. It was entitled something like "Artistic Perspective and the Creation of Alternative Realities". I have it here, somewhere – it's really very interesting. But what Franck essentially said was that when an artist paints a picture, despite the fact that it is two-dimensional – that is, flat – his creation of *visual* depth takes on a reality of its own.'

Vincent drained his already empty brandy glass (for the second time) with an ostentatious gesture. It was excellent brandy, and he would very much like to have been offered a little more. But Dr McKinnon kept his hand firmly around the neck of the brandy decanter as he went on talking.

'The theory is by no means a new one,' he said. 'It has its roots in the psychic and psychological studies carried out in Vienna in the 1930s. You may have heard of Meissner's theory of imaginative manifestation; or, even if you haven't, you've certainly heard of Jung, and his collective unconscious. Meissner and Jung worked together for several years and corresponded a great deal, and eventually in 1933 they decided that there was distinct if arguable evidence that people and places created in novels and paintings, *if readers or spectators believed in them with sufficient conviction*, could actually manifest themselves in the real world. They could take on physical form – sometimes not very substantially, so they would appear as no more than ghosts – but at other times very solidly.'

He smiled to himself. 'It's rather like Peter Pan asking if enough children believed in fairies to keep Tinkerbell alive. Because, after all, what are we made of, we human beings? We are nothing more than physical collections of electrically charged particles. And what is our imagination made of? *Abstract* collections of electrically charged particles. And, believe me, in terms of simple physics, there is but a hair's breadth between the hand that you can imagine and the hand that you can actually shake.

'Meissner became convinced that people out of books and paintings actually live among us: fiction and art made flesh. He was sure that many houses and places described in books or created in imaginative paintings – *once they had been mentally pictured within the collective unconscious of a sufficient number of people* – actually came into being. Somewhere in the world, there *is* a Shangri La.'

Vincent sat back. He was beginning to suspect that Dr McKinnon was not going to be able to give them much in the way of practical help. He had tried to listen so far with as little scepticism as possible, trying to assure himself that Dr McKinnon might know what he was talking about. But characters out of novels, coming alive? Houses, out of fictitious landscapes, suddenly appearing in the countryside? Shangri-La?

But then Dr McKinnon stood up and pushed his book back into its place on the upper shelf, and said dryly, 'Plenty of Meissner's colleagues thought he was mad. After a while, even Jung disassociated himself from the work he had done with Meissner. Perhaps Meissner *was* mad. Certainly, it is difficult to believe, for instance, that Castle Dracula is actually mouldering away somewhere in Transylvania, just because a great many people can imagine it.'

'You're right,' said Jack. 'It *is* hard to believe.'

'Ah,' said Dr McKinnon, 'but you have already seen for yourself the power of that portrait, so you'll have to admit that there must be some kind of unusual influence at work here. And, I do believe this: that paintings *do* constitute more than the sum of their colours and their pigments. An artist *does* create on his canvas some form of alternative reality, and it *is* possible for people like the Grays, who have entered into an extraordinary psychic and spiritual transaction in order to separate their bodies from their souls, to retreat completely into that alternative reality. To vanish, as it were, into their own paintings.'

Jack said, after a pause, 'All right. Let's just suppose for one moment that they can do that. Is there any way of pursuing them, once they've disappeared?'

Dr McKinnon pouted, in deep uncertainty. 'Theoretically, I suppose, anyone who wanted to pursue them could have *his* portrait painted, and then enter into the same psychic transaction.'

'But that would mean that *his* soul would be separated from *his* body, too,' said Charlotte.

'Yes, indeed, it would,' Dr McKinnon agreed. 'Whosoever decided to go after the Grays would have to make the same commitments that *they* did, to eternal life, without the benefit of a soul.'

'Couldn't we just destroy the portrait?' asked Jack.

'Well, naturally, that is one alternative. But the Grays are not naive. They have been surviving for too long to allow themselves to be caught undefended. They have a hostage, in the shape of Mrs Montag –'

'*Blat*,' said Vincent. 'Mrs Mon*blat*.'

'Ah, yes, Mrs Monblat,' said Dr McKinnon. 'And already the Grays have put you into the position of having to decide if you are prepared to sacrifice her life as the price for getting rid of them. I assume that if Mrs Monblat *hadn't* appeared in the picture, you would have burned it by now?'

'Yes,' said Vincent. But then, frowning a little, he said, 'No.' He wasn't quite sure why, but something about the idea of destroying the Waldegrave portrait disturbed him. He began to wonder why his grandfather had never destroyed it; why his father had never destroyed it. He knew that they were men of their word, and that if one of them had promised the Grays that the portrait would remain safe, then they would have felt honour-bound to make sure that it did. But it seemed strange that Vincent's grandfather hadn't destroyed the portrait as soon as he had suspected that the Grays were murdering people for the pleasure of it. And it also seemed strange that he himself should feel any qualms. He was prepared to wait until Laura Monblat was rescued from the Grays, but once they had managed to do that, and the Grays were alone in the portrait, why should he worry if they burned? They were utterly depraved: murderers and torturers and blasphemers. And yet – and yet – he didn't know. He couldn't understand his reluctance. He turned to look at Jack, but Jack hadn't noticed that he was doubtful. Jack raised his empty brandy-glass instead, and said, 'Cheers.'

Dr McKinnon said, 'The Grays, I imagine, if they were ever to take possession of that portrait, would disappear for several years, especially since they seem to have stirred up so much trouble and alarm. They could remain concealed in the portrait for as long as they wanted, until all of us were long dead. Then they could re-emerge, and reoccupy their bodies, or even presumably the bodies of others. I remember my own father telling me that one should never sleep in a room in which a portrait hangs, in case the spirit from the portrait emerges in the night, when you are deeply asleep, and takes over your body. You will then find that *you* are hanging on the wall, trapped in the portrait, while the spirit that was once inside the portrait occupies the person that was once you. Have you noticed that in the wards of Roman Catholic Hospitals, there are no portraits, except of Christ and the Virgin Mary? Well, that is why. It dates from a Papal instruction of 1873, from Pius IX. *Ab insidiis diaboli, libera nos Domine.* Rescue us from insidious demons, O Lord.'

Vincent said, 'Is there anything we can do to extricate Laura Monblat from the picture? The Grays put her in there, surely there must be some way of getting her out.'

'Only by the method I described. Having your own portrait painted, and pursuing them into their alternative reality.'

Jack cleared his throat. 'I think we may have to negotiate our way out of this one, Vincent. Maybe contact the Grays, call them up, and ask them what it is that they want. Treat it like a regular police hostage situation. Unofficially, of course. I wouldn't be able to call up a squad – not on the evidence we have so far.'

Vincent was thoughtful. 'Supposing we tried to cut Laura Monblat out of the picture – I mean, with scissors. What effect would that have?'

'It would kill her, I expect,' said Dr McKinnon. 'It may possibly kill the Grays, too, but there isn't any certainty of that. You see, the portrait's reality depends on it remaining whole, as the artist created it.'

Vincent then turned to Jack. 'Here's a hard question, Jack. Supposing this was a hostage situation. Supposing the Grays were terrorists, holed up in a house someplace, and you knew that you couldn't get them out without risking the life of their hostage. You also knew that if they got away, they would almost certainly kill more people. What would you do?'

Jack lifted his hands. 'The usual understanding is that every possible effort should be made to rescue the hostage without jeopardizing police lives unnecessarily, or endangering the civilian population.'

'In other words?'

'In other words, although nobody ever admits it, the immediate apprehension of dangerous criminals is generally considered to be a marginally higher priority than the lives of any hostages they might be holding.'

Jack hesitated for a moment, and then he added, 'It depends, to a certain extent, on the hostage. The police public relations department is usually called on to make an assessment of public reaction if a particular hostage were to die. Like, they wouldn't let Michael Jackson or Billy Graham go to the wall, if *they* were being held hostage; but they wouldn't worry quite so much about Joe Blow or Jane Doe.'

'My God, that sounds cynical,' said Charlotte.

Jack shook his head. 'It isn't as cynical as it sounds. Every reasonable effort is always made to save the life of every hostage. But there are times when you have to shut your eyes and go in shooting, and pray that nobody innocent gets hurt.'

Charlotte said, 'You're debating a woman's life here. You can't destroy that portrait, not if it means hurting Laura Monblat.'

'*We* know that,' said Vincent, 'but do the *Grays* know that? Remember they have no conscience, no pity, no genuinely human feelings. They've been living without them for years now – do you think that they can remember what it was like to feel a pang of concern for somebody they hardly even knew?'

Dr McKinnon said, 'You're right. You may have a point. But if I were you, I'd keep a very close eye on your family, Mr Pearson. If the Grays are uncertain about Mrs Monblat's value as a hostage, they may seek to take another hostage, even closer to home.'

Vincent suddenly thought of the Waldegrave portrait, standing in the living room on its easel. He suddenly thought of Thomas, walking home alone through the snowy woods, after spending the morning with Susie Foster. He could hear his own words echoing in his ears, *'If we're not home by the time you get back, just make yourself comfortable. There's* Ghostbusters *on the video, and plenty of Coke and cookies in the kitchen. Stack up the fire. We won't be late.'*

He said to Dr McKinnon, 'Could I use your phone, please?'

Dr McKinnon looked surprised, but then he said, 'Certainly. There's an extension in the hall.'

Vincent went quickly out into the musty hall, and stood in the multicoloured light from the stained-glass window over the door and dialled his own number at Candlemas. The phone rang and rang and rang, but nobody answered. He propped the receiver under his chin, and leafed through his small black leather address book, until he found the Fosters' number. He dialled that, and waited. After almost a minute, the Fosters' maid answered the phone.

'Hallo? This is Vincent Pearson here. My son Thomas was spending the morning with Susie.'

'That's right, Mr Pearson, he was.'

'Did he leave? Or is he still there?'

'Oh, he left, Mr Pearson, round about an hour since.'

An hour, thought Vincent. He had his snowshoes; maybe he could have taken a detour, just to try them out. But an hour?

Damn it, he thought, stop worrying. Thomas is a big boy now. But he couldn't help thinking of yesterday's séance, and all that chopped flesh and bright crimson blood flooding out of Pat's stretched-open lips.

He went back into Dr McKinnon's library. 'I'm sorry,'

he said, 'I have to get back to New Milford. Dr McKinnon – thank you for everything. Charlotte, Jack – I'm sorry to rush you.'

'Is everything all right?' asked Charlotte.

They drove back across Connecticut in gathering darkness. When they reached Manchester, Jack had himself patched through on his radio to his headquarters, and he told Norman Goldberg to send an officer round to Candlemas, to check that everything was okay. 'And no half-assed looks down the driveway, neither. He goes up to the house and he rings at the bell and he speaks to the boy, and makes sure that he's a hundred per cent.'

'Yes, sir, Sheriff.'

They were almost out of Hartford when Norman called back.

'Is Mr Pearson there with you, Sheriff?'

'Affirmative.'

'Well, I don't want to cause him any unnecessary distress, but the house was found with the front door wide open, fires burning, but nobody around.'

'Ask him about the portrait,' Vincent demanded, feeling himself go cold. *They may seek to take another hostage, Mr Pearson, even closer to home.*

'He says he doesn't know nothing about no portrait.'

The snow flew at the Cherokee's windscreen as fiercely as white locusts. Vincent said, 'Send him around there again. Tell him he has to check.'

Jack picked up his radio-microphone again, and said, 'Send him back, Norman. We need to know if there's an oil-painting there, in the living room, draped in a bedspread.'

There was a crackle, and a pause, and then Norman came back. 'He's here now. He says he saw the bedspread. It was lying on the floor. There was an easel on top of it, an artist's easel. That was all. No portrait.'

Vincent took a deep breath and sat back in his seat. 'Jack,' he said, 'drive me straight to Darien.'

Jack looked at him intently. 'Do you think that's the best idea?'

'Drive me to Darien, for Christ's sake! Those bastards have got hold of the picture, and they've taken my son, too!'

Twenty-six

Darien, 23 December

They arrived outside the gates of The Wilderlings, but the gates were closed and shackled together with a heavy-duty chain. It was snowing furiously now, so that they could scarcely see what they were doing, but they climbed out of the Cherokee and made their way round to the side of the house, where the wall was lower. They scrambled over it, and struggled their way through a wide snowdrift, three feet deep; Vincent in front, Jack close behind him, and Charlotte trying her best to keep up.

They reached the front door, and Vincent pounded on the knocker. The echo barked out across the snowy garden, but there was no reply. Vincent pounded the knocker again and again, but there was still no response.

'Three alternatives,' said Jack, lifting his fingers. His nose was red from the bitter cold. 'Either they've left; or else they're not answering; or else –'

Vincent finished his sentence for him. 'Or else Dr McKinnon, for all his nuttiness, was right; and they've escaped into the portrait, with Thomas and Laura as hostages.'

'It's so crazy!' Charlotte screamed. *'You're acting like it's true! How can it possibly be true?'*

'What else can I believe?' Vincent retorted. 'You saw

what happened to Pat. You saw what happened to Laura Monblat. They killed Edward, to get that portrait. Do you think I'm going to stand around and let them kill Thomas the same way? God damn it, Charlotte, I know it's impossible, but what other explanation has anyone given us?'

Jack said, 'I'm breaking in. There's a crowbar in the wagon. Keep on knocking, just in case there is somebody there, and they're asleep.'

Jack waded and leaped his way back through the snowdrifts, like an outgoing surfer, while Vincent and Charlotte waited outside the front door. Vincent knocked again, half-heartedly, but he knew that there was nobody there. The wind sighed briskly around the side of the house, and ice particles sizzled against the porch. Up above them, the sky was relentlessly dreary: the kind of sky which promises you that summer will be late this year, if it comes at all. Christmas was only two days away now. And Thomas had gone.

Jack came back, and without a word, began to lever open the double doors. Oak splintered, hinges complained, and at last the central lock sprang apart, the bolts burst, and the left-hand door juddered open.

'It's a technique,' Jack said tersely. 'You have to pick the correct point of leverage.'

Vincent was the first to step into the darkened hall. He hesitated at the top of the marble steps and called, 'Hello? Is there anybody there?' But the house was empty and silent and dusty; a smug house, that guarded its own secrets, and would continue to guard them, even when developers eventually came and smashed down its brickwork.

Jack said, 'Call them again, huh? We don't want to be guilty of trespass.'

414

Vincent called, but there was no reply. Jack looked around, and then said, 'I guess it's okay.'

'You don't want to be here, do you?' Vincent chided him.

'I'm here,' said Jack. 'Isn't that enough?'

'Well, what the hell's wrong?' Vincent wanted to know. 'The Grays killed your friend George Kelly; you know that. They killed Elmer Tweed, too, and they kidnapped Laura Monblat. What more do you want, before you bust them?'

'If you really want to know, I need evidence,' Jack retorted. 'I need the kind of testimony that can stand up in court. How do you think a judge is going to react, if I bring a man like Dr McKinnon on to the stand, with all his theories about characters from books and paintings coming to life? What do you think a smart and expensive defence lawyer is going to make of that? Think about Melvin Belli, my friend, because that's about the league of lawyer that the Grays can afford. "Oh yes, Dr McKinnon, characters out of books can come to life, can they? So where are Raggedy Ann and Raggedy Andy living right now? Palm Springs?"'

'For Christ's sake!' Vincent shouted at him. 'Evidence, is that all you care about? What about justice? These freaks took my son! You're the sheriff, aren't you? Elected and sworn, to protect and to serve! Well, protect, damn it! And serve!'

At that moment, however, Charlotte said, 'Look,' and they turned their heads across the hall and saw it for the first time, standing on a gilded easel, swathed in purple drapes: the Waldegrave portrait.

Vincent walked across to it with mechanical steps and stood staring at it. 'They did take it,' he said. But he was incapable of saying out loud what he really meant, and what he had immediately seen. Next to Laura, at the very edge of the picture, pale and staring, stood Thomas: his own son Thomas, in a black velvet Victorian suit with knickerbockers and a white lace collar, staring and submissive, painted in the immaculate style of Walter Waldegrave.

Charlotte came up beside him, and took his hand. 'Oh, God, Vincent,' she said. 'I'm so sorry.'

'They're insane,' said Vincent. He felt as if someone had hit him in the face with a ten-pound hammer. *'They're insane!'*

He turned round to Jack and shouted, 'There's your evidence, for God's sake! My son, in that painting! You want to show *that* to one of your judges? Is that proof enough? Why the hell didn't you kill the whole damned family while you had the chance?'

Jack came up and inspected the portrait carefully. He touched the painted image of Thomas, and it was quite dry. 'I don't know what to tell you,' he said. 'I'm sorry, believe me.'

Vincent said, 'I'm going to search the house. Maybe they've got him tied up somewhere.' He strode across to the foot of the staircase, and shouted out, 'Thomas! Are you there, Thomas? Thomas!'

Charlotte suddenly said, 'There's a note here, Vincent, look.'

Vincent turned around. On a small mahogany side-table with twisted legs, there was a plain cream vellum envelope. He went across and picked it up. It was addressed in lilac-coloured ink to *V. Pearson, Esq.*

'They planned this, God damn it,' swore Vincent. He tipped open the envelope, and shook out the letter inside.

It read,

The Wilderlings

Dear Mr Pearson,

As you will see, we have reclaimed at last the portrait which was always rightfully ours. You will never understand the suffering that your grandfather and succeeding generations of Pearsons imposed on us; and it is only because we are a sentimental family that we have not taken revenge on you.

'*Sentimental,* for Christ's sake,' Jack put in. He had been reading the letter over Vincent's shoulder. 'What do they mean by sentimental?'

The letter went on,

We have taken your son with us, as a precaution. He will be kept quite safe, we assure you; just as your family kept this portrait quite safe. You should understand, however, if you do not understand it already, that any attempt by you to damage or destroy this portrait will result immediately in your son's death or serious injury.

You should resign yourself to the fact that you will never see your son again, and that we have gone quite beyond your reach. You may search for us all over the world for the rest of your life, and never find us.

Leave the portrait where it is. If you try to take it away, we shall punish your son severely. I think you know how severe we can be, when taxed.

The portrait will be collected by our agents after the Christmas vacation, and stored in proper conditions.

We are satisfied now that justice has been done.
We wish you solace in your loss.

Respectfully,

Maurice Gray

Vincent read the letter again, and then handed it to Jack, so that he could examine it more closely. 'What do you think?' he asked, calmer now.

Jack said, 'This line here, about going beyond our reach. Do you think they've actually managed to do what Dr McKinnon was talking about? Do you think they're actually *in* there, inside of that portrait?'

'You're asking if I believe something that's absolutely impossible. The trouble is, it's the only reasonable explanation there is.'

'They could simply have left, and taken Thomas and Laura Monblat away with them,' Charlotte suggested. 'I mean, perhaps they've gone to South America, or Mexico, or someplace like that.'

Vincent turned around, and looked at the dark and musty hall, with its breeze-blown draperies of cobwebs. 'No,' he said. 'I think that Dr McKinnon was right. I think they're still here. I can feel them.'

They made a search of the upper floors of the house, from the gloomy attics with their oval windows which overlooked the snowy and derelict gardens, and the dusty rococo bedrooms with their strange and claustrophobic perfumes, to the operating room with its marbletopped table and rows of immaculate surgical instruments. At last they arrived back in the hall, where the painting stood.

'That's it,' said Jack. 'If they're anywhere here at all, they're inside the painting.'

'I think I'm going to have an hysterical screaming fit,' said Charlotte. 'I mean, I know it was my idea to go talk to Dr McKinnon. But imaginative manifestations? People going in and out of paintings?'

'McKinnon mentioned something else, too,' said Jack. 'He said that when the people went inside the portrait, into that what-do-you-call-it –'

'Alternative reality,' said Vincent.

'That's right. When they went into that alternative reality, they left their bodies behind and kind of stored them, like meat. So – if it's true, if any of this is true, and the Grays have disappeared inside the painting – then their bodies must be somewhere in the house. Does that make sense?'

Vincent nodded grimly.

'Where would you think?' asked Jack. He unwrapped a piece of gum and began to masticate the sugar out of it. 'The cellar, maybe? We haven't looked in there yet.'

Charlotte took hold of Vincent's arm again. 'Please, Vincent, this is all getting out of control.'

'No, no,' said Vincent. He was beginning to feel more determined. After the initial shock of seeing Thomas in the portrait and knowing that the Grays had kidnapped him, he was prepared to take some positive action now, no matter how bizarre it might be, to get his missing son back.

They found the cellar door under the stairs – the same cellar door through which George Kelly had emerged into the hands of Maurice and Henry Gray. Jack located the light-switch, and one by one they went cautiously down between chilly plastered walls, into the vaults beneath the house. 'They don't make cellars like this any more,' said Jack, his breath smoking in the cold. 'Look at those arches.'

'Look at those cobwebs,' Charlotte shuddered.

Their footsteps were grinding and noisy on the concrete floor. They passed one chamber after another, peering at wine, and furniture, and tea-chests of china. Charlotte delved into one of the boxes and brought out an exquisite gold and blue plate. 'Look at this. Royal Worcester, probably a hundred and fifty years old.'

They found the storeroom filled with paintings. Vincent looked through five or six of them, and said, 'These are amazing. Bonnard, Vuillard, Denis. All first-class Nabis; worth anything up to a million and a half each. Look – there's a Moreau. He was a Symbolist. And that's a Signac.'

'Some collection, huh?' asked Jack.

'That's the understatement of the eon. These paintings are probably worth more than two or three hundred million dollars, if the rest of them are even half as good as these, which they probably are.'

They found chamber after chamber crowded with the relics of a family life that had outlived itself by seventy years. They found pots and jars and boxes and riding-tack and even parts of an early De Dion automobile engine. They found some leathery fabric carefully folded between sheets of yellowed tissue paper, and none of them wanted to touch it in case it was human skin. But there was no sign of the Grays, and there was no sign of Thomas or Laura.

'Maybe we should try the stables,' Jack suggested.

They went outside, through the back door. The gardens were derelict and frozen. The sky was clamped over them like a pewter plate. Their feet squeaked in the snow, and Jack cleared his throat two or three times, because the cold made his nose run.

The garages and the stables and all of the out-buildings were deserted.

Jack stood in the snow with his hands in his pockets and his face contorted with frustration and cold.

'What did Dr McKinnon say? They would probably hide their bodies in places where you wouldn't usually expect to find people.'

'Do you think they buried themselves?' asked Vincent.

'They wouldn't have had time. And, in any case, as soon as the snow melts, somebody's bound to see where they did it. And, in any case, none of them are here, and if one of them had buried the others – which he would have had to – where is he? Or she, of course. I forgot. I mustn't discriminate.'

Their breath smoked. They looked all around them, trying to think where fourteen people might quickly and easily conceal themselves. It was then that Vincent glimpsed a slight darkness in the snow, in the centre of the lawn.

'What's that over there?' he asked Jack, shielding his eyes.

'I don't know. Some kind of ornamental pond, looks like.'

Vincent peered at the pond through the snowy twilight. 'Where do criminals throw guns away, when they don't want them any longer? Where do gangsters drop bodies? Where is the last place on earth that you'd think of looking for anybody who was hiding from you?'

They trudged quickly across the lawn until they reached the edge of the pond. Most of the surface was thickly frozen over, but the darker area which Vincent had noticed from the opposite side of the garden had recently been smashed. It was already freezing back over again, and the water in it was an opaque porridge of slush; but in the past few hours somebody had obviously considered it worth their while to break through a crust of ice that was over four inches thick, in a perfect circle, only three feet in diameter, and then leave the hole to freeze over again.

In spite of the snow, Vincent got down on to his hands and knees, and strained his eyes to see what was happening under the water.

'Give me your flashlight,' he told Jack, and Jack obediently handed it over. Vincent shone the flashlight from side to side, illuminating ice, and goldfish, and trailing strands of weed.

He angled the light down deeper, and it was then, with the greatest dread that he had ever experienced, that he saw the face. His own son's face, as white as a fish's belly, staring up at him from four feet under the surface of the freezing pond. Next to Tom, holding him close in a cold and motherly embrace, lay Laura. And there was Belvedere, too, and Henry, and Netty the crippled girl. A tangle of arms and legs, chilled and white beneath the surface of the water. They had obviously hoped that their bodies would be concealed during the winter by ice and snow, and during the summer by a subaquatic ceiling of lily-pads and dancing reflections and trailing streamers. Both summer and winter had been intended this year to serve these aristocrats of death and immortality in the way that summer and winter had served them so far for nearly a century, and always would.

Deep in the gelid water, with her face against a bank of weed, Vincent saw Cordelia; and there, lying close by, his face greenish and drawn, lay Maurice.

'I guess we should fish 'em out,' said Jack, taking the light from Vincent and playing it from one side of the pond to the other. 'This is a massacre.'

'Not yet it isn't,' Vincent told him. He stood up and beckoned, and Jack reluctantly followed him. Vincent was shivering from cold, and from the shock of having seen Thomas under the surface of the pond. He kept telling himself that Thomas wasn't dead, that none of them were dead, that they had all escaped into the portrait. But there were moments when disbelief kept yawning beneath his feet, and he began to think that it would all end here, as a mass drowning in a squalid Connecticut pond, with bodies being brought up dripping by the coroner's department.

Charlotte came out of the house, looking for them. Jack beckoned her over. 'They're all in the pond,' he said, wiping his nose with the back of his hand.

'Not Thomas?' asked Charlotte, aghast.

Vincent nodded. 'He was fourteen years old,' he said, with furious dullness. 'That's all. Fourteen years old. Why the hell didn't I take him down to Seekonk with me?'

Confused, horrified, Charlotte said, 'Are they – are they dead? Are they all drowned?'

Vincent turned away from the pond. 'They're not dead,' he said, in a voice constricted with emotion and phlegm. 'This is where they've chosen to conceal their bodies, that's all, while they escape. I guess they could have found somewhere more secure, but they probably didn't have very much time. What's more, they probably didn't realize that we knew what they could do.'

'At least,' he added, 'what we *hope* that they can do; for Thomas's sake, and for Laura Monblat's.'

'You really think that they've escaped inside of their picture?'

'God knows,' said Vincent.

'But couldn't we take out the Grays . . . drag them out of the pond . . . and shoot them or something?' Charlotte asked. She was as frantic as Vincent was despairing.

Vincent shook his head. 'Maurice Gray said it all in his letter. The Grays have gone way beyond our reach.

423

What you see here are simply their bodies. They themselves, their spirits, everything they really are, *they're* still free. They don't have to worry about being arrested, or growing old, or growing sick. They can do whatever they like; and whenever they like; to anybody they like.'

They walked back towards the house. Vincent was tormented by the urge to run back to the pond and pull Thomas out of the freezing water. *That's my son in there, my only son, lying cheek-by-jowl with half-decayed perverts and murderers.*

But he knew that there was only one way in which Thomas could be saved. And Laura Monblat, too. So he led Jack and Charlotte back into the house, feeling light-headed and shocked and impossibly unreal, but still determined.

Back in the hall, Jack said, 'Okay – what are we going to do? Are we going to run with Dr McKinnon's idea, or what?'

Vincent said, 'We don't have any choice. If we don't pursue the Grays into their own painting, then we're never going to get them back. You heard what Dr McKinnon said: it's an escape route. They could stay hidden inside it for years and years, until we're all long dead and forgotten. We daren't touch the painting, because Thomas and Laura are in it, and we daren't touch any of those bodies, because they'll punish Thomas and Laura in retaliation, no question about it; and you know what kind of people they are.'

'So, what do we do?' Jack repeated. 'We get in after them. But how?'

'I'm going to call Aaron Halperin,' said Vincent. 'He's the quickest and the most competent professional artist that I know. I'm going to ask him to come down here, right now, and paint my portrait. Charlotte – you call Dr

McKinnon again. Ask him to read you the whole Latin ritual that was used to separate a person's soul, so that one part of it went into a portrait and the other part stayed with their body. And, please, make sure that you get it right. One mistake, and it may not work.'

Jack said, 'Listen, Vincent. I'm the investigating officer here. Don't you think that *I* ought to be the one to get in there after the Grays?'

Vincent emphatically shook his head. 'That's my son there, Jack. And besides, what is the Litchfield County Police Department going to do with a sheriff who lives for ever? Not to mention your wife.'

He took out his telephone book and called Aaron in Bantam. Aaron sounded slurred on the phone, and Vincent found it hard to make himself understood.

'Vincent? Where are you calling from? I rang you at home. I was going to ask you over to try out my new plum brandy. I call it Slithervitz, on account of it only takes two glasses and you're slithering all over the floor.'

'Aaron, this is urgent. You remember the Waldegrave portrait?'

'My dear Vincent, how could I ever forget it?'

'Well, something's happened. Something serious. I want you to drive down to Darien, bring your paints, and paint a portrait of me, full-length, right now.'

There was a long pause, punctuated only by the suppressed thunder of Aaron's breathing. 'A portrait? *Now?* You're out of your mind! It's Christmas Eve practically!'

'Aaron,' said Vincent, 'never in my whole life have I needed anybody as much as I need you now. Whatever you ask, I promise I'll pay it. I'll tell you what – you can have those pen-and-ink sketches by Charles Wilson Peale, and ten thousand dollars besides. But for God's sake, Aaron, I need you. It's life and death.'

Aaron was silent for a very long time. Then he said, 'I'm drunk, you know.'

'Well, call a taxi, in that case. I'll pay the fare. But get on down here, please. I'm at a house called The Wilderlings, just north of Darien on the New Canaan road. Will you please do it?'

'But *why*, Vincent? Why do you want your portrait painted so urgently? You know, having your portrait painted, that's never anything *urgent*.'

'Today, Aaron, it is. I promise you. You'll understand why, when you get here.'

Aaron hesitated for a moment, and then he said, 'I've just talked to the family. The family consensus seems to be that I should stay here, and that if you want a portrait of yourself so desperately, you should go to the photo booth in Woolworth's.'

'Aaron,' Vincent told him, 'you remember Van Gogh?'

'Van Gogh? What about Van Gogh?'

'I'll tell you what about Van Gogh. Van Gogh is still in the Waldegrave portrait, but now Thomas is, too.'

'*Thomas?* Oh, God, they didn't –'

'No, Aaron, they didn't hurt him. Not yet, as far as I can tell. But the chances are that they will, and I want him out of there.'

There was more hesitation, and then at last Aaron said, 'I'm coming down there, Vincent. Give me a couple of hours. I have to get some paints and a canvas together, but then I'll be on my way.'

'Don't forget, take a taxi if you want to. I'll pay.'

'Okay. Listen! I'm okay. A couple of hours, that's all, if you can wait that long.'

'I'm counting on you, Aaron.'

After Vincent had finished talking to Aaron, Charlotte called Dr McKinnon again. Dr McKinnon was offhand and reticent at first. He was not a man who was used to being walked out on; and he was not a man who suffered the psycho-spiritual quandaries of others – not happily anyway.

'I was left with the *clear* impression,' he said, 'that none of you quite believed what I was saying.'

'Dr McKinnon,' Charlotte pleaded with him, 'the Grays have abducted Mr Pearson's son.'

'That is a matter for the police, I would have thought.'

'Dr McKinnon – they've taken him into the picture.'

Prickly silence. Then, 'Is this a practical joke, young lady? I began to suspect as much, this morning.'

'No joke, Dr McKinnon. I promise you. But I need to know the ritual: the ritual for allowing people to live for ever, while their portraits grow old.'

'*Over the telephone?*' Dr McKinnon protested. He was obviously scandalized.

'Dr McKinnon,' Charlotte protested, 'we really don't have any time. Believe me, if I could come over there myself, or send you a personal letter, then I would. But all I need is the words. Please. And any special instructions.'

Dr McKinnon said, 'This isn't very regular, you know. The rituals are secret, and have been for five hundred years. To read them out to you over the telephone –'

'Dr McKinnon,' Charlotte snapped at him, 'for God's sake, get off that old academic hobby-horse of yours. This is the twentieth century, and people need help.'

'Well, look here,' Dr McKinnon expostulated. 'I don't have to put up with that kind of talk, I'll thank you.'

All the same, he stayed on the line. Charlotte said,

'I'm sorry, Dr McKinnon. I'm panicking, that's all. Please. It's the very last hope we have left.'

Dr McKinnon was silent for so long that Charlotte had to say 'Hello?' to make sure that he was still listening. Vincent watched her closely, and raised one querying eyebrow, but Charlotte waved her hand to indicate that Dr McKinnon was still there, and that he was apparently considering her request.

'You have an actual problem there?' Dr McKinnon asked, at last.

'Yes, Doctor. An actual problem.'

'Well,' said Dr McKinnon, 'I hope I'm not being taken for some kind of monkey here. Wait up, and I'll go find the book.'

Charlotte covered the mouthpiece with her hand, and whispered to Vincent, 'He's going to do it.' Vincent said, 'Thank God.'

Slowly and pedantically, Dr McKinnon read out the words of the ritual, and Charlotte, who had once been an excellent secretary, wrote it all down in faultless shorthand. The Latin was difficult and archaic, but Dr McKinnon read every word out with explosive relish.

When he had finished, Charlotte said, 'I don't know how to say thank you, Doctor.'

Dr McKinnon half snorted, half coughed. 'Use the ritual to good effect, that's all. And when you have rescued your people, well, let me know about it.'

'Yes, sir. You're an angel.'

Once Charlotte had written out the Latin words in longhand, Vincent scanned them, and said, 'Okay. All we need now is the portrait, and then we can get after them.'

Vincent and Charlotte stayed close together while they waited for Aaron. Jack found the boiler, and got it going again, in case the temperature dropped severely during the rest of the afternoon. The Wilderlings echoed with extraordinary creaks and shuffling noises while the pipes heated up. Jack at last appeared from the cellar, wiping his hands on a large swathe of cheesecloth. He didn't look at the Waldegrave portrait any more; none of them did. The fear of what might happen if they failed was too great.

Jack was also conscious that he wasn't behaving at all like a sheriff. He should have called the Darien police long ago, and had The Wilderlings sealed off and thoroughly searched for drugs, bodies and concealed weapons. But Jack had already gone too far along the road, as far as believing in the Grays was concerned, and now there was no turning back. An official search would inevitably turn up the bodies in the pond, and if the medical referee attempted any kind of autopsy on them, the consequences would be bloody and disastrous.

Jack could just imagine it: Maurice Gray threatening to cut from Thomas each and every equivalent piece of flesh that the medical referee cut off his relatives.

By the time Aaron arrived, it was dark. He came struggling through the snow with his box of oil-paints under his arm, and smiled to Vincent and Charlotte testily.

'I hope you realize I'm a saint.'

'Do they canonize Jews?'

'St Aaron of the Immutable Palette. Now, what's this all about?'

They showed him the Waldegrave portrait, with its new additions, Laura and Thomas; and then they took him down to the pond, and showed him the tangle of chilled white bodies.

'All right, already,' he said, at last, swallowing, 'I understand.'

'Then paint me,' Vincent insisted.

'But you know what this means, if I paint you; and if you say that ritual. You're going to live for ever, aren't you, like them? You're going to lose your soul, Vincent, and how are you going to get it back? Thomas, he's already lost his. What kind of life is he going to live, even if you rescue him? He's going to be a killer, skinning people to stay young. And are *you* going to be the same?'

'Aaron, for Christ's sake just let me cross that bridge when I come to it. Right now, my son's being held by some family of homicidal perverts in some imaginary place, where I can't even reach him. Now, please, paint my portrait, and let me save him, at least.'

Aaron methodically opened his box of paints and laid out the brushes.

'Aaron, do you understand what I'm asking?' Vincent protested.

Aaron nodded, and took out his palette and his sticks of willow charcoal. 'I know what you want, Vincent, and I'll do it for you, for sure. Don't fret. I'm as scared as you are.'

Vincent sat in a large brown velvet spoonback chair which they had dragged in from the music room, and crossed his legs so that he was comfortable; and Aaron began to sketch. The outlines of Vincent's head and body began to appear on the canvas, then his legs. Quickly, Aaron went over his charcoal outlines with a thin wash of crimson, painting deftly and accurately. After this, he rubbed in the background colour, and the constructional tones around the forehead, the sockets of the eyes, the cheekbones and the side of the nose.

Painting with yellow ochre, viridian, light red, black and white, Aaron speedily produced a vivid portrait of

Vincent's head: his dark curly hair streaked with grey, his straight nose, his deep-set eyes, his strong jaw. The clock struck nine, and his brush was still flying, filling in tones and highlights and areas of unexpected shadow. By two o'clock in the morning the portrait was almost completed, although Aaron's hands were cold now, and he was exhausted, and it was taking him longer and longer to finish each detail.

At four, Aaron suddenly flung down his sable brush, and said, 'That's all I can do. I'm sorry.'

Vincent rose stiffly out of his chair, where he had been sitting for the past three hours bundled up in his overcoat. He examined the still-glistening portrait, and then he laid his hand on Aaron's shoulder.

'Aaron, I always said that you were a genius. This proves it. Whatever happens, forget restoration. Paint portraits. You'll be rich.'

'I think I need a drink,' said Aaron, in a hoarse voice. He stood up, and stretched his shoulders, and waggled his fingers.

'Now for the ritual,' said Vincent.

Charlotte said, 'Now?'

'That's Thomas in there, Charlotte. That's my son.'

'The painting is still wet.'

'It doesn't matter,' said Vincent. 'Let's do it.'

'Where have I heard *that* phrase before?' commented Jack. 'Oh, I know. Gary Gilmore.'

'The ritual,' Vincent repeated. He was too tired to argue.

Charlotte handed him the piece of paper on which she had written the same words that, ninety years ago, had given the Gray family the gift of immortality. Vincent's hands were shaking as he took it, and he had to breathe in steadily before he started to recite.

Sanctum suum Spiritum per concedat agere Dominus
nobis quod. Superatis nequitiam multimodam eorum
uobis in prius cum, imperabitis daemonibus aliis in recte
etenim tunc . . .

Even in its shortened form, the ritual was very long. It included not only the exorcism, in reverse, but an endless passage about the powers of time and the powers of creativity, and how the forces of the world were pinioned in four different quarters, Evil, Purity, Selflessness, and Jealousy.

Jack and Charlotte watched Vincent closely while he recited these words. But at the end of them all, he was still there, still tired, with his head bowed; and the portrait remained on Aaron's portable easel, with a slight run of viridian sliding down his left cheek. The early morning wind blew chilly and insistent through the broken front door; a pattern of snow had already crossed the threshold, like the spines of a Catherine-wheel. The huge house creaked as the boiler began to cool down again, neglected of fuel, and outside the world was white and hard and difficult to look at, as it almost always is, on Christmas Eve, in Connecticut.

'It's not going to work,' said Jack. He had known, all along, that it wasn't going to work. He had known, all along, that Dr McKinnon had been fifteen per cent too eccentric to be true, with all of his talk about people and houses and landscapes coming alive. There were not many times in his life when Jack felt like poking the muzzle of his .38 revolver into his mouth up against his palate, although every policeman now and again feels like doing it; but tonight, for some reason, he could have done it. The cold, uncomfortable pressure of steel, and then oblivion.

Vincent kept his eyes closed. Nothing had happened;

432

he hadn't been transported into another reality; but somehow the words had given him an extraordinary sensation which he knew was right. He turned round, still keeping his eyes closed. Now, he didn't know which way he was facing. But that wasn't important. The important thing now was to *walk forward*, straight ahead, into the darkness that clustered behind his own eyeballs.

Charlotte and Jack and Aaron saw him walk quite easily and methodically across the hall, out of the front door, and into the early morning snow. Jack called, 'Vincent! Are you okay?' but there was no answer at all. Charlotte hesitated for a moment, and then ran to the door, and looked out across the blindingly white garden, and he was gone. His footprints continued for three or four paces beyond the porch, and then vanished.

Jack came up behind her, and laid a hand on her shoulder. 'He's done it,' he whispered. 'He's gone. He's fucking immortal.'

Twenty-seven

Maurice Gray was sitting in the crimson parlour smoking his pipe when Thomas came in and stood close to the fireplace and stared at him. Maurice was discomfited. He didn't like anybody staring at him when he read the newspaper, especially boys, and even more especially, unfamiliar boys. He tried to read a long paragraph about President Arthur's plans to acquire Pearl Harbor as an American naval base, but in the end he had to shake his paper out and say, 'Yes, sir? Anything you want?'

'Please,' said Thomas, 'may I go home?'

Maurice sighed with melodramatic impatience. He laid his paper down on the floor, the ultimate gesture which a disturbed father uses to make his son feel guilty. *You have disturbed the Almighty Perusal of the News, my boy* (as if the course of history could be changed by anybody's father failing to peruse the news). *But, speak, and I shall suffer.*

'I don't know where I am,' said Thomas, his lower lip unsteady, although he refused to cry. 'I don't know what's happening to me.'

'Well,' said Maurice. 'I believe that I can settle both of those uncertainties, although whether you find the answers satisfactory or not is up to you. You are at

434

The Wilderlings, in Darien, Connecticut. It is Christmas Eve. Tomorrow, there will be presents, and goose, and plum dumplings, and all the sweets that boys enjoy. And what is happening to you is that you have come to live here with us, since you were recently made an orphan, and you are about to embark on a very satisfactory and rewarding life.'

'An orphan?' asked Thomas.

Maurice smiled, and twiddled his fingers together. 'What else do you call a boy who has no living parents?'

'But my father's alive. My mother's alive.'

Maurice shook his head, almost tetchily. 'Not a bit of it, Thomas. Neither your mother nor your father have yet been born. Look out of the window, Thomas, and tell me what you see.'

Thomas walked to the window and parted the heavy lace curtains, with their patterns of peacocks and flower-baskets. Outside the window, he could see the snow, and the drive, and the gates of The Wilderlings. But in the roadway beyond, he could see the horse-drawn sleighs, and ladies with sweeping coats and thick fur muffs, and gentlemen in tall hats.

Maurice stood up and approached the window, and fastidiously cleaned his nails with the sharp point of a small silver pen-knife.

'This is the year the picture was painted,' he said. 'We have returned there, for the time being, because we are children of the picture. We are inside the picture; inside! And you, with the assistance of Uncle Belvedere's artistry, are inside it with us.'

'I want to go home,' Thomas insisted. He still couldn't be sure if this was a nightmare or not; but he was determined to get home, even if it meant nothing more complicated than waking up.

'No,' said Maurice. '*This* is your home. *This*! You are

part of our family now. In fact, I think you should meet them, so that you know them better.'

'I just want to go home,' Thomas repeated.

But Maurice genially ignored him, and took hold of his arm, and led him through to the hall, which was shining and bright, and arranged with bronze Greek statues of muscular young men with perfectly formed bodies preparing to throw the javelin or the discus, or to run the marathon. Maurice remarked, 'Did you know that the word *gymnast* comes from the Greek word which means, *one who exercises naked*?'

Thomas was reluctant, but Maurice's grip on his arm was bitingly strong, like a lobster. He forced Thomas upstairs, along the landing, and up yet another flight of stairs, where dismal landscapes were hanging, views of Münster during a thunderstorm, and heavy seas off Heligoland. At last they arrived at a wide doorway, carved with fruit, which had once been painted but was faded now, as if from listlessness. Maurice knocked, and smiled at Thomas while they waited, his smile like a diluted nitric acid.

The doors were opened from the inside by a private nurse. A withered old woman in a white apron and a white wing hat, which drooped because of an insufficiency of starch. She whispered, 'He's sleeping. Please don't wake him.'

They tiptoed in darkness across a huge bedroom that smelled of disease and liniment. They arrived at the head of the bed, where Algernon Gray, the father of the family, lay awkwardly propped up, but asleep. He was snoring quietly, as if he were at peace with the world.

What horrified Thomas, however, was that his face was crawling with maggots. They wriggled in and out of his nose and poured into his mouth, and made his sparse white hair ripple as if it were being blown by an unfelt wind.

'He's very sick, you see,' Maurice remarked, with apparent unconcern, 'and Mother's the same. But now we have the portrait back, we can have it restored; and *they* will be restored along with it. Father and Mother. God bless them.'

Thomas couldn't think of anything to say. He felt frightened and nauseous and desperately lonely. *This must be a dream, mustn't it? Please, somebody, tell me for sure!*

'It was *your* family, you see, the Pearsons, which caused all of the problems,' said Maurice, leading Thomas out of the bedroom. 'They were friends of the Grays in the 1890s. They were always going to parties together; they were always going boating together. Your father's great-grandfather was always visiting The Wilderlings.'

'He had *maggots*,' Thomas whispered, in terrible awe.

Maurice squeezed his hand. 'Maggots, yes. Maggots! But none of us are quite what we were. It's sad, isn't it? Rather melancholy, when you come to think of it. I've often thought of writing poems about it, the sadness of dying. But here, of course, we don't die – although we do spend more time than we ought to, keeping ourselves in condition.'

They descended the main staircase and walked along the downstairs corridor, and went into the kitchens. There was nobody there at the moment. The copper pans hung shining, in order of size; the silver spatulas gleamed like fresh sardines hung up to dry.

'We were always a close family, you know,' Maurice told Thomas, his face half concealed by the hanging pans. 'If one of us caught the flu, well then, we *all* caught the flu. Some diseases became quite admirable family occasions: a cause to celebrate. You'll never guess! Hooray! I think I've caught the German measles! Break out a bottle of Gewürztraminer!'

Maurice hesitated, and then he said more seriously, 'Nowadays, it is becoming harder and harder for us to survive. We are outcasts, we know that, even if other people have managed to accept us. Without the portrait, we were lost; we had no control over our own destiny. But we have it back now, and we can restore ourselves.'

Thomas obviously didn't understand. Maurice offered him a high-backed stool, and leaned himself against the kitchen range, his arms crossed, and said, 'We wanted youth. What was so terrible about that? We wanted to stay as we were: young and bright and joyful. And we did. It was only when your great-grandfather intervened that we began to suffer. He stole the portrait, and kept it under lock and key; and then he sent us to Europe, as exiles. That was in 1911: a year which is yet to come, in this portrait. And which never *will* come, because portraits stay as they are, on the day they were painted. Young, vibrant, and alive.'

Maurice went through the cupboards and found a bottle of kir. He poured himself a very small glass, and knocked it back in one gulp.

'The portrait has to stay close to those who commissioned it, you see, because every now and then, to prevent ourselves from ageing too drastically, we must return to the year in which it was painted, *through the painting itself*. You might say that it is like going to a health farm to be rejuvenated. As years go by, you see, as each of us grows farther and farther away from the day when we *should* have died, our strength grows weaker and our youthful appearance begins to need some attention.

'Everything went well, until your great-grandfather

stole the portrait. Then, we had to rely for our survival not on revisiting the portrait itself, as we had before, but on changing skins every two or three months, to keep ourselves presentable to the outside world. Many innocent people died because of that need. We killed them; but I lay the blame for each of those deaths firmly at the Pearson family door. If the Pearsons hadn't meddled, then the Grays might very well have hurt no one, offended no one, and remained *la crème de la crème* of Connecticut society.'

Maurice rubbed his forehead with his fingertips in a gentle circular motion, as if he were beginning to feel the first pangs of a migraine. 'The portrait is essential to our survival. To disappear inside it, each of us has to physically touch his or her own image on it. And, amazing, here we are! Sitting in the kitchen, talking to each other, in 1883. But you're young. You must be getting bored. All this talk of rejuvenation, and influenza, and the sadness of lives that have long outlived their usefulness. No wonder God sends us down to Earth for such a short time! Nobody is capable of making decent conversation.'

Thomas said, 'I want to go home.'

'My dear fellow,' Maurice told him. 'From now on, this *is* home. At least, for as long as I say so. You have no other way of getting back, except through me, so you had better accept it, and be nice. If you weren't here, your father would probably set fire to our portrait and burn us alive; but you are here, and so is Laura, and, well, we're quite reasonably protected, wouldn't you say? Hm?'

'I thought you had killed Laura,' said Thomas, which was probably the single most sophisticated remark that he had made all day.

'Killed her, my friend? Certainly not; although she

does have certain drastic decisions to make about her own life, as do all of us.'

'Such as?'

Maurice smiled smugly. 'She has to decide whether she wants to be Henry's servant for the rest of her life, which is almost immortal, or whether she wishes to sacrifice her skin to save my mother from losing her looks altogether.'

Thomas said, 'That's all she can choose? That's terrible! That's exploitation!'

'And this is 1883, my dear boy; before the word exploitation was in common currency, especially among boys of your age. My God, you're a do-gooder, aren't you? Just like your father.'

Maurice stroked Thomas's hair, but Thomas jerked his head away. 'Let's see where Laura is,' Maurice suggested. 'It might be amusing to see what Henry has in store for her today. Do you want to come? Or do you want to sit here all day and sulk?'

Maurice left the kitchen and walked through to the music room. Thomas felt that he had no alternative but to follow. He was conscious that the air in the house was strangely hazy, as if everything were seen through the finest of muslins. There was a musical box playing somewhere, some long-forgotten tune; and he could hear a woman singing.

> And should you gather lilies
> Beside the sliding stream;
> And should you breathe the perfume there
> In times that make you dream . . .

In the music room, Henry was sitting at the piano, his hair tousled, a black Russian *papirosi* cigarette dangling unlit between his lips. He was wearing full morning dress, complete with grey silk tie, although he had taken off his coat and hung it over the back of the chair. He wasn't playing the piano: he was only staring at the sheet-music, a complicated piece by Chopin, a black forest of semiquavers.

Laura was sitting in a small upholstered armchair, her hands in her lap, rigid and silent. She turned to look at Thomas as he came into the room, her liquid eyes made misty by the hazy atmosphere, but she said nothing. She was wearing a severe black floor-length dress, which fastened in the front with scores of tiny black buttons.

'Well, cousin,' said Henry disconsolately. 'What is the grand decision?'

Maurice systematically clicked his knuckles and looked around him with that pained James Mason expression of his (and James Mason not yet born, nor dead). 'I don't think that there has ever been any serious dispute about it, Henry. The girl must go to Mother.'

'Tomorrow, I suppose?'

'Tomorrow is Christmas Day. I hardly wish to . . .'

Henry played a series of chords. 'Of course not, Maurice. I know how delicate your stomach is. And, of course, since it would be better for Mother to have her sooner, rather than later . . .'

'Yes, well, this afternoon would be suitable,' said Maurice.

Henry revolved on his piano stool and said loudly to Laura, 'Do you hear that, my angel? This afternoon, you are to be skinned! All for the sake of Maurice's mother, who is not at all well.'

Thomas stared at Laura in horror, but Laura remained expressionless. Maurice laid his hand on Thomas's shoulder and patted it, and said, 'It is a wonderful thing, you know, regeneration. Laura will have saved my mother's life, and live again, in her. We are always very grateful.'

Henry took out a box of matches and lit his cigarette. There was a sharp smell of burned sulphur and Balkan tobacco. 'Maurice considers his gratitude to be reward enough for anything. You may die in agony; but as long as Maurice is grateful, what of it?'

'Come now,' Maurice said to Thomas. 'We have a fascinating library upstairs. Perhaps you would like to while away the afternoon by the fire, and read some encyclopedias. Then we shall ask Cook to bring us some crumpets, and we shall toast them, and eat them with plenty of butter and jam.'

There was nothing that Thomas could say or do. Frightened and meek, he allowed Maurice to guide him out of the music room and up the stairs.

'You mustn't be concerned for your own safety,' said Maurice, as they walked along the landing. 'Now that we have the portrait back, we need to restore ourselves only once. That means that we need only one more gentleman, for Father; and possibly one more young lady, for my sister Cordelia. It isn't *really* necessary for Cordelia to have anybody else, but she is so vain about her appearance!'

Just as Thomas and Maurice went into the library and closed the door, the front door of the house opened cautiously and Vincent stepped in. It was warm in the hall, and the snowflakes on his shoulders died almost immediately. He hesitated, and listened; and he could tell by the crackling of the fires in every room, and by the aroma of tobacco and pot-pourri, that Dr McKinnon's theory was correct, and that he had actually managed to penetrate the creative existence of the Waldegrave portrait. There was an unusual quality to the air, and when he looked around the hall, the furniture and the statues all seemed distorted, as if he were seeing them through curved glass. The light was blurred, and the conversations that he could hear sounded peculiarly flat. But apart from that, here was the house, and here was he; and there was nothing to deny the 'reality' of either of them.

There had been no sense of travelling in time or space when Vincent had walked out of the front door and into the garden. He had taken three or four paces, and then turned round again and walked back in.

Carefully, Vincent tiptoed his way across the hall, until he reached the open doors of the music room. Henry was leaning against the keyboard of the piano, with his back to Vincent, and Laura was standing by the window, staring out at the snow. Her hair had been brushed up, Victorian-style, and she was wearing tortoiseshell combs in it.

Vincent glanced behind him, to make sure that nobody else was around. He was breathing heavily, with tension and determination. He loosened his necktie, and then quietly tugged it off and wound the ends of it tightly around his hands, like a garotte.

Henry was saying, 'Nobody knows what it was that Chopin saw in Konstancja Gladkowska. Why did he love her so much? Why didn't he marry her? And, of course, nobody can ask him now.'

Vincent stepped boldly through the open doors of the music room, his necktie raised between his fists. At that moment, Laura turned around from the window and saw him. She raised her hand to her mouth and stared at him in surprise.

'What's the matter with you?' Henry asked her. 'You look as if you've seen a ghost.'

There was a moment when Vincent was sure that

Laura was about to point to him and give him away, and he was still too far away from Henry to reach him before he could turn round to defend himself. But then Laura suddenly looked away and said, 'It makes me sad, the story of Chopin.'

'It makes you sad? What an extraordinary thing to say!' Henry exclaimed. He half rose off his piano-stool, but then he sat back again – and that was when Vincent came up close behind him and whipped the necktie right round his throat.

Henry lurched sideways. The piano-stool crashed on to the parquet floor. Henry twisted and struggled, and he was strong. Vincent could feel the muscles in Henry's shoulders straining against his thighs. But Vincent wrenched at the necktie with all the strength he could manage, and kept his grip relentlessly tight, and knew that if he loosened it, or let go, then he was finished.

Henry roared and gargled, his neck bulging, his face crimson, his eyes protruding. He kicked his legs around, trying to lash behind him so that he could knock Vincent off his feet. His grey pumps scrabbled and clattered at the floor. But Vincent tugged tighter still, grunting with the effort of it, and pressed his knee forcibly into the middle of Henry's back to prevent him from getting up.

Abruptly, Henry began to cough maggots. Small bursts of them at first, scattered across the floor, twisting and writhing. But then his whole body convulsed; and with a stomach-wrenching heave, he brought up thousands of them, glistening and wriggling in deep, soft heaps.

He collapsed, face-down, and Vincent prayed that he had finished him off. There seemed to be no substance to him at all now; his body was little more than a skeleton, flaccidly draped in fine, pale skin. The maggots began to crawl painfully away from him,

444

abandoning their host and their home, and presumably seeking someone else's body to occupy. Vincent brushed half a dozen of them off his hands and out of his sleeve, and he had to shake his necktie two or three times to get the last of them off.

'Laura,' he said, and crossed the room and took hold of her hand. 'Laura, it's Vincent Pearson. Don't you remember me? Vincent Pearson. I own the gallery where Edward used to work.'

'*Edward . . .*' murmured Laura.

Vincent said, urgently, 'You have to get out of here, Laura. They intend to kill you. Laura, listen to me!'

'Is Edward here?' Laura asked vaguely. She frowned at Vincent as if she found it difficult to focus on his face.

'Edward – Edward is outside,' Vincent told her, with sudden inspiration. 'Come on, quickly, and I'll show you.'

Doubtfully, dragging her silk-slippered feet, Laura allowed Vincent to tug her out of the music room, and into the hall. He opened the front door for her, and said, 'There! Just outside! Hurry, or you might miss him!'

'But it's cold out there,' said Laura. 'It's cold and it's snowing, and Henry said that I wasn't to go anywhere. Henry said –'

Vincent took hold of both Laura's wrists and dragged her out on to the porch. 'He's there!' he screamed at her. 'Go and find him!'

Confused, shivering, rubbing her wrists, Laura stepped out into the snow. At first, Vincent was frightened that nothing was going to happen, that there was no way for them to escape from the painting. But as she walked out across the garden, Laura's black dress began to fade to grey, and then to look almost transparent. Within a matter of moments, she had vanished, and there was nothing to show that she had been there,

445

except for the tracks of her slippers, suddenly disappearing into nothing.

Now Vincent had to look for Thomas. He went back into the house, and began to open up doors, one after the other, searching for his son. He looked into the music room again, but it was empty. Most of the maggots had crawled away, and were teeming into the hems of the velvet curtains for warmth. He tried the kitchen, but that too was deserted. Then he suddenly burst into the morning room, and came face to face with Willa and her daughters, and the crippled Netty.

Willa screamed. 'Who are you?' she demanded. 'How dare you come trespassing into our house!'

Vincent hesitated to begin with. These were girls, after all. Children. And one of them was crippled. But he knew what he was here for: to destroy the Grays. The continuing lives of these girls had been bought with the flayed skins of other children, God only knew how many, over the years. They had lived far longer than they should have done, in any case, and at what cost to their victims. Hours of agony, days of fear and not even a consecrated grave. The victims' spirits were still trapped at The Wilderlings, waiting for release, and they would only reach the next life when the Grays themselves were dead.

Vincent went a little mad. It had to be done, but he could do it only in a fit of righteous hysteria, when his natural sense of justice and mercy was blotted out by red-eyed rage. He picked up the heavy brass-knobbed poker from beside the fire, and with a single swing, he hit Willa on the side of the head, just above the ear, where her lacy bonnet was tied. Then he hit her again, as she fell, at the back of the neck; and even if she wasn't dead, she would never walk again.

The girls screamed. Netty clutched at her mahogany

wheelchair in terror, and shook her head from side to side. Emily and Ermintrude tried to hide behind the curtains, but Vincent struck at the curtains again and again, until Emily dropped into sight, concussed, and Ermintrude fell to her knees and begged for mercy.

Vincent killed them, somehow. Such an act of violence was completely out of character. But he knew that there was nothing else left for him to do. It was like clubbing seals. Ermintrude knelt in front of him, and he beat her twice, so that her skull broke. Netty, he dragged from her wheelchair, and threw face-down on the floor, and hit her as hard as he could on the back of the head. The knob on the end of the poker must have weighed at least two pounds, and she jerked, then lay still. There was blood and lace-trimmed Victorian dresses everywhere, like the casualty ward of a doll's hospital. Willa groaned, and lifted one hand, embellished with diamond rings. Then her hand fell back again.

Vincent stood in the doorway, his chest heaving with the effort of what he had done. *My God,* he thought, *I've killed them all. But just supposing this isn't some other reality; supposing I've gone crazy, and just think that this is some other reality? Supposing these were all ordinary, innocent girls; and I've cudgelled them all to death?*

He didn't have long to wait, though, before the proof appeared that he was justified in having killed them, and that he was not deranged. The girls' skirts and pantaloons began to stir and ripple, as if they were waking up again. Their sleeves shifted; their petticoats rustled.

Vincent cautiously lifted up Netty's body with the blackened tip of the poker, and there they were, in their thousands. The maggots which had infested the Gray family, ever since the day when they should have died. In just a few minutes, the whole of the morning room

447

was alive with them, curling and uncurling, twitching and crawling; until Vincent retreated in disgust and closed the door behind him.

At the same moment, however, Cordelia appeared at the head of the staircase, right in the act of powdering her face. She saw Vincent at once, and snapped her powder compact shut.

'Maurice!' she called. She turned around, and started to hurry along the landing. 'Maurice! For God's sake, Maurice! Vincent Pearson is here! Maurice!'

Still brandishing the poker, Vincent ran across the hall and surged furiously up the stairs. As he reached the top, he was just in time to see the black hem of Cordelia's dress disappearing into the library, like the fin of a vanishing shark. He jogged along the landing until he reached the library doors, and then he stopped, listening. The last thing he wanted was to be caught by surprise, or to have Thomas hurt.

'Maurice Gray?' he called harshly.

There was no reply.

'Maurice Gray, this is Vincent Pearson! I want my son, Mr Gray, and I want him now!'

He was just about to try to kick the library doors open, when they were opened for him from inside, and Cordelia appeared. She stood white and silent, regarding him intensely with those eyes like mirrors.

'Where's my son?' Vincent demanded.

'Well, well,' said Cordelia, stepping out on to the landing and circling around him. 'So you're Vincent Pearson. So like your grandfather, you know. Both in looks and in moral recklessness. That is, you recklessly apply your morals to the lives of others, without a thought for the consequences.'

Vincent raised the poker. 'If you don't tell me where my son is, I'm going to kill you, here and now.'

Cordelia smiled with faultless frostiness. Then she opened the library doors a little wider. Vincent could see a fireplace, a hearthrug, on which an encyclopedia lay, opened at a page about praying mantises, and a chair. Beyond the chair, there was a panelled door, which was half ajar.

'Your son has gone on a journey with my brother Maurice. A fascinating journey, to other lands! And I can promise you, here and now, my dear, that you will never find him. You might as well resign yourself to returning to your own humdrum existence; and to forgetting about the Grays for ever.'

Twenty-eight

Darien, 24 December

Vincent crossed the library and looked into the open door. Beyond it, there was a narrow spiral staircase. 'Where does this lead?' he demanded.

'It leads to almost anywhere you wish,' said Cordelia airily.

Without asking her anything else, Vincent went through the doorway, and rapidly began to descend the staircase. It was constructed of mahogany, beautifully carpentered, and it had obviously been intended to give the original master of the house a secret way out (perhaps from his creditors) or a secret way in (perhaps for his mistresses). It was dark and dry and it smelled of furniture polish. Vincent remembered as he clattered down the stairs that this mid-Victorian house was only twenty or thirty years old, in the alternative reality of the portrait.

There was a heavy door at the bottom of the staircase, and when Vincent pushed it open, he found himself in the cellars. There were gas-lamps burning, so Maurice Gray had obviously come down this way.

'Thomas!' called Vincent. 'Thomas! Can you hear me, Thomas! It's Daddy! Thomas, shout if you can hear me!'

He waited, and listened, but there was nothing. He walked swiftly along the central corridor that ran the length of the cellar, trying the doors, but all of them were locked. At last he reached the metal-clad door behind which the Grays' art collection was stored. It was open. Only a quarter of an inch, but it was open.

Vincent hefted the poker, and warily stepped inside. It was dark and cool and silent in there; and all he could see was the faint gleaming of the gilded frames.

'Thomas?' he whispered. 'Thomas?'

At first, there was no reply. But then he heard the smallest and faintest of voices; and no matter how small and faint it was, he knew at once that it was his son.

'*Dad* . . .' A voice so small that it sounded as far away as the sea heard in a seashell.

'*Dad . . . help me . . .*'

Vincent listened and listened, but he couldn't make out where the calling was coming from. How could Thomas possibly sound so far away, when the room was only thirty feet square? Unless – unless he *wasn't* in the room, not in the normal sense of the word. Because what had Cordelia said upstairs? '*Your son has gone on a journey.*' And how else could anybody go on a journey, within the confines of this stone-built cellar, unless they entered the paintings here, in the same way that Vincent had entered *this* painting?

'Thomas!' Vincent shouted. 'Thomas, can you hear me?'

'*Faint . . .*' came the reply.

Vincent furiously searched through stacks of canvases. 'Thomas, give me a clue, for Christ's sake! Where are you? Thomas, where are you?'

'*River . . .*' Thomas called. '*Reeds, and grass, and . . .*'

It sounded as if Thomas had suddenly been cut short. Perhaps Maurice Gray had told him to stop shouting. *River*, thought Vincent, desperately. *River, reeds, and grass. God Almighty, there are scores of landscapes here.* He worked his way, sweating, through nearly twenty pictures, stacking them all to one side.

It was then that Thomas gave him a vital clue. In a voice so tiny that it could have been nothing more than the settling of a fly on his shoulder, Vincent heard the words, 'White . . . clock . . .'

White clock. River, reeds and white clock. And there was only one painting that included all of those characteristics, as far as he could remember. *A View of Dennisburg*, painted in 1854 by Charles K. Barraclough. It must have been sold by the Grays before they left Connecticut in 1911, because it was now on display at the Brightwell Gallery, in Philadelphia. But this was 1883, and so the painting would still be here. Maybe Maurice Gray had chosen to escape into it, simply to confuse him.

Vincent found it easily. After all, Maurice Gray must have been in a hurry when he came down here. A large painting of the Heron River, bordered with reeds; and in the far distance, that distinctive white clock-tower.

Vincent peered closely at the painting; and there, on the bridge, hand in hand, he could make out the figures of a man and a boy, running.

He closed his eyes. He touched the surface of the painting with both hands. The oil-paint was smooth and cool, and still faintly aromatic. He didn't know whether it was necessary to recite the words of the exorcism. If it was, he would have to go back into his own reality and get them. But he kept his eyes tightly shut; and he prayed to God that he could enter the painting; and he thought of nothing else but saving Thomas. Surely that would be enough.

The painting began to feel rough, then dry, then stalky. Suddenly a wind was blowing, and there was the chaff-like rustling of reeds. Suddenly it was afternoon, in spring, and the sky was as clear as bright blue grass. Vincent stood up, and he was knee-deep in grass, by the eastern bank of the Heron River in Delaware; and there, not more than a quarter of a mile off, was the small shoreline town of Dennisburg, with its famous white clock-tower and its clustered orange rooftops.

Seagulls wheeled and circled overhead, and there was a strong smell of salt in the air.

Vincent began to run. He was still clutching the brass-knobbed poker. His feet crackled through broken bracken, heaps of riverside shingle and derelict herons' nests. It took him only five minutes to reach the white-painted wooden bridge, but by the time he got there, the man and the boy had gone. He crossed the river and walked along the wooden-boarded sidewalk that lined the opposite bank. There were small neat fishermen's cottages here, with yellow nasturtiums blowing in tubs, and nets hung up, and large zinc washbowls for cleaning fish.

An old woman in a white headscarf was leaning on her front fence. She stared at Vincent openly, and he realized that he was something to be stared at, in his Bijan suit and his Turnbull & Asser shirt, carrying a long brass poker.

'Did you see a man and a boy pass this way?' he asked the old woman.

'Where *you* from?' the old woman asked him, in return.

'New York. Did you see them?'

She pointed along the boardwalk. 'Might have gone that way, if it's worth anything.'

Vincent took out his wallet and gave her a dollar. He thought that five dollars might be rather too much, in 1854. The old woman stared at the money, and stared at him, and then went back into her cottage, so that she could continue her staring through the window, from a safe distance.

Vincent continued along the boardwalk, which soon petered out into sand and grassy scrub. There was no sign of Thomas, or Maurice Gray. But Vincent kept on going, until the ground began to rise into sand-dunes, and he could see the grey glittering breast of the Atlantic Ocean, off to his right. Near the horizon, a fishing-smack leaned over, its sails white and vibrant in the afternoon sunlight.

He topped one more sand-dune, and then he saw them, still hand in hand, hurrying along the shore. His heart expanded and adrenalin surged through his body, because it was Thomas; he recognized the colour of his hair and the black velvet Victorian suit that the Grays had given him to wear.

Vincent was tempted to shout out, but he restrained himself. He jumped and bounded from one sand-dune to the next, keeping low, ducking his head whenever he thought that Maurice Gray might turn around. Soon, he was almost abreast of them, leaping through the tufty seaside grass; and it was then that he broke his cover and ran diagonally across the sand towards them, whirling the poker over his head, so that it whistled, and at last screaming out, 'Thomas! Thomas! It's Dad!'

Thomas turned, and immediately tugged himself away from Maurice Gray's grasp. He ran back towards his father, his arms and legs pumping, his face clenched in that furious sports-day expression of childish concentration.

Maurice Gray stood where he was, tall and dignified, in morning dress, his spats stained dark with sea-water, his grey hair lifted by the Atlantic wind.

'Well,' he said, 'my nemesis.'

Vincent was too much out of breath to answer him;

too furious; too crazy. Thomas stayed a little way behind him as he circled Maurice Gray, whirling the poker, listening to the way it whirred and whistled.

'Do you intend to strike me?' asked Maurice. He lifted his left wrist and carefully buttoned his grey kid glove.

Vincent walked right round Maurice, behind his back. Maurice was just turning his head to see what he was doing when Vincent lashed him across the side of the neck; a blow so fast and hard that it bent the shaft of the poker.

Maurice clapped his hand to his neck and said, 'Good Lord,' and then fell on to the sand, on his side. He lay there with his eyes open, not yet dead, while Vincent stood over him, still breathing hard.

'You'd better finish me off,' said Maurice. 'I can't stand to look at the sea, from this point of view. It reminds me how fragile we are.'

Thomas looked away, with his hands in his pockets, which is a gesture that all boys use to try to show their fathers that they disapprove, and that they're frightened, and that they can't understand what's happening.

Vincent struck Maurice on the back of the head, four times. It was probably three times more than necessary; but in Maurice's case, Vincent wanted to make absolutely sure.

Maurice lay sprawled on the sand, his arms and legs twisted at ungainly angles. Blood seeped from his scalp and filled up a small white cockleshell that was lying close beside him.

Vincent took hold of Thomas's hand and led him quickly away, along the shore. He didn't want Thomas to see the maggots that infested Maurice's body come pouring out; although twenty yards along the beach, he glanced around himself, to make sure that they had.

From this distance, they looked like nothing very much at all. Just as if somebody had spilled a sack of white rice across the sand.

Thomas said, 'You killed him.'

'Yes. I had to. He wasn't actually real. Not in the way that we are.'

'How do we get home?' asked Thomas.

Vincent squeezed his hand and smiled. 'We keep our fingers crossed, and say a prayer.'

They walked back through the town, and across the bridge, and down through the reeds by the river. The old woman in the headscarf had seen them pass her window, and out of curiosity had followed them, at a distance. She was standing on the bridge shading her eyes against the sun when they vanished from sight altogether, like ghosts. She had no way of telling that she herself only existed in a painting, which a hundred and thirty years later would be hanging on the wall of the Brightwell Gallery, in Philadelphia.

Vincent and Thomas took one more step through the reeds, and the day began to fade and grow darker; and, holding hands, they felt a strange sensation of sliding forwards and downwards, as if they were descending a glacial escalator.

'We'll be safe now,' Vincent told Thomas, in a slow and fuzzy voice.

Quite suddenly, however, the day brightened again, and they found themselves walking along a brick-paved street. The houses were quite unfamiliar, with flat rendered façades and green-shuttered windows. There were church bells pealing somewhere, and dogs barking, and, from somewhere close by, an extraordinary hollow clattering noise which sounded like hundreds of wooden spoons being rattled against the ground. Up above their heads, the clouds billowed like the sails of old-fashioned galleons, and the wind blew up dust and glittering specks of straw from the roadway.

'Where are we?' asked Thomas, frightened.

Vincent looked around. There was a butcher's shop across the street, with huge orange-skinned ox carcasses hanging outside on hooks. The sign above the shop announced *Vleeswaren*, in faded gold letters. 'That's Dutch,' said Vincent. 'We must have come the wrong way.'

Thomas anxiously tugged his hand. 'Don't let's go on; let's go back.'

'Thomas,' Vincent told him, 'I don't know *how* to go back. Don't you realize what this is? This is another painting.'

'But if we walk back to where we came into it?'

'We walked back to where we came into the Dennisburg painting, didn't we? And all that did was to bring us here. Maybe if we can find out what picture this is, that might help.'

Two nuns with white-winged wimples came bustling along the street towards them. As the nuns approached Vincent went up to them, and called, 'Pardon me, sisters. Could you give me some directions, please?'

They stopped and stared at him in perplexity. One of them had the pale oval face of a saint; as pretty as a religious effigy. The other was blind in one eye, and had lips that were formed into a permanent snarl.

'*Parlez-vous français?*' asked Vincent.

'*Oui, monsieur.* Do you need assistance?'

'My son and I, we're lost. I wonder if you could tell us what town this is?'

'Leiden, monsieur. Is there anything else?'

'Yes. Do you know of any painters who live here, any artists?'

'*Non, monsieur.* Only the monks.'

Vincent said, 'You're very kind. Could you do one more thing for me?'

'Of course, *monsieur.*'

'Could you please tell me what year this is?'

'What year?' the snarling nun asked him suspiciously. She was evidently beginning to believe that he was a lunatic, especially since he was dressed in such a peculiar way.

But the pretty nun said gently, 'This is 1631, monsieur,' and lowered her eyes bashfully, and hurried her sister away.

Vincent stood where he was, his hand pressed against the side of his neck as if he were trying to stem the flow of blood from an artery. Thomas stood watching him, biting his lips.

'My God,' said Vincent, at last. 'Sixteen thirty-one. That means that Rembrandt is still alive; although I don't remember Rembrandt ever having painted anything like this. Besides, I don't think the Grays ever *owned* a Rembrandt.'

'What are we going to do?' Thomas asked him miserably.

'I think the best thing we can do is take a look around. Now listen, don't panic. Don't get upset. We've got each other, haven't we? And we've beaten the Grays. All we have to do is work out a way to get back.'

They turned the corner of the street, and they saw then what was causing the clattering noise. There was a market in the town's main square, with scores of stalls under flapping white awnings; and it was the wooden clogs of all the shoppers and the stallholders and the running children that was setting up the noise.

Cautiously, doing their best not to attract attention, Vincent and Thomas walked through the market. There were stalls heaped with shining yellow cheeses; fish stalls, with smoked herring and pickled elver; bread stalls, with coarse brown loaves as large as wheels. Most of the stallholders wore leather caps or head-scarves and long leather jerkins, but there were a few more elegantly dressed men around the square, with wide-brimmed hats, and cloaks, and calf-britches. Vincent was struck by the dullness of the women's dresses, in faded pinks and dusty browns, and remembered that the dyestuffs available to fabric-makers in 1631 were very limited.

The aroma of the cheeses and the smell of the fish blew through the market-place on the afternoon wind. Vincent found it strange that nobody seemed to be talking, or crying out their wares, in spite of the fact that their clogs were making so much noise. It was almost as if they were miming the parts of seventeenth-century Dutch townspeople, and Vincent found their silence extremely disquieting.

They had nearly reached the brick-fronted town hall when they were hailed by an ugly-looking man in a brown cape and a lopsided leather cap. He walked directly up to them, dragged off his cap and bowed impudently low.

'What is it?' asked Vincent.

'Yoop thar,' the man grinned at them.

'What?' asked Vincent. '*Parlez-vous français?*'

'Nee, nee,' the man replied, shaking his tangled curls. 'Yoop thar.' And he pointed to a second-storey window, at the left of one of the houses that fronted the square. A yellow-washed house, with leaded lights, and numbers announcing that it had been built in 1611.

Vincent frowned at the house, and, as he did so, he saw a hand waving at the window.

'Yoop thar,' the leather-capped man repeated, and

beckoned Vincent with a hand that had lost two of its fingers. 'Kom, kom, yoop thar.'

'He means "up there",' Vincent told Thomas. 'He wants us to go with him.'

'Kom, kom,' the fellow insisted.

But Vincent raised both hands. 'We don't know anybody here. We're strangers. Do you understand that? We don't know that man, whoever he is. You're making a mistake.'

'Winson?' the fellow demanded, pointing at Vincent. 'You Winson?'

'That's right, I'm Vincent. But how on earth did you know that? And who's that, up there at the window?'

'Kom,' the fellow repeated.

Vincent shrugged. 'We don't seem to have any alternative. Let's go see who it is.'

They followed the leather-capped man along by the town hall steps and across the side-street that led to the yellow house. The fellow opened the front door for them and ceremoniously waved them inside with his cap. Vincent kept his hand on Thomas's shoulder and stepped carefully into the hall.

The interior of the house was dark and musty. Through a side doorway, Vincent could see a young woman with an embroidered bonnet sitting at a desk, sewing. A small songbird chirruped in a cage on the wall beside her. The scene reminded him strongly of an interior by Vermeer, but the nuns had told him that this was Leiden, not Delft, where Vermeer had lived; and again he doubted whether the Grays had been sufficiently wealthy to own any Vermeers.

They crossed the black-and-white tiled hall, and the fellow in the leather cap hopped ahead of them upstairs. The staircase was solid oak, heavy, and carved with fruit. Their feet sounded flatly on the bare oak treads. At the top, there was an oval window, through which Vincent could see the branches of trees waving in the wind, like swimmers waving for help.

They were guided along the shadowy upstairs landing, until they reached a door at the very end of the house. The leather-capped man knocked on it loudly, and then opened it for them. 'Kom,' he nodded.

Vincent and Thomas entered the room. It was white-washed, low-ceilinged, with diamond-leaded windows looking out over the wind-flapped awnings of the market-place. The floor was polished oak. There was a desk, with an upright chair, and a silver inkwell with a plumed pen standing in it, as if somebody had recently been writing, although there was no paper there.

By the window, against the light, stood a tall figure in a hooded brown velvet robe. He was standing at a three-quarter angle away from them, so it was impossible for them to see him clearly. He was very softly humming a tune, which Vincent did not recognize. It sounded repetitive and medieval, one of those quaint songs about the harvest, or the fish, or the cow that never gave milk.

'You sent your man for us,' said Vincent, in a strained voice.

There was a moment's silence, and then the hooded figure nodded and said, 'Indeed I did.' His words were very indistinct, as if he were speaking with his mouth full.

'I don't think it's impertinent of me to ask who you are, and why you want to see us,' said Vincent.

'Of course not,' the figure replied. 'But I would have thought that my identity was self-evident.'

The figure turned and drew off its hood. Thomas screamed in terror.

It was Maurice Gray; still alive, but with his grey

scalp clustered with clots of drying blood, and maggots teeming around the neck of his robe and around his hairline and dropping from the corners of his mouth. His eyes – which had always looked mirror-like and dark – now gleamed silver, as if they had been filled up to the brim with mercury.

Vincent seized Thomas's arm and made for the door; but the leather-capped man was waiting for them, grinning with a mouthful of rotting stumps, holding up a large-bladed cleaver. He swung the cleaver from side to side, and cackled.

Maurice took two or three heavy-footed steps towards them. A pellucid maggot squeezed out from between his lips and tumbled on to his cloak. There were even maggots squirming up inside his nostrils.

'I killed you,' Vincent insisted. 'I killed you on the beach at Dennisburg.'

Maurice smiled, and said, almost indulgently, 'Would that you had. But I am the inheritor of everything which the Grays have stood for, these past hundred years. The strength of the family is invested in me, Mr Pearson, and I am a difficult man to dispose of.'

He raised one hand, with maggots dropping out of his open sleeve. 'Do you like this painting? I must say that I have always rather cared for it myself, despite the dullness of its subject-matter. It was painted in 1631 by Gerard Dou, who was a pupil of Rembrandt. A most meticulous painter; something of a forerunner to Vermeer. The quality of the light is so interesting, don't you think?'

Vincent said, 'All we want to do is get out of here. Now, will you please let us go?'

Maurice stared at him with those blank silvery eyes. 'The Pearsons have been the curse of my family ever since we met. You don't seriously believe that I am going to let you escape? You can stay here for ever; that's probably the punishment most appropriate for a pretentious art-dealer like you. Trapped in a seventeenth-century townscape of unsurpassed dullness.'

He paused, and brushed maggots from his collar. 'Better still, perhaps, I should have you hacked to death by my friend here, and fed to the dogs of Leiden.'

Vincent took a step towards the man in the leather cap. He glanced at Maurice, and then he glanced towards Thomas.

'Thomas,' he said, in a level voice. 'Do you remember the old one-two?'

'What?' asked Thomas, petrified by Maurice's grisly appearance.

'The old one-two, Thomas. You remember. Back on the lawn at Candlemas.'

Thomas turned and stared at him. Vincent wasn't at all sure that he understood.

'The boy is justifiably frightened,' said Maurice smoothly. 'Death, after all, is very greatly to be feared, wouldn't you say?'

But Vincent immediately swung backwards, catching the man in the leather cap by surprise. He seized the fellow's grimy wrist in both hands, banging his hand furiously against the side of the door, so that the man yelled out and dropped his cleaver. The fellow was strong, but Vincent pushed him backwards; and just as he did so, Thomas dived on to his knees and crouched over, the old one-two, and the man stumbled over him and fell flat on his back on the floor.

Vincent scrabbled around on the floor, and picked up the cleaver. He brandished it at Maurice Gray, and Maurice instinctively raised both arms above his head to protect himself.

'*Dad! No! Dad! You can't!*' Thomas shouted hysterically. But fiercely and blindly, Vincent chopped down at Maurice's arms, feeling the heavy metal blade strike soft decaying tissue, then bone. He struck again and again, until fragments of flesh and velvet began to fly around the room in a storm. There was scarcely any blood; only a kind of dark glutinous treacle, which stuck to the blade of the cleaver with every stroke.

Maurice soundlessly fell on to his knees. His mutilated arms dropped to his sides. Now Vincent chopped into the back of his skull, severing his ears, half scalping him, leaving his head looking as if it had been flayed, and torn at by animals.

He would have hacked him into pieces, but Thomas held on to his arm, and shrieked at him, '*Stop! Stop! You've killed him! You've killed him! Dad! Stop. Dad, you've killed him!*'

Vincent at last threw down the cleaver with a peculiarly diffident sideways toss, and stood staring at his son like the lunatic which the nuns had believed him to be. The man in the leather cap cowered in the far corner of the room, and when Vincent looked towards him, he tugged his cap right down over his forehead and stammered, 'Nee, nee, nee!'

The body of Maurice Gray collapsed sideways on to the floor, his silver eyes wide open. The shoulders of his gown began to stir as the maggots poured out of him. Vincent held up his hands and stared at them. He had never hurt anybody before today. Now he was a wholesale killer.

'Dad, come on, let's go, Dad,' Thomas begged him.

Vincent nodded, and followed his son into the corridor. He was so dazed by what he had done that he scarcely noticed the subtle transition from daytime to night; and that suddenly the corridor wasn't boarded beneath their feet, but carpeted, and that there were flickering blue-grey lights up ahead, and the booming of unfamiliar voices.

'Where are we?' Thomas asked him, and reached out to take hold of his hand.

Vincent stared into the darkness, willing his eyes to become accustomed to it. He could see a narrow entrance up ahead, partly draped by red curtains. He thought he could see somebody standing there, a woman perhaps, although she was wearing trousers. The lights kept shifting and flickering, and the booming voices continued. There was a strong smell of cigarette-smoke in the air.

'This is a movie theatre,' Vincent told Thomas. 'Maybe we're back in the present. Come on, let's take a look.'

They walked the length of the corridor, until they reached the auditorium. It was a big, shabby, New York cinema, with garish yellow walls and peach-coloured lights. Under the lamps stood a blonde-haired usherette in a blue trouser-suit, studiously picking at the two-day-old nail-varnish on her fingers. She looked up at them as they came in, and said, 'Tickets?'

Vincent pretended to search in his pockets, taking the opportunity to look around. He could see by the way that the audience was dressed that this wasn't the present day. The men wore coats with wide lapels, and the women mostly seemed to have dresses and jackets with shoulder-pads. Nineteen-forties, maybe; or late 1930s. The movie that was flickering on the screen confirmed it. Robert Donat, in *Goodbye, Mr Chips*. As far as Vincent could recall, that was 1939, the same year that *Gone with the Wind* had won the Oscar for best picture.

'Do you have a ticket or dontcha?' the usherette wanted to know.

'Well, I think I must have dropped it,' said Vincent. He laid his hand on Thomas's shoulder. 'I'll go back and see if I can find it.'

They walked back along the corridor and up the stairs. Thomas asked fearfully, 'Do you know where we are?'

'It looks very much like *New York Movie*. That was a painting by Edward Hopper, 1939.'

'But how do we get out of it?' Thomas begged.

'I don't know. But the Grays did it; and so there has to be a way.'

They reached the foyer. It was night-time outside, and through the gleaming windows Vincent could see a busy New York street crowded with Hudsons and Plymouths and Packards. The foyer was almost deserted, except for the girl in the box-office counting out the money she had taken, and two spotty young men smoking cigarettes and waiting for their dates to come out of the ladies' room.

'What do we do now?' asked Thomas.

Vincent was about to suggest that they took a walk along the street outside when the red-painted door marked *Theatre Manager* opened up, and a young man with a short brilliantined haircut stepped out and said, 'Mr Pearson?'

Vincent stopped, and squeezed Thomas's hand. 'What is it?' he asked sharply. 'How do you know who I am?'

'I wonder if you would step into the manager's office for a moment, sir?'

'I don't think that I care to, thank you.'

The young man smiled. 'The manager could assist you, I think. You *are* looking for a way out?'

Vincent hesitated. Then he said carefully, 'Yes.'

'In that case, sir, please step this way.'

Reluctantly, Vincent followed the young man into the manager's office. There was a wide veneered desk, a row of pens and an empty leather-backed chair. On the wall were twenty or thirty signed photographs of the stars.

'The manager will be right with you, sir, if you don't mind waiting.'

The door closed behind them and Vincent and Thomas stood in the office in silence, feeling lost and desperate and tense.

'Do you really think that the manager might be able to help us?' asked Thomas.

Vincent shrugged. 'I haven't any idea. I don't even see why he should be interested. A movie-theatre manager? But, well, I don't know – it seems like life inside these paintings has a different kind of logic from ordinary life. Did you notice how quiet all those people in that Dutch market-place were? None of them spoke. Maybe it's something to do with the way the artist painted them.'

They were still waiting when the lights in the office suddenly went out, and they were plunged into total darkness. Vincent groped behind him for the door-handle, but when he jerked it down, he discovered that it was locked. Thomas said, 'Dad – where are you? Dad!'

'Hold on,' Vincent reassured him. 'Let me just find the light-switch.'

He felt his way awkwardly along the wall, but he couldn't locate a light-switch anywhere. He touched the manager's collection of framed photographs, and they clattered loudly in the darkness.

Thomas said worriedly, 'Dad – are you okay?'

'I will be, as soon as I can find the lights.'

They heard the key turn in the lock. Both of them froze, and held their breath. The door-handle squeaked, and then the door swung open.

'Oh, my God,' Vincent whispered.

Silhouetted in the doorway was a tall figure dressed in what looked like a tuxedo. Vincent could just make out the gleam of his shirt-front. A smartly dressed cinema manager, in charge of a cinema that existed only in a painting. He lifted his hands and tugged his cuff.

'You're the manager?' Vincent asked him.

The figure stepped forward. 'I am many things, my friend. I play many parts. Today, I am playing the role of the vengeful pursuer. An intriguing role, that of the vengeful pursuer, wouldn't you say?'

The lights abruptly blinked on, and Thomas gasped in shock. The cinema manager was Maurice Gray. His head was hacked down to the bone; all that remained of his hair was a few bloody tufts. His hands, in spite of his immaculate cuffs, were chopped and raw. And he crawled with maggots, everywhere. Even as Vincent stared at him in utter horror, they were devouring the scarlet scraps of flesh that still clung to Maurice's cheekbones.

Maurice Gray advanced towards them. His eyes were blank, as if he could no longer feel anything or think anything. 'The vengeful pursuer,' he said; and he reached into his inside pocket, and with a theatrical gesture, produced a surgical scalpel. 'Have you seen what one of these can do to human flesh? It can slice through to your liver without your feeling it. It can take off your face, *zzik!* just like that, and leave it lying on the floor.'

He took another step forward. Vincent, tugging at Thomas's arm, retreated round the desk.

'You cannot escape me anywhere,' Maurice whispered. Maggots began to drop out of the side of his skeletal jaw. 'You cannot escape me, even in Hell.'

Vincent seized the arms of the leather-backed chair, hefted it up over his head and threw it as hard as he could, straight at Maurice's chest. Maurice staggered, and then stumbled. Vincent vaulted over the desk and kicked out at him, sending him sprawling. Maurice flailed at him with the scalpel, cutting open the side of his shoe; but then Vincent kicked him again, right in the ribs. Maurice coughed maggots. Vincent picked up the fallen chair, held it up for a moment and then slammed it down with a sickening crack on Maurice's head. Maurice's skull broke open like a china jug, and for one terrible moment the shattered pieces boiled with maggots.

Vincent stepped back, breathing harshly.

'Is he really dead now?' Thomas asked him.

Vincent desperately shook his head. 'I hope so. God Almighty, I hope so.'

It was then, however, that he became aware of another figure standing in the doorway. She was slender, and elegant, and dressed in black. Her face was even more luminous than usual. It was Cordelia Gray, and she stepped into the room with all the elegance of a Connecticut thoroughbred.

'You have destroyed my brother at last,' she said, in a sibilant whisper. 'Perhaps you are feeling proud of yourselves.'

She knelt down and touched Maurice's shoulder. 'He was a man of great breeding, you know. I don't think you really understand what you've done.'

Vincent said, 'This is the finish of it, Miss Gray. We want to get out of this picture and back to reality.'

'Reality? You deserve to stay here for ever, for what you have done.'

Vincent grasped her wrist and wrenched it round. 'You're going to show us how to get out of here, and that's all.'

He had never felt a wrist so brittle and so thin. He felt as if he could snap it with one twist of his hand. But Cordelia Gray stared at him in absolute contempt.

'You may release me,' she said.

Vincent shook his head. 'Not until you take us back.'

'I refuse to take you back.'

'Do you want me to break your arm?'

'Will you let go of me? If you don't let go of me, I'll –' Cordelia shook herself loose and stood up, and just when Vincent thought she was going to say something, she wrenched open the office door and hurried away across the foyer.

'Quick!' Vincent urged Thomas.

Together, they ran across the foyer and out through the shiny glass doors. They found themselves in the street, on a warm evening in New York City, in early fall, with the cars honking and the sirens wailing and the pavements clamorous with shoppers and sightseers and home-going typists.

Vincent glimpsed a black figure stalking towards 36th and Fifth. 'There!' he said, and began to jog after her. Side by side, he and Thomas ran across the Avenue of the Americas, rousing a battery of car-horns; but they managed to keep Cordelia Gray in sight. They ran through the acrid smoke of bagel stands; jostled past shoppers; pushed aside beggars and street-musicians and newspaper sellers. Up above them, the lighted mosaic of the Empire State Building shone through the clouds. But all the time, urgent as a sewing-machine bobbin, the black figure of Cordelia Gray pushed her way through the crowds.

On the corner of 38th Street, Vincent was almost run

over by a brand-new 1939 model DeSoto Custom S6. The driver wound down his window and yelled at him, 'What are you, dreaming?'

But as they approached 39th Street, Vincent caught up with Cordelia and seized hold of her arm.

'Let me go!' she breathed furiously. 'You've killed my brother, isn't that enough?'

'Take us back,' Vincent demanded. 'Take us back, before I twist your goddamned arm off.'

'You haven't even worked it out yet, have you?' Cordelia mocked him. 'You're like an infant. You can't even do it for yourself.'

'Miss Gray, you're going to take us back,' Vincent threatened her.

'My dear man, I don't have to *take* you back, you can do it for yourself. This is your spirit, not your body. Instead of rushing from one painting to another, all you have to do is close your eyes and realize that you're back; and then you will be.'

'I want you back with me.'

'How can I guarantee that? And why should I guarantee anything?'

'Because I'm going to keep hold of your arm, and I'm not going to let you go.'

'You're a swine, Mr Pearson. A swine of the very first order.'

Without any warning, the New York pavement vanished from under their feet and they were standing isolated in a hot and glaring desert, with strange constructions of wood leaning on the horizon. Melting slug-like creatures slid all around them, and cannon barked and banged like dogs. Vincent recognized an allegorical painting by Salvador Dalí; but, almost as soon as he did so, they were pitching on the deck of a sailing-ship, in mid-Pacific, with the wind screaming through the rigging and the timbers growling beneath their feet.

'*Dad!*' shouted Thomas, clinging on to his arm.

Vincent knew then that Cordelia was playing with him, that she was showing him just how much of an innocent he was. He gripped Thomas's hand, and closed his eyes, and thought to himself, *This must stop. We're not really here at all. We're back in Connecticut, in our own time, in our own reality, and this is nothing more than sorcery.*

His face was lashed with freezing spray. The ship heeled and tossed, its decks running with foam, its halyards cracking; and then suddenly he was deluged with icy-cold water. But it was stagnant water, cold and still, and when he opened his eyes and saw the murky grey outlines of bobbing bodies, he realized with a paralysing shock that he was down at the bottom of the ornamental pond at The Wilderlings, surrounded by the fleshly remains of all the Grays.

He broke the surface, rearing out of the slush like a sea-lion gasping for air; and right beside him, Thomas surfaced, too. Shouting, shivering, he waded over to Thomas with the bodies of the Grays bumping and nudging his legs. He seized his son in both arms and lifted him out of the water on to the snowy bank, and then heaved himself out.

The sky was dark now, and the first few whirls of another storm were beginning. They took three or four paces across the lawn, and then, shaking and trembling, scarcely able to articulate, Vincent said, 'We're back, damn it! At least we *should* be back.'

As if to reassure him, a 737 thundered overhead, its lights flashing, making its first approach to Bridgeport airfield. 'We're back,' said Vincent triumphantly.

'Now, let's go in, and burn that goddamned picture.'

They waded through foot-deep snow, until they reached the house. Then they pushed open the back door and walked through to the hall. Their shoes were filled with freezing water, and they squelched as they walked.

'We're here!' Vincent shouted. 'We've done it! We've made it!'

They walked straight into the music room; but the *tableau vivant* that met their eyes had obviously been especially prepared for them, only moments before. Charlotte and Aaron were there, one at each end of one of the Grays' old sofas. Laura Monblat was there, looking shocked and shaken, but alert. But none of them smiled when Vincent and Thomas came in through the door, nor raised their hands in welcome. Because Cordelia Gray was there, too, locked in what looked like an unholy embrace with Jack Smith, her black gown clinging wetly to her body, water running all around her high-heeled shoes, her hand holding a shining surgical scalpel up to Jack's throat.

Vincent quietly told Thomas, 'Stay well back. Don't say anything.' Then he stepped into the middle of the hall and confronted Cordelia, his hands on his hips.

'It's all finished,' he told Cordelia. 'Thomas and Laura are back with us, here. You have no hostages. We can destroy the portrait, and you with it, any time we want to.'

Cordelia visibly shuddered.

Vincent approached her and held out his hand. 'Your family tried to do something that was humanly impossible, Ms Gray. I think you have to recognize that it's all over now. Would you please give me that knife?'

'And what do you intend to do with me?' Cordelia asked him sharply. 'Beat me to death, the way you beat all my poor cousins to death? Strangle me, the way you did Henry?'

Vincent said, 'I think you should remember what you and your family have been doing, in order to stay alive for so long.'

Jack said to Cordelia, 'If you give evidence, you could wind up with twenty years inside, nothing more. With remission, that could be ten.'

'Give me the knife,' said Vincent.

Cordelia shook her head. 'You have killed my brother, Mr Pearson. You have murdered my cousins. A poor little crippled girl, with her head crushed! I refuse to submit to your vigilante justice, any more than I intend to submit to your ridiculous twenty-year sentence! Should I *thank* you for that?'

Quite coolly, Vincent walked across to the Waldegrave portrait. Cordelia watched him carefully, her scalpel still shimmering a quarter-inch away from Jack's Adam's apple. Jack said anxiously, 'Vincent – will you please not do anything rash? I think this lady means what she says.'

Vincent reached into his waistcoat pocket and produced a small silver penknife, the one he usually used for probing into layers of canvas and paint. He opened out the blade, and held the point of it just a fraction of an inch away from Cordelia's painted face.

'If you so much as scratch Sheriff Smith, Ms Gray, then I will have no hesitation at all in sticking this knife into your portrait. And you know what *that* will do to you, don't you?'

Cordelia was silent for a second, and then she laughed out loud: high and brittle, like breaking glass.

'Yes, I do, Mr Pearson – but do you know what it will do to *you*?'

'She's bluffing,' said Charlotte, under her breath. 'What does she mean?'

'I'm not so sure,' said Aaron. 'Hear her out.'

Cordelia said, with supreme satisfaction, 'You have probably asked yourself, Mr Pearson, why your grand-father didn't ever destroy the Waldegrave portrait. After all, he may have been an honourable man, but he was also a moral man; a man of considerable social conscience; and you know what they say about promises made with murderers and thieves – one almost has a duty to break them. With one match, he could have obliterated all of us.'

Vincent said nothing, but his hand began to waver over the portrait of Cordelia and he glanced towards Charlotte anxiously.

'Similarly,' Cordelia went on, 'you have probably asked yourself why my father Algernon was prepared to leave the Waldegrave portrait in your grandfather's custody, knowing that the fate of himself and his wife and his family was in the hands of somebody else. Don't you think he should have fought your grandfather a little harder? Why did he agree to go into exile, with such comparative meekness?'

'I think you'd better say what you have to say,' Vincent told her.

'I intend to,' Cordelia retorted. 'You see, the Pearsons and the Grays were always very good friends. Sometimes, they were *more* than good friends. Your great-grandfather, Mr Pearson, used to come round calling almost every weekend.'

'My great-grandfather said nothing about that in his diaries.'

'He wouldn't have done, Mr Pearson, because the reason your great-grandfather came calling almost every weekend was me.'

'What the hell are you talking about?' Vincent asked her fiercely.

'Let me make it plain,' smiled Cordelia, and the hand that held the scalpel against Jack's throat remained as steady as if it were cast out of alabaster. 'Your great-grandfather and I were lovers, Mr Pearson; in those days when I was still beautiful and still untouched by – what shall I call them? – our little white friends from the graveyard.'

'You were lovers? You're out of your mind!'

'I have photographs to prove it, Mr Pearson. Pictures of your great-grandfather and me, yachting off Sherwood Island; letters; gifts, signed with love. There was one long wonderful summer, and by the end of that summer, I was pregnant. It was a scandal, I suppose, especially in those days; but the Grays were always considered to be rather a scandalous family, albeit *la crème de la crème*. I refused to go to a doctor, because I loved your great-grandfather so much, and the following year, I gave him a baby boy.'

The silence in the hallway of The Wilderlings was intense. Vincent could sense what was coming, he could feel it, that dark train rushing through the night, but he had to know for sure. 'Go on,' he said, with a dry throat.

'I couldn't look after the child, of course. A single mother? In those days, the idea was ridiculous. I didn't want to look after it, either. There were parties to go to, as there always will be. But your great-grandfather didn't object, because his marriage had been childless. He and your dear dead great-grandmama took my son and reared him as their own. So you see, your grandfather was my son; and your father was my grandson; and *you*, Mr Pearson, God bless you, are my great-grandson.

'*That* is why your grandfather couldn't destroy the portrait. And *that* is why my father accepted your

476

grandfather's assurances that the portrait would be kept safe. Of course, none of us knew at the time how essential it would be for us to stay in communion with the portrait. As years went by, and our condition grew increasingly desperate, we begged your grandfather and your father again and again to let us have the portrait back, so that we could restore ourselves; but they refused, every time, and threatened to expose us for the murders we were supposed to have committed. There was nothing we could do but remain in exile and try to survive the best way we could.'

'So, if I stab the portrait now?' asked Vincent. 'Then what happens?'

'If you stab the portrait now, you will destroy me. I will be grave-dust and bones, in front of your eyes. Yes, and maggots, too, because that is all I am. That is what your family have made me. I have continued to exist only through courtesy of Walter Waldegrave. The way you see me now is the way I was, just before I met your great-grandfather. And if you destroy me now, the historical chain will be broken, and your grandfather will never have existed; and nor will your father; and nor will you.'

Charlotte said, 'Vincent –'

But Vincent looked round at Thomas, and suddenly understood what it would mean if he were to vanish, as if he had never existed. Thomas would vanish, too. Lost in some unborn limbo, where souls wait hopelessly to be conceived, and time and love have no meaning whatsoever. Eternity, he thought, had no attractions.

He folded away his penknife. 'All right,' he said. 'You can keep the portrait. And you're welcome to whatever punishments God gives you.'

Cordelia smiled, and took the scalpel away from

Jack's throat. 'I suppose this has ended decently,' she said.

Jack stepped quickly away from Cordelia, and then turned to Vincent. 'I don't know whether you saved my life there or not, pal. Pat predicted I was going to meet some beguiling lady, and that I was going to have to watch out.'

Vincent said quietly, 'I think there was some mutual life-saving, all round.'

Charlotte held Vincent close, as if she never wanted to let him go, but knew that she had to. Vincent stroked her hair, although he had the strangest feeling that now she knew that Cordelia Gray was his great-grandmother, he had somehow lost her. Their embrace was not the embrace of lovers any more, but of friends; and of friends who would gradually distance them-selves, too. Maybe, after Christmas, he would call up Meggsy.

Aaron said, 'Don't forget your own portrait, Vincent. Those things are dynamite, as far as I can tell.'

Vincent went over and picked up the portrait that Aaron had painted. It was still sticky, so he held it by one corner.

'You *were* devious, weren't you?' said Cordelia, with that chilly smile of hers. 'I suppose it runs in the family.' She touched her fingertips to her lips, and blew Vincent the coldest and most abstract of kisses.'

They left The Wilderlings, and walked across the snowy garden. Vincent glanced only once towards the ornamental pond. The bodies of those Grays whose spirits he had killed would rot there now, among the weeds. Those who had survived his vengeance would one day rise out of the water again; but that was something he didn't want to think about. As he looked, a bedraggled creature came slinking across the snow towards him, crying pitifully because of the cold. It was Firework, the reincarnation of Van Gogh. Vincent held out his arms for the cat, and it jumped up, shivering, as if it already knew him. He stroked the cat's wet furry head.

The last that Vincent saw of Cordelia, she was standing in the lighted doorway, one arm raised against the lintel, watching them. He supposed that it was some sort of a consolation that, now the Grays had the portrait back, they wouldn't need to kill anybody for skin, any longer. And the two most murderous and licentious members of the family,' Maurice and Henry, were both dead.

They drove back to New Milford, and on the way, Jack stopped the Cherokee by the side of the road, and they all shook hands, and kissed, and congratulated themselves.

'What about that portrait of yours?' asked Jack, as they drove on northwards through the early hours. A subdued carol was playing on the radio, 'The Holly and the Ivy'.

Vincent held it up, and looked at it. 'What about it?'

'Well, when you had the portrait painted, you made the same kind of pact that the Grays did, didn't you? Now, the portrait's going to grow old, and you're going to stay young.'

Vincent laughed. 'Not me, my friend. Old age is going to overtake me gradually and naturally. I have seen immortality, and it doesn't work.'

When they got back to Candlemas, Jack came in for a glass of Christmas Eve champagne, and then he went home to Nancy. Vincent and Charlotte and Thomas sat around the fire and talked about the Grays and what had happened that day, until the logs burned down and the chilly draught began to blow down the chimney-stack. It was only two hours before Christmas Day. They had no presents to give each other, so they went to bed and slept until it was time for them to go out to lunch.

Twenty-nine

After Christmas, Vincent went back to New York, and Thomas went back to Margot, and Charlotte went back to MOMA. Spring came, and the gardens of Candlemas were crowded with blossom. Mrs Miller came and cleaned the house, and Vincent spent Easter there, with Thomas and Meggsy. Jack called in, and one evening they got drunk together and laughed a lot.

Summer passed, like a hot and golden wheel. Then fall, with its dying leaves and its strong, sad colours. Winter came again, and Vincent returned to Candlemas, alone this time, because Charlotte had gone to Vancouver, to live with a young Canadian architect called Zeke, and it was Margot's turn to have Thomas for Christmas.

Vincent sat in front of the fire, drinking Irish whiskey and listening to Mozart. The portrait that Aaron painted for him had been framed now, and hung over the mantel-shelf. Vincent looked up at it, and raised his glass, and said, *'Prost!'*

He frowned then, and looked at the portrait more carefully. He stood up and went close to the fireplace, and stared at it for almost five minutes. On one side of the portrait's head, the left side, there was white hair, quite a conspicuous streak of it. Yet – when he turned to the mirror – there was no corresponding streak in his own hair.

'*No,*' he whispered.

He spent the whole night awake, staring at the portrait. In the morning, a few minutes after seven o'clock, he called the Grays' number in Darien, and waited for an answer. He wasn't even sure what he wanted. Reassurance? Comfort?

But a monotonous recorded message told him, '*The number you have dialled . . . 203–667 9904 . . . is out of service. Please refer to your directory . . . The number you have dialled . . .*'

Epilogue

Tite Street,
7 September 1891

My dear Oscar,

I have just finished reading your draft story (at midnight, no less!) and I must confess that it is thrilling and alarming in the extreme (apart from being most exquisitely written).

However, my legal friends from New York (who were dining with me only yesterday) tell me that the Grays of Connecticut, apart from being *very* wealthy are also *very* litigious; and if you were to breathe even a whisper of *l'affaire Waldegrave*, they have no doubt at all that the Grays would sue, and ruinously.

They suggest that, if you *do* wish to make literary capital out of this remarkable tale, you alter it sufficiently so that the Gray family cannot find reasonable grounds for action. In other words, you could alter the family portrait to the portrait of a single individual, and alter the name somewhat.

Anyway, please consider it, because the notion is most original and eerie; and it will certainly leave me trembling in my bed for months to come.

Your devoted friend,

Charles Petrie

Enclosed, the manuscript of *The Picture of the Darien Grays*.

HAMMER

Hammer has been synonymous with legendary British horror films for over half a century. With iconic characters ranging from Quatermass and Van Helsing to Frankenstein, Dracula, and now the Woman in Black, Hammer's productions have been terrifying and thrilling audiences worldwide for generations. And there is more to come.

Leading actors including Daniel Radcliffe, Hilary Swank and Chloe Moretz are now following in the footsteps of Hammer legends Sir Christopher Lee, Peter Cushing and Bette Davis through their involvement in new Hammer films.

Hammer's literary legacy is also being revived through its new Partnership with Arrow Books. This series will feature original tales by some of today's most celebrated authors, as well as classic stories from more than five decades of production.

Hammer is back, and its new incarnation is the home of smart horror – cool, stylish and provocative stories which aim to push audiences out of their comfort zones.

For more information on Hammer,
including details of official merchandise, visit:
www.hammerfilms.com

ALSO AVAILABLE IN ARROW/HAMMER

Mirror
Graham Masterton

'One of the few true masters of the horror genre'
James Herbert

It is said that a mirror can trap a person's soul . . .

Martin Williams is a broke, two-bit screenwriter living in Hollywood,
but when he finds the very mirror that once hung in the house of a
murdered 1930s child star; he happily spends all he has on it.
He has long obsessed over the tragic story of Boofuls, a beautiful
and successful actor who was slaughtered and dismembered by
his grandmother.

However, he soon discovers that this dream buy is in fact a living
nightmare; the mirror was not only in Boofuls house, but witness to
the death of this blond-haired and angelic child, which in turn has
created a horrific and devastating portal to a hellish parallel
universe. So when Martin's landlord loses his grandson it is soon
apparent that the mirror is responsible.

But if a little boy has gone into the mirror, what on earth is going to
come out?

'Masterton is a crowd pleaser, filling his pages with sparky,
appealing dialogue and visceral grue'
Time Out

The Pariah

Graham Masterton

'One of the few true masters of the horror genre'
James Herbert

The quaint seaside town of Granitehead seemed like the perfect place for John and Jane Trenton to start their life together. But disaster strikes and Jane and their unborn child are killed. John's grief is total, so when he starts to see the ghostly apparition of his wife he almost welcomes this supernatural phenomenon.

Yet all is not what it seems, and this sinister spirit is not Jane, but something evil and terrifying. In a bid to rid himself of this horrific spectre he soon finds that many more in the town have been victims of unwanted visitations. And when he discovers the body of a local busybody, impossibly impaled on a still hanging chandelier, he knows something must be done.

As he searches for an explanation he uncovers a link to a mysterious ship, lost around the time of the nearby Salem witch trials. For three centuries the rotting wreck of the David Dark has lain beneath waves, but an awful secret is concealed in the chill waters . . .

ALSO AVAILABLE IN ARROW/HAMMER

The Witches

Peter Curtis

'Flesh-creeping'
Daily Telegraph

Walwyk seemed a dream village to the new schoolteacher, Miss Mayfield. But dreams can turn into nightmares.

When it becomes clear that one of her pupils is being abused by her grandmother, Miss Mayfield is determined to do something about it. But Ethel won't say anything, despite the evidence of Miss Mayfield's own eyes, and someone seems to be actively discouraging her from investigating further. As she tries to get to the truth of the matter, however, Miss Mayfield stumbles on something far more sinister: Walwyk is in the grip of a centuries-old evil, and anybody who questions events in the village does not last long.

Death stalks more than one victim, and Miss Mayfield begins to realise that if she's not careful, she will be the next to die . . .

First published in 1960, *The Witches* was made into a classic Hammer film in 1966, starring Joan Fontaine and directed by Cyril Frankel, who has written an exclusive foreword for this new edition.

'Intensely suspenseful, powerfully underplayed,
subtly authoritative'
New York Times

ALSO AVAILABLE IN ARROW

Mist Over Pendle

Robert Neill

The witches are amongst us...

Seventeenth century England is a place of superstition and fear.

Deep in the Forest of Pendle, people have been dying in mysterious circumstances. The locals whisper of witchcraft, but Squire Roger Nowell, in charge of investigating the deaths, dismisses the claims as ridiculous. Until a series of hideous desecrations forces Roger and his cousin Margery to look further into the rumours. And what they discover brings them face to face with the horrifying possibility that a coven of witches is assembling, preparing to unleash a campaign of evil and destruction . . .

Robert Neill's novel is a classic tale of witchcraft set in a wild inaccessible corner of Lancashire and in a time when the ancient fear of demons and witches was still a part of life . . . and death.

arrow books

THE POWER OF READING

Visit the Random House website and get connected with information on all our books and authors

EXTRACTS from our recently published books and selected backlist titles

COMPETITIONS AND PRIZE DRAWS Win signed books, audiobooks and more

AUTHOR EVENTS Find out which of our authors are on tour and where you can meet them

LATEST NEWS on bestsellers, awards and new publications

MINISITES with exclusive special features dedicated to our authors and their titles

READING GROUPS Reading guides, special features and all the information you need for your reading group

LISTEN to extracts from the latest audiobook publications

WATCH video clips of interviews and readings with our authors

RANDOM HOUSE INFORMATION including advice for writers, job vacancies and all your general queries answered

Come home to Random House

www.randomhouse.co.uk